D0451293

PRAISE FOR ELAINE BARBIERI'S PREVIOUS BESTSELLERS

TATTERED SILK

"A powerful story that evokes every human emotion possible...pure reading pleasure...a must read."
— *Rendezvous*

WINGS OF A DOVE

"A magnificent love story." — *Rave Reviews*

DEFIANT MISTRESS

"Ms. Barbieri's wonderful writing is a marvelous mingling of sensuality, passion, and adventure."
— *Romantic Times*

UNTAMED CAPTIVE

"A five-star read! Elaine Barbieri has proven that romance is well and alive!"
— *Affaire de Coeur*

DANCE of the FLAME

ELAINE BARBIERI

"Elaine Barbieri is an absolute master of her craft!"
—Romantic Times

"Yea, *husband*. Anything you say, *husband*." Sera's tone was caustic. "Are those the words you would have me speak?"

Tolin's gaze remained cold. "They will suffice for now."

"Oh, will they! I hope you will remember their ring, because you will not hear me speak them again! And if you think that during this journey I will wait on you hand and foot—"

Tolin's voice took on an ominous tone. "You will do exactly what I tell you to do. You will defer to me in all things as a good wife should, and you will not again behave so foolishly as to flaunt yourself with another man so others might suspect the vow between us."

"You are insane!"

"And you are a fool!"

"How dare you!"

Sera gasped as Tolin moved in a lightning flash. The white world around her lurched suddenly upside down as she was snatched from her feet and tossed over his broad shoulder.

ELAINE BARBIERI

DANCE of the FLAME

LEISURE BOOKS NEW YORK CITY

A LEISURE BOOK®

June 1995

Published by

Dorchester Publishing Co., Inc.
276 Fifth Avenue
New York, NY 10001

Printed in the United States of America.

*To the love that made me believe in the happy ending—
we did it together, hon.*

DANCE of the FLAME

Dance of the Flame

Winds of change blew across Orem Proper, the heavily forested land of clear streams and jagged hills, where the debris of a bitter civil war lay rotting beneath a brilliant blanket of fallen leaves. In the beautiful, bucolic land a deceiving peace reigned. Recollections of the war between the rival Royal Houses of Neer and Rall remained hidden in the memory of those who would not allow themselves to forget. . . .

THE PROPHECY
"Spirit of Neer confined in flame,
Crescent reborn to come again,
Vessel to seek, wherein the key
To bring the House of Rall to knee."

Prologue

The Country of Orem

The shadowed tower room was silent as Fador of Rall cradled the glittering crystal sphere in his palm. Mesmerized, he watched the captive flame within as it danced in sinuous appeal. The matchless hues of red and amber-gold writhed and swayed, falling and rising again as they flickered into infinity in the faceted glass.

The flame called out to Fador in a siren call heard by his ears alone. The words were a whisper . . . a promise . . . a sigh. They enthralled and seduced him, reducing him to trembling as his mind conjured up the image of the woman whose spirit was confined in the flame—the magnificent Versa of Neer.

Versa, whose beauty and courage had been unequaled.

Versa, who had raised within him a carnal hunger so voracious that it would not die.

Versa, of whom only the flame remained.

His bearded face intense, his dark hair glinting in the meager light, Fador caressed the crystal with a shaking hand. He had pursued a relentless course in the savage civil war that had raged in Orem. He had conquered Versa's ruling House of Neer, and his lust for the total annihilation of Neer had been satisfied. The House of Rall now reigned supreme in Neer's stead, and as Rall's leader, he—Fador—was omnipotent!

His triumph was absolute. But his *lust* remained.

Suffering an aching, palpable need that he could neither sate nor deny, Fador railed at the irony of a fate that held him captive as he was captor. The flame danced more brightly, mocking his torment, and he cursed aloud, longing with an intensity close to pain for the courage to smash the precious crystal against the stone floor and stamp out the taunting flame forever!

But he could not. Fador's throat was tight, his distress profound. No, he could not extinguish the flame and still Versa's spirit forever. Because . . . Fador swallowed, his anguish acute. Because . . . *he loved her.*

REBIRTH

"Spirit of Neer, confined in flame, Crescent reborn to come again . . ."

Chapter One

Orem Proper, five years later . . .

A fragrant summer breeze stirred the forest of Orem Proper, shifting the night shadows. Pale slivers of moonlight filtered through the cover of trees, weaving an undulating pattern against the lovers lying in tight embrace below. Rasped endearments and soft sounds of passion broke the silence of the leafy bower as the handsome warrior pressed his loving assault on the young woman in his arms.

Tears streaked Sileen's cheeks as she met Angor's dark-eyed gaze. Reading an emotion therein that matched her own, Sileen clutched him closer. She knew the harsh truth behind this matchless moment. A warrior serving the

House of Rall could not cleave to a simple maid such as she for a lifetime, despite the rapture now raging between them. But her love for Angor was intense, and his passion would not be denied. This was the moment supreme, and she consoled herself that in this time and place— however briefly they might be together—Angor loved her, too.

Sileen indulged her love. She returned kiss for kiss, caress for caress, knowing that when all was over and done, she would cherish the memory of this night forever.

Angor . . . her love, her life. She gave herself up to his loving.

Filnor's heart pounded with youthful jubilation as he climbed the winding stone staircase toward the forbidden tower room. Smiling, he congratulated himself on his ingenuity. He was so clever—far more clever than Fador, his frowning father, deigned to credit him! He had proved his resourcefulness this night by slipping away from the lively congregation feasting in the great hall of the castle below without attracting the notice of his father, whose scrutiny of him in the past year had intensified discomfitingly.

Resentment flashed across Filnor's handsome young face. At the age of eight, he was no longer a child and he would not be treated like

18

one! He would not allow Fador to refuse the rights due him as heir to the House of Rall!

In his mind's eye, Filnor again saw the flame.

Filnor's determination grew. He had been well educated in the history of Rall's rule. He could recite in minute detail the events of the great war that had destroyed the House of Neer and brought Rall to the throne years earlier. He could name every battle, every step his father had taken toward victory. Not even the whispered rumors of his father's fascination with the beautiful Versa of Neer had escaped him.

Filnor knew something, however, that no one else knew.

He knew that the whispered rumors were true.

A familiar excitement rising within him, Filnor recalled the countless times he had peered through the crack in the tower room door and watched as his father held the precious crystal in his hands. He had recognized his father's bemusement, his inability to tear his gaze from the flame that danced hypnotically within the crystal.

And Filnor had understood.

For the flame was beautiful.

A frown remarkably similar to his sire's flashed across Filnor's countenance. It was not fair! Fador had forbidden him entrance to the tower room simply because he had asked to hold the crystal! Did his father not realize that the flame called out to him as well?

Or did his father simply not care?

Filnor's frustration mounted. Fie on Fador! Fie on his sire's jealous possessiveness of the crystal and the flame within! He would hold the crystal as his father had held it. He would feel its weight in his palm. He would experience its warming heat—this night, this hour, before another day dawned!

Pushing open the great oak door of the tower room, Filnor paused briefly on the threshold. Lanterns hanging from the high, vaulted ceiling cast a flickering glow on the familiar tapestries adorning the gray stone walls, on the fur rugs covering the floor, on suits of armor worn in a time long past, and on the massive, ornately carved desk and chair that occupied the center of the room.

Of all there was within, however, Filnor saw only the barred niche high on the opposite wall where the flame encased in crystal beckoned.

Moving quickly to the massive desk, Filnor pressed the concealed hinge for the secret drawer. His breath caught in his throat as the drawer opened and a small brass key within glinted in the dim light.

Filnor picked up the key. He clutched it tightly as he dragged the chair toward the barred niche just above his reach. He was breathless with anticipation as he stretched up to insert the key into the grill lock.

The door of the niche sprang open as Filnor turned the key, allowing him an unrestricted view of the flame at last.

Beautiful. It was beautiful. . . .

Reaching inside, Filnor withdrew the crystal. Enthralled, he gazed into the iridescent flame. But he did not converse with it in the low, sensuous tones he had heard his father use. Nor did he rail at it, or mock it, as his father had sometimes been inclined to do. No less bewitched, however, he smiled into the flame, warmed by the rapturous shades reflected against its translucent prison as it floated in mesmerizing display.

The sudden sound of a step behind him . . .

A hissing intake of breath . . .

Snapped from his avid scrutiny of the beauteous flame, Filnor turned to see.

"Father!"

Fador's bellow of rage resounded in the tower room at the same moment that the crystal's heat surged hotly in Filnor's hands, scorching them. Crying out aloud as the orb slipped from his grasp, Filnor stiffened, incredulous with horror as the crystal shattered against the stone floor.

Paralyzed with fear, Filnor watched as the freed flame ignited the dry rushes scattered nearby to become sudden, angry tongues of fire. He held his breath as Fador snatched up a bear-skin rug a few feet away and threw it over the blaze. He gasped aloud as Fador cursed and shouted, stamping at the persistent flames licking out at him.

When a final, curling spiral of smoke signified that the last spark had been extinguished, Fador turned to face Filnor at last. Unable to control the tremors that shook him, Filnor knew he would never forget the look in his father's eyes at that moment. For in their lifeless depths, Filnor saw a reality more terrifying than any he had ever known—the irreversible truth that darkness would forever prevail in Fador's soul without the flame that had been his prisoner . . .

. . . and his love.

Unseen by father and son, a glowing cinder, the last remnant of the captive flame, rose on a gust of air that carried it through the open window of the tower room into the forest beyond.

The jubilant spark drifted upward on the warm air . . . bobbing, dancing . . . elated to be free!

Sileen's pale hair was damp with the heat of passion as she writhed at the wonder of her lover's touch. Angor's hungry lips moved against her aching breasts, bathing them with his kiss, and she gasped again. His hands cupped the virgin mounds and Sileen drew him closer, arching her back, encouraging his loving ministrations as she had during the long, heady moments past. But somehow, that intimacy would suffice no longer.

Angor pressed himself full upon her naked flesh, and a new exaltation dawned within Sileen. The time had come! She would soon be a part of Angor as she was meant to be! She would soon give to him what she had given no other man. That act would seal forever the sanctity of their joining, the love that brimmed in her heart, and the beauty she had waited to share with him alone!

"Sileen . . ."

"I love you, Angor."

Angor's craggy face flushed with passion. Sileen saw the love, and she saw his hesitation, however brief, the second before he thrust full and deep within her.

A soft groan escaped Sileen's lips as she clasped Angor close. Ignoring the fleeting pain, she reveled in her joy at the knowledge that it was this moment for which she had been born.

Angor's hard male warmth was tight against Sileen's soft female flesh as the rhythm of loving began. The growing splendor was almost more than she could bear, and Sileen closed her eyes as she matched the cadence of Angor's ardent assault.

So enraptured was she that Sileen did not see the glowing cinder floating high above them. Nor did she see the cinder drift slowly downward to hover over her impassioned face.

Knowing only the exhilaration of Angor's final, surging thrust, Sileen caught her breath, breathing in the waiting spark as she joined her lover in soaring culmination.

Breathless and still moments later as Angor lay replete upon her, Sileen slowly opened her eyes. She slid her arms around her lover, absorbing his impassioned whispers.

Enveloped in the soft afterglow of love, Sileen was unmindful of the spark within her gradually growing to flame.

Content in her lover's arms, Sileen was ignorant of the unexpected life that spark would bring anew to . . .

. . . the House of Neer.

Chapter Two

Sileen walked laboriously along the cobbled marketplace lane, clutching her shawl around her. She paused to avoid the sudden surge of people between the open stalls where craftsmen plied their trades, backing up against a half-brick, half-timbered house identical to many others lining the way. The early morning traffic of the village was brisk as she resumed her pace and approached the public square. The growing din of merchants hawking their wares, the haggling of matron and maid bargaining over merchandise displayed, and the crush of peasants scrambling to sell their produce was familiar.

But Sileen was not deceived by the facade of normalcy that prevailed.

Glancing around her, she saw the desperation behind the smiles. She sensed the tension that accompanied each exchange of coin. She saw the cracks in the veneer that marked the steady deterioration of the good life formerly lived in the towns and villages of Orem Proper, a deterioration which had begun to accelerate after that fateful night months ago.

A chill unrelated to the temperature of the sunny morn moved down Sileen's spine. She paused at a busy intersection as a rumbling wagon loaded with empty barrels moved past, her hand sliding to the distended abdomen beneath her sober robe. The babe within her moved at her touch, and a sad smile flickered across her lips. Aye, the babe—the fruit of her night of love—was all that remained of the grand passion she and Angor had shared.

Sileen closed her eyes in a moment of weakness before resuming her step. She needed to put the past behind her. She should take solace in the realization that she had been saved from dire circumstances and shame when she was allowed to retain her position in the small tavern where she was employed instead of being thrown into the street because of her condition. She ought to be grateful that the proprietor and his wife had taken pity on her and had allowed her to work in the kitchen, out of sight, where she might not be ridiculed for her submission to the ardor of a handsome warrior who was no more.

For Angor was dead, killed in an exchange with highwaymen only scant weeks after that loving night.

Her throat tight, Sileen caressed the great protrusion she carried before her. That fateful night . . .

Strangely, that night, which had had such a profound effect on her life, had marked a change with far more sweeping consequences for Orem Proper.

Orem Proper had always been the better of the two worlds of Orem. But some said it was no longer.

Some said that Orem Minor—the bitter-cold land of snow and ice an endless journey away, where only Minor Oremians could survive because of the physical adaptations they had made—was now the better of the two worlds, simply because Fador's rule had less effect on life there.

Sileen knew that was not true.

Fador's prejudices against Minor Oremians were legend. The cold reality was that were it not for the priceless zircum present in the mines of Orem Minor, Fador and the House of Rall would have seen Minor Oremians erased from the face of Orem forever. But Orem Proper was dependent upon zircum for the enhancement of everyday life, and the Minor Oremians were the only people physically capable of mining the precious substance without suffering gradual and irreversible physical impairment.

Rumors continued to circulate about an incident in the tower room of Fador's castle on that same night long months ago when Angor and she had consummated their love. There were stories of a great loss incurred by a fire there, and about Fador's rage at his son for the part the boy had played in it. Fador's uncontrollable grief had manifested itself in the harsh measures he had visited upon Orem in the time since.

Hardships unknown under the House of Neer had grown in every quarter. Cruel taxes and oppression of simple liberties had taken their toll. The hungry grew legion. Unreasonable curfews were viciously enforced. Crime proliferated in the forests, the streets, and the highways. The gibbet was applied at Fador's whim . . . and no woman was safe from Fador's rapacious needs.

The fire in that tower room had released a demon in Fador, and Orem reeled under that demon's rule.

Sileen's waddling gait slowed. Her fair brow furrowed. Strangely, she had seen a flame often in her dreams since that night with Angor in the forest. But its heat had not threatened her. Instead, it had consoled her in her grief, it had given her courage to go on when she had felt she might not prevail—and it had given her hope.

Pausing beside the fountain in the square as exhaustion became abruptly overwhelming, Sileen dipped her hand into the water there and patted it across her forehead. She was determined to complete her errand for Matra. Kind Matra had become the mother she had never known during her adversity. Yet, Sileen felt the need to prove to the dear woman that she could still earn her way so that when the babe came she might—

Struck suddenly with a wrenching pain, Sileen gasped aloud. She turned to search the crowded street around her for a familiar face, but she saw none. Another pain followed as a flow of hot liquid gushed unexpectedly from between her thighs.

Panicking as the sunlight of the early morning streets seemed to dim and the world around her began slipping away, Sileen struggled to catch her breath. She saw it again then, flickering brightly before her mind's eye.

The flame . . .

It lent her joy where there had been panic. It gave her strength where there had been trepidation. It brought a smile to her face, however weak her step, as Sileen drew in a stabilizing breath, turned, and started slowly, deter-

29

minedly, back in the direction from which she had come.

Fador opened his eyes gradually, with caution. He grunted at the rays of bright morning sunlight streaming through a slit in the window hangings, then cursed the stabbing pain in his head that ensued, as well as the faithless servant responsible for allowing a breach in the darkness of his room. He was not yet ready for morning.

Fador grunted again. That faithless servant would pay. . . .

Turning in afterthought, Fador looked at the sleeping woman lying beside him on the broad feather bed. Her features, obscured by long, tangled hair covering her face, were unrecognizable. He frowned as he picked up a fiery lock that lay against her bare shoulder. It was brittle and coarse, the color obviously altered, and he gave a derisive snort. What was her name? Jewel . . . Jena . . . Jerla? He did not recall. Nor did he care. She was merely another in a long line of women who had sought to win his favor with their bodies, going so far as to adopt the hair color he was known to favor in order to gain his attention.

Fador's frown darkened. Somehow, the color of the sleeping woman's hair had not seemed so garish when he had been in his cups the previous night. He remembered thinking that in the limited light of his room, it had taken up a color similar to the streaming tresses he stroked nightly in his dreams. It galled him to realize that his judgment could have been so impaired.

Throwing back the fur coverlet, Fador drew himself to his feet. He stretched to his full height, unmindful of his nakedness as he walked to the garderobe and jerked open the door. He entered and relieved himself, his frown enduring as he emerged minutes later and approached the washstand in the corner.

The image reflected in the mirror there displeased him. Long months of dissolute living had left their mark. The handsome planes of his face were shadowed and his dark eyes blackly ringed. Even the raven sheen of his thick, wavy hair appeared to have dulled. As for his beard, it was shapeless and unkempt.

Stepping back, Fador scrutinized himself in the broader view. He grunted again, satisfied to see that the dissipation visible on his face had not touched his powerful, tightly knit frame. His shoulders were still broad and regal, despite his present physical discomfort. His body still retained the muscular composition of the victorious leader who had overwhelmed and destroyed his enemy years earlier. There were no visible signs indicating that in his heart he—

Suddenly furious at the direction his

31

thoughts were again taking, Fador turned viciously toward the bed behind him and the woman snoring lightly there. Beside her in a few swift steps, he grasped the coarse, dyed locks and jerked them roughly. His rage knew no bounds when she responded with a harsh protest, and he pulled the woman to the floor by the tawdry strands, ignoring her screams as he then used her hair to drag her to her feet.

Her bloodshot eyes fearful, the woman uttered a rasping plea. Almost retching at the foul smell of her breath, Fador thrust her sharply backwards.

"Get out of here, cow! You've served your purpose! But I warn you, do not regale others with a tale of the hours you spent within these walls! If you do, you will do so at the expense of your life!"

The frightened woman stumbled in her haste to depart, and Fador assessed her nakedness through a new haze of fury. Heavy, sagging breasts . . . broad hips . . . quivering thighs . . . and dull, *brown* eyes. Where was the woman he had seen in her the previous night?

Revulsion twisted Fador's lips as the woman disappeared through the doorway with a flash of heavy buttocks. Turning with a rapid movement that set his head to pounding, Fador walked to the window and thrust it open to breathe deeply of the fresh morning air.

His gaze lingered on the land below him.

All belonged to him, as far as the eye could see and beyond.

A familiar surge pulsing through him, he shouted out in ringing declaration, "Orem is mine!"

Fador's triumphant tone rang in the silence of the morning, but the sound echoed hollowly in his ears and in his heart. The bitter truth was that there was no cure for his pain, and consolation was now beyond him. He could no longer hold the captive flame in the palm of his hand as Versa's spirit, however tormenting, infused him with life. He could no longer stroke the faceted glass, dreaming of the woman who had set his heart afire although their flesh had never met. He could no longer peruse the magnificent flame, knowing that in its brilliant, unyielding glory, Versa was his alone.

And he could not forget her.

Turning back to the washstand with a furious flourish, Fador picked up the pitcher there and poured its contents over his head. He stood motionless as the water streamed down his body and dripped onto the fur rug beneath his feet. Moments later he reached for his clothes, striving to strike from his mind the recurring image of Filnor's youthful horror as the crystal crashed to the floor of the tower room.

Filnor . . . his son . . . his heir . . . the offspring of the only woman he had taken to wife, the woman who had had the grace to die upon birthing Filnor, thereby setting him free. . . .

Fador breathed deeply in an attempt at control. He needed to keep in mind that he would never again marry, that no woman save the one who was forever lost was worthy of him, and that Filnor would succeed him in rule.

He needed to make Filnor strong.

And he needed to forgive.

Hot rage suddenly surged through him as the full scope of his loss returned mercilessly once more, and Fador turned toward the door with a feral growl that came from the soul. But he would not forgive now. Now, he would hunt and kill and debauch until he had burned from within him all memory of the fiery hair he had never stroked with passion, of the gold eyes that had never glowed for him, and of the lips that had never said his name with love!

Fador slammed his chamber door closed behind him and made his way below. Reverberating in the sharp crack of sound was the echo of a truth Fador could neither conquer nor ignore.

In winning all, he had lost all, and joy was forever beyond him.

"Bite down, I tell ye! Quickly, now! It will ease the pain!"

"Nay! Take it away, Seetra!"

Sileen's hand was rough and sure despite its trembling as she pushed away the shriveled bark the midwife sought to press between her lips. Regaining her voice after another wrenching spasm passed, she rasped at the small, hawk-faced woman who refused to give ground, "I will not have my senses dulled with your potions! I will see my child born. I will feel her emerge from my body! I will know the joy of her birth so I may keep it always with me, a clear memory that is not impaired by—"

Pausing as another spasm assumed control, Sileen looked imploringly at the plump woman standing worriedly a few feet away.

"Matra . . . tell her. I need nothing to help me bear this, the sweetest moment of my life." Uncertain of the cause for the urgency she felt deep inside her, Sileen implored once more, "Matra, please . . ."

Closing her eyes as Seetra stepped back from the bed at last, Sileen opened them again to see Matra looking anxiously down at her.

"Sileen, my child, your time may be long. You may suffer much."

Clasping Matra's trembling hand, Sileen attempted a smile. "Nay, it will not. Do not worry, Matra. There is little to fear. The child will come when it is ready, and the rest will follow."

"My dear . . ." Matra's full chin trembled.

"Were that it was always so easy. Five times I sought to bear my husband's seed, and five times the new life was snuffed before the babe's first cry."

"Not my babe."

"My very dear, how can you be so sure?"

"Because I know."

Long minutes passed as the pain swelled more strongly, stealing her breath, and Sileen felt a strange awareness come over her. The child was coming, but she knew no fear. Within her a glow had come to life, masking the pain. She saw a glittering spark within her mind. She watched it grow. She felt its glory spreading through her, a wonder like none she had ever known. She experienced its explosive joy, a massive thrust, and then—

An infant's wail! The voice of her child! Loud and clear, the sound rang within Sileen with a resplendence unlike any she had ever known.

"A girl! It is a girl!" Matra's round face was wet with tears. "She is a glorious babe! She—"

Her exclamations cut off, Matra gasped aloud. Her shock was reflected on the midwife's wrinkled face as the old woman halted her work abruptly.

Apprehension expanded within Sileen.

"I want to see my babe. Matra!"

"Nay, not yet. We must bathe her first . . . scrub her clean."

"Now, Matra!"

Her hands trembling as Matra handed her the babe, Sileen looked down into her beautiful daughter's face. Her heart singing, she viewed features so small and delicate as to appear unreal, skin pink and clear despite the stains of birth, eyes of a curious gold—infant perfection so complete that she—

Then she saw it.

Glancing up with fear, Sileen saw the same trepidation reflected in Matra's eyes and in the gaze of the silent midwife.

"Matra, how can this be?"

Responding in her stead, the midwife spoke softly in a voice trembling with awe.

"There can be no doubt of it! The rose-colored crescent on the babe's thigh—I saw it twice before while in service to the Royal House of Neer. The first crescent was on the thigh of the infant Traka, daughter of Vern and Heiress of Neer, who grew to womanhood only to be slain by the sword of Rall. The second was on the thigh of Versa, daughter of Traka, born in the moment of her mother's last breath, her tenure ended by the sword of Rall before the line could be continued."

Seetra's eyes grew wide. "Yet the crescent lives, signifying that the line survives with a new Heiress of Neer!"

"No, she is *my* child!" Sileen clutched her

babe tightly. "She is mine!"

The old midwife drew closer. Her eyes assumed a distant glow as she responded softly, *"Child of your body, there is no doubt, but the mark of Neer is born without. . . . "*

"Don't speak to me in rhymes, old hag!" Fear turning to panic, Sileen attempted to rise. "I will take my child far from here, where she will be safe from witches' tales such as yours!"

"Nay, wait . . ." The midwife's knobby hands were gentle as they closed around Sileen's arm. "Do not be afraid to accept the evidence in clear view. Instead, close your eyes. . . . " When Sileen hesitated, the midwife's lips parted in an encouraging, toothless smile. "Close your eyes, my dear, and tell me what you see."

Somehow unable to refuse, Sileen closed her eyes. She saw—

Her eyes snapping open, Sileen stared at Seetra in shocked silence.

"She was beautiful, wasn't she?" The old woman's tone was filled with pain. "Hair a fiery red, eyes a radiant amber, there was no beauty to match Versa of Neer's, and no voice as sweet as hers when she spoke your name."

Startled as the ancient midwife recounted the vision she had just seen, Sileen gasped, "How did you know?"

The old woman's eyes drooped slowly closed. She rocked gently from side to side, her voice taking on a singsong cadence as she recited:

"Spirit of Neer confined in flame,
Crescent reborn to come again . . .

". . . Vessel to seek, wherein the key,
To bring the house of Rall to knee. . . ."

"What is this nonsense!" His handsome face livid, Fador faced Zor with growing rage. The ancient magician's small black eyes blazed from a wizened face overwhelmed by the snow-white hair that marked his extended years as Fador continued harshly, "You are a demented old fool, and the rhyme you recite is nothing but a child's amusement!"

"Nay . . . nay . . ." Zor clasped his hands before him, closing his eyes and becoming so still that he assumed the appearance of a specter as he continued softly, "I see it again, as I did in the darkness of my sober dwelling."

"That filthy cave where you choose to reside—"

"The abode that sustains me, which has granted me the power to guide Rall as I have through your sire's time and his before him, through the great war and the destruction of Neer—the abode that endowed me with the power to contain Versa's spirit in flame as a gift to you."

"A gift to torment me so I might know no peace!"

"Nay, nay. In doing so, I was but a servant of the prophecy! I am still its servant—and yours—and as such, I report to you what I see."

"Damn you!" Aware of Zor's powers, powers which he had resented since childhood and sought to deny, Fador urged, "What did you see?"

"I saw the crescent reborn this day! A female babe with the crescent of Neer on her thigh . . . a child lying in the arms of a young mother with yellow hair."

"Fool! The Heiress of Neer's hair was a flaming shade, not a pale hue!"

"Child of her body, there is no doubt . . . but the mark of Neer is born without . . ."

Fador stared at the wizened figure standing so motionless before him. He could no longer deny the powers possessed by this man whose loyalty to Rall had been sworn in blood long years before his birth.

A deeper rage rising, Fador shouted, "Nay! Versa, once conquered and once destroyed, will not rise to plague me again!" His hands fell heavily on Zor's fragile shoulders and Fador shook the old man roughly. "Tell me where I might find this child—this wonder child born of a bloodline that exists no more."

Opening his eyes, Zor pinned Fador with new intensity. "Seek, and you will find the royal child in the arms of her fair-haired mother, on a birthing bed that lies within your realm. The prophecy—"

"The prophecy be damned! The prophecy ends this night, for it is *this* night that I will bring Neer to its final rest, never to rise again!"

Signaling the guards nearby, Fador paused a moment longer. Intensely sober, he scrutinized the seer, the man of inexplicable powers. He whispered harshly, "As old as you are, as feeble as you are, you have never failed Rall. So I will act on your word. But, old man, should you ever mislead me . . ."

"They are coming! They are coming!"

Sileen turned toward Matra as the older woman entered the bedchamber at a run. Her face devoid of color, Matra halted abruptly at Sileen's bedside, her gaze dropping to the babe who lay wrapped in a blanket in the crook of Sileen's arm.

"The soldiers—they've reached our lane! They're searching house by house, looking for newborns."

Sileen's arm tightened around the still babe. "Don't be afraid, Matra. All will be well. My babe will not fall to a soldier's blade."

"But I am afraid for *you*, Sileen! The soldiers will—"

Startled at a sudden pounding at the door, Matra took a step backward. Her back to the

41

bed, she shielded Sileen with her body at the sound of the outer door splintering under a heavy thrust and running footsteps down the hall. She gasped aloud as three soldiers entered, swords drawn, and advanced toward the bed.

Within moments, heavy hands were fumbling at the babe's blanket as Sileen protested, fighting off the merciless touch that bared the child's cold limbs. She heard the man's gasp as the crescent birthmark was revealed, heard as he called back to the men behind him, "Summon Fador. Tell him we have found the babe."

"Whatever babe you seek, this is not the one!" Sileen attempted to cover the child. "This babe is mine! She is the daughter of a warrior such as you, Angor of Tristle, who was killed by highwaymen he attempted to subdue!"

Her hands shaking, Sileen was still struggling to cover the babe when a tall man stepped into view. Dressed in a royal robe marked with the scrolled R of Rall, he was dark and handsome despite the evil he exuded.

Seeing death in the man's gaze, Sileen went abruptly still.

Fador stood momentarily aghast in the doorway of the small bedroom to which he had been summoned. Silent, he assessed the beautiful, fair-haired woman in the bed and the bundle that lay in the crook of her arm. The scene was exactly as Zor had described it.

Advancing toward her, Fador halted the woman's protest with a glance as he reached down to uncover the babe. He suppressed a gasp. The crescent birthmark was unmistakable on the infant's thigh, but Zor had not told him that the babe was—

"Dead!" Fador's jaw locked with anger the moment before he spat, "There is no life in this babe!"

"That cannot be true!" The young mother's pale eyes widened incredulously as she attempted to remove the babe from Fador's grasp. "She was well and strong only moments ago! She cannot be dead! Take your hands from her!" Succeeding in thrusting Fador's hands away, the woman rasped, "I will give her back her breath! Go away!"

Disgust swelled within Fador at the woman's hysterical outcries. Turning to the guards behind him, he instructed, "Take the babe and throw it on the pyre burning in the square."

"Nay!"

The young mother's screeching protest rebounded in the small room, drawing Fador's frown as he faced her once more.

"Cease your senseless protests! You may lay your babe's death at your own door, for it is most assuredly the result of the ignorant customs you followed in birthing her. But I tell you now, her death was sealed in any case, for no female child bearing the mark of Neer will survive in Orem—this night or evermore!"

Fador ignored the woman's piercing scream as the dead babe was wrenched from her arms. He turned toward the door with a step that did not falter. Unmindful and uncaring of those who watched in silent horror as he reached the great pyre burning in the square, he smiled with satisfaction as the body of the babe was tossed into the flames and was consumed.

Sobering, Fador glanced back in the direction from which he had just come. The reflection of the billowing flames imparted a demonic glow to his dark eyes as he addressed his personal guards in a voice deceptively soft for the evil it conveyed.

"Kill the woman. She has borne one babe with the mark of Neer. I will not have her bear another."

His guard moved to carry out his command and Fador mounted his horse. Heedlessly scattering those in his path, he turned the animal back toward the castle and signaled the remainder of his force to fall in behind.

Frightened shouts and the clatter of horses' hooves overwhelmed the sound of Sileen's brief scream as a sword pierced her breast moments later. Even as her blood drained onto the birthing bed beneath her, Fador dismissed her from his mind and rode recklessly back toward his castle—the victor once more.

Unknown and unseen as the funeral pyre of the dead babe burned brightly in the square and the last spark of life left Sileen's still form, Seetra moved briskly down a shadowed lane nearby. In her deceptively frail arms, she clutched a small bundle.

Seetra, formerly midwife to the Royal House of Neer, bound in its service by an oath of fidelity and love, hissed a soft hushing sound as the babe she carried gave a soft cry. Glancing up at the house just coming into view, she fought to suppress her hatred for the vicious Fador. She had seen the glorious Traka give Versa life. She had then seen Traka lose her own. She had remained at Versa's side until Versa had grown into a woman of such incredible beauty, courage, and worth as to cast all others into insignificance in her shadow. She had witnessed the treachery which had brought down the House of Neer. But unlike her dear Versa, Seetra had survived.

Her aged heart weeping with remembered pain, Seetra clutched her priceless bundle closer. Versa's life had been stolen from her, but she would not allow this babe who lived with Versa's spirit—this new Heiress of Neer—to suffer the same end.

45

Seetra's small eyes grew moist. She had recognized the hand of fate in the birth of another female child shortly after the infant heiress she now held was born—another female child who died after only a few breaths. She had hastily marked that child with a rose-colored crescent and taken it to Sileen's bed. Her heart had ached at the destiny she had foreseen for the loving Sileen as the new mother tearfully relinquished her child, sacrificing herself as she accepted the lifeless infant in her babe's stead.

A single tear trailed down Seetra's wrinkled face. She had no doubt that Sileen would not survive the hour, but she dared not concern herself with anything but the babe she carried. The child was the only remaining hope for those who had suffered Neer's destruction, those who longed for the return of rightful and compassionate rule, and those who, like her, would remain loyal to the Royal House of Neer until they breathed their final breath.

Seetra glanced apprehensively around her. The dwelling she sought was only a few more yards away, but she did not fool herself that the babe was safe. She knew only too well that Zor's powers still guided Rall and that the deception practiced this night would eventually be revealed to him. She also knew that Fador's rage would be great, that he would stop at nothing to find the babe, and that there was no place, save one, where the infant would be safe.

Breathless from her rapid flight, Seetra turned into a narrow alleyway, emerging at last in a dark yard where a wagon awaited. Her throat tight, she looked at the woman standing beside it, then handed the child into her care. The woman climbed up onto the wagon with the help of the burly driver, protesting when Seetra refused a helping hand up as well.

"Nay, I dare not accompany you," Seetra spoke in quick reply. "I am too old to survive the journey you undertake, but even if I were not, my presence would endanger the child. Go now with haste and courage, and remember that the future—the very life of Orem—lies in your arms."

The import of Seetra's words was reflected in the gaze of the sober driver as he slapped the reins against the back of his team, and in the eyes of the matron whose silent gratitude registered deeply within Seetra's heart.

Not allowing herself the satisfaction of watching the wagon slip into the darkness beyond, Seetra turned to retrace the path she had taken minutes previously, walking as quickly as her aging legs would carry her. It was time to return to Matra, to see who had survived this momentous night, and to weep and to rejoice at the sweet secret that, however briefly, was theirs alone.

* * *

Sitting stiffly atop the rough wagon as it bounced along the cobbled streets, Millith held the babe with a gentle yet unyielding hand. She had known when Seetra approached her that this journey was the reason that she had survived the destruction of the House of Neer.

Her throat tight as she viewed the babe's angelic, sleeping countenance, Millith knew that innocence was no protection from the wrath of Fador. She glanced at the wagon bed behind her, where produce from a nearby farm covered the heavy fur robes and layered clothing which would provide the protection needed from the cruel cold of Orem Minor—Orem Minor, where Zor's all-seeing eye would be blinded by the reflected power of the zircum lying beneath the surface of that frozen land.

Millith took a steadying breath, thrusting aside her fears. The House of Neer had powerful friends in Orem Minor who would keep the babe safe. She would rely on the hand of fate to deliver her and the babe safely to them, and to intercede so the babe would not suffer the same gradual debilitation of all other Proper Oremians who attempted to remain there.

As for herself—Millith clutched her cherished bundle tighter—she cared little. All life within her had died with the House of Neer, only to be revived when Versa's spirit had been reborn. She was expendable.

The babe whimpered and Millith cooed to it gently.

Uneasiness reigned over the great, dark cave which was Zor's dwelling place. The glossy, cavernous walls gleamed in the flickering light as Zor stood his ground, his expression impassive despite his astounding declaration of a few moments previous.

Zor's sober words drove Fador to outrage as he rasped, "Is this the important message you called me to this dank, stinking abode to impart, old man—*that the crescent of Neer still lives?*" Fador made a harsh, scoffing sound. "Is your brain so addled that you may speak only in riddles, or is it your purpose to incite me?"

Zor's pale face tightened at Fador's demeaning words. "Royal Rall blood flows in your veins, and for that reason I serve you, but I give you warning. The powers I place at your disposal are to be neither ridiculed nor ignored. They must be heeded if Rall is to survive."

"Senile old fool! Rall will survive, if for one reason alone—that there is no one left to challenge it!"

"Fador errs. The crescent survives."

"Again the crescent! What good is a crescent without flesh and blood—a body and mind to bring it to life?"

"The crescent lives in the body of the babe."

"The babe is dead, old man! I saw it blue and cold—without life—several nights past. I saw the crescent on its thigh! I traced the cursed mark with my finger before I ordered its lifeless form thrown into the fire! Are you telling me the babe survived its own death and a fiery grave as well, and is now back to haunt me?"

Zor held Fador's raging gaze without flinching. "My seeing eye has been clouded, but the amber crystal that gives me sight cleared briefly and I saw that the babe still lives."

"Impossible!"

Zor's stillness grew to anger. "Will you believe only if you can see as well?" Zor nodded. "So be it. Come with me."

Turning, Zor did not see the resentment that flickered across Fador's countenance as he motioned his guards to remain behind, then followed Zor into a dark corner. Nor did Zor see Fador's resentment deepen as Zor picked up the amber stone atop a rough pedestal there.

Turning back to Fador, Zor curled his long, gnarled fingers around the stone. He stroked it gently, whispering, "Look into the stone, Fador of the House of Rall, and I will call the power to serve you. Look . . . and see. . . ."

Fador gazed into the stone as he was bidden. The amber crystal remained cloudy to his view even as he felt the warmth radiating from them, the power held in abeyance, the energy that he could not quite seem to—

Fador's breath caught in his throat as he glimpsed a fleeting vision within the amber crystal. He saw the babe with the mark of Neer brightly emblazoned on its thigh—a babe alive and well!

Choking on the bitter truth of Zor's claim, Fador took a sharp step backwards, then another. Moments later he strode stiffly from the cave toward the waiting horses, one thought foremost as he mounted and signaled his guards to take up the rear.

The icy wind howled and screeched, a frigid blade that penetrated Millith's fur robes with the ease of a zircum shaft. Stealing her breath, benumbing her mind, the gusts flayed her face with sharp pellets of snow as the leaden sky overhead grew as ominous as the trackless wilderness that stretched out in a blanket of unrelenting white to the horizon.

Glancing at the driver of the wagon seated beside her, Millith struggled to recall their entrance into this merciless land—a day, a week, a month earlier, she was uncertain which. Burton's face was masked with ice. The realization that she doubtless wore the same grotesque veil caused Millith to slip her heavily wrapped hand under her furred robe to the sling where the

51

babe lay cradled against her body.

Her frozen features unable to reflect her relief, Millith inwardly smiled. The babe was still active and well, protected by her body heat—but for how much longer?

Gasping as the first of their heavily wrapped horses stumbled in his step, Millith turned a frightened look toward Burton. When the second horse stumbled, then fell to its knees, Millith's heart fell as well.

Moments later, both animals abruptly surrendered to the relentless elements, and Burton stepped down into the knee-deep snow to help her down beside him. It occurred to Millith as she took first one stiff step, then another in the icy drifts, that it was somehow ironic to have come so far, only to see the flame of Neer expire in the foreign, frozen land she had hoped would nurture its new life.

The raging wind abraded Millith as she clutched her robe tighter around her and struggled forward, sheltering the child beneath her clothing. She was not certain when she realized that Burton had fallen and could not rise, and that she had fallen and lay helpless as well. The rabid whine of the wind faded, overwhelmed in her mind by the whimper that emerged from beneath her robe.

Helpless to appease the plaintive cry, Millith drifted slowly into a world where the snow no longer fell. She did not feel the gentle touch that lifted her onto a fur-wrapped travois. Nor did she see the sober, silent figures who took up her weight and trudged steadily onward.

The silent tower room high over Orem Proper vibrated with Fador's fury as he viewed the trembling boy who had been delivered to him there. The click of the door became a lethal sound as it closed behind Fador's personal guard, leaving Filnor alone under his father's glaring perusal.

Fador seethed. The search for the babe had ended in failure—a failure that had been compounded by Zor's inability to bring the infant back into view in his mystical stone. Only one thing was certain.

The babe survived.

All but crazed with frustrated wrath, Fador addressed his son. His voice quaked with the power of his rage.

"In your pride and youthful arrogance, you, of my own flesh and blood, have done me greater injury than all those who sought my downfall! Through your disobedience, the House of Neer lives once more! You have cost me dearly, a price I was not prepared to pay. For that reason, I now tell you this. . . ."

Fador took a threatening step closer to his cowering son. "From this day forth, you will put the amusements of childhood aside. Your education, your training, your every thought and deed will be directed toward one purpose and one purpose alone—the eradication of the House of Neer and all who bear its mark! It will become your sole reason for existence as it was mine before you. From that path you will not stray—at the cost of your name, your heritage, and your life!"

In a land far away, a warm room glowed with the greenish hue of zircum heat as an icy maelstrom assailed the frozen landscape. A babe lay silent in its cradle therein. Under a servant woman's watchful eye, the babe breathed easily in a restful sleep. She was a beautiful child, a special child. She was a child marked by destiny to be the House of Neer reborn.

THE QUEST

"Vessel to seek, wherein the key,

To bring the house of Rall to knee."

Chapter Three

Orem Minor, twenty years later.

With eyes of glittering gold, fiery hair streaked with strands of platinum and amber, Sera was tall, slender, as graceful as a willow. She was teacher, healer, and the Royal Heiress of Neer fully grown.

Sera walked briskly across her chamber, her diaphanous robe flaring out behind her. She stopped abruptly beside her desk to stare down at her journal.

Day had dawned an hour earlier. Its silver rays had barely penetrated the heavy curtain of snow still falling beyond her bedchamber window, but Sera had spared little thought for the frozen landscape covered with a fresh blanket of white as she arose. Instead, she had dressed quickly, feeling anew the sense of urgency that had grown consistently stronger since she had attained adulthood a few months previously. That urgency allowed her little rest from the driving thought that she must finish the important work she had begun.

The pale green of zircum heat tinted the austerely furnished suite, lending its hue to the delicate fabric of the robes Sera wore. They had been woven especially for her of a zircum fiber that insulated her pale flesh against the unrelenting clime of her adopted land. Having worn similar apparel from childhood, she did not question the unique properties of the cloth. Instead, she accepted her special circumstances and the considerations afforded her as the norm, receiving them as she had all others since arriving in this frozen land as a fugitive babe—with gratitude and love and a sense of purpose renewed by each dawning day.

Frowning, Sera scrutinized the written page. Her abilities as a healer had come gradually, starting when she was little more than a child. Led by a silent call, she had discovered that the precious zircum mined below the surface of Orem Minor held special properties in her hand. She was certain that she had not yet learned the full extent of its power. She believed that a greater revelation was yet to come, but the ability to treat illness and to cure was presently gift enough. It was a favor she had felt bound to record in her journal, noting each healing step so that others similarly gifted in the future might find the way easier. To that purpose she was presently dedicated.

"Permission to enter, Sera?"

Sera looked up from her journal at the sound of the familiar voice. Momentarily annoyed at the heavily robed servant who had been at her side since birth, Sera responded with a familiar twitch of her lips.

"One might think you a stranger to me by your insistence on formalities, Impora. Tell me, does that mean I must respond to you in kind? Or may I speak to you as I have all my life, as I have since I carried my joys and fears to your knee from the moment I said my first word?"

Impora's face creased into a soft smile, and Sera's annoyance faded as she marveled once more at the countenance of Minor Oremians, so unlike her own. Contrary to opinion held outside their frozen domain, she saw beauty in leathery skin that was never young, never old, from the day of birth. The gentle, fixed stare of eyes with pupils permanently contracted had become dear to her. She knew that those aberrations, brought about by countless generations of exposure to the extreme conditions of Orem Minor, had allowed Minor Oremians to survive—indeed, to thrive—under conditions that caused relentless physical deterioration in all Proper Oremians who attempted to live in their difficult world.

But Sera also knew that the true beauty of Minor Oremians came from within, in their sensitivity and generosity of spirit, and in the desire for peace which was inherent in their race.

Sera's frown returned. Although she had never strayed from Orem Minor, she knew that the peace Minor Oremians sought was tenuous. The friendly co-existence between the two worlds of Orem had been shattered by the policies of Rall. Fador's cruel prejudice against Minor Oremians had taxed them greatly under his rule and would have proved fatal to their race if not for the zircum in Orem Minor's mines which only Minor Oremians were able to extract.

That fact had been brought home only too clearly to Minor Oremians by Fador's attempt to replace them in the mines with rotating crews of Proper Oremians shortly after he assumed rule. The heavy toll on his miners' lives had ultimately caused Fador to abandon the project. Minor Oremians had never lost sight of the reality, however, that Fador's intolerance was deeply ingrained and that he could just as easily decide to cast aside such considerations and implement the same policy again in the future. Dependent upon supplies from Orem Proper, and unable to live elsewhere, Minor Oremians would not survive.

Sera reached for the pouch at her waist. The inner heat of the powdered zircum within surged responsively to her touch.

Zircum, the might of Orem's blades. Zircum, the heat of Orem's fires. Zircum, the productivity of Orem's fields.

Impora walked closer, and Sera waited for her to speak. She saw the regret in Impora's fixed gaze as it met hers.

"I bring you Millith's regrets for disturbing you in your studies."

"Millith?" Sera tensed. "Is Millith unwell?"

"Nay. Millith would not have you become unduly alarmed."

"Then something *is* wrong!" Sera tensed. "Tell me what it is so I may prepare the necessary potion."

"My dear Sera." Impora's gaze was compassionate. "The hard truth is that our friend Millith is beyond your healing skills."

The heat of tears rushed to her eyes, and Sera clutched the hand Impora extended in consolation. Her tone was anguished.

"It is not just, Impora! Millith has sacrificed

61

all for me, yet she suffers while I flourish. I have been granted the power of healing, yet I cannot cure her!"

"You give her relief from her physical difficulties. . . . "

"I want to *cure* her!"

"It is too late."

"But she is dying because of me!"

"Yea, because of you."

Sera's gaze lingered on Impora's sober face for long moments. She knew that Impora's words had not been voiced to inflict pain.

Releasing Impora's hand, Sera thrust away her sorrow. She raised her chin and her gold eyes glowed with familiar fervor.

"By the royal blood of Neer that flows within me, I give you a solemn promise that neither Millith nor any of you who have done so much to bring a threatened babe to womanhood so that she might fulfill her destiny will have sacrificed in vain."

Turning abruptly, Sera strode toward the door. Within moments she was walking down the corridor, her purposeful step ringing behind her.

The frigid wind whined louder. Snowflakes gusted, becoming icy whirlwinds that abraded Tolin's numb face as he turned stiffly in the saddle to survey the panorama of relentless white enclosing him. He saw vast, frozen hills that were starkly barren; a leaden, sunless sky; and dark clouds rolling ominously closer in silent confirmation that the tribulations he faced in this harsh, unyielding land would not relent.

Rocked by another howling blast, Tolin assessed the caravan crawling through the mounting drifts behind him. His pale eyes emotionless, he saw horses stumbling and drivers huddled under heavy robes, both appearing to have lost direction and will. A snort from his destrier drew Tolin's attention to the mount that had served him through countless battles. The powerful animal was faltering. The great wolfhound walking a few feet from his horse's hooves whimpered, and Tolin's concerns deepened.

Attempting a steadying breath only to have it snatched from him by the brutal wind, Tolin felt impotent. He had fought battles too countless to recall. He had shed blood and had felt his own blood flow. He had lived a life of service and had died inside when he could serve no more. Yet fighting, killing, serving, reveling in victory and seeking strength in defeat, he had never faced an enemy as impervious as this world in which he now traveled.

Glancing again at the caravan behind him, Tolin knew that it, and he, could not last much longer.

Dismounting as the great warhorse beneath him swayed, Tolin grasped the animal's reins. His faithful wolfhound moved stiffly to his side as he shouted to the caravan behind him. His voice was lost in the wind, and he called out again. The drivers' heads rose toward him in an effort that appeared to expend the last of their strength as he waved them onward.

Numb, unable to feel the ground beneath his feet, Tolin trudged forward as a weak whinny echoed on the wind. He looked back toward the sound to see that one of the horses in the caravan had fallen. As he watched, another fell, then another and another. He saw the drivers dismount to walk only a few steps before collapsing as well.

Gradually, all were still.

Tolin felt a wild, unexpected urge to laugh. The scene was reminiscent of a battlefield where all were slain without a drop of blood.

A battlefield without blood, a world without hope.

Tolin paused in his rambling thoughts as his destrier gave a soft whuff of sound and slipped to the ground. Kneeling beside him, Tolin stroked his brave steed's frozen muzzle as his wolfhound moved to lie close by.

A battlefield without blood, a world without hope . . .

. . . a fitting end for one such as he.

Dance of the Flame

* * *

Sera mixed one herb, then another. Adding a pinch of zircum, she poured the potion into a cup and stirred it. Turning, she held it out to the woman reclining weakly on a chaise behind her. Her command was gentle.

"Drink this, Millith." At the woman's hesitation, she urged, "Come now, it bites the tongue but will give you ease."

Her features were so drawn as to appear skeletal, and her skin so gray that it appeared void of life, but Millith responded with a flicker of a smile. "My dear Sera, you are so clever and so wise . . . why are you unable to mix a potion that will *ease* me and *please* me as well?"

Sera laughed aloud, a musical sound that widened Millith's smile as she accepted the cup. Shuddering as she drained it dry, Millith rasped, "All right, I've drunk your devil's brew. In a few moments I will be well and strong enough again to do my morning tasks."

Sera's smile slowly faded.

"Sera, my dear," Millith said, beckoning her closer. "Come, sit by me so we may speak."

Hardly aware that Impora had slipped quietly out of the room, drawing the door closed behind her, Sera accepted the hand Millith offered her. She gripped it tightly as she sat.

"My lovely Sera." Millith's dull eyes grew moist. "You must not be sad because the bloom

65

of health has left my skin. I am old—"

"You are not! Had you resided in Orem Proper these many years you have spent at my side, you would still be robust and active, and you—"

"And I would have been the woman I was before you were placed in my arms as a babe that fateful night, a woman whose sorrow had stolen the life from her heart." Millith paused for breath, then continued, "You are beautiful, Sera. I did not believe I would ever say these words, but you are as pleasing to the eye as the woman whose spirit gave you life—perhaps even more so." Millith hastened to add, "But as you are like her, you are also unlike her in ways that have reminded me time and again that your heart and mind are your own. For that reason I have hesitated to speak of the restlessness I have sensed in you of late. You are anxious to begin, yet—"

"Yet I wait."

"And the waiting chafes you sorely."

Sera nodded, marveling again at Millith's ability to read her innermost feelings.

Millith's gaze became moist once more. "My heart is torn. Were you the daughter of my body as you are the daughter of my heart, I would speak the words I am tempted to say. I would tell you to remain in this land where you are protected by those who love you and where you serve a useful purpose unlike any before you."

"You speak of my ability to heal." Sera shrugged. "I record my efforts daily and will pass the results on."

"To someone who would have the knowledge, but not the power?"

"Mayhap."

Millith's wan face grew tight. "Then there is the part of me that would see you fulfill the destiny for which you were born."

Sera stiffened, her gaze growing slowly distant. "I am a woman in waiting, Millith. When my time comes, I will know."

Millith paused. "Yea, you will know."

Those words appeared to fatigue Millith. Clutching her hand tighter, Sera whispered, "Sleep now. I will return later."

The older woman's eyes drooped as Sera walked quickly to the door. She pulled it closed behind her as the first tears fell, blinding her to the tall figure who approached to slip his strong arms around her and draw her comfortingly against his robed chest.

Leaning into the familiar embrace, Sera drew heavily from its consolation as she whispered, "She's worse, Serbaak, and I cannot help her."

"You help her by your presence and with your love. Millith does not need more."

"Oh, Serbaak . . ." Sera looked up at the sober

Minor Oremian. Handsome, with a noble carriage and strength of feature that set him apart from others of his race, he was the man of compassion and honor with whom she had been raised. He was the brother of her heart, her confidant, and her friend.

Sera questioned, "How do you always seem to know when I need you?"

"I have told you many times, but you choose not to believe me." A smile tugged at Serbaak's lips. "I read your mind."

Sera's response was a familiarly indignant protest. "You do not!"

"Oh, ho! You dislike that thought, do you?" Serbaak's smile widened as he touched a teasing fingertip to her temple. "What shameful secrets do you have in there that you seek to conceal from me?"

"If you could read my mind as you claim, you would know, would you not?"

Serbaak laughed aloud. The sound reverberated in the corridor, drawing a responsive smile from Sera as he countered, "Perhaps I seek to confuse you—to see if you would lie to one who grew up beside you and who is closer to you than a brother, to one who—"

"—who has sought to tease my private thoughts from me since I was a worshipful child!" Sera's eyes narrowed. "And to one who never pretended for a moment that he would return similar confidences."

"Oh, Sera!" Serbaak raised his dark brows in mock astonishment. "Surely you would not expect a man of my experience and years to share his innermost thoughts with a young, inexperienced maid?"

"A man of your *years*?" Sera's eyes widened. "You have seen but six years more of life than I!"

Serbaak's generous lips twitched. "Ah, yes, but what full, rich years they have been!"

"Oh, pooh!" Sera waved her hand with disgust. "You irritate me beyond measure when you play the swaggering fool!"

"Perhaps that is true." Serbaak slipped his arm around her with a quick wink. "But there are times when I am able to make you smile when otherwise you would not."

Drawing her away from Millith's door, Serbaak urged Sera down the corridor at his side as he continued, "Of course, if you really want to know what I am thinking, you could attempt to read *my* mind as I read yours."

A reluctant smiled tugged at Sera's lips. "Pooh to you again, Serbaak!"

"So speaks the sage Heiress of the House of Neer."

"Serbaak!"

Laughing, Serbaak coaxed Sera onward.

* * *

The echo of his laughter had long faded from the corridor as Serbaak approached the great room where Alpor awaited him. He walked quickly through the maze of loosely structured chambers, corridors, and tunnels connecting the major domiciles of the primary village of Orem Minor. Morning was quickly advancing into afternoon and he was behind in his scheduled duties.

Serbaak's broad shoulders grew still under his sober robes. His responsibilities to Alpor, his father and the unofficial Minor Oremian spokesman, grew greater each year and were critical to Orem Minor's survival. The need to maintain steady production from the mines below their land was crucial, for Fador's greed was insatiable. It sometimes appeared to him that their relentless ruler would not be truly satisfied until his demand for the precious zircum so far outdistanced Orem Minor's ability to supply it that he would doom his Minor Oremian subjects to failure and the penalties certain to follow.

Serbaak's strong jaw hardened. He had little recollection of the specifics of Minor Oremian life under Neer's benevolent rule, but he remembered that it was sweet. The two worlds of Orem had functioned in harmony then, complementing each other and contributing to each other's needs in an easy exchange that was not governed by threat. Foodstuffs and raw materials unavailable in their harsh climate were transported into their land by the same caravans that transported zircum out in return, with those who made the dangerous journeys liberally compensated for the risks they undertook in the trafficking. It was a system that had benefited all, and which all easily accepted.

But the animosity between the ruling House of Neer and the rival House of Rall came to a virulent peak with the advent of Fador of Rall. Sad was the truth that the two royal houses had been on congenial terms in a time long past, until a powerful leader embarked Rall on a divergent path of cruelty and destruction that the ruling House of Neer disdained. The power of Rall's diabolic bent captured many under its spell, however, strengthening Rall until it ultimately challenged Neer for reign with the intent of the total annihilation of Neer.

In the civil war that ensued, Rall's relentless evil prevailed in the person of Fador.

Of Neer, only Sera remained.

Under Fador's rule in the time since, both worlds of Orem had suffered, and the exchange between Orem Proper and Orem Minor had become so unbalanced that the mines below were forced into constant activity so Minor Oremians might simply survive.

The sweet life had become more bitter each day.

Having come of age under those difficult circumstances, Serbaak had accepted the responsibilities with which his father charged him, responsibilities often painful to fulfill for the hardships they imposed on his people. The only ease granted him had been the knowledge that his people understood the source of the pressures he put upon them and his certainty that when the time came for him to guide them in Alpor's stead, they would accept him.

It was that realization which raised Serbaak from his sleeping couch with zeal each day, along with the knowledge that within the heart of Orem Minor, hope still lived in the person of Sera of Neer.

Dear Sera . . . *his* Sera, who had entranced him as a babe, who had amused him as a child, and who, as a woman, filled his heart with love.

The sharp pain of that concealed love made Serbaak pause.

Sera, whose love was beyond him in so many ways . . .

Serbaak's brief smile was touched with sadness. But Sera was not beyond the easy bantering between them, the closeness that had developed over the years, or the spontaneous irritation that surged each time he teased her.

For all her powers, however, Sera did not know that behind his teasing lay another sober truth.

Serbaak's smile slowly faded. He was uncertain when the link was first made—when Sera's distress was first transmitted over the distance between them. He knew only that her cries had echoed in his dreams as a child, drawing him to her when she was ill or in the throes of a nightmare from which she could not awaken. His sensitivity to her needs had grown through the years.

That same sensitivity was the gift that had drawn him to her earlier that morning so he might take her in his arms and comfort her when she emerged from Millith's chamber. The price he paid for the gift, however, was steep. For he suffered Sera's despair, and he felt the same need that drove her to fulfill the destiny that would eventually take her from him.

Serbaak thrust that painful thought from his mind as he paused before the great-room doors. Suddenly alarmed by the anxious voices and sounds of frantic activity beyond, Serbaak tensed.

Uncertain, he pushed the doors open.

Walking through the echoing corridor at a pace just short of a run, Sera turned toward the frowning male servant at her side. She had been astonished when he had appeared at the door of her chambers to summon her minutes earlier. She was incredulous still as she addressed him breathlessly.

"You are certain—of the entire caravan, only *one* survives?" Sera's hand tightened on the herb sack she carried, continuing as they turned another corner, "Caravans usually number forty drivers or more, with twice that many animals to draw the wagons. Yet you say—"

"Only the one survives." The servant's expression was grim. "His condition is so poor that Alpor asked for your immediate attendance."

Sera's stomach tightened. "Alpor himself summoned me?"

The servant's affirmative nod deepened Sera's concern. Her adoptive father, Alpor, was a man of honesty, intelligence, and limitless compassion. For her own protection, he was also the man who had forbidden her contact with any and all caravans journeying into their land. Surely the situation must be dire if he now broke his own cardinal rule.

The servant's voice was soft in response. "Alpor said that only you can surmount the obstacle in the path of the injured man's care."

"The obstacle?"

Sera reached the open doorway of the great room and turned inside, only to halt abruptly at the incredible scene she beheld. Standing motionless in a half circle around a still figure, she saw Alpor, Serbaak, and three servants, their expressions tense. Between the two, holding the attention of all with a slavering growl, was a huge beast unlike any she had seen before. Larger and more heavily muscled than a wolf, uglier than any domestic animal she had ever known, it blocked access to the man whose fur robe was still encrusted with ice.

The sound of her entrance turned the attention of the men toward her. The beast snarled savagely at her as she queried softly, "What is happening here?"

Alpor answered, "This man is the sole survivor of an unscheduled caravan. That he is still alive is doubtless due to this beast, who was found lying atop him, warming him with his body heat. The animal and the man were transported here together—which appears to have proved a mistake, for now the beast has miraculously regained his strength and will allow no one near his master."

"And you could not overpower the animal without injuring him."

"Nay."

"So you called me."

"Your affinity to animals, Sera—"

"I know."

Placing her sack on a table nearby, Sera turned back toward the beast standing threateningly a few yards away. A chill ran down her spine as his small eyes flicked in her direction. He growled more menacingly, and the hair on his spine stood up in a stiff ruff. The power of the beast was unmistakable. If he should turn on her . . .

Meeting and holding the animal's feral gaze, Sera sensed his fear and panic at his master's condition. She felt his instinctive need to protect the inert man. Her heart softened toward the great brute as her admiration for his loyalty and courage grew.

Taking a step forward, Sera offered the animal her hand, palm upward in a sign of peace, but he maintained his menacing stance. He shifted position subtly as she took another step, his powerful muscles tense, ready to spring, but Sera did not fear. She had read his simple mind and transmitted her thoughts. She knew he would understand that she was no threat to his master.

Within inches of the beast's glinting fangs, Sera paused. She touched his head with her fingertips, and the animal fell back abruptly to lie in silent scrutiny of her at his master's side.

The moment of peril past, Sera looked at the motionless form on the travois for the first time. Still clad in frozen fur outerware, he lay stiff and still, his face totally lacking in color. Sera realized that death hovered very near the unknown man. Her reaction was immediate as she turned to the servants behind her.

"Quickly, carry this man to my chambers where I may treat him."

When the servants hesitated, looking at the animal nearby, she admonished, "There is no need to fear the beast. I have calmed his anxieties. While your purpose toward his master remains pure, you are safe from his attack."

Her annoyance grew when the servants still hesitated. Sera addressed the animal softly.

"Friend . . ."

The beast stood abruptly as she continued, "These three of faint heart must be coaxed to do my bidding."

In a flash of movement that defied the eye, the beast was behind the three servants. A rough growl moved them quickly toward his master, and within moments they had lifted the travois and were walking toward the door.

Glancing at Alpor as she followed, Sera saw an almost fatherly pride in her skill reflected on his face.

"What will you need to treat this man?" Serbaak asked.

"Hot water for both bathing and consumption, the pots of salve marked with my sign that are stored in the cellar room, clean cloths . . ."

Serbaak nodded, adding, "I will have the servants bring additional fur robes to raise his body heat."

"Robes will not be necessary. I will use a coverlet from my coffer."

"A coverlet of zircum cloth for this man?" He shook his head. "The cloth is yours alone. It scorches all other skin on which it lies."

Sera's response rolled off her tongue without prior thought. "This man will bear its heat well. But haste is imperative if he is to survive."

Sera paid no heed as Serbaak's instructions to the servants rang in the corridor behind her, followed by the sound of running feet as they hastened to his bidding. Her attention was fixed again on the unknown man as the travois turned a corner ahead.

Afternoon had stretched into evening and evening into night, and still Sera labored. Her delicate features tense, her slender body covered by perspiration, she closely scrutinized the elixir she mixed.

Herbs carefully cultivated in her domed garden, honey from the land of Orem Proper, water drawn and warmed from the depths of Orem Minor's wells, and powdered zircum, ground by her own hand.

Sera stirred the swirling mixture again, frowning. Three times this day she had slipped this potion between the stranger's blue lips and had rubbed his throat until he swallowed. He had not yet responded, and her consternation had grown.

Walking back to the bed, cup in hand, Sera stared briefly down at the man who lay naked except for the small clothes that covered his male parts and the translucent coverlet thrown across him. Her heart began a ragged pounding as she perused the motionless, powerful body she had spread with warming salve throughout the day. The broad shoulders and chest into which she had massaged the heat of life moved with shallow breaths; the sinewy arms lay lax at his sides; the long, muscular legs rested motionless against the bed linens. She had been strangely affected as she felt the might of this man's form lying quiescent under her hands.

Her gaze shifted to focus on the stranger's right hand, Sera saw again the heavily scrolled letter R marking the skin there, and her throat tightened convulsively. She had seen that symbol many times in her dreams.

Her gaze shifted to the man's face, and Sera felt her stomach knot. Yes, she knew who he was. He had been easily recognizable once his fur outer garments had been removed, for there could be few so chillingly formidable in appearance as he, even in his unconscious state, and fewer still of such overwhelming muscular proportions. The scar that marked the man's cheek in a fine line from eye to lip, and the countless others on his body, were the badges of a warrior. The wolfhound lying silently beside his bed and the destrier delivered nearly frozen to the stables below were warrior's beasts. His shoulder-length hair was silver-gold in color, and she had no doubt that beneath those darkly lashed, unmoving lids were gray eyes as cold and lifeless as ice.

Of the few who might match this man's description, there could be fewer still who bore the scrolled letter R identifying the personal guard of the Royal House of Rall.

Her expression tight, Sera slipped her arm under the warrior's neck, raising his head as she pressed the cup to his mouth. The great beast beside the bed stirred as his master mumbled a brief sound, but she paid neither the beast nor the man any mind. The fearless warrior had protested each time she had forced the bitter elixir between his lips. In that way he was no different than the gentle, loving Millith, who suffered because of this man's master.

Pressing the cup relentlessly against his lips, Sera waited until the elixir had been completely consumed before allowing the warrior's head to slip back against the bed.

Yea, she knew who he was . . . and she would wait and see.

Tolin stirred from his tormented sleep. Straining to raise the heavy weight of his lids, he opened his eyes slowly. The throbbing ache in his limbs distracted his mind as he attempted to focus on the unfamiliar chamber in which he lay. Large, sparsely furnished, as devoid of color as the landscape which had threatened to consume him, it would have appeared similarly void of life had it not been for the pale, greenish hue which appeared to warm and encompass all.

A familiar whimpering beside him drew Tolin's attention the moment before a wiry canine head slipped onto the bed beside him. Satisfaction surged within him. Gar had survived.

Managing to move his hand, Tolin rested it briefly against the animal's stiff fur. A flicker of motion in the doorway drew his attention from Gar's responsive whine as a woman stepped unexpectedly into view.

A flash of heat in the cold, a burst of color where there had been none, the woman moved quietly and with grace, her long, slender limbs and smooth curves clearly outlined under her sheer garments. The woman's supreme beauty contrasted sharply with the stark surroundings, and Tolin reacted acutely to her sensual stimulus, despite the dulling veil that shrouded his mind. The woman turned abruptly toward him, and Tolin's foggy mind grew incredulous.

Could it . . . could it truly be she?

Hair of a fiery tone, eyes of brilliant gold . . .

The woman moved closer and Tolin's gaze dropped to her thigh. Spontaneous rage soared as he identified her.

His rage ebbing as abruptly as it had swelled,

Tolin allowed his eyes to droop slowly closed. It was too late. Tolin, the cutting edge of Fador's personal guard, no longer existed. He had sacrificed his name along with his home, lands, and all he possessed when Fador's lust for power and carnage had become unconscionable. In throwing down his arms and resigning from the service of Rall, he had become a nonentity, a being without purpose, a wanderer with no life in him.

Drifting into unconsciousness once more, Tolin was struck by the irony of the moment. The truth had been revealed at last, at a time when it meant nothing at all to him.

Sera turned abruptly toward the pallet behind her. The warrior's eyes were closed, but she sensed that he had been studying her.

Walking quickly to his side, Sera scrutinized him intently despite the exhaustion that dragged at her body and mind. He was breathing more easily and his color was returning.

He would survive.

She would *make* him survive . . .

. . . for the time she had awaited was now upon her.

Chapter Four

Sera awakened, her mind abruptly keen and clear as she glanced through the window at the scene beyond. The heavy snow continued falling as it had since the unconscious warrior had been delivered into her care three days previously.

Throwing back her coverlet, Sera stood up, a sense of apprehension suddenly overwhelming her. Her patient had responded peculiarly to her ministrations during that time, staring at her with those frozen gray eyes, withholding conversation or comment of any kind as his periods of consciousness gradually lengthened.

Strangely, Sera knew he had been aware of her attentions even when death hovered close by. Strange also had been the spark within her that had come to life during those tense hours, steadying her through her exhaustion, urging her to greater effort, and guiding her curing hand.

Aware of how close her patient had come to succumbing, Sera had respected his silence and remained silent as well, going so far as to direct all visitors out of earshot before any discourse between them began.

Sera recalled Serbaak's concern when she had refused his aid and the help of the servants sent to her. She knew she had hurt his feelings by allowing him only brief access to the room. But she had the sense deep inside her that all hinged on what would transpire within the next few days and the certainty that in holding the life of this man in her healing hands, she also held her own fate.

For three days, she had labored over the warrior in silence, but somehow she sensed that this day—

Anticipation suddenly acute, Sera abandoned her cursory grooming and strode toward her outer chamber. Caring little that she still wore her sleeping garment, a robe more translucent than her usual apparel, she stepped into the doorway and halted abruptly. Her breath caught in her throat as the towering figure, standing erect and strong with his warrior beast at his side, turned to regard her with his lifeless, gray-eyed stare.

That same lifeless gaze moved to the fiery profusion of her unbound hair with an almost palpable touch, then trailed slowly downward, as if noting every detail—the heavy fringe of dark lashes surrounding the golden glow of her eyes, the exotic rise of her cheekbones, the smooth slope of her jaw, the curve of her lips. The intimate perusal descended further, stroking her neck and shoulders, the rounded swell of her breasts, her flat, narrow waist, the sweet curve of her hips, then the long, slender length of her legs before returning to linger a fraction longer on the warm delta between her thighs.

Angry at the responsive heat the warrior's gaze elicited within her, Sera raised her chin, boldly returning his stare.

How dare he! She was not a swooning maid who would fall at this man's feet when faced with his bold assessment or the blatant masculinity he so arrogantly displayed as he stood before her clad in a breechcloth! Nor would she allow him to believe for a moment that he intimidated her with the sheer size and breadth of him, or the power he so effortlessly exuded despite his recent debility.

She had seen him in his weakness. She had fed him, bathed him, and smoothed every inch of his imposing frame in her ministrations, leaving not an inch of him unattended. And if there had been times when her hands trembled

85

as they massaged the life back into his smooth, hard flesh—if her heart had pounded, leaving her strangely breathless under his silent scrutiny as she was even now—she knew it was only because she sensed his pivotal role in her destiny. For she was Sera, Heiress of Neer! As such, she was beyond the common reaction of woman to man.

Sera's voice was as frigid as her stare when she finally spoke.

"Have you completed your evaluation? Would you care to tell me what you see?"

"What I see?" The warrior's voice was unexpectedly deep, almost a growl as he regarded her scathingly. "I see a scantily clothed woman standing brazenly before me as I study her body. Since you have not come to me so revealingly clad before, and since you have done so this morning when my strength would almost certainly be fully returned, I can only conclude that it is your desire to seduce me. If it is, I tell you now that no further artifice is necessary. I will accede."

Sera's fair skin flamed. "The noble warrior flatters himself!"

Contempt registered briefly in the strong lines of the warrior's countenance. "Surely you are not one of those maids of pretended virtue who demands compliments and cajoling words before copulation. Would you have me adhere to formalities and speak the obvious as others doubtless have before me, by telling you that you are a beautiful woman?"

Incited beyond restraint, Sera advanced furiously into the room. "Nay, you need not speak *the obvious*. Nor do *I* feel it necessary to say what others have doubtless said to *you* many times before—that you are woefully lacking in the most meager of sensibilities—for that is obvious, too! Instead, I say simply, in words even *you* cannot misconstrue, that time spent in paying compliments to me would be wasted. I am as far above such female considerations as I am above the weaknesses of the flesh!"

Coming to a halt so close to him that she could feel the intense male heat emanating from his body, Sera repeated, "I ask you again—what do you see when you look at me?"

The warrior's cold eyes narrowed as they dropped directly to her thigh. His voice rang with an emotion formerly suppressed.

"I see a woman whose flesh is stained by the mark of infamy, a woman whom I formerly believed merely a legend created by those in Orem Proper who cling to the last remaining vestiges of opposition to Rall's rule."

"Infamy, you say!" Sera's temper soared. "Surely infamy is more truly represented by the letter scrolled on your hand than by the mark I wear!"

The warrior gave a hard, unexpected laugh. "So you would have me believe! Is that the reason for your ardent care—the hope that you might persuade me you act out of a heart that is kind and pure?" He laughed again with a sound that contained no mirth. "Nay, devoid of sensibilities I may be, but I am not fool enough to believe that beauty is innocence, no matter how supreme that beauty may be. I did not doubt your ulterior purpose from the moment my eyes first touched upon you. Nor did I doubt that you would eventually tell me what you expect from me for the services you have rendered."

Sera trembled with outrage. "Yea, I will tell you what I want of you, but I will ask a question first—one so direct that even one of your deviant bent of mind will have no difficulty responding. I would have you tell me if you agree that my ministrations to you—ministrations that filled both the day and night hours of the three days most recently past—brought you back from the edge of death."

Cold gray eyes turned frigid. "Yea, you saved my life."

Sera inwardly smiled. Seeing victory within her grasp, she continued softly, "What I ask of you, then, is simple. I would have you return my favor by performing a service."

"You waste your breath!" Frigid eyes turned to ice. "My days of service are over!"

Incredulous at his reply, Sera rasped, "Do my ears deceive me, or did you say you would sacrifice your honor by refusing repayment of a debt?"

"My *honor*?" The warrior's harsh bark of laughter was as sharp as a blade. "I have no honor! It was stripped from me the first time I plunged my knife into the heart of one man at the command of another." The warrior's lips twisted into a snarl. "But you may be sure that if honor still held any meaning for me, I would not be fool enough to believe it would be well served by helping the sorceress who seeks to enslave Orem!"

"Sorceress!" Sera was aghast. "Can it be that you are honestly unaware of the folly you speak? Were I the sorceress you claim me to be, would I have worked to exhaustion during the long days and nights recently past, employing my skills as a healer, to save your worthless life? Would I now seek your *willing* aid? Or would I have enchanted you into health with a magic spell and veiled your mind so you *must* obey me?"

Sera's smile was grim when he did not reply. "Would that it could be so. Instead, I must endure your supreme insolence and ingratitude in order to obtain your aid!"

"I will not participate in the downfall of Orem!"

"You, of all men, have played a greater part in Orem's downfall than I ever could!" Sera's lips tightened as she proceeded, "You are the warrior named Tolin, are you not—he who was called Death's Shadow while in Fador's service?" She nodded. "Yea, I recognized you. Your reputation has scorched even Orem Minor's frozen reaches! Has your intimate proximity to the mayhem Fador induced so benumbed your mind that you fail to realize that Fador's endless lust for power and riches takes Orem rapidly along the path toward the downfall you decry? Fool! You have but to step outside this chamber to see how the people of Orem Minor live. Good, honest people at the mercy of Fador because of the harshness of this land, they are driven and oppressed until they can manage little more than to survive. Judging from word which filters to us by way of the caravans, Orem Proper does not fare much better under Rall's rule."

Pausing to catch her breath, Sera continued, "But even if you would repudiate the evidence before your eyes—if you would deny honor—you cannot refuse an opportunity to unite Orem and restore it to the peace and harmony its people deserve. You can do that by helping me to fulfill the prophecy so that I, the true Heiress of Neer, may be returned to my rightful position."

Tolin's cold eyes mocked her. "What position is that, heiress?"

"You know that answer as well as I!"

"I know only that I will no longer agree to destroy for any cause!"

"I do not ask you to destroy! I ask you to help restore life to Orem. I ask you to protect a life which will be endangered—*mine*."

"Your life will not be endangered if you give up this mad scheme to depose Fador."

"To do that would be to deny life—the life for which I am fated!"

Sera spoke again into the silence that ensued. "My requests are simple." She raised her hand, briefly covering Tolin's eyes with her palm as she continued, "I ask you to use the sight my ministrations saved to keep me safe from my enemies until I am back within Orem Proper."

She grasped his muscled arm. "I ask you to use the strength restored to this arm by my skill to aid me in my quest—to deliver me safely to those who await my return."

Dropping her hand back to her side, Sera concluded, "These two things I ask of you, and nothing more."

Fire and ice met as their gazes locked, and Sera felt the chill that encompassed Tolin's heart. Never more certain that the ruthlessness, brute power, and knowledge this man possessed were the perfect shield against Fador's threat, she demanded, "What is your response?"

Silence stretched long and tense between

them before Tolin responded abruptly.

"I will deliver you to your destination in Orem Proper and nothing more."

"That is all I ask."

Tolin's handsome, scarred face was colder than death as his deep voice rumbled the words of a bargain struck.

"Then it is done."

His gaze narrowing as the ravishing Sera of Neer left the chamber without another word, Tolin felt a familiar heat soar. Cursing aloud, he reached for his clothes.

Nay, there was no doubt. She was a witch after all.

Slipping his undergarment over his head, Tolin pulled it down roughly. He noted the sweet scent of recent laundering and realized that the Heiress of Neer had let nothing slip past her. She had tended him in his illness. She had smoothed the pain from his body with soft, relentless hands, the thought of which still warmed him. She had fed and given him comfort, remaining at his side without interruption until health was fully restored. Through it all, she had bathed him with the gaze of those glowing eyes, and in doing so had kindled a fierce fire within him that he could not dispel.

Tolin's short bark of laughter was hard.

Sera . . . Heiress of the Royal House of Neer.

Neer . . .

Tolin's mind slipped back to the dim memories of childhood, to a time when the sound of that name had sent chills down his spine. It had been during the great civil war, a period of bloodshed and fear for Orem. He had been hardly more than a babe, the son of a fallen warrior of Rall whom he could not remember. He had been carefully guarded from the turmoil by his mother, but the sounds of the tortured and dying had hung on the wind, as had the black smoke that had covered the land. He recalled that he had rejoiced along with his mother when she had come to him and breathlessly exclaimed that the House of Neer had fallen, that Fador— the great, incomparable Fador—now reigned.

Strangely, his mother had lived only a few years after that day. There one moment, gone the next, she had left him an orphan to be handed over to the service of Filnor of Rall because of their like age and his warrior heritage. Educated and reared at Filnor's side, he had shared Filnor's life, a life which had changed forever after a fateful night in the tower room high above Orem Proper.

Tolin's eyes briefly closed. Sharing Filnor's life as well as his punishment, his childhood had come to an abrupt end that night. A new education had then begun—and sometime during the years that followed, Filnor's mission had become his own.

93

Frowning, Tolin reached for the warrior's garments he had retained as his manner of dress, the leather vest and leggings tailored specifically for his powerful proportions. He remembered the day Filnor and he had first donned the traditional clothing. Fador had stood in silent observance of the ceremony, his impressive figure distinguished by his royal colors and the letter R emblazoned on his garments. But Fador had remained expressionless and remote despite the great import of the occasion.

A chill crawled down Tolin's spine. That had been a day of firsts, for it had been that day when he first realized that the rumors of Fador's unwaning resentment toward his only son were true.

Tolin's eyes iced once more. He had fought long and hard at Filnor's right hand in the years that followed. He had served Fador with cruel dedication—quelling uprisings, conquering anew, tracing and silencing every whispered hint of the return of Neer.

Tolin's broad frame stiffened as he strapped his leather jerkin closed.

He had cut a bloody swath across the land until the wash of blood became a flood that drowned the last flicker of life within him.

Tolin's jaw clenched tight as he was revisited by the memory of Fador's contempt and Filnor's fury when he announced the surrender of his commission. Filnor's scathing verbal attack still rang in his ears.

Coward! Traitor! Fool!

The camaraderie and brotherhood of years was dispelled in that moment, never to be restored. Looking back at Filnor and Fador one last time as he turned away, he had seen only hatred in their eyes. Strangest of all, however, was his realization that in the glare of Filnor and Fador's disdain, he had felt nothing at all.

Glancing at the doorway through which Sera of Neer had disappeared minutes earlier, Tolin reached for the sword that lay nearby and strapped it to his waist.

During the years he had served Rall, he had devoted himself to eradicating all traces of the faceless, nameless "Heiress of Neer."

But the heiress was faceless and nameless no longer.

Standing fully clothed at last, pale hair touching broad, leather-clad shoulders, strong features hard, light eyes grim, Tolin silently acknowledged that he was now that same Heiress of Neer's only protection from the shadow of death that still stalked her.

Gar's soft growl was a warning that confirmed a sudden, instinctive awareness within Tolin. He whirled back toward the doorway, sword slashing from its scabbard.

*   *   *

Serbaak halted abruptly at the glint of steel in the leather-clad warrior's hand. He remained in the doorway, studying the fearsome stranger with silent animosity. Neither the speed nor the spontaneity of the man's aggressive movement had escaped him. Nor had he missed the grizzled canine at the warrior's side, or the look in the man's gray eyes which declared that a blade which had drawn much blood would not hesitate to draw more.

Serbaak knew he should not have expected anything else. His contempt soared as he spoke.

"You may calm your fear. I am unarmed."

The stranger's deep voice was similarly chilly. "I *have* no fear."

Serbaak's strong jaw locked. He did not doubt the claim was true. A step forward started the huge canine to growling again, to which he responded, "Call off your animal. My presence here threatens neither you nor him."

Serbaak paused, the need for explanation grating on him as he continued, "It appears that you and your canine protector are unaware that we of Orem Minor do not share the same combative tendencies as our counterparts in Orem Proper. We do not carry weapons, nor do we indulge in intimidation."

The warrior's sword remained unyielding. "What do you want of me?"

"You are so sure I came here to ask something of you?"

"You did not come here to see Sera of Neer, of that I am certain. You are too conscious of her comings and goings not to have known that she is not here."

"What if I came from the other direction and did not see her depart?"

"But you did not."

Serbaak nodded, acknowledging, "Nay, I did not."

The sword slowly sank to the floor. Moments later it was sheathed.

Serbaak entered the chamber as the warrior Serbaak knew to be called Tolin addressed him.

"Your face is not unfamiliar. I saw you many times in the doorway while I was still afflicted. I also saw Sera of Neer dismiss you each time you came."

"She did not dismiss me!" Serbaak's temper flared at the man's deliberate affront. "In her concern for your uncertain condition, she asked that we converse outside."

"So"—The pale eyes narrowed—"those of Orem Minor who are above weapons and intimidation are not above anger."

Serbaak's dislike for the sullen warrior soared as he introduced himself more formally. "My name is Serbaak. The people of Orem Minor look to my father, Alpor, for guidance and call him their spokesman. You have lived these past days under my father's roof. His food and drink have sustained you and allowed you to grow strong again."

The warrior's gaze tightened. "Am I to be told a second time this day that a favor given requires a favor in return?"

"Nay. I ask no favor of you."

Serbaak seethed. He neither liked nor trusted this man of the lifeless eyes and the killing spirit. He did not approve of Sera's plan to put her safety into his hands, and he feared for the outcome of her quest if she persisted in doing so. He had expressed his concerns to her countless times over the past few days, voicing them so adamantly that Sera had directed him out of the room so he might not disturb her patient's recuperation.

Were Sera another woman—a Minor Oremian such as he—Serbaak would have stilled her objections with the warmth of his kiss and drawn her into the comfort of his arms, holding her there, gently and safely, all the days of their lives.

But Sera was not another woman. She was a woman of destiny, and for that reason Serbaak spoke again with a harshness of tone that set the great beast at Tolin's side to growling once more.

"My purpose in coming here was to make a declaration of purpose to the warrior who has served Rall so well that his dubious fame precedes him."

The warrior stiffened. "Rall is my master no longer."

"You have shed blood in Rall's name!"

"I have fought Orem's enemies."

"Sera of Neer is not Orem's enemy!"

The man did not deign to reply, sending a hot flush to Serbaak's distinctive skin and intensifying the piercing gaze of his eyes. "I tell you again, *Sera of Neer is not Orem's enemy*! She is the hand that will lift the oppression under which Orem lives. She is the spark that will return joy to Orem's people. She is the life Orem has awaited, and she is Orem's only hope for survival!"

"Fool!" The warrior spoke in a scathing hiss. "With every word you speak, you reveal how deeply the woman has bewitched you!"

"Yea, she has bewitched me." Serbaak's words grew gradually stronger. "I, who have known Sera of Neer from a babe, who have grown to adulthood at her side, who have come to know the inner workings of her heart—I, who value her above all other women—tell you this. I do not know why Sera has chosen you to lead her home, for it is a privilege and an honor that is far above you. I do know, however, that should you betray her, should you lead her astray in any way, the death of Orem will doom your soul to the darkest reaches of eternity!"

An extended silence was followed by Tolin's emotionless reply.

"I *have* no soul."

The truth of Tolin's statement clear, Serbaak responded levelly.

"My only recourse, then, is to speak of *my* destiny. It is reflected in these words I speak now, words which burn into *my* soul when I pledge to you that should you betray Sera of Neer, I will follow you to the ends of Orem, and before my final breath is breathed, I will see the last drop of blood drain from your veins into Orem's doomed soil."

"So"—The warrior's gaze grew mocking—"Minor Oremians are above weapons and intimidation . . ."

"But not above avenging the life of one who is Orem's only hope for survival!"

"You take me for a fool!" The warrior's expression was suddenly savage. "You would avenge the woman, not the ideal!"

"My heart would avenge the woman." Serbaak's voice became a lethal pledge. "But my hand would avenge all else."

"So speak you, who have never shed a drop of blood!"

"So speak I, who would make the first drops of blood I shed the last."

The silent tableau that remained in the wake of Serbaak's somber words was shattered by the approach of a light step in the corridor beyond. Serbaak turned toward the doorway as Sera stepped into sight. A great tenderness welled inside him as her tentative gaze touched his. He approached her and took her hand.

"Your patient is strong again, Sera. You have done well."

Departing shortly afterward, Serbaak did not bid farewell to the warrior who stood cold and silent behind him.

Chapter Five

Dawn filtered through the continuing storm, shedding its muted glow on the caravan assembled within the gates of the primary village of Orem Minor. The low, dimly lit buildings were covered with a growing mantle of white and appeared silent and serene, belying the frantic activity of the past hour as the caravan prepared to depart.

His hooded fur robe already encrusted with a thin layer of frozen snow, Tolin scanned the assemblage. His narrowed gaze drifted unconsciously toward the rise of ground behind the village where Orem Minor's largest zircum mine—the destination of regularly scheduled monthly caravans from Orem Proper—lay barely visible to the naked eye. He had learned during his two weeks of residence that smaller mines and their corresponding villages stretched in a chain across the frozen terrain, each with its own schedule of caravans, and that each mine and village worked to capacity to meet Fador's demands.

Tolin recalled the exhaustion he had read on the miners' lined faces. He had learned that such was the rule rather than the exception in this hard land, contrary to the deliberate lies propagated by Rall in Orem Proper. He had carefully counted the ore wagons in the caravan with which they would travel. Simple calculations proved that Orem Minor was producing ore in amounts that far exceeded Rall's claims—amounts that did not justify the continued rationing and rapidly escalating price of the valuable substance under Fador's rule.

So precious was zircum to Orem Proper that without it, the fuel of Orem Proper's fires burned with little heat, the soil of Orem Proper's fertile fields lay barren, and the metals of Orem Proper's mines were all but useless.

Zircum was an enhancement of Orem's life that had become so necessary to its survival that Tolin had not considered, even for a moment, that Fador's greed had risen to a degree where he might withhold it from his people for personal gain. Nor had he considered that Fador encouraged the hatred of Proper Oremians for their counterparts in Orem Minor because of his own despicable prejudice.

A chilling blast rocked him, and Tolin glanced up at the sky. He saw no end to the blizzard that raged around them. Determined that the disaster which had struck him on the journey to Orem Minor would not be repeated, he had insisted that certain precautions be taken with this caravan. The wagon runners had been sharpened to allow travel with greater ease and speed in the snow, the protective mantles for the animals had been improved, and an additional wagonload of supplies had been included for the journey.

The caravan master had followed the charges with open resentment, but Tolin would not have expected else. He had known men like the arrogant, heavily bearded Rockwald before. He knew he could easily handle the man's ire, but he also knew that to make the man suspicious of him or the beautiful "wife" with whom he would be traveling would be dangerous.

Tolin recalled Rockwald's scrutiny of the wagon that Alpor had ordered prepared to transport Sera and him back to Orem Proper. Without any obvious luxury, the attention to detail offered uncommon comfort, to which Rockwald had reacted with open contempt.

Taking the opportunity to seek Tolin out in private, Rockwald had goaded him with a mocking rise of his brow. "Are you certain your wagon will be comfortable enough to meet your needs? After all, there is only *one* feather mattress and *two* fur coverlets. Surely *two* mattresses would be better, or *three* coverlets." Rockwald's lips had drawn into a deliberate sneer. "Mayhap you have a personal problem. Mayhap your wife complains of your ability to cushion her ride and warm her properly through the night."

Tolin had pinned him with a frozen gaze, responding, "Rather than concerning yourself with my wife's needs, it seems to me you had better concentrate on the needs of your drivers and animals, who both appear much the worse for wear after their lengthy trek here."

"*I* am the best judge of the needs of my men and beasts, not you!" Rockwald's expression had grown livid. "You forget, *I* arrived here with my entire caravan intact, unlike you who, along with your wife and personal beasts, were, however strangely, the sole survivors of the caravan in which you traveled!"

Tolin's massive frame had tensed beneath his heavy robes. "If you imply foul play on my part . . ."

"Nay . . . nay!" Rockwald had retreated as Tolin's stare turned deadly. He had continued in a more solicitous tone, "That was not my thought! I merely wished to point out my superior experience in traversing this frozen wasteland."

"You have made more journeys through this land than I—that I will not dispute—but keep one warning in mind." Tolin's stare had intensified as he grated, "Both my wife and I are innocent of wrongdoing in the disaster of our arrival in Orem Minor. For you to insinuate aught else, either here or upon our return to Orem Proper, will prove a costly error."

Tolin had turned away then, dismissing the man with a silent curse.

Looking up, Tolin cursed again as Sera's slender, fur-clad figure moved into sight in a dimly lit doorway. Serbaak stood close beside her as he too often was, and Tolin's stomach clenched with a harsh emotion he was finding increasingly difficult to dismiss. Shouts of imminent departure turned Tolin to see that the last of the precious cargo had been loaded. The drivers had already mounted their wagons and the horses stood snorting and blowing, their breath frozen puffs on the air.

Man and beast were poised and ready to begin the agonizing journey ahead . . . and still Sera lingered.

Anger exploded within Tolin. Fool! Was she not aware of the danger in her extended farewell to Serbaak? Did she not see that the charade of husband and wife necessary for her protection was threatened by the emotion she so obviously displayed? Was she so obtuse that she did not realize that a man such as he would never allow his woman to linger in the arms of another man?

Fury overwhelming him, Tolin strode rapidly toward the two figures in the doorway. He was a short distance away from Sera of Neer when he saw the marks of tears on her cheeks.

His stomach knotting more tightly than before, Tolin continued his angry advance.

"I beg you one last time to reconsider." Serbaak's voice quaked with the concern Sera read in the sober lines of his face as he continued, "It is unwise to put your life in the hands of any stranger, Sera, but it is *foolhardy* to entrust it to a man such as Tolin, who has no life or hope within him."

Sera's anguished expression revealed the sadness of her farewells to Alpor and Impora and the devastating effect of her final adieu to Millith, who would not live to see her return. She replied with difficulty.

"My dear Serbaak, can you not understand? I have no recourse but to follow my destiny."

"To follow destiny without a viable plan to accomplish all it entails is madness!"

"Madness?" Sera paused in response. "Is it madness to know that the voice within me, the flame that gave me life and has guided my path to this day, will not desert me? Is it madness to believe with utmost certainty, as I stand poised to be thrust into events decreed by fate, that all will be provided for?"

"Sera . . ." Serbaak's expression grew pained. "There are so many things that lie still unexplained to you . . . as to us all. The total devastation of the House of Neer leaves those details forever a mystery. With the fate of the Royal Advisors of Neer uncertain, you may yet arrive in Orem Proper to find yourself totally alone."

"The Royal Advisors are alive. Of that I entertain no doubt. As for the rest, the prophecy will guide my way."

Not questioning the basis of Sera's conviction, Serbaak continued earnestly, *"Vessel to seek, wherein the key* . . . the prophecy is vague, so unclear that the actual vessel for which you are to search is not defined!"

Sera's eyes of moist gold held Serbaak's anxious, fixed stare as she began in a voice husky with solemnity, "My dearest Serbaak, why can you not comprehend my faith in the destiny toward which I travel and the voice within me which guides me there? Why can you not understand my willingness to risk all in my supreme confidence that the vagaries of the past will eventually be revealed in full to me—somehow—when the time is ripe, so I may protect myself from their inherent dangers? How can you ask me to suffer your painful uncertainties, when I know within my heart that you endure them all for naught?"

"Sera, once you leave the soil of Orem Minor, the protection which shielded you all of your life will no longer prevail."

"The Flame of Neer will prevail."

"Within you, yea! But without, you will be defenseless!"

"Tolin will—"

"Tolin *of Rall*! His very name bespeaks treachery and bloodshed!"

"His given word will remain his bond."

"A man who rejects his soul has no bond!"

Serbaak's torment was more than she could bear. Sera pressed her fingers against his lips to hush his tortured words, even as she rasped, "Serbaak . . . my dearest friend . . . I beg you to take courage in my conviction that the step I now take was preordained, and in the knowledge that the pain I now suffer is untouched by fear and is only the pain of separation from those I love."

Echoing shouts from behind alerted her to the imminent departure of the caravan, and Sera leaned full against Serbaak's broad chest. Their arms intertwined as she realized fully, for the first time, the true extent of her loss in leaving him. Serbaak . . . her brother, her confidant, her friend . . . somehow she had not anticipated that she would suffer their farewell so deeply.

Drawn from her thoughts by the sound of a step behind her, Sera was about to turn when she was wrenched from Serbaak's grasp and jerked roughly backwards to meet Tolin's fierce countenance.

Startled, her golden eyes snapping wide the moment before they turned hot with fury, Sera halted Serbaak's angry advance with a warning glance. Dwarfed by Tolin's great size, she felt only outrage as she hissed, "Are you truly as mad as your actions would indicate? By what right do you lay your hand on me?"

"By what right?" Tolin's lifeless gaze dripped ice. "By the right of a husband."

"A husband! So that is the part you play!" Sera sought to subdue her surging ire. "I warn you, do not take your role too seriously, for I will not suffer your oppressive ways!"

"And I warn you"—Tolin's menace reverberated in the narrow distance between them—"you risk *my* life as well as your own with this game you have foisted upon me, and I will not have you dismiss it lightly! Were it to become known that I transport the Neer crescent back to Orem Proper—"

Sera's gaze narrowed. "That fact will become known only if you betray me."

"Could you possibly be so much a fool?" Tolin

111

was incensed. "Look around you! Tell me what you see!"

The heat of Tolin's response turned Sera to survey the scene of impending departure—wagons in line, drivers mounted, and caravan master with whip readied to start them on their journey. Her face flushed hotly despite the bite of the wind when she noted that all eyes were turned in their direction.

"Yea, heiress." Tolin's gaze slashed her. "It is not I who would betray you! You would betray yourself by lingering in another man's arms, thereby mocking the union that supposedly exists between us!"

"Another man's arms? Serbaak is not *another man*! He holds a special place in my heart!"

"A heart that Fador would wrench from your body with a merciless hand if given the chance!"

Serbaak took a heavy step forward as Tolin growled, "Stay back! If you value this woman's life, you will follow through with this farce so I may convince those behind me that she is *mine*!"

His jaw taut, Serbaak advanced no further. Aware of the price Serbaak paid for his compliance, Sera looked at Tolin with eyes blazing.

"Yea, *husband*. Anything you say, *husband*." Sera's tone was caustic. "Are those the words you would have me speak?"

Tolin's gaze remained cold. "They will suffice for now."

"Oh, will they! I hope you will remember their ring, because you will not hear me speak them again! And if you think that during this journey I will wait on you hand and foot—"

Tolin's voice took on an ominous tone. "You will do exactly what I tell you to do. You will defer to me in all things as a good wife should, and you will not again behave so foolishly as to flaunt yourself with another man so others might suspect the vow between us."

"You are insane!"

"And you are a fool!"

"How dare you!"

Sera gasped as Tolin moved in a lightning flash. The white world around her lurched suddenly upside down as she was snatched from her feet and tossed over his broad shoulder. Her head dangled against his back as she raged in protest and her booted feet kicked wildly against his chest. She saw the doorway behind her slip into the distance as Serbaak stood there stiffly unmoving. She was still protesting at the top of her lungs, her arms and fists flailing, when she was released unexpectedly to land in an astonished heap in the back of a nearby wagon.

Righting herself, momentarily disoriented, she saw that a fierce wrath had replaced the ice in Tolin's gaze. He spoke in a whispered hiss.

"You will stay here! You will neither leave the

wagon nor speak a word to the driver without my permission. You will remember that for all the world now knows, *you belong to me*. For that reason, you will not behave in a way that will bring scorn down upon me, for if you do, you will bear my wrath."

"I will not suffer your threats!"

Tolin took a step closer. "Threat or warning, the truth is this. You had best heed my words, for I will not hesitate to use the weight of my hand to enforce my will if I am given no choice."

"Nameless son of a dog!"

"Nay. My heritage is known. Only *yours* is suspect."

About to launch herself forward in attack, Sera was halted abruptly by the sound of an approaching step nearby. Her gaze jerked to the bearded man she knew to be Rockwald, the caravan master, and she snapped her mouth closed.

Rockwald halted at the rear of the wagon, laughing aloud as he slapped Tolin's shoulder heartily. "That is the way to put a woman in her place! She will not taunt you again, I wager." Glancing back at her, Rockwald then winked at Tolin. "She is a beauty, all right, and from the look of her, a lively piece in bed as well. If I were you, I would make her pay the price of her flirting when you are settled beneath your robes tonight."

Clenching her teeth to keep back her angry retort, Sera looked at Tolin. She saw his gaze flicker toward her before he stated flatly, "Nay, Sera will not play that game again. Is that not right, Sera?"

Sera did not respond.

"Is that not right, Sera?"

Tolin's autocratic tone rebounded in Sera's ears as she nodded stiffly in response.

The lifeless grey of Tolin's gaze challenged her. "I did not hear you."

A silent moment passed before Sera managed stiffly, "That is right."

"That is right, *husband* . . ."

Another pause; then Sera grated, "That is right . . . *husband!*"

Rockwald's laughter rang once more. "Yea, that will do!"

Inwardly seething as Rockwald and Tolin strode away, Sera sat rigidly. The caravan lurched into motion at the crack of Rockwald's whip and began lumbering forward as Tolin reappeared mounted astride his great warhorse with his wolfhound trotting at his side.

It occurred to her as Tolin took up a steady pace directly behind the wagon, his emotionless face almost hidden in the fur of his hood, that behind her were not two warrior beasts, but three. Her fury soaring, Sera pulled down the flapped closure of the wagon, abruptly cutting them from view.

* * *

Suffocating from emotion held sharply in check, Serbaak watched as Sera's caravan gradually disappeared into the heavy veil of falling snow. Fists clenched, he closed his eyes.

The voice sounding quietly close by was unexpected.

"Would that I could have spared you this anguish, my son."

His eyes snapping open, Serbaak beheld his father's strained countenance—the lined face with features so similar to his own, the graying hair once as black as his, the eyes still sharply bright. He read pain in those bright eyes as Alpor continued, "It did not occur to me when Sera was brought to me as a babe those many years ago that by accepting her into my house, I might be consigning you to the sorrow of a love that could never be."

Serbaak's brow furrowed. "Nor did I realize that my feelings for Sera were so apparent."

"They are not apparent to all, my son. Just to those close enough to you to feel your pain."

Serbaak's frown deepened. "I suppose you think it foolish of me to suffer a hopeless love."

"Nay." Alpor's graying brow became similarly knit. "Masters of this hard land we have become—masters of our hearts we will never be. Most difficult of all for me at this moment is the realization that I, who inadvertently brought this despair upon you, have no consolation to offer you—save one."

Alpor paused, then continued slowly, "We have been accorded a great privilege, you and I, one which we have upheld with honor. We have nurtured the future of Neer within our bosom. You and I, in different ways, had no choice but to love Sera. Nor did we have any choice but to let her go."

Serbaak's throat moved convulsively, his agitation supreme. "I am worried. The warrior, Tolin, cannot be trusted."

"Sera trusts him."

"She despises him, and he treats her badly."

"She trusts him."

"If he betrays her—"

"You will sense it if he does."

Serbaak was momentarily taken aback at his father's perception. "So, you know of that also!"

"Yea, unlike Sera, I have been aware of your link to her since you were children. Our dear Sera—a matchless gift and an exquisite burden."

"Nay! Never a burden!"

"The burden was in knowing that we were given a priceless treasure we were never meant to keep. All that is now left to us is to be grateful for the time that treasure was ours."

Serbaak's deep voice trembled with the words

he had not formerly dared to speak. "She will not come back to us, Father."

"Nay, she will not."

Alpor's soft confirmation was the final blow. Serbaak turned away.

Serbaak's heavy footsteps echoed down the corridor. In the sound drummed a thought that provided him both comfort and despair—that although Sera and he had said farewell, they would never truly be apart.

The icy wind blew in earnest, whipping the falling snow into numbing whirlwinds that assaulted the caravan mercilessly as it continued through the storm. Uncertain of how many hours had elapsed, knowing only that the day had been long and the moments of rest brief, Tolin followed steadily behind the wagon marked as his own.

His features a frozen mask, he stared at the rear curtain of the wagon which had not lifted since Sera of Neer had flung it down in his face. In truth, he was glad it had not. His fury was so great that he was not sure how he would react to the sight of her.

In retrospect, he realized he should be grateful that Sera's flaunting of her Minor Oremian lover had allowed him to dictate the tone of the interaction between them from the outset of their journey. It could be no other way, for the danger of the present situation was acute. Sera's beauty drew the eye, attracting attention where other women might find neglect. Strangely, the near violence of their exchange in full view of the others and Sera's eventual submission to him, however feigned, had established a distraction that he now realized would work to their advantage. Sera was accepted in the eyes of all as a troublesome wife whom Tolin ruled with a heavy hand. There would be little suspicion that a woman kept so cowed by her husband could be the Heiress of Neer, who was born to rule.

But, *Sera . . . cowed?*

Tolin's frozen lips twitched. So much the fools they, who believed what could never be.

The wind gusted more strongly and Tolin's steed whinnied in protest. Tolin patted the warhorse's strong neck. He had not believed the brave animal had survived their excursion into Orem Minor those long weeks ago, but he was relieved that he had, for there was no truer beast—save the one that now trotted at his side. Within the hour, both worthy animals would be rewarded for their loyalty with all the comfort he was able to afford them in this frozen wasteland.

Tolin paused in his thoughts. He, too, would soon be rewarded, but his reward would be from a commitment reluctantly made, when he would retire to the wagon and lie beside the warm body of the beauteous maid now concealed by that damnable curtain. It mattered little to him that her eyes were golden daggers that sought to pierce his heart. To the world around them, she was his wife.

Tolin gave a low snort. He would have little enough comfort during the torturous time of travel ahead. He had decided during the endless, frozen hours just past that he would make liberal use of the few comforts afforded.

Sera, his wife.

Yea . . . *his wife*.

Soft sounds, loving sounds . . . a wisp of perfumed scent . . . a gasping breath . . .

The woman in his arms responded eagerly to Serbaak's loving as her flesh moved warmly against his. The bedchamber Serbaak had come to know so well was lit by candles that lent a gentle glow as the woman gasped again, drawing his head down to her breasts. He felt her hands move gently in his hair as she encouraged his intimate ministrations. He heard her speak softly in the ardent tone he had come to know so well.

"I knew you would come to me tonight, Serbaak." Teesha's voice was breathless. "I suffered at your absence from my chamber, even while I consoled myself with the knowledge that you visited no other woman to fill your needs."

120

Serbaak drew back from the comforting warmth of Teesha's body, disturbed. He looked up at the angular face he knew so well. He saw straight dark brows over bright eyes with pupils permanently contracted, small features, and warm lips always eager to welcome his. Teesha was his mistress. He treated her well and cared for her. Their association was passionately strong. He recalled the first time he saw her, after she had migrated from the furthest of Orem Minor's villages upon the death of an older husband. She had been alone, impoverished, and without support when she entered service in his father's household.

Serbaak stroked a dark wisp of hair back from Teesha's face, recalling that awareness between them had been instantaneous. Somehow, Teesha had sensed his need, and he had sensed hers. Somewhere in the course of the interaction between them, mutual solace had turned to loving. In the intimate liaison they had struck, each had found rewards, and yet . . .

Serbaak began tentatively, "Teesha, surely you know—"

"Yea, I know." Teesha swallowed, disturbed at Serbaak's discomfort. "I have always known how deeply you value me, just as I have always known you were not free to love."

Serbaak remained motionless, uncertain. He felt a special tenderness for Teesha, but he had

121

never misled her. He did not love her. Nor did he want *her* to love *him*.

Speaking softly, Serbaak replied, "You are a source of great comfort to me, Teesha. I have come to depend on the time we spend together, but . . ."

A slow panic entered Teesha's eyes. "You need say no more, Serbaak. It is enough for me to have you close . . . to know I am a part of you, however briefly. You are a source of comfort beyond measure to me."

"As you are to me." Serbaak paused, searching Teesha's face more closely. "But mayhap the time we have spent together has—"

Teesha slipped her hand over Serbaak's lips. "Nay, speak no more. The time for speaking is past. The time for loving has begun."

Serbaak allowed his gaze to linger moments longer. As always, Teesha sensed that this was not a time for words. As always, she offered the only solace that would dull the ache within him.

Serbaak drew Teesha close. He stroked her dark hair as hair of a more brilliant hue persistently filled his mind. He kissed her closed lids as gold eyes that had touched his heart haunted him. He pressed his lips to hers, knowing he would find a respite there that he would never find with others he loved so well.

Serbaak accepted Teesha's consolation, offering the same in return . . . while in his heart he mourned a precious gift that was lost to him forever.

Outside Sera's silent, primitive conveyance, the snowfall and the long first day's journey had come to a simultaneous end. Drawn to a halt for the night, the wagons had been grouped into several small circles, in the center of which the draft animals had been confined to afford them shelter from the icy wind. A simple meal of smoked meat, dried fruit, and a tepid herbal drink had been delivered to Sera's wagon. She had consumed it without enthusiasm and retreated to the bed as the mumbled conversation of the drivers outside the wooden walls gradually stilled.

Steeped in her enforced silence, Sera had jumped when the wagon flaps slapped open abruptly and Tolin entered. Sera recalled the frigidity of his glance as he stripped off his furs. There was little conversation between them, but as close as he had stood in the limited space of their wagon, she could not help but notice that crystals of ice still clung to his brows and heavy lashes, that endless hours of exposure to the elements had lent a blue tinge to his skin, and that exhaustion was obvious in the shadows under his lifeless eyes.

Smarting at the arrogance that flashed briefly in those eyes, Sera had averted her gaze as Tolin stripped unashamedly down to his small clothes despite the icy chill. Then he threw back the fur coverlets and slipped boldly underneath beside her.

A tremor again shook Sera at the remembered shock when Tolin's naked flesh had brushed her arm. She had momentarily regretted dispensing with her outerwear for the night, although she had known her zircum sleeping garment and coverlet would provide protection enough beneath the fur robes.

In the hour since that time, however, an unexpected problem had emerged to prohibit sleep—and it continued to astound her, that of all the difficulties she had anticipated facing on a prolonged journey under intimate circumstances with this man, so simple a matter could have escaped her.

Simply put, she could not fathom how she had not realized that Tolin's superior weight would drag down the mattress they shared, that it would become an exhaustingly constant, uphill battle to remain on her side of the bed!

Sera inwardly groaned. Her briefest moment of relaxation in the past hour had caused a relentless downward slide to Tolin's side. Yet she was determined not to yield.

Nay, she would not lie dutifully pressed against that emotionless beast's bulk.

Nay . . .

Sera yawned.

Nor would she allow her resolution to be affected by her deep weariness, by the longing to close her eyes that grew stronger by the minute, or by the increasing weight of her heavy eyelids as sleep hovered near. She would resist the call of the sweet, dark void lying just beyond her reach.

Sera resisted even as consciousness slowly drifted away . . . as her eyes slowly closed . . . as . . .

Tolin abruptly shifted his weight.

Sliding flush against Tolin's side, Sera jumped as if scorched at the meeting of their flesh. She heard Tolin's angry snort the moment before his arm locked around her, holding her where she lay despite her struggle to escape him. His cutting whisper struck her suddenly motionless.

"You may surrender your virgin pose, heiress! You forget that I saw the warmth of your farewell to your Minor Oremian lover. I know you are no stranger to the touch of a man's body. But you may set your mind at rest. I have no designs on your white flesh. I merely seek to stop your squirming so I may find a few hours of restful oblivion before our journey begins for another day."

Furious when Tolin refused to surrender his hold, Sera rasped in return, "I will not comment on your offensive assumptions! I will only say that I would expect no more from a crude barbarian such as you—who, unlike a man of Serbaak's fine sensibilities, has doubtless never known a noble emotion in his life!"

Tolin's warm breath brushed Sera's cheek as he drew her tauntingly closer. His muscular frame crushed her softness, sending a tremor down her spine as he whispered, "Yet you sought the aid of this crude barbarian in your quest, when you might have chosen any one of the many others who came to Orem Minor before me." Tolin's tone took on an unexpectedly silken quality as he continued, more softly than before, "Enlighten me, heiress. Why did you choose me for the great honor of delivering you home?"

"You may rest assured that my decision had nothing to do with your personal qualities!" Sera's reply was cold. "My reason was as I told you before. I recognized you upon your arrival, and I knew only one who had been in Fador of Rall's intimate service, and knew him well, would be able to deliver me safely from him if the situation arose."

Tolin's response was cautious. "You condemn my service to Rall, yet you would use the skills I employed there to aid your purpose."

"I would."

"So you admit it."

"I *admit* . . ?"

Holding up his callused palm so Sera might view it clearly, Tolin impaled her with the sensuous heat of his peculiarly light eyes. "You have made it clear that you are willing to dismiss the blood that stained this hand in the service of Rall when this same hand may serve your purpose." Tolin lowered his hand to stroke her cheek with unexpected gentleness as he then purred, "Would you also dismiss the blood that stained this hand if it were to caress you with tenderness . . . if it were to stroke your sweet flesh with growing warmth . . . if it were to start your heart to pounding and—"

Tolin's titillating whisper halted abruptly. His expression suddenly alert, he curtailed her response with a sharp glance, then raised his hand to snap his fingers twice in quick succession before turning back to her with a soft command.

"Kiss me, heiress—now—as if your life depended upon it, for it surely may!"

Gasping as Tolin slipped himself unexpectedly atop her, Sera was struck breathless by the intimate male weight of him, by the confusing message in the clear eyes looking down into hers. The potency of Tolin's kiss stunned her as his lips separated hers, as his tongue swept her mouth in a sweet caress, as he slid her arms up to encircle his neck, holding them there, deepening his tender assault until they clung of their own accord.

Overwhelmed by the sheer masculine power of him so gently displayed, Sera felt herself slowly succumbing to the unexpected wonder of the moment when—

The slap of the wagon flaps and the ensuing rush of cold air jarred Sera from her mesmerized state. Stiffening as Tolin turned sharply toward the familiar figure outlined in the opening, she was unable to move as Tolin held her fast in their intimate posture, demanding, "What do you want, Rockwald?"

"What do I want?" Rockwald's laughter rang sharply on the frozen silence. "Yours was the only wagon that has shown a hint of movement during the hour past. When the rocking and jostling became intense, I decided to see for myself what was going on in here! Of course, now that I have . . ." The slow tensing of Tolin's frame sent a shiver coursing down Sera's spine as Rockwald laughed again. ". . . I find myself so envious that I begin to wonder if you would be willing to share your—"

The subtle movement of Tolin's hand toward his sword sent Rockwald quickly backwards. His laughter took on a nervous tone. "Nay—nay, this is but a friendly visit! It was not meant to offend. Sleep well—sleep well. Morning will be quick in coming."

Dropping the wagon flap abruptly, Rockwald disappeared from sight. The sound of his quick, crunching step in retreat returned Sera's gaze to Tolin's tight expression. Sliding abruptly from atop her, Tolin grated in response to her unspoken question, "Rockwald's suspicions have been temporarily sated. He has seen us intimately engaged and believes you to be my wife—or my mistress—whatever suits his depraved mind more."

"He was suspicious of me?"

Tolin's lips curved scornfully. "The Heiress of Neer—the chosen one Orem awaits—you are in greater need of protection than even *I* believed!"

Flushing at the affront, Sera raised her chin. "You would have me believe you anticipated Rockwald's intentions?"

"They were apparent to all eyes but yours! Then when Gar warned me of his approach—"

"Gar? I heard no warning."

"Nay, you did not."

Snapping his fingers thrice in quick succession, once more than he had minutes previously, Tolin turned toward the rear of the wagon as the flaps separated unexpectedly and the huge dog leapt inside. The beast lay beside the mattress upon silent command.

Tolin turned back to Sera. "You need not worry that Rockwald will return."

Startled when Tolin reached for her once

more, Sera twisted from his grasp. "You have saved the hour, and in doing so fulfilled the promise of protection that I was wise enough to extract from you. But I warn you, do not take your part too seriously, *husband*. Rockwald may now be convinced that I am your wedded slave, but *I* am not."

Tolin's whispered response was unexpectedly husky. "Your arms were warm around my neck and your lips sweet, heiress. There is much comfort we may afford each other during the long, cold nights to come."

Furious at the slow trembling that began deep inside her as Tolin's gaze caressed her brow, her cheek, the line of her jaw, then moved to linger on her lips, Sera responded hotly, "The Heiress of Neer is immune to such needs!"

Tolin's gaze turned abruptly cold. "Yea . . . how dare I forget?"

His broad back turned to her moments later, and Sera felt a slow flush transfuse her. Her own words returned hauntingly.

The Heiress of Neer is above the weaknesses of the flesh!

Well, it was true, was it not?

Was it not?

Sera's stomach tightened. It had better be. Trembling, somehow bereft, Sera turned her back as well and closed her eyes.

* * *

130

Stirring in a sleep that had been long in coming after his conflict with the haughty Sera of Neer, Tolin became slowly conscious of a soft warmth pressed tight against him. The glint of fiery hair tucked beneath his chin met his gaze as he opened his eyes. Its delicate scent assailed him. He stirred and the female warmth moved closer, a fragile sleeping garment the only obstruction between the rounded breasts pressed against his chest and the long, slender legs lying curved against him.

Drawing back slightly, Tolin looked down at Sera's matchless features relaxed in sleep. So . . . what her waking mind disclaimed, her sleeping self could not.

Anger returned. So much the fool she!

Anger fled. So much the fool he. Curling his arm around her, Tolin drew Sera closer, for comfort when there was little, for consolation when there was none.

Chapter Six

A hint of fragrance lingered in the air. The lamps were turned low in the deepening twilight. Diaphanous curtains undulated gently at the window of the opulent boudoir as the sky of Orem Proper clung to the last glorious streaks of the setting sun.

Filnor's lips twitched in a hard smile as soft, sensuous music drifted from the courtyard below. He had no doubt that Kiray had arranged for the musicians' presence there after he sent word of his intended visit, just as she had provided the crystal dish of spiced honey on the table beside the broad, lavishly draped sleeping bench and the bowl of choice fruit nearby.

Filnor felt a familiar hardening in his groin as he recalled his last visit to this particular chamber. Kiray had been especially pleased to see him because of his extended absence from her quarters. She had fawned over him, inventing new ways to please him, telling him she did not believe the stories of his most recent bloody foray against the enemies of Rall.

Filnor's smile broadened as he recalled the manner in which Kiray's dark eyes had widened when he proclaimed the stories to be true, boasting that he had personally annihilated many in the pocket of growing resistance to Rall's rule in a nearby province. Her creamy skin had flushed when he told her that he had ordered the earth charred black where the battle had raged, as a reminder of the cost of revolution and a lesson to all who might think to follow the same path, and that he was proud to have served Rall so bravely.

And he was.

Annoyance nudged. He did not like being kept waiting. He had a need to satiate his carnal needs after yet another extended foray in the provinces.

Filnor took an impatient step. His image flickered in the gilt-edged mirror on the wall nearby, but he paid it little mind. He knew the glass would reflect hair that was thick and dark, arched brows over eyes so black as to appear bottomless in depth, a perfectly shaped patrician nose, full lips, and white, even teeth that often flashed in a smile of superficial warmth. He knew his countenance was handsome enough to stir even the coldest of feminine hearts, while being thoroughly masculine and unmarked by battle as well.

Filnor drew his impressive frame slowly erect. He was well aware that as he stood garbed in his well-worn leathers, his stature was that of the ultimate warrior. He had earned that stature by the sweat of his brow and the strength of his sword. And unlike some, he had never regretted a single life he had extinguished in his service to Rall nor a drop of the blood he had spilled.

Unlike some . . .

Memories that had turned as bitter as gall flashed across Filnor's mind, raising his agitation. He saw two boys of a like age and size who had been commonly raised, one dark-haired and the other fair. Friends they had been, exchanging confidences, sharing the penalties and rewards of youth, growing and training for their futures in the service of Rall. Together they had donned their warrior leathers for the first time. Together they had drawn their first blood. Standing shoulder to shoulder with their swords, they had left all in awe of their fearsome might in battle.

Filnor's bitterness deepened. But the fair-haired one began to change. His gaze grew cold as his services to Rall grew to be in great demand, as he wreaked glorious destruction upon command, and his accomplishments in that regard became legend.

And then . . .

Coward . . . Traitor . . . Fool!

Fador's mouth tightened with a sharp twitch. A friend who was no longer a friend was an enemy. The wrong that had been committed could be set right only by the sword!

Yea, *unlike some*, he would never regret his service to Rall. It was his birthright. He had grown stronger and wiser with every drop of blood that had been shed in Rall's name. And if women could not resist him, the reason was simple. Rather than his good looks, it was the savagery within him that drew them—the barbarity they sought to conquer. Fools that they were, they did not realize that they would never do more than ride the tempest which they sought to tame!

Filnor knew there were some who credited his appeal to women to heredity. Instead of acknowledging the inner power he had so carefully cultivated, they reminded him that his father held the same relentless appeal to the fairer sex, despite his advancing years. To that, Filnor had but one response. Fador's day was waning, while his own had barely begun.

A sound in the other room interrupted Filnor's thoughts as he turned with a scowl, awaiting Kiray's appearance. Her passion for him had elevated her to the position of his favorite whore, but it appeared that only he appreciated the dubious honor of that title. In the pink haze of adoration through which Kiray so obviously viewed him, she failed to see a simple truth—that however great the effort she expended in his behalf, she would never change the fact that *a whore was a whore, after all.*

Filnor turned toward Kiray as she moved into view. Black hair hanging long and straight down her slender back, brown eyes glowing with anticipation, her lushly feminine curves concealed by a filmy garment that fluttered with her step, Kiray approached. In a moment her warm, moist mouth was tight against his, her body hot and ready as she moved sinuously against him.

Drawing back from him abruptly, her breast heaving with a passion she barely subdued, Kiray whispered, "I have waited anxiously for your return, my love." Kiray's long fingers stroked his cheek as she appeared to read in the tight lines of his face the fatigue unrelated to his physical state that he had come to expunge. She whispered, "I have many delights in store for you this night . . . some that I have dreamed of with such great anticipation that it is difficult for me to restrain myself."

Raising herself on her toes, Kiray licked sensuously at Filnor's lips, an impassioned tremor shaking her as he cupped her head with his palm and crushed her against him for a savage foraging of her mouth. Her cheeks flushed as she drew herself back with obvious reluctance, Kiray continued, "But I would not have this moment marred by the stress your important duties have caused you. I would have you relaxed so we may prolong the moments . . . enjoy them to the fullest . . . *savor* them together. . . ."

Her voice dwindling as she slipped her hand into his, Kiray drew Filnor forward. Following reluctantly, irritation surging at the whore's maneuverings, Filnor could not help but respond to the inner heat of her that seemed to flow from her fingertips as she drew him into an alcove and ordered the curtain drawn back with a sharp clap of her hands. Motioning to the fragrant bath prepared there, Kiray whispered huskily, "For you . . . and for me."

The music from the courtyard throbbed erotically on the scented air as Kiray worked with trembling hands at the closure of Filnor's leather jerkin, then slipped it from his shoulders. As she drew the white shirting beneath from him and discarded that as well, she proceeded to bathe his powerful chest with her tongue. Licking and tasting, nipping and biting, she groaned with growing abandon as Filnor responded with escalating heat, manipulating her rounded breasts to the point of pain as he scraped the hardened nipples with his callused thumbs.

Stepping back abruptly, her dark eyes smoldering, Kiray worked with an effort just short of frenzy at the closure of his leggings, making a soft, mewing sound when she was finally able to slip her hand inside to take his rock-hard member in her hand. Her breathing rapid, her eyes half-lidded with the white-hot fervor that consumed her, she manipulated him with sensuous expertise, raising herself to gnaw again at his lips, to slip her tongue inside his mouth, to search each moist hollow until she left him gasping.

Her ministrations stilling abruptly, Kiray waited until Filnor's gaze dropped to meet hers before she whispered again in a sweet, singsong voice, "Tell me what you would have me next do, Filnor. Tell me how I may sate the need within." She grasped his throbbing member more tightly, then slid her hand down its shaft to grip the testicles beneath. He caught his breath as she urged, "You have but to say the word, Filnor . . . tell me."

His patience short as salacious emotions soared, Filnor gasped, "Do not tease me, witch, or you will pay the price!"

A sound of elation escaping her lips as she observed his loss of control, Kiray rasped, "Fear not, my handsome warrior, for the best is yet to come."

Slipping his leggings from his hips with experienced hands, Kiray went suddenly silent. Filnor felt the appetite within her soar as he stood naked and fully engorged. She dropped to her knees before him with a feral growl and closed her mouth over the throbbing shaft she had raised to full passion.

Motionless, unable to move, Filnor groaned with increasing intensity as Kiray worshiped his manhood with voracious hunger, stroking and fondling, tracing the fine blue-veined lines with her tongue, then drawing from him deeply and fully until his brief shout of ecstasy echoed vibrantly in their intimate bower.

Taking long moments to draw his breathing under control, Filnor looked down at last to see Kiray still crouched before him. Her flushed cheeks were streaked with tears, so great was her joy at having pleased him.

Filnor inwardly sneered. The whore's intoxication with him was almost amusing. She loved him, as had so many women before her. Fool that Kiray was, she was incapable of realizing that all which transpired between them—and she herself—meant nothing to him past the stimulation of the moment.

But the stimulation of the moment was divine, and Filnor did not object as Kiray urged him into the warm bath, as she bathed his body with the same care with which she had worshiped it minutes earlier. Leaning back against the tub's rim, Filnor allowed Kiray her pleasure as she left no spot untouched, as she lathered him with scented soap, massaging his scalp with her long fingers, smoothing his neck and shoulders, kneading the muscles in his chest and arms with expert care. The long length of his legs did not suffer her neglect, nor did a single toe as she scrubbed each with ceaseless ardor, taking them into her mouth to suck them with pathetic fervor.

The gaze Kiray raised to meet his at last was again inflamed to a carnal frenzy as she reached below the water line to cup the lax male member floating there. Separating his legs, Filnor allowed her full access as she raised him to full tumescence once more.

A lust laced with contempt rising in him, Filnor rose from the tub to lie on the prepared couch nearby at Kiray's urging. He allowed her the physical homage of her desperate adoration as she accommodated his myriad sensual needs, groaning softly as she poured a fragrant oil onto his back and massaged the tight muscles there, as she stroked and softened, missing not a single knot of tension in the long column of his spine and firm buttocks.

Noting that Kiray was shuddering visibly when she urged him to his back to continue her ministrations, Filnor forced himself to remain still as she smoothed and petted with new purpose, her trembling fingers gratifying each point of masculine sensitivity, each personal preference, until his member ached for the release soon to come anew.

Stripping suddenly to the flesh, Kiray mounted him with a vigor unmatched by any woman he had ever known, and only then did Filnor give her the ride she sought, a wild, unbridled race to culmination that left her enraptured shrieks echoing on the perfumed silence of the chamber.

But the witch was not yet done.

Appearing determined to outdo all her former efforts, Kiray slipped to the sleeping bench beside him and prepared him a concupiscent repast—honeyed fruit dipped with her own fingers to be eaten from the table of her creamy flesh.

Determined to make the libidinous witch howl, Filnor consumed the repast voraciously and savagely as her groans and cries rose. Stopping short only of the warm delta Kiray offered him, maintaining his silent determination to share that feast with one woman alone—one he knew so well although they had yet to meet—

Filnor raised himself above Kiray to plunge deeply within her. Her sudden rasp echoed as her legs wrapped around him, as he plunged again and again, groaning loudly when he reached culmination once more.

Breathless, Filnor fell back to the surface of the sleeping bench. He frowned at the loving words Kiray whispered into his ear as she caressed him, pressing herself tight against him. Fool! Did she not realize that she had served her purpose? He had had enough of her!

Issuing a harsh command, Filnor thrust Kiray away the moment before sleep overwhelmed him.

Fador paced the familiar tower room with a furious step as the twilight beyond the window deepened.

Where was he, damn him!

His countenance twisting into a mask of fury, Fador seethed. Handsome features no longer youthful were further coarsened by years of debauchery and drink. Hair once gleaming a deep, dark hue was peppered with the silver of passing years. Skin once firm and clear was robbed of color and permanently cast in downward lines of cruelty that could no longer be disguised.

Drawing himself up to his full height, Fador squared his stance with instinctive hauteur.

Aware of the deterioration that marked his face, he also knew that neither his mind nor his will was similarly affected and that his body was still strong and able. He still hungered for female flesh with an appetite that belied the passing years and found little difficulty in summoning a response in return.

When all was said and done, he knew that he was more than a match for the arrogant young fool he now awaited.

Where was he?

Damn him!

Filnor opened his eyes to the familiar, scented room and the reality that twilight had slipped into night. Annoyed that he had spent longer in his sexual pursuits than he had intended, he looked to the sleeping couch beside him. It was empty.

Filnor shrugged. So much the better. The adoring whore too often annoyed him with her simpering ways when he had finished his business with her.

Drawing himself to his feet beside the sleeping bench as the music in the courtyard resumed, Filnor stretched. Yea, the eager harlot had done her work well. The tension was gone from his frame. It irritated him to realize, however, that although his carnal appetite had been satisfied, an unidentifiable need remained.

Thrusting the lingering dissatisfaction aside, Filnor reached for his clothes. Fully dressed moments later, he started toward the door, only to turn abruptly at the sound of a rustling step behind him. He halted as Kiray stepped unexpectedly out of the shadows.

Black hair gleaming in the limited light, dark eyes half-lidded, Kiray approached him slowly as the music filtering into the room swelled. Her lushly familiar curves concealed only by a glittering gossamer veil, a single jewel sparkling at her throat, Kiray raised her hands gracefully over her head, her rounded breasts boldly displayed as she began swaying sinuously to the throbbing rhythm. Tiny bells on her fingers and ankles punctuated the erotic movements of her dance as she writhed and twisted around him with mesmerizing gyrations. The tempo of the music mounted as it became increasingly savage and taunting.

A familiar heat surged as he observed the carnal witch's dance with increasing fascination, and Filnor felt his blood rise to a slow pounding. The ache in his groin increasing despite himself, he attempted once, twice, to capture Kiray only to have her whirl from his grasp.

Filnor tensed, his frustration turning rapidly to anger. So, the whore had had her fill and now thought to tease him, to torment him, to taunt him past restraint—to make him squirm!

When he failed to capture her a third time, Filnor was possessed of a sudden rage. Did the bitch now think she controlled him so well that she could make him *beg* for her favors?

Nay, that would never be!

Catching Kiray's arm in a vicious grip, Filnor heard her pained grunt as he tossed her roughly to the floor. Lust and fury savagely mingling, he ripped away her fluttering veil, his expression feral as he stripped away his leather leggings and threw himself upon her.

Kiray's cry of protest as he plunged roughly within her exulted him, and he laughed aloud. Yea, this was the satisfaction that had been left wanting!

Plunging again and again, Filnor was aware of the exact moment Kiray's protest turned to passion, when she began rising to his thrusts, and he cursed viciously at the loss of a gratification only barbarity allowed. Driving deeper, harder, he heard Kiray's growing complaints, her increasing moans, her cries of pain.

Passion soared.

He—Filnor—was *master*!

Lust erupting in a guttural shout, Filnor shuddered with a soaring gratification all the more powerful for the violence that had accompanied it. Collapsing upon Kiray at last, Filnor noted after long moments that her body shook with sobs.

Perverse enjoyment drew a tight smile to Filnor's lips as he raised Kiray's tear-streaked face to his.

"Crying, Kiray? That is a strange way to show pleasure. I am disturbed, for if the pleasure should end, I would most assuredly find another who would enjoy my attentions more."

"Nay!" Her damp eyes widening, Kiray shook her head. "I . . . I did not realize I had raised your passions to such a volatile extreme. That is all. The fault is mine if there was discomfort."

Filnor's smile became a vicious sneer. "Yea, the fault is yours."

A sudden pounding on the chamber door diverted Filnor's attention as he shouted, "Who disturbs Filnor of Rall's private hour with this woman?"

The response was clear despite the door between.

"Fador of Rall summons Filnor to him."

"Tell him—"

"Fador's orders are to accept no delay."

His face flushing, Filnor stood abruptly. The woman lying on the floor below him dismissed from his mind, he reached for his leggings. Dressed in a moment, uncaring that Kiray still lay naked where he had abandoned her, he opened the door. Exposing her without concern, he grated, "I will tell him myself!"

Striding down the corridor ahead of the silent

messenger, Filnor gave the chamber he had left and the woman in it no more thought than to slam the door behind him.

Chest heaving, eyes aglow with menace, Fador faced his angry son. Dismissing his guards with a sweeping motion of his arm, Fador waited for the click of the door to echo against the stone walls of the tower room before addressing Filnor in a low, ominous tone.

"So, you come at last to make your report, my son."

"Yea, I come." Filnor responded in a tone rife with fury. "I come to ask by what right you summon the Heir to the House of Rall under duress!" Filnor took a threatening step forward that was not missed by his sire as he rasped, "I will not be treated as less than I am! I will be treated with the respect due my station and with the respect I have *earned* with my ready sword and a dedication to the purposes of Rall that are beyond question!"

Fador paused, his lips twisting into a familiar grimace as he scrutinized his son's livid countenance.

Anger drawing closer to the surface, Fador demanded in a sudden, resounding tone, "You have been abroad on the land for a fortnight in a pursuance of reported unrest, yet you made no attempt to convey your findings to me upon your return."

Filnor's jaw ticked. "The unrest has been suppressed in the usual manner."

"Has it, *my son*?" Fador paused again for restraint. "Have you suppressed it so well that you feel no need to report to your father?"

"You know very well what transpired! The suspected conspirators will never open their eyes to the light of another day! Once more I have protected you from your enemies, as I have all my life!"

"Nay . . . not *all* your life!"

Filnor's gaze grew rabid. "So it is *that* again!" Motioning to the barred niche on the wall that stood empty in silent reminder of a fateful night long past, he continued hotly, "The flame of Neer! Will you never cease to mourn its loss? Will you never cease to hold my childish lapse against me? Does it make no difference to you that I am your only son and legal heir, and that my loyalty and devotion to the crest I will someday inherit is without blemish? Can you not see that I have served you to the full extent of my limits and beyond, pursuing your enemies and shedding their blood without remorse, and that in serving your every command I have proved there is no one on the face of Orem you may trust more than you may trust me!"

Fador sneered.

Filnor's angry flush drained. "Your thoughts

will never be more clear."

His heart devoid of compassion, Fador felt only a familiar anger soar. "You, who are my only son and heir, you who have served me to the full extent of your abilities, you who obey my every command and seek to prove to me that there is no one on the face of Orem whom I may trust more than you . . . you who claim the future of Rall . . . You are Rall's greatest enemy!"

Filnor's jaw clenched before he gritted a reply. "The flame—"

"Yea! The flame!" Fador's resounding response echoed against the domed ceiling of the room. "In your false, arrogant pride—a pride you still boldly brandish—you have never accepted true responsibility for that black night so long ago, when you released the only true threat that Rall will ever know to its rule!"

"That was years ago! The flame was extinguished! I saw you stamp it out myself!"

Fador began a slow trembling. "The flame was reborn!"

"Nay! That is an old wives' tale, instigated by Zor and perpetuated by the last remaining few who refuse to surrender allegience to Neer!"

Fador's trembling grew stronger. "The old wives' tale is true." His bearded cheek twitching, Fador rasped, "I had a dream—"

"A dream?" Filnor's tight expression went

momentarily lax. "A dream, Father? You called me here—enraged, railing at a mistake committed in childhood—because of a *dream*?"

Barely controlling the hand that swept to the silver dagger at his belt, Fador growled, "I warn you, *my son*. It is only the fact that common blood runs in our veins which saves you from my blade—but a few words more and my restraint will expire."

Fador advanced to within an inch of his son's white face as he spat, "I had a dream!" Glaring, he continued, "In that dream a great, pale bird of prey soared in the sky above my head. As I watched, it circled closer and closer. My bow was powerless against it, as were the slings and warrior nets of my guards. I was unable to evade it as it circled lower over my head . . . and then I saw, clenched in the raptor's claws . . ."

Fador paused, his chest heaving, his throat tight. ". . . I saw a glittering crystal." Fador swallowed. "Within it was a flame."

Sensing Filnor's skepticism, Fador warned, "Mind your words, Filnor, for a careless utterance now may yet cost you your life!"

"Is that all that happened in this dream?"

"Damned fool that you are, was that not enough? Are you too dense to understand what the dream portends? Are you too blind to see what must be done?"

When Filnor's silence was his only response,

Fador grated in a voice filled with hatred, "You who are the cause of this great jeopardy to Rall will seek out this raptor! You will find it and crush it, and with it, the fragile crystal it carries!"

Filnor's face twitched. Fador saw his obvious distress, as well as the hand his son raised tentatively toward him before allowing it to fall back to his side in a gesture of futility. "Where will I find this raptor, Father?"

Fador's countenance took on an apoplectic hue. "Again a question when it is an answer I seek!"

Stepping back from his son, Fador ordered in a thunderous voice, "I charge you this night, Filnor of Rall—seek out and destroy the flame! I will suffer you to indulge no priority before it, for now or evermore! Is that understood?"

"Yea, it is understood."

"Then our interview is ended!"

His powerful frame trembling, Fador turned abruptly away. The silence that followed, stretching long and thin between the two men, was breached by Filnor's rasping whisper.

"Can you never forgive me, Father?"

A sterile hush ensued.

The sound of Filnor's shifting step sounded as he awaited his father's response—then his abrupt retreat, and the harsh snap of the heavy oak door closing behind him when there was no reply.

As the echo of Filnor's departing steps died away, Fador looked upward at the barred niche. He shuddered, knowing that the true source of his torment was neither anger nor fear, nor even contempt. Instead it was the memory of the boundless anguish he'd known when he extinguished the flame.

The flame that had been his life.

The flame that would take his life.

The flame that could be his life . . . if it were his once more.

The personal chamber of Alpor, spokesman for Orem Minor, was austere. Its simple furnishings and spartan decor reflected the personality of a man supremely dedicated to the responsibilities of his position. In the open ledgers on his desk, and in the endless columns of figures, lay the evidence of a tyrannical rule he could not shed. And in his erect stature as he stood in the midst of all was evident the determination that his people would survive.

Behind the strength evinced in Alpor's sober countenance, however, lay his concealed pain as he approached his son, who had entered moments earlier.

The green glow of zircum heat tinted the solemn lines of Serbaak's frown as he spoke with obvious sorrow.

"I bring word that Millith surrendered the last

153

spark of life within her this morn."

A sad smile touched Alpor's lips. "That noble woman has been relieved of her burden at last. We should rejoice that Millith's spirit has finally been released from a body which no longer served her needs, my son. I am sure she would want us to view her departure from us in that way."

"Her last words were of concern for Sera."

"Where her heart abided."

"I could not give her mind rest, Father, for my concerns matched hers."

"You must not torment yourself, my son." Placing his hand on Serbaak's robed shoulder, Alpor continued softly, "It is not Sera's destiny to be thwarted before her quest has truly begun."

Serbaak shook his head, his expression darkening. "If I could only be sure."

"Surely your lack of certainty is proof enough." Alpor's tone grew brighter. "Were Sera in deep distress, you would know."

"The time has stretched long since she departed. Mayhap she has traveled too far for my perception."

"There is no distance that surmounts your special bond."

"But if she were stricken swiftly, without foreknowledge or pain . . ."

"Serbaak, my son"—Alpor's countenance

154

grew strained—"Were that so, the void within you would be complete."

"If I could but see her now and know she has not been abused."

"Sera . . . abused?" Alpor's elderly face creased in a smile. "Nay."

"Or betrayed."

The smile faded. "Nay, I think not, but in any case, Sera's time is at hand. With its arrival has come an end to our stewardship of her cause."

"Our stewardship may well be ended"—Serbaak's gaze strayed—"but my devotion has not. Like Millith, my mind will not relinquish thoughts of her."

"And Teesha?"

Serbaak's gaze snapped back to meet his father's. "Teesha's contract with me is clearly drawn, Father. She fills a need that bears no relation to my concerns for Sera."

"My words were a question, my son, not an accusation." Pausing, Alpor continued, "I but hoped you might find one who would be able to help you to—"

Anticipating his father's words, Serbaak interrupted with a single word in response.

"Never."

Alpor dropped his hand to his side. "We must put Millith to her final rest, and when we do, we must keep in mind the cause for which Millith sacrificed all. In your concern for Sera, you must remind yourself that she has been touched by destiny, and that although she is beyond our reach, she walks the road that was laid for her before she was born. We must celebrate as she is doubtless celebrating now. Serbaak, my son"—Alpor's intense gaze grew bright—"if you could observe her now, you would doubtless see Sera descending the slopes toward Orem Proper with the caravan, smiling as she says . . ."

"... *I am uncomfortable!* I have ridden astride this bulky beast with you since early morn and have had enough! I demand that you put me down so I may return to the wagon!"

Tolin's hand tightened at Sera's waist, pulling her back more snugly against the muscled wall of his chest as his great destrier trudged relentlessly onward through the snow.

Sera's temper soared. Turning to look up at the handsome, emotionless face that had become as familiar to her as her own during their many days of traveling, she grated, "Do . . . you . . . hear me?"

Her stomach tightened spasmodically in a way with which she had grown exasperatingly well acquainted as Tolin's frigid gaze dropped slowly to hers.

"Must I instruct you again in the proper behavior of a loving and obedient wife? I warn you. I grow weary of the task."

"Not as weary as I! Put me down!"

Tolin's scarred cheek twitched. "Not yet. Instead, I will remind you that rather than protesting the intimacy we have shared this morning long, an *obedient and loving* wife would be grateful for her husband's attentions."

"Grateful for hours of discomfort? I would rather walk!"

"Yea . . . walk . . ." Tolin's gaze narrowed as he deliberately lowered his head to brush her mouth with his. At her stiffening, he directed, "Smile, wife. Your lord and master has deigned to show his affection for you. You should be appropriately grateful."

"Grateful *again*?" Sera gritted her teeth in a smile as she prepared herself for the same reproval Tolin had spoken so many times before.

Tolin pressed his lips against Sera's ear, giving his warning hiss in the guise of a loving whisper. "Watch yourself, heiress. Surely you do not believe I enjoy this game we play. If you will look back into memory, you will recall that it was *you* who asked me to deliver you safely home, and *I* who sought to evade the dubious honor you bestowed upon me. It seems, however, now that you have obtained my pledge, you have it in mind to thwart all my efforts to accomplish the goal you have set me to. I warn you, heiress, I do not take my given word lightly."

157

Sera gasped, astounded. "I did nothing to thwart you!"

Tolin nibbled softly at her ear in a way that sent chills racing down Sera's spine despite his angry response. "You did nothing but make your true feelings obvious to all as you played the part of princess of the realm more convincingly than that of loving wife! Even now Rockwald's gaze strays to you with renewed suspicion. You will do well to demonstrate how loving you can be."

Forcing back her spontaneous response, Sera turned stubbornly toward the passing terrain, focusing her gaze without comment as if the countryside held consuming interest. In reality, she saw not a single rise of the endless snowladen panorama while she considered the truth of Tolin's words.

The journey was endless. Days and nights of unchanging landscape had begun blending one into another until she was truly uncertain how many had passed. The sameness of the days was deadening: weary animals drawing heavy wagons, drivers alternating their posts, one driving, the other trudging alongside through the deep snow, Rockwald riding his much-abused mount in unrelenting scrutiny of all that transpired. Day after day, everything the same.

Nay, that was not completely true. A slight difference in the weather had become perceptible during the last few days. The hours of daylight had begun to lengthen, first by minutes, then by hours. The storms had relented in favor of a crisp cold that had become tempered with a show of brilliant sunlight for a few brief hours each day. The air had lost its ability to numb the mind, and in its place was a cold that was invigorating.

For that reason, Sera had taken to dismounting from the wagon during those brief periods of sunlight so she might walk beside the rattling conveyance and stretch muscles cramped by inactivity.

Sera gave a short snort. For some reason, Tolin's impassive countenance grew stiffer after those brief periods, and his gaze colder. She supposed she should have become accustomed to the insolence of his raking stare, but she had not.

Sera raised her chin in silent defiance. She had suffered the enforced intimacy with Tolin during this period with grace. Accepting the need for their charade, she had shared her sleeping quarters without complaint. She had accepted the conditions and berated neither herself nor Tolin when she awakened each morn either tucked snugly against his side or fitted intimately into the curve of Tolin's body, his powerful chest against her back and his strong arm draped across her waist. She had reluctantly admitted to herself that her sense of security was complete when so confined, knowing she might otherwise be helpless against unknown peril. She had even accepted the presence of Tolin's powerful wolfhound at her side whenever she slipped from his view. Strangely, she had found herself becoming accustomed to her canine companion, and for the first time the word she had first extended to the beast—"friend"—now rang true.

But such did not hold true with the animal's master. She had taken care not to extend the intimacy of their common bed beyond the moments spent there, choosing instead to adopt a formal attitude that befitted the mission on which she was bound.

A tremor moved down Sera's spine. If she had come to experience a strange sense of loss when Tolin occasionally arose before dawn and left her to awaken alone in their common bed, or if the male scent of him lingering on the linens where he had lain stirred a warmth deep within the core of her, she had decided it was best ignored.

When all was said and done, she had discovered that the great, handsome warrior with the lifeless eyes bore inner scars far deeper than those outwardly marking him. In his impervious gaze, she had read the uncontestable truth that those scars marked a brutal amputation of joy and hope that lamed him more cruelly than physical impairment ever could. During the long days and nights of their journey, she had grieved for his deprivation even as she detested the man he had become.

She had tried to keep her distance from him, but he seemed to delight in forcing contact between them. He had done so again that morn when she had slipped down from the wagon to stretch her aching limbs, only to be snatched up onto his saddle to assume the role of the simpering, adoring wife she was supposed to be.

Tolin continued his surveillance of the surrounding terrain, his breath fanning her cheek, his lips brushing the cool skin there with the casual air of lord and master that rested so comfortably on him. The role of simpering slave, however, fit *her* poorly.

Sera inwardly seethed.

Were she but a man . . .

Were he a different man . . .

Tolin inwardly seethed.

Tightening his hand as he held Sera forcibly close to him on the saddle, Tolin surveyed the horizon with the eye of a hunter, keenly aware of the peril ever lurking for the woman seated before him. Yea, the ice maiden, the Heiress of Neer who was above weaknesses of the flesh, but who raised unbearable temptation in others.

161

His agitation rising even in retrospect, Tolin recalled the casual strolls alongside the wagons Sera had instituted as the days had grown gradually warmer. So casual was the manner in which she stripped back her furred hood as her blood warmed, allowing her fiery tresses to lift in the breeze as they caught the sun's rays and the attention of every masculine eye. So confident was she as she trod through the snow, her inherently graceful form tantalizing despite her heavy robes. So careless was the composure of her flawless features, a beauty so perfect that it stole the breath. And so vain was she, believing herself so far above the men around her that not a one of them would dare touch her.

But the men of the caravan did not share her view. Their lust was obvious. Nor did Rockwald consider her above his attention, as he analyzed the tenor of relations between them, persistently seeking out the flaws in their intimate performance.

Tolin's jaw locked painfully tight. The imagined delights of Sera's female form taunted him even now, but never more than when she lay beside him in their common bed each night. An unrelenting yearning to taste her sweet flesh had come to life inside him.

A low, silent curse sounded abruptly in Tolin's mind. *Had come to life* . . . that was the cause of his bitter resentment. He had been numb inside, but Sera had awakened a confusing welter of emotions within him.

Yea, the witch had enchanted him, and somehow Rockwald had sensed his emotional turmoil. Unless Rockwald's suspicions were permanently dismissed before Orem Proper was reached, the man would surely relay word of the recently arrived red-haired woman with eyes of gold who was not what she pretended to be.

The approach of Rockwald's laboring mount nearby alerted Tolin to the man's continued scrutiny. His jaw hardening, Tolin knew there was only one way to convince Rockwald that the heiress was his woman . . . to do with as he chose.

Sera jumped as Tolin's broad hand slipped unexpectedly under her fur robe from behind her, claiming her breast. Turning furiously toward him, she saw the warning in his cold eyes the moment before his other hand cupped her chin to hold her fast and his mouth claimed hers.

Tolin's kiss deepened as he held Sera powerless under his heady assault. The stroking of the sensitive virgin crest of her breast sent unexpected tremors of heat radiating raggedly through her as his mouth moved expertly against hers, separating her lips. She was drowning in the unexpected wealth of emotions burgeoning to life as his seeking tongue met and caressed hers, as his hand stroked and petted, as—

The sound of a hooting male voice from the line of wagons jerked Sera abruptly back to reality, her face flaming.

"How dare you!" Not daring to strike Tolin's hand from its soft rest, Sera hissed, "Remove your hand from my breast!"

"Nay, heiress . . ." Tolin's gaze swept her with unconcealed heat as he whispered in return, "I dare not spoil the scene of our loving interlude as Rockwald watches."

"Rockwald again?" The color of Sera's cheeks deepened as she controlled the urge to glance up. "It seems to me that Rockwald's observance is a poor excuse for the liberties you take since he is unable to see your hand in its intimate pursuits."

"Mayhap not . . ." Tolin's gaze dropped to her lips, his eyes darkening rapidly as he whispered, "But he can see the effect it produces . . . the fire in your eyes . . . the way you warm to my kiss . . ." Tolin's hand moved to her other breast and Sera's eyes briefly closed as he cupped it tightly. "And he can see the heat that builds within me, and in you as well, as I stroke you."

Her heart fluttering wildly beneath Tolin's experienced touch, Sera attempted confirmation of Rockwald's scrutiny.

"Nay, do not look back. You betray your thoughts. The need to convince Rockwald that we are what we claim grows critical."

"Critical?" Growing increasingly breathless as Tolin's hand roamed freely, massaging and teasing, straying to her rib cage and then slowly below, Sera whispered hoarsely, "Critical?"

His mouth drawing upon hers in short bites, Tolin rasped between ragged breaths, "Your coldness to me has been noted, heiress."

Tolin teased her lips with his tongue as Sera sought to catch her breath. Yea, she had been cold to him . . . purposefully cold.

"Last night I heard Rockwald confide to his man that something was amiss between us— that if a woman such as you truly belonged to a man such as I, you would not be allowed to grow so distant."

Tolin's mouth grazed her eyelids, her brow, the curve of her ear. "Are you cold to me now, heiress . . . ?"

Sera gasped, unable to respond as Tolin drew her back farther against him, his hand sinking unexpectedly beneath the waist of her undergarment to the warm delta untouched by any man before. His seeking fingers explored with gentle persistence until he found a point that sent a jolt of pleasure surging through her. He then whispered, ". . . For I am not cold to you."

Tolin was breathing heavily. Sera could feel

the rise and fall of his chest against her back as his hand moved in intoxicating persuasion. "There is a heat within me that wants more . . . much more."

Fighting to maintain her equilibrium, daring not to withdraw from Tolin under Rockwald's scrutiny, Sera rasped, "Nay . . . nay . . ."

"Yea . . ." Drawing his tongue along her lips, Tolin urged, "Purr for me, heiress. I would hear you purr your pleasure."

Sera felt the hot surge of moisture that bathed Tolin's fingertips as he captured her mouth once more, as his stroking grew more intense. His consequent growl sent a tremor coursing through her as he forced apart her legs to allow greater access to his delving hand.

Ripping his mouth suddenly from hers, Tolin drew back abruptly. So stunned was Sera by the progress of events that had slipped so rapidly beyond her control that she was uncertain of the exact moment when Tolin dismounted and swept her down into his arms.

Turning toward their wagon as it moved steadily forward a few feet away, Tolin covered the distance in a few rapid steps. He lifted her up and placed her on the mattress inside. He was inside with her, kneeling, leaning back to draw the flaps closed, when Sera glimpsed Rockwald riding in their direction.

Tolin's rough hiss started her trembling

anew. "Rockwald approaches. A convincing performance now is paramount, heiress."

Not waiting for Sera's response, Tolin thrust off his fur robe and stripped away his leather leggings. Reaching for her furs as she lay motionless, he ripped them off as well. He did not hesitate as he separated the zircum robe beneath and whipped away her undergarment with a careless hand.

Halting abruptly as his gaze dropped to the creamy flesh exposed to his view, Tolin whispered hoarsely, "So my eyes behold at last that which has grown familiar to my touch through these long nights." He paused. "You are beautiful, heiress."

His gaze jerking behind him at a sound close by, Tolin lowered himself quickly upon her. Sera caught her breath as his mouth covered hers, preventing her scream, her gasp . . . her sigh. . . .

Tolin slid Sera's arms around his neck, a low groan sounding silently within him as her rose-crested breasts touched the bared flesh of his chest. Heated elation brimmed as he slid his hands into Sera's hair, the hair he had longed to strain through his fingers from the first moment the gleaming strands had met his sight. He dragged his callused fingertips against her scalp, her temples, the smooth contours of her cheeks. He heard her gasp. He felt her sigh. He knew Rockwald was close by, but the thought slipped from his mind as he pressed his mouth more deeply into hers.

Yea, this was what he had wanted! He was holding this woman—this chosen woman—as he had held her in his dreams. He was touching her as he had longed to touch her. He was tasting her flesh. He could feel the wild pounding of her heart as she strained against him. But it was not enough.

Slipping his hands lower, Tolin brushed the moist delta between her thighs, finding the bud of her passion that he had stroked earlier. His body responding hotly to her gasp, he whispered, "Purr for me, heiress . . . purr. . . . The sounds of your pleasure are sweet to my ears. Let me hear your voice so I may join you in tender harmony as our lips meet."

His gaze tight on Sera's matchless countenance, Tolin saw the flush of color that transfused her skin, the separation of her lips that allowed a soft, groaning sigh to escape. The sound sent his senses reeling as he stroked her more boldly, raising the sound to a heated pitch.

The wagon flaps clapped open with a startling sound that jerked Tolin abruptly from his impassioned task. Cursing his brief lapse, Tolin slid his hand to the dagger he had shed with his leather leggings, turning in a fluid movement that shielded Sera's nakedness with his body as he met Rockwald's lecherous grin.

His voice a feral growl, the edge of his blade glinting, Tolin addressed the intruder with unrestrained menace.

"Once again you force your presence upon me in a private moment! My patience grows thin, Rockwald! Were you not essential to the successful return of this caravan to Orem Proper, I tell you now that I would not hesitate to send my blade on the course it so desires."

"Oh, so?" Rockwald's grin grew slowly savage. "Was not your wanton display in the sight of all an invitation to a man such as I, deprived of a woman's company during our long journey, to visually enjoy what now progresses?"

Tolin's lips drew into a contemptuous sneer. "So, you are one of those pathetic few who must observe copulation in order to obtain the satisfaction of the act."

"Nay, I am not one of those!"

Feeling Sera tense beneath him, Tolin pressed, "What kind of man are you, then?"

Rockwald's expression grew lewd. "I am a man who will pay well to follow you upon the female flesh you now shelter from my view."

Feeling Sera's shudder, Tolin responded with a perverse bid to torment, "How much do you offer?"

Rockwald salivated openly. "Thirty castars!"

Tolin laughed.

"Forty!"

Another laugh.

"One hundred!"

"One hundred, eh?" Enjoying retribution for weeks of merciless frustration, Tolin waited until Rockwald's sudden, aggressive step drew his harsh snarl.

"Fool, stay where you are! There are not castars enough in all of Orem to persuade me to share this woman. She is mine and mine alone!"

Tolin's hand tightened convulsively on his dagger as he continued with menacing finality, "Having said that, there is only one thing more I will add. If you are wise, you will not again invade my privacy, for if you do, I will see that you never again feel the need for this woman— *or any other.*"

Rockwald's color grew florid. He stood staring at Tolin, his chest heaving, before he slapped the wagon flaps abruptly shut and disappeared from sight.

In the silence of his departure, Sera spoke slowly, her words filled with contempt.

"You low, nameless cur . . ."

Tolin turned back to the woman still lying beneath him. She was no longer purring.

Thrusting Tolin from her with a strength born of flaring rage, Sera withdrew sharply.

Her eyes spat gold fire as she clutched her zircum robe closed.

"You are lower than the lowest mire that mucks the road."

Driven by an unknown demon within him, Tolin responded coldly, "I am but the man you sought to deliver you home—no more, no less. It was my intention to make you understand, once and for all, that I will honor my given word to deliver you safely to your destination, but only on my terms."

"What terms are they, Tolin of Rall, Master of Whores? Instead of offering my services to that salacious beast, would you have me sell my wares to every man in this caravan?"

"My terms would be far simpler than that tiring exercise." Tolin's gaze grew tight. "Instead, from this moment on I would have you as my *loving* wife before all who look upon us. You will ride with me each day as you did this morn, seated before me. You will cling to me. You will seek my touch, my lips, my gaze."

Sera's graceful brows arched with anger. "Is that *all*?"

"And you will kiss me upon demand—as you have never kissed another. As you will kiss me now . . ."

"I will not!"

"You will! And in that way you will demonstrate to me how much you desire to be delivered to fulfill your 'destiny.' "

"There are no words to describe the depth of your depravity! Nor are there words to express how I despise—"

Tolin interrupted Sera's scathing tirade. "I am waiting."

I am waiting.

Sera felt a surging hatred rise. Tolin . . . a demon in male form!

She slid closer to Tolin, suddenly determined to beat him at his own game. She would have no more difficulty maintaining the pretense of loving exchange between them than he! It mattered little to her that their lips might touch and their bodies press. She was Sera of Neer, this man's equal in every way!

Releasing the zircum fabric of her robe, Sera allowed the garment to fall open. The cold air touched the creamy flesh of her breasts as they were again exposed, but she paid the chill little mind. Rising to her knees instead, she moved closer to Tolin as he kneeled at the edge of the mattress. His gaze was narrowed, assessing, as she moved closer still.

Sliding her arms boldly around Tolin's neck, Sera raised her gaze to his. Her lips parted of their own accord and her eyes closed as the rosy crests of her breasts brushed the golden-brown hairs on his chest. Tolin's quick intake of breath as she leaned flush against him was the signal she sought to press her mouth to his. Slanting her lips, she took full measure of his mouth, curling her hands in his heavy, pale hair so she might draw him into cooperation should he withhold himself from her.

But Tolin did not withhold. Instead, his arms went around her, wrapping her tight in his embrace. Crushing her against him, he moved his palms over her back, smoothing and seeking, slipping down to cup her firm buttocks, pressing her female delta against his groin where the fine material of his breechcloth did little to hide his burgeoning tumescence.

Within moments Sera neither knew nor cared that Tolin had slipped her zircum robe down around her waist, that his hand had slipped between them to caress her breasts, that the game she had begun was again slipping from her grasp. Instead, she was lost in the world of flesh against flesh, heat against heat, of glory tasted but not yet fully indulged. Seeking Tolin's response to her kiss as hungrily as he sought hers, she invited him to taste the honey she offered with a whispered moan.

Gasping as Tolin abruptly released her, Sera stared with disbelief as he turned to reach for his leather leggings. Clothed a moment later, he turned back to face her, dispassionate amusement briefly twisting his lips as she struggled to raise her zircum robe to shield her nakedness.

Incredulity soared as Tolin stated flatly, "You perform well on command, heiress . . . so well that it may save your life."

Gone in a moment, Tolin left behind only the echo of his cruel words as Sera of Neer cursed the day he was born.

His eyes closed, his wizened face still, Zor strained to attain control. The damp confines of his abode were chilled, but he felt only the supreme exertion of the effort he expended in seeking to clear the relentless curtain from his mind.

The visions were there, taunting him. They called out in voices too soft to discern. They danced before the doors of his consciousness, flitting away before he could respond.

Knowing unrelenting torment as the haunting specters continued to elude him, Zor walked deeper into his cave. His step faltering, he felt the weight of years pressing heavily upon him. His had been a life of service as yet unfulfilled. Dedicated to his mentor, a seer with powers so far superior to his as to leave his own pale in their wake, he had sought all his life to prove himself worthy of that great man's faith in him. Upon his mentor's death, he had known he could prove worthy in only one way.

Like his mentor before him, Zor had sworn

his allegiance to Rall. In the time since, he had served the proud, often difficult masters of Rall to the full extent of his powers.

But difficult times had come upon him. The veil that had fallen across his mind after that fateful night in the tower room so long ago had dimmed his sight. He had lamented his loss, calling out with all the skills at his command for its return.

His appeal had remained unanswered—until now.

He was not truly certain when the veil had begun clearing. Sometime during the weeks past, the shadows had become images not yet defined. Driven by the need to see them more clearly, Zor approached the amber stone awaiting him. He stroked the surface with trembling, blue-veined hands, raising his voice in incantation. His words grew in power as he chanted, as the heat of the stone increased, expanding, forcing away the veil, consuming it, until—

The vision was gone!

Screeching aloud with frustration, Zor pulled at the white hair at his temples. How many times must he look, only to see nothing?

Yea, the veil was lifting. What lay yet unknown was whether—Zor shuddered—whether it would rise *in time*.

Chapter Seven

The familiar rattle and sway of the wagon lulled Sera as she came slowly awake. Morning light filtered through the rear flaps as she blinked, then raised her hand to brush the sleep from her eyes. Her hand freezing in midmotion, she looked abruptly toward the mattress beside her.

He was gone.

Sighing, Sera pushed a wisp of hair back from her brow as she allowed her thoughts to ramble over the events of the journey now nearing its end.

The day a week earlier when Rockwald tried to buy her services had marked a turning point in the interaction between her and Tolin. Accepting the validity of Tolin's concerns, she had heeded his warning while despising the man who offered it. She had done her best to quell Rockwald's suspicions with the displays of loving affection Tolin demanded. She had told herself that the demonstrations were a burden she must bear in order to walk the road for which she had been fated.

But the burden was heavy indeed.

For Tolin was a consummate actor, totally convincing in his stance of watchful husband. She was unable to step out within view of others without his arm slipping possessively around her. He appeared never to tire of touching her, of tasting her lips, while demanding the same of her in return. Were she not aware of his real motivation, she would have been tempted to believe there was true warmth behind his facade and true jealousy behind the gaze that accosted any man of the caravan who attempted so much as a glance her way. He was so proficient in the part he played that there were times when she almost—*almost*—forgot that the passion of his kiss was feigned, or stirred by nothing more than pure animal lust.

The sham was abandoned, however, when Tolin and she were confined in the seclusion of the wagon they shared. Their common bed aside, she maintained a stiff formality between them, knowing that the heart of the man whose physical warmth surrounded her through the night was as cold and sterile as the frozen land she had left behind. And if the long, dark hours of night raised, however briefly, a wish that it was not truly so, that thought was promptly banished by the first light of morn and the first touch of gray eyes that were cold and lifeless once more.

Sera drew herself to a seated position, noting that the air had lost still more of its chill. Their slow descent from the frozen plateau of Orem Minor had brought about rapid changes in the few days most recently past. The daylight hours had grown longer than any she had ever experienced, and the air warmer than she had ever known. The sun remained visible from the early hours of morn until the hour when most Minor Oremians would already have retired to their sleeping couches. Here and there brown spots of soil had begun appearing through the snow until the landscape had changed from the pristine, ever-renewing white of Orem Minor to a dazzling display of color.

Color, color . . . she had been astounded by the color increasing around her with every mile they traveled! She had been mesmerized by the flora and fauna becoming visible. She wished she could share their beauty with Millith and Impora, who would be similarly delighted, but she longed most of all to share them with Serbaak. She knew his thoughts would reflect her own if he could see the wonder of trees, bushes, and occasional flowers in shades too varied to name; of brightly plumed birds often filling skies of endless blue in squawking flocks; of small furred animals darting from cover to cover, their coats ranging from pale hues of gray and brown to more luxurious growths that rivaled the shade of her own fiery locks; and of larger animals of different sizes and shapes, some lumbering, some fleet of foot, who regarded their relentless caravan with expressions that ranged from suspicion to disdain.

A chill passed down Sera's spine as she recalled the lethal sound of arrows hissing to their mark as they felled the unsuspecting prey that had given them their first fresh meat since the inception of their journey. Recognizing necessity, she had nonetheless been stricken by the joy of the kill she had witnessed in the eyes of the hunters in their caravan and the excitement that the flow of blood had induced.

Her stomach again revolting, Sera briefly closed her eyes. All was not beautiful in this world being unveiled to her. Despite the years spent in solemn preparation for her mission, she knew she had much to learn.

Sera rose, automatically completing her primitive toilette, knowing that a few minutes hence she would be expected to appear at the back of the wagon to smile lovingly at her "husband" for the benefit of watchful eyes. She discarded her zircum garment and reached for the more sober attire necessary now that she had traded her fur robe for a woolen mantle. The gown was of a simple fabric far less luxurious than any attire she had previously worn, and it was cut in a style meant to emulate the common dress of the women of Orem Proper. The garment somehow depressed and inspired her simultaneously. Its somber color and lack of ornamentation recalled the present submission of the House of Neer, while reminding her of the brilliant promise of Neer's future which presently lay just beyond her reach.

Fully dressed, Sera squared her proud shoulders determinedly. To achieve the future she must survive the present.

Her hand on the wagon flaps, Sera paused momentarily, then thrust them aside. The distinctive clap of the folds drew the gaze of all nearby in her direction, but Sera was conscious only of the mounted figure a short distance away. Tolin held her motionless with the steel gray of his gaze. She saw his strong features tighten, whitening the fine scar marking his cheek. Then he dismounted with the fluid strength and confidence that marked all his movements. The morning sunlight glinted on his pale hair as he clasped his mount's reins in one hand and advanced toward her, drawing the great warhorse along behind him without effort. She recalled the ease with which those strong arms had supported her during long days astride. She remembered their warmth as they held her protectively close through the dark nights.

Yea . . . she remembered.

A disquieting tremor moved down her spine as Tolin neared. Sera clamped her teeth shut with a smile so tight that it approached a grimace. A little while longer and she would be free of this man and of unwanted thoughts of him as well.

Yea . . . just a little while longer.

Tolin walked toward Sera, his gaze fixed as she stood outlined in the wagon opening like a brilliant flame confined within tarnished glass. He silently cursed. Was the woman so foolish as to be unaware of the picture she presented as she stood framed in a shaft of morning sunlight for all to see? Did she not realize that her common attire emphasized her brilliant beauty by the sharpness of contrast, carving her image so deeply into the mind as to make her unforgettable? Did she not see that to impress herself so profoundly into the memory of the men of this particular caravan was to destroy any chance of her arriving in Orem Proper without comment?

A glance around him confirmed that his thoughts were not without foundation, and Tolin's frustration surged anew. Why could Sera of Neer not have been a solemn, drab piece easily ignored by all, instead of a beauteous witch whom all desired? He would then have had no difficulty in delivering her safely to her destination—nor would he have had to fight the arousal he continually felt whenever she was near.

The memory of long, silent nights returned to Tolin—nights almost beyond bearing while Sera lay vulnerable to his lustful desires, nights spent in wakeful frustration while the steady breathing of Sera's undisturbed sleep mocked him.

Yet, it was not his physical desire for Sera of Neer which most disturbed him, or his constant conflict with the often sharp-tongued, self-contained woman of destiny she claimed to be. Rather, it was his increasing susceptibility to the innocence, the naivete, and the endlessly diverting facets of the woman within Sera. It was the untouched inner woman Sera sought both to conceal and deny who caused him true torment. That inner woman had turned spontaneously to him in need. She had given her life over to him, trusting him instinctively despite the blood that stained his sword and the harsh words that often rang between them. He knew just as instinctively that Sera had never faltered in that trust. She had slept in his arms, warmed to his touch, revealing ever so fleetingly in a parting of her lips, in a flicker of her eye, in a momentary tremor of uncertainty, a vulnerability that had somehow become his own.

Tolin's broad shoulders stiffened. He disliked being vulnerable. He resented Sera's penetration of the armor he had so effectively raised around his emotions. He was determined to mend the break.

Realizing as he neared that Sera's welcoming smile stiffened more into a grimace with every step he took, Tolin's spirits perversely rose. The pose of subservient wife grated on Sera with the same intensity that his increasing frustration taunted him. They would both be grateful when their association ended.

As he reached the wagon, Tolin raised his arms toward the grimacing heiress. He caught her easily as she slipped down into his embrace. Her sweet, female warmth was both pleasure and pain.

Yea . . . very soon.

Muted sounds of laughter from the public room below rumbled through the heavy oak door of the meeting room as Filnor surveyed the filthy beggars awaiting his address. His handsome face twitched with disgust. Raggedly dressed, they were also personally unclean. The stench of them was almost beyond bearing.

Filnor took a short step backwards. It galled him to be forced to again employ these vermin of the streets. Had he his choice, he would rather see them swept forever from the face of Orem. But he had no choice.

Filnor counted. Five had responded to his summons, though he had originally called eight. His temper flared as he addressed the small, rodent-faced fellow who was their unofficial leader.

"It is long past the appointed hour. Why have Sittle, Pitts, and Werto not responded to my summons?"

Molta's gap-toothed grin flashed. "Sittle and Werto took the journey of no return two weeks past at the hands of your own soldiers, Master Filnor. Caught stealing a few buckets of grain from the royal stable, they were. The pity of it, two good men slain for a few buckets of grain."

"Yea, two good men," a tittering voice piped from the rear, "who tried to steal the royal mounts along with the royal grain."

The burst of laughter from within the group revealed that little sorrow had accompanied their friends' unexpected demise. More contemptuous than amused, Filnor pressed, "And the whereabouts of Pitts?"

Molta shrugged, then scratched the sparse

gray strands lying limply on his greasy brow. "Word has it that Pitts met up with the wrong woman, a wily witch who neglected to tell him that she carried the pox. On last report, his male member had turned a purple hue that was astounding!"

Another round of laughter left Filnor similarly unaffected as he raised a haughty brow. "So, your number wanes. Unfortunate, for I have use for the eyes and ears of even those churlish louts."

"Ye need them not, Master Filnor." Molta took a bold step toward him that sent Filnor's hand to his sword.

"Nay, I pray you, do not act in haste!" Molta sputtered. "I but meant to assure you that whatever your quest, we will be happy to pursue it. In truth, it is not often that the heir to the royal house seeks out those such as we."

The veracity of the man's words cut more deeply than intended as Filnor dropped his hand slowly to his side. His mental promise to himself that he would soon see the last of them sustained him as he proceeded slowly, "I have called you here because word has come to the House of Rall that an enemy approaches."

"An enemy?"

A buzz briefly ensued within the squalid group, halting abruptly as Filnor continued, "An unidentified enemy intends to infiltrate the

House of Rall for its foul purposes."

Another bout of buzzing set Filnor's nerves on edge, bringing a harshness to his tone. "I would have you whose eyes and ears are so keen watch closely for unusual occurrences or suspicious strangers, male or female, as you travel the streets and byways. I would have you report immediately to me should anything occur, with the promise of suitable reward."

"Suitable reward, Master Filnor?" Molta's smile flashed once more. "And what might that suitable reward be?"

Enraged at the vile cur's effrontery, Filnor responded in a menacing growl, "You dare to press me for specifics? I will not be challenged!"

"Nay, nay, I meant no challenge!" Molta's rheumy eyes popped wide at Filnor's flaring anger. "I meant no harm!"

His temper controlled once more, Filnor snapped, "It is enough for you to know that the payment will suit the endeavor, but I promise you this"—His dark eyes glowed with a fanaticism seldom displayed—"should your band keep my confidence, all will share in a reward that will far exceed your fondest imaginings. This word I give in the name of Rall. However . . ."

Seeing sudden caution visible in the eyes of all, which was the reaction he had sought, Filnor continued, "I give you fair warning that should any one of you betray me, *all* will share the same punishment."

Complete silence ensued until Filnor spoke once more. "He who would bring honor upon himself, brings honor to all. He who would betray brings all to the same untimely end. The choice is yours. Now, leave me!"

Filnor's eyes were black wells of anger when the click of the door closing behind the foul crew concluded the interview. In his wild obsession, Fador had again forced him into dealing with the lowest scum of the streets. He would not easily forgive his father's imposition upon his royal personage. Nor would he forget, and when the day came . . .

The stench in the room suddenly oppressive, Filnor walked abruptly to the door and threw it open. The cool morning air rushed in from the entrance below, giving temporary relief. He breathed deeply. He would go to Kiray now. She would be grateful for the opportunity to please him once more.

Walking rapidly down the stairs, Filnor approached the front door of the inn. An unfinished thought returned to linger pleasurably in his mind.

Nor would he forget . . . and when that day came . . .

The warm morning sun raised the sheen of perspiration to Tolin's brow. He had been walking along the trail beside Sera for the past hour. He had told himself that he was simply availing himself of the opportunity to stretch the stiffness from his legs, but he knew that was not truly so.

Tolin glanced beside him. Sera had cast off her outerwear in response to the morning heat. Even in the rough, shapeless garment she wore, Sera's slenderness, her inherently graceful step, drew all eyes. As he watched, the breeze molded the simple garment against her feminine curves, and his agitation swelled.

The men were salivating.

Slipping his arm around Sera, Tolin noted the chill in her gaze which was not dispelled by her smile. That smile . . . He knew every man in the caravan envied him that smile, yet only he knew the truth behind it.

Suddenly weary of his thoughts, Tolin looked up at the trail ahead. Had circumstances been different, he might have enjoyed the morning walk. The countryside was beautiful, but he knew it was the woman at his side, not the passing terrain, that had fascinated him during the hour past. Despite her attempt to conceal her interest, it was clear to him that Sera was entranced with the sights and sounds around her. The simple song of the willow bird had drawn a smile, its sudden flight a startled gasp that had widened her eyes into saucers of brilliant gold.

The unexpected flare of a dragon flower, its scarlet petals sweetly scented, had held her enthralled. It had been another morning of discovery for Sera of Neer, whose world had formerly been one of gray skies, white landscapes, and the green hue of zircum heat.

A sudden honking overhead alerted Tolin to the flight of great striped geese the moment before Sera stopped abruptly, raising her hand to shield her eyes as she followed their rapid departure from sight. Curling his arm more securely around her, Tolin urged her forward. When she looked up, he warned, "You betray yourself with so open an appreciation of those things you would have others believe you have viewed countless times before."

Sera glanced around her as she resumed her step. The interested stares of the drivers turned her back to him with a frown. "I had not realized I was so obvious."

"Heiress." Tolin's reminder bore a note of unconcealed irony. "There is nothing you do on this caravan that goes unobserved."

Sera's nose twitched. "The plight of being the solitary woman amongst so many men."

"That, too."

Sera's brow rose. "You are saying I am not playing my part well?"

"You have occasional lapses."

"Which you are quick to point out to me."

"I am but fulfilling my pledge to you to the best of my ability."

"Such nobility."

"Nay, I make no claim to nobility."

"Such—" Halting abruptly, Sera gasped at the appearance of a black-masked raccoon at the edge of the trail. She watched as the small animal moved more clearly into view, his elaborately striped fur gleaming as he stretched in a patch of sun. Her awe was ill-concealed as she whispered, "How beautiful! I have seen drawings of such animals in my studies, but I had not realized that they—"

Sera's words jerked to a stop as a deadly hiss sounded and the raccoon jerked suddenly upward with the force of the arrow that pierced its heart. Her choked cry piercing his heart as surely as the arrow that left the animal lifeless a few feet away, Tolin turned toward the caravan behind him with a growl of rage. Rage turned to blood fury at the sight of a fellow snickering at Sera's distress, a bow still hanging carelessly from his hand.

Tolin covered the distance between them with rapid steps. Wrenching away the offender's weapon, he rent it into firewood with a swipe of his sword, then grasped the fellow in a choking grip, raising him above the ground to hold him helpless as he grated, "You have taken your amusement at the expense of someone I hold dear. It is only the supreme ignorance of your act that now saves you from my blade. But I give you fair warning. Another offense—however small—will cost you your life!"

A hearty thrust sent the man sprawling in the dirt, but Tolin did not waste time in contemplation as the fellow scrambled to his feet and quickly disappeared from sight. Instead, he strode back to Sera, sliding his arm around her as he urged her off the trail.

Protected from prying eyes by a surrounding wall of greenery, Tolin turned to Sera. Her distress rebounded deeply within him. His voice dropped to a whisper as he stroked an errant wisp back from her pale cheek.

"The animal's death was instantaneous. It felt no pain."

"It is dead because of me—killed to shock or impress, I do not know which—but because of me nonetheless."

"Death is a part of life."

"But wanton killing is not."

Sera's words struck a spot forever raw within Tolin, hardening his response. "It seems to me that you, of all people, would need to prepare yourself for the slaughter that will soon prevail in your name."

Sera's eyes flew up to his. "You err if you think I return to Orem Proper to bathe its soil in blood!"

"There can be no other outcome should you press your claim."

"You know not of what you speak, Tolin of Rall!" Her fair face flushing, Sera said, "I have not waited twenty years, studying and preparing myself with relentless dedication for the duties I will assume, so I might bring a bloodbath to my people. That is not my intention!"

"It is not *your* intention that concerns me." Tolin's frustration returned. "Time grows short, heiress. We will soon arrive at the primary village of Orem Proper and the need for plain talk grows dire. You have proved clearly this morn that even the wanton slaying of a dumb animal offends you. It bleeds your face white and doubtless sickens your stomach."

Sera swallowed spasmodically, confirming his observation, but Tolin felt little satisfaction as he continued, "What will you do when you see the battlefield run red with the blood of your followers? Will you retch and run away, causing their blood to have been shed in vain? Will you waste their lives, heiress? For if you will, it is far better that you disavow your claim now, before a single drop of that blood has been shed."

"I will not have the blood of my followers run in my name, I tell you!"

"Mayhap *you* will not—but *Fador* will."

"It is not my destiny to shed the blood of my people!"

193

"But it is *Fador*'s destiny!" Grasping Sera's shoulders, Tolin shook her roughly. "You say you spent most of your life preparing for this journey you now undertake. You say you are ready to assume rule of Orem, thereby restoring the House of Neer to its rightful place. Look at me, Sera!" Tolin shook Sera again when she sought to avoid his gaze. "Do you really believe Fador will not fight your ascent to his throne with every ounce of strength, every drop of blood in his body? Do you truly believe that should Fador fall, Filnor will not take up his sire's sword and fight his sire's fight to the death rather than fall to his knee and accept your reign? If you believe that to be so, you are more the fool than I ever considered you to be!"

"I am no fool!"

"Nay, you are not." Tolin's gaze narrowed as he drew back to assess the beautiful flushed face so close to his. "But if you are not, what *are* you, heiress?"

"I am the hope of Orem!"

"So you say, but there is only one way you can assume the rule of Orem without bloodshed." Tolin's strong jaw twitched as his gaze narrowed. "If you *are* a sorceress, after all."

"A sorceress?" Sera laughed aloud. "Yea, I am a sorceress who has borne the weight of your oppression these many weeks for the sheer joy of it!"

"Mayhap you concealed your powers so they could be used at a more propitious time."

"Fool, my strength does not lie in enchantment!" Sera's golden eyes glowed. "My strength comes from within! I say to you now, Tolin of Rall—"

"I tell you again—Rall is no longer my master!"

"And *I* tell *you* that my power comes from the flame of life within me that will not die! That flame has spoken to me from the time I was old enough to recall. It has encouraged me, instructed me, and guided my path. I serve it now as I have served it all my life. In doing so, I seek benign retribution for Sileen, the mother of my body, who was slain to give me life; for Versa, the mother of my spirit whose time was shortened so cruelly; and for the House of Neer and those who lost their lives in its name. Nor will I be satisfied until the threat of the House of Rall is abolished from Orem forever!"

Tolin's sudden laughter rang in the wooded glade, a sound devoid of mirth. "All this you would accomplish without the shedding of your people's blood!"

The fine line of Sera's jaw hardened. "I say again, I will not have Neer's throne marked by the blood of her people!"

"Then you will never rule!"

"I will!"

Exasperation soaring, Tolin rasped, "It is imperative that you listen to me and believe what I am to say, heiress. You do not know Fador as I know him. He is a man unlike any you have ever known. He is without joy, without mercy, without remorse. He is a man who lives solely for the power he wields, a man who would sacrifice all rather than surrender it. You play with fire when you seek to depose him!"

The peculiar gold of Sera's eyes became intense. "I *am* fire."

Tolin studied the beauteous woman standing before him, slow realization dawning as her words reverberated in his mind. She who had been brought to the brink of tears by the death of a small animal a short time earlier was gone. For all her obvious youth, for all her delicacy of form, the woman now standing proudly in her stead was as formidable as the sword that lay sheathed at his side. Her mind was as sharp as its cutting edge, and her will as strong as its blade.

Sorceress?

Nay.

The flame of Neer?

Mayhap.

The future ruler of Orem?

Not while a breath of life still remained in the House of Rall.

Eyes of icy gray locked with those of fiery

gold. Yea, this woman needed him—more than she knew.

That thought registering deep inside him, Tolin took Sera's arm. Without another word, he turned her back in the direction from which they had come.

The wagon rumbled along the rutted trail beneath her, but Sera did not peer out through the swaying flaps to stare at the brilliance of the setting sun as she had been wont to do in the days of their journey most recently past. In a few swift moments, hours earlier, the joy had been stolen from the beauteous day by the hiss of the arrow that had penetrated the heart of a small, furred animal—and her own as well.

Secluded in her wagon as she had been since Tolin and she left the leafy bower and their tempestuous discussion behind them, Sera raised long, tapered fingers to temples throbbing with the anxiety that raged within.

What will you do when you see the battlefield run red with the blood of your followers?

The harrowing words echoed in Sera's mind. The throbbing in her temples increased as a reality untouched by the words of the prophecy registered clearly. Tolin, for all the unsparing harshness of his words, had spoken the truth. Despite her years of study, there was so much she did not know about the past, so much she did not truly understand about Rall, yet she had embarked upon a rendezvous with destiny that endangered the lives of all who believed in her, as well as the future of Orem itself.

Sera's eyes suddenly welled. She could not proceed steeped in such ignorance any longer.

Nay!

She needed to understand her enemy.

She needed a clearer vision of the path she walked.

She needed to know *more*.

Those needs a slashing shaft of pain she could no longer bear, Sera closed her eyes. She pressed her fingers tighter against her throbbing temples as she prepared herself to appeal to the source within that had never failed her. The wagon rattled relentlessly onward as she spoke at last, her voice a fervent whisper that echoed from the well of torment deep inside.

"Versa, essence of the flame that gave me life . . . help me. The path I now travel, the new world I am destined to rule in your stead, is foreign to me in so many ways. My studies have left me ill prepared for the cruel inconsistencies of this land. There is a golden warmth here that is absent in Orem Minor, yet the hearts of so many are cold. A profusion of beauty and color astounds the eye in every quarter, yet harshness and brutality abound. Joy appears forever absent from the soul. How can this be?"

Desperation choked Sera's voice, causing her to pause in her plea to the silent flame within. Her hands dropping to her lap, she clenched them tightly there, opening her eyes to the dim light of the wagon as she strove to bring full comprehension to the mysteries confounding her. "Help me, Versa. Help me to understand the bitterness of my people. Help me to comprehend the hatred that prevails. Help me to view the heart of Rall so I might see its threat more clearly. Reveal the past fully to me so I might approach the future with true awareness. Help me to save my people, Versa. Help me . . ."

Sera's impassioned entreaty lingered on the solemn silence.

Help me . . .

Help me . . .

Somehow unprepared as the flame within surged hotly in response, Sera caught her breath. She remained silent and rigidly still as the mists of the past rose in an unexpected swell and began swirling before her view. Pale spirals of zircum green enveloped her. They cushioned her in their wavering gyres. They incited her with expectation, urging her to surrender, to breathe deeply as they took her back . . . back . . . back. . . .

Gasping, Sera saw her!

Versa, the mother of her spirit—young and beautiful, startlingly similar to her in appearance, yet with an individuality of feature that set them apart—stood in a castle room that grew suddenly brilliantly clear. The silent tableau sprang to life as Versa turned sharply, agitation marking her expression as she addressed the thin, white-haired woman beside her.

"Is there no end to Rall's treachery, Seetra? Must I be forever cursed with Rall's lust for rule?"

The midwife's aging face grew grave. "A lust for rule that is unrelenting . . . yea, for even now Rall's solicitors range far and wide in the provinces, fomenting discord and rebellion."

Versa's royal robes flared out behind her as she assumed an angry, pacing step. She appeared to speak as much to herself as she did to the small woman who watched her with obvious distress. "Why, Seetra? Are my people so blind that they cannot see the devious bent of the House of Rall? Has Fador so enchanted them that they can no longer see the truth?"

"Fador has given them a new truth."

"What truth? That given the opportunity, he would use them as they have never been used before to achieve his lust for dominion? That he has no feeling for them beyond the power they might grant him as their ruler? That the promises he makes will all fall by the wayside when he attains the position of rule he covets? Why do they believe him?"

"The weak believe him, but there are many who recognize the supreme benevolence and right of Neer's rule and will never turn their back on it."

"Many ... who remain cautiously silent while Neer's detractors grow more vociferous each day."

"Your army awaits your command."

"Yet some within the ranks are also increasingly drawn to Rall."

"One cannot discount the strange fascination of evil, Versa. Fador knows that fascination well and uses it to his advantage. He has allowed his army to steep itself in iniquity while holding it aloof from retribution on all quarters. His army is drunk on the debauchery and excess that he so cleverly wields, and like the drunkard who glories in his vice, his warriors look to a future of continued satiation of physical desire that Fador promises will be theirs if they but follow him. He allows their corruption to infect others with the same carnal appetites, and he revels in their debasement, knowing that because of it, his warriors have become his slaves."

"An evil that corrupts ... and kills ..."

"Your royal guard remains steadfast to a man."

"Yea, that stalwart few ... but what of the

good people of Orem?" Versa's expression grew pained. "Do they, too, grow corrupt?"

"Nay, but they are helpless against the power of Fador's evil. You are their only hope."

"I . . ." Versa's delicate jaw hardened. "Were that the strength of my forces were not compromised by the pox that so recently razed my army in the provinces, a sickness that continues to weaken it more with each passing day."

"Pox? Nay, clever poisoning, instead."

Versa gasped. "No man would sacrifice hundreds for the sake of his own glory!"

"Fador would."

"If I were sure . . ." Versa's jaw grew rigid. Her eyes of golden citron grew hard as she turned to face Seetra squarely. "I will seek out the Royal Advisors now, and I will have them confirm these words you speak. If they prove true, I will raise my royal guard and those of my army still standing and lead them to confront Fador myself!"

"Nay, Versa! Fador but awaits the opportunity to snuff the life of Neer and to exterminate the royal crescent forever! If you must dispatch your army, it is imperative that you remain behind at a point of safety."

"Never!"

"Versa, I implore you . . ."

The exquisite planes of her countenance growing impassioned, Versa responded to the old woman's plea with a determination laced with regret for the pain inflicted with her words.

"My dear Seetra, you who saw my mother gasp her last breath at the same moment she gave me life—you who remained at my side to nurture me in her stead while the threat of Rall remained ever looming—surely you know what I must do. I have studied and trained all my life, inwardly sensing that with Fador's coming of age would come the true test of my ability to rule. It pains me that I have been ineffective against his deception and the slow eroding of Neer's power that he has accomplished."

"It is not Fador alone that you combat. It is the power of evil, aided by the incantations of Zor, which held you impotent!"

"But I can remain impotent no longer! Seetra, can you not see that the ultimate test approaches? I am the bearer of the royal crescent! As I was born to rule, I was also born to lead in the conflict now looming ever nearer. I am a warrior, born to the sword and trained in the wielding of a zircum blade that has never failed me!"

"Yea, a blade that has never failed, yet a blade that has never confronted Rall."

"I cannot shield my blade from that which my warriors would face in my name!"

"Versa, should you fail—"

"Should I fail?" Versa stiffened, resolution

written in the taut lines of her slender form. "I will never surrender Orem to Rall."

"But—"

"*Never*."

"Versa—"

Versa placed her hand on Seetra's frail shoulder, her expression softening as she felt the old woman's shuddering. "First things first, Seetra. A visit to my advisors. Confirmation, then discourse, with confrontation the last resort. I would not have the blood of my people needlessly shed."

"Versa, I beg you . . ."

"Confirmation, then discourse, Seetra."

The mists rose again before Sera's eyes, obscuring the castle room and the images she had seen so clearly. Motionless in its thrall as the hazy vapor again enveloped her, Sera saw a forested tableau loom in its stead. Two handsome figures stood facing each other there, but the golden sunlight streaming into the leafy bower did little to soften the fierce emotions that surged between them as the tall, bearded man clad in warrior leathers addressed the slender, flame-haired woman who faced him without fear.

"Incredulity leaves me speechless!" Her eyes wide, Versa studied the man standing opposite her, missing not the sheen of raven-black hair carefully trimmed, aristocratic features tightly drawn, a broad, proud stature that bespoke the royal lineage of a time long past. Her gaze came to rest on the ruthlessness that shone from eyes as black as ebony as she rasped, "How dare you plead this private meeting with me, only to insult me with your depraved offer to betray the trust of my royal house!"

"Your royal house? You choose to forget that Rall's is a royal house as well!"

"A royal house of a time long past! Rall, in its greed and partnership with the black arts, relinquished its right to rule! The natural disasters that overwhelmed our land in the wake of Rall's rule, and the emergence of Neer, benevolent and strong in the devastation that followed, declared Neer and the bearer of the crescent the chosen ruler of Orem for all generations to come! In the many lifetimes that followed, Orem's progress and prosperity have confirmed the right of Neer's rule over and again! Nothing has happened to change that, and nothing ever will!"

"You err, Versa." Fador's bearded cheek twitched with the volatile emotions he suppressed as he continued with tenuous control, "Lacking a leader of sufficient strength, Rall lay inept and powerless those many generations, but it is inept and powerless no longer. In my person, Rall will be restored to its former glory!"

"Nay!"

"Yea!" Fador covered the distance between them with rapid steps that brought him so close to Versa's slender frame that the two almost touched. His gaze fervent, he rasped, "You know as well as I that the fruit of my surreptitious labors nears harvesting and that Neer's rule nears its end. Nor is there need for me to confirm that a confrontation is soon to come in which Rall and Neer will determine by the sword which house will rule. In such a conflict, true victory may be achieved in only one way."

"So say you, who knows no path but the shedding of blood!"

"So say I, who sees the future for what it will be!"

Clasping Versa's shoulders with his hands, Fador drew her abruptly close, his dark eyes suddenly bright with an ardor that bore no relation to a lust for rule as he whispered, "Versa, can you not see that I would not have your blood shed so I might reign? You are too beautiful to have the life within you sacrificed. Your mind is too keen, your spirit too brave, and your body too warm to be laid waste in that way. Nay—I have in mind a future far more suited to the heated core of you, the force that draws me relentlessly to you even now, as it has since the day I first viewed you in my youth. You were meant for a future at my side, my consort as I rule Orem in the name of Rall—a future in which the common people of Orem live their lives in service to us as we were meant to be served. In that future we will function unhindered by common bounds, indulging and exploring the pleasures of the flesh to the fullest, seeking satiation of our most carnal desires, denying ourselves nothing in the sampling of sweet, forbidden fruits, knowing that the supreme power of life and death lies in our hands even while we are held untouchable by reparation of any kind for our acts."

"Unhand me!"

Startled as Versa's command cut sharply into the impassioned words of his suit, Fador remained motionless.

"Unhand me, I said!"

Fador's hands dropped to his sides as Versa stepped backwards, shuddering with revulsion. "Vile, degenerate wretch . . ."

"You do well to watch your words, Versa."

"You seek to corrupt me as you would corrupt Orem."

"I seek only to give you pleasure, to share with you—"

"Liar! You seek only to *gain* pleasure, the pleasure of knowing you have defiled Neer as you have defiled all else that your hands touch!"

"You speak a fool's words, Versa! Neer's rule weakens more each day, while the power of Rall grows! You know as well as I that I offer you the only hope that remains to you, yet you shun the truth!"

"Truth!" The exotic planes of Versa's face grew tight. "You are a stranger to truth, Fador! It is you who shun it, not I! Were you to accept the truth, you would see that your lust for power and the perverted depths to which you sink to achieve it will destroy the very land you seek to rule!"

"Orem destroyed? Nay! It is only Neer which will fall—never to rise again!"

"Nay, it is Neer's destiny to rule! So it has been decreed by prophecy!"

"Prophecy? There is only one prophecy that Fador of Rall accepts, and that is one which he himself declares!" The sharply sculpted planes of his face hardening, Fador went on, "And so I prophesy to you now, Versa of Neer, that the offer you disdain in this bower casts in stone the fall of Neer and the shedding of the last drop of Neer's blood. It is a prophecy to be altered in only one way. . . . "

Versa's gaze burned with impassioned fury. "Leave me, Fador."

Ignoring her command, Fador dropped his lascivious gaze to Versa's mouth, continuing, "That prophecy will be negated only by a plea for mercy from your soft lips. . . . "

"Leave me!"

Taking a sharp backward step as Versa's ringing command resounded in the forested glade, Fador stared at Versa's flushed countenance in seething silence. A rabid hiss his only response, he turned abruptly on his heel, and in a moment was gone.

The mists of zircum hue returned, whirling with increasing intensity, erasing the scene and revealing a great room in a cavernous cave, its dark walls slick with moisture that trailed to the stone floor in glittering streams as two men, one in youth's prime, the other thin and wizened with age, faced each other in heated confrontation.

"She will change her mind, I say!"

"She will not!"

"Addlepated fool! How dare you contradict me?" Fador's handsome face was florid with rage as he raked the aged seer with his gaze. His contempt was clearly displayed as he assessed Zor's white flowing hair and beard, his colorless skin, and the common robes hanging limply on his bony frame. "You are old! Your seeing eye dims and your senses falter. The juices of life are dry in your veins and you are unable to recall the force of youth that once flowed there! Versa will change her mind, I tell you! She will not allow her life to be ended prematurely for the sake of a people who will never know gratitude for such sacrifice!"

"Versa is a product of Neer! Her goals bear no resemblance to those you pursue!"

"Stupid old man! There is only one true goal for one who leads a royal house! Power, and all it entails!"

"Nay."

"Yea! And even if it were not so—if Versa were committed to the lofty, aesthetic goals which are the fodder of fools, she is too wise to allow all she has to offer to be sacrificed on the altar of futility! She is aware of the steady draining of her power. She knows that should a confrontation come, she cannot emerge victorious!"

"So you would believe. But in truth, Versa sees another path. I have employed the seeing eye you so openly scorn, and I have seen the conflict that rages within her. Her conflict is not the result of a lascivious offer made in a forest bower. Instead, it is derived from her innate desire for direct confrontation with Rall and her realization that to follow that inclination will result in the shedding of blood."

His gaze narrowed, his breathing heavy as he sought to control his emotions while considering Zor's words, Fador managed a stiff nod. "As always, spare grains of truth lie amongst the chaff of your words. Versa is courageous. She does not suffer intimidation. At her own request, she trained with warrior apprentices in her youth until she became as proficient with the sword as any warrior in her guard, for all her fragile frame. It was during such a training session that I first saw her as a boy. I recall with utmost clarity even now the ferocious glory of her charging advance, the skill with which she wielded her blade, the elation sparking in her eyes as she claimed easy victory over her male combatant, and the youthful splendor of her as she stood beautiful and proud. It was in that moment that I knew—as I know now—that there was no woman on the face of Orem worthy of the man Fador of Rall would one day be, save Versa of Neer. And I vowed that one day *Versa would be mine!*"

Fador drew his powerful frame erect. His handsome face creased into a hard smile as he continued more softly than before, "That time has come. I will not allow Versa to slip away from me."

"You may have no choice."

"Fie on you, old man! The choice will be mine!"

"Yea, you may have a choice . . . of sorts. You may yet come to the moment when you must choose between the power you covet and the woman you covet as well."

"I will have both! If you persist in seeing else in your cloudy crystal, I charge you now, as you are bound by your solemn vow to serve the House of Rall, to effect its change!"

The old seer's small eyes tight on Fador's livid countenance, Zor responded, "I can aid you in one of the two quests you pursue—but not both. So, in answer to the charge now given, I ask you, Fador of Rall, which path would you have me clear for you? The path to ultimate rule, or the path to—"

His breath escaping in a gasp as Fador thrust him sharply backwards to strike his back against the cave's glistening wall, Zor was unable to continue as Fador hissed, "Enough! I will listen no more! Orem *and* Versa will be mine!"

Striding angrily from Zor's rough abode, Fador left the elderly magician breathless in his wake.

The spirals of time again shifted, blocking the glossy, cavernous walls from Sera's view, holding her prisoner within its grasp as yet another scene grew gradually clear.

She saw a castle chamber lit by the light of dawn creeping through narrow windows. On one side were walls hung with maps of Orem's two climes, a desk piled high with official papers, and a case overflowing with countless books that reflected hours of devoted study. In the middle was a great fireplace in which a fire flamed brightly. On the opposite side was a broad bed with hangings marked with the royal seal of Neer. A wardrobe lying open revealed a surprisingly limited number of robes bearing the same crest, stored beside garments of more sober intent. A pedestal mirror seldom used for vanity's sake alone was positioned nearby.

Standing still amidst it all was Versa, who came to life with an abrupt pacing step that reflected the same anxiety evinced in the tense lines of her countenance as she glanced toward the window and the brightening light of dawn. Versa turned at a sound behind her, drawing herself erect as Seetra entered.

The old woman's expression was stiff as she clutched a missive in her hand. She hesitated long moments before handing it over to Versa's scrutiny.

Breaking the seal marked with the crest of Rall, Versa breathed deeply, preparing herself as she read:

"Versa of Neer,
The time of Neer's rule approaches its final hours. The provinces lie under the command of Rall as Neer's army remains weakened by sickness and ineffective against Rall's superior force. The people of Orem hide themselves in their homes, awaiting the outcome of this fateful day.

Fools that they are, they flounder in uncertainty even as the future of Orem looms abundantly clear.

You know that future as well as I, Versa. It is a future that we will share if you will but surrender Orem to the House of Rall, if you will swear allegiance to Rall in its omnipotence, if you will accept Rall's infallible wisdom as your own and vow the abandonment of Neer forever.

A difficult choice? Neer has already been abandoned and you are alone. Only your royal guard remains, a force sadly inadequate against the vast number of Rall's warriors massing even now within striking distance of your castle gates.

Nay, the choice is not difficult. Surrender is your only recourse.

You must make that choice by mid-point of the day that is now dawning. If you do not, choice will be taken from you.

Rall's banner will fly from the castle ramparts this day, whatever path you choose.

I await your word.

Fador of Rall."

Versa looked back at Seetra's pale face, her hand twitching on Fador's missive, the moment before she crushed it in her fist and cast it into the fire.

"Caution, Versa! Do not dismiss Fador's words too lightly!"

"Dismiss his words? Nay, I do not! I read them and I eschew them, but I do not dismiss them! I see them for what they are—the voice of evil seeking to taint the minds of all who would heed its siren call."

"You must not be too harsh. You must consider—"

"Consider? Seetra, you forget that I committed the history of Orem to heart, memorizing each devious step Rall took in its heinous days of rule, each diabolic act committed, recording within my mind the devastation that resulted from a reign so debased that it left Orem reeling in its wake. That evil has arisen again, Seetra, no matter the handsome face and appealing stature its standard bearer presents. To surrender to that evil is to become part of it. I will not surrender Neer to Rall, for I will not dishonor Neer's name with Rall's infamy!"

"But Fador will—"

Placing her hand on Seetra's frail shoulder as she had once before, Versa whispered, "Try to understand. I cannot allow myself to look past the evil that now confronts me. As Orem's leader and the bearer of Neer's crescent of rule, I must defend the truths it represents. I must

215

have faith that the prophecy written long before my time will not desert Neer in its hour of trial, and I must do all in my power to shield the principles of Neer from the precepts of darkness that assault it." Her voice briefly failing, Versa added, "Seetra, please try to understand."

The old woman's response was a brief sob the moment before she enclosed Versa in a trembling embrace. Leaving moments afterward, Seetra drew the chamber door closed behind her as Versa walked to her desk and seated herself there to take her quill in hand.

Arising from her desk a short time later, Versa strode to the case nearby. There she removed some books, exposing a jeweled sheath secreted behind them. Carrying the sheath back to her desk, she carefully rolled the scroll over which she had labored and slipped it inside.

That task completed, Versa turned, striding toward the wardrobe on the opposite side of the room. She drew the doors open and reached inside.

Tears welling, she withdrew her warrior leathers.

Moisture filled Sera's eyes as well. A zircum haze clouded the scene, only to clear moments later, exposing the great room of a castle—stone walls hung with brilliant tapestries, floors covered with fur rugs, and brilliant pennants boldly displayed beside the throne. Frantic activity reigned. Sounds of battle echoed from the castle walls. The hiss of flying arrows, the clashing of swords, the unmistakable whistle of flaming projectiles launched again and again accompanied the shouts of advancing warriors as they raised their battle cries amid the calls of the wounded and dying.

Uncowed, Versa stood slender and proud, as if born to the warrior leathers she wore. Her expression solemn, she assessed the five sober men dressed in the dark robes of the learned, then addressed them each in turn.

"Nako, my faithful principal advisor; Gorum, second in authority over this eminent group; Dorball, Ektra, Whit, three who round out the circle of knowledge and wisdom which has guided me during my reign, five men faithful and true—"

"Five who have failed you." His lined face marked with the pain of the impending moment, Nako continued, "Five unable to stem the tide of evil that Fador raised until it now stands outside our gates ready to inundate us all!"

"Nay, Nako, do not distress yourself with useless recriminations. Your faithful circle has proved its skill and dedication to Neer in countless ways as you pursued a path of integrity and devotion to its people. Years of devotion are not negated by the beast that now slavers at our gates. In truth, your service to Orem and to Neer has not yet ended. There is a final task with which I would charge you."

"You have but to ask, Versa, and it will be done."

Nako's impassioned response, earnestly reflected in the expressions of the men beside him, brought a fleeting moisture to Versa's eyes. Turning to the nearby stand to pick up the jewel-encrusted sheath lying there, she looked briefly at each of the other advisors in turn before placing it in Nako's hand, solemnly charging, "As I entrust you with this sheath, I entrust you with the future of Orem and all those who would follow me. Guard it with your life. Hold it safe for me, knowing that within lies the only true life Orem will ever know. Promise me you will do this."

Emotion quaking in his voice, Nako responded, "So I vow."

Nako's words were echoed over and again by each of the dark-robed men surrounding Versa. Swallowing against another rise of emotion, Versa continued, "Go then—quickly, before the gates fall."

"Nay, we cannot! We will not abandon you!"

"You do not abandon me! You aid me in my moment of trial in a way no others may!"

"Nay—"

"Go!"

Turning to the guard nearby, Versa commanded, "Take them to the underground tunnel. Hold them there until the sounds without indicate that the gates have fallen. Bide time until the beast bays at my door, until the sounds of fury are at full height, before spiriting these good men into the forest beyond. Guide them to safety, remaining at their side until they have no further use for you, knowing full well that as you serve them, you serve Orem and Neer as well."

Turning back to her advisors once more, Versa attempted a smile with her parting words. "You have not seen the last of me, or of Neer. You will yet serve us both again. Of that, I give solemn promise."

The emotional scene faded unexpectedly from Sera's view, to be replaced with a scene of raging conflict that caught her breath with horror. Clashing swords, shrieking cries, wounded and dying spilling their life's blood onto the stone castle floor even as the crash of splintering wood announced that another section of the castle had been penetrated.

And then she saw Versa.

The tower room was the final bastion of safety within the castle walls. Versa retreated up the steps, her remaining guards behind her. She turned as a cracking sound below indicated that the door had fallen. Rushing footsteps and the sudden appearance of Fador's elite, their leathers bright with gore, raised Versa's sword to clash once more.

Striking, feinting, wielding her sword with dauntless courage, Versa waged noble battle as her men fell one by one under the onslaught of the superior force. She backed up into the tower room, gasping, her strength failing as she swung her sword again and again, as the clash of blades grew harder to withstand and the stone floor ran red with the blood of her last guards.

Alone against the wall, her fiery mane a brilliant contrast to her ashen pallor, Versa clutched her zircum blade. She allowed its strength to fill her anew as Rall's elite surrounded her, panting with lust for the kill as their captain pressed, "Do you yield, Versa of Neer? Do you yield to Fador and to Rall?"

Glancing at the loyal men who lay dead at her feet, Versa sneered. "Yield? Do you believe the Crescent of Neer would do less than the brave men who sought to shield her from the jackals of Rall? Nay! I will not yield!"

"Do not be a fool, Versa!" Pushing his way through Rall's bloodied throng, Fador approached to a point just beyond the thrust of her blade. "Neer is vanquished! It will never rise again! Yield! Embrace Rall and you will save your life!"

"Never!"

"Think what you say! You have but one chance more!" Fador's face took on an apoplectic hue as he hissed, "Yield! Yield!"

Versa's response was a flashing thrust of her blade that forced Fador unexpectedly backwards. Gasping aloud when a burning pain penetrated her midsection, robbing her breath, Versa tumbled to the floor even as Fador withdrew his sword.

Standing over her for a brief moment, Fador grated, "Fool you are, Versa of Neer! And as a fool, you die!"

Turning to the men around him, Fador ordered, "Leave her where she lies!"

Versa closed her eyes as heavy, shuffling steps retreated and faded into the silence of the tower room, as her breathing grew strained, as life began ebbing.

A spark within suddenly flaring, Versa forced open her eyes.

Nay! She would not surrender her life!

Not yet! Not yet!

Turning at the sound of a scraping step beside her, Versa struggled to keep the encroaching grey mist at bay as a wizened face appeared above her, small, black eyes intent as they gazed down into hers.

Her breath fading, Versa rasped, "Zor . . . I knew you would come. You are enemy of Neer, but servant of the prophecy . . . bound to it, as am I."

"I am here."

"With my last breath, I declare . . . I will never surrender Neer to the evil of Rall. My spirit . . . my spirit remains. . . . "

Versa's words faded.

The brilliant gold of her eyes glazed over.

Her breathing stilled.

Zor swiftly withdrew a faceted crystal from the sack at his waist. Placing it over the heart of Versa which beat no more, he raised a gnarled hand to the power which had served him many times before. His voice growing in strength, he summoned all the mystical powers at his will, reciting an ancient incantation that caused Versa's bloodied form to convulse sharply the moment before a brilliant flame burst to life within the sealed crystal!

Taking the crystal into his hand, Zor turned, leaving behind the fragile, bloodied shell that had once been Versa of Neer, carrying the captive flame . . .

. . . the spirit that had been Versa's life.

. . . the spirit that would not surrender.

. . . the spirit that would give life once more.

Tears streamed from Sera's eyes as the whirling mists of the past faded from her view, leaving only the last flickering image of the captive flame.

She had witnessed Versa's life.
She had witnessed Versa's death.
And now she knew.

The last flickering light of the captive flame lingered before Serbaak's eyes as the images of the past that had so unexpectedly inundated his mind abruptly faded, as he fought to suppress the emotion still prevailing.

"Speak to me, Serbaak."

Serbaak returned to the present with a jolt. Glancing around him, he saw shadows dimly lit by the glow of zircum lamps, in a chamber with which he had become increasingly familiar since Sera's departure. He felt Teesha's caressing touch on his arm as she lay beside him.

"Tell me what is wrong, Serbaak."

The torment in Teesha's gaze increased his own as Serbaak rose to his feet. Unmindful of his naked state, he walked to the window to gaze out upon a landscape that gleamed silver-white in the unusually clear night. Before his eyes, however, was another scene, a bloodied tower room strewn with the bodies of a loyal few, in the midst of which lay a lifeless, flame-haired figure so similar to that of Sera of Neer's that it all but rent his heart in two. It was a scene painfully engraved on his heart, which would remain forever as clear as the room in which he now stood.

And then he felt Sera's anguish.

Its onslaught was sharp, almost debilitating. It was accompanied by a sadness, the depth of which he knew Sera had never experienced before. He knew just as suddenly that as he had shared the press of the past with her in those harsh minutes, her grief would be forever his as well.

Serbaak closed his eyes. This most recent vision had not been the first since Sera had left Orem Minor. Some clear, some uncertain, Serbaak knew only that Sera's torments were many. Joy one moment, pain the next, then anger that soared to fury. Sera's distress had come to him across the miles. There was no escaping it.

But this last was almost more than he could bear.

"Serbaak . . ."

Turning to the woman who stood beside him as unashamedly naked as he, Serbaak attempted a smile. Silver moonlight caught the midnight sheen of Teesha's hair as it lay unbound against her back. He raised a hand to stroke the silken locks, sliding his fingertips along the line of her shoulders, finally cupping her chin gently, with regret. Teesha was beautiful and warm and giving . . . but she was not Sera.

"You are thinking of her again, aren't you?"

Long past the point of denial, Serbaak attempted a smile. "Without intent, I have been unfair to you, Teesha. I have been thinking long and hard on my treatment of you. It occurs to me that perhaps it would be best if I—"

"I do not wish to hear those words!" Her slenderness suddenly tight against him, Teesha raised her face to speak in a gentle whisper. "She has slipped away from you, Serbaak. Not born of this place, she was never meant to remain."

"I know."

"She has gone home. She will not return."

"I know that, too."

"You must put her from your mind."

"I cannot."

"You must try."

Serbaak paused. How could he explain that the bond he had believed severed had returned stronger than before? How could he make Teesha understand that he had felt Sera's frustration, expecting it; that he had suffered her discomfort, expecting that as well; but that her pain, experienced so sharply, was magnified a thousand times within him until it almost overwhelmed him? How could he make Teesha see that while Sera's future remained uncertain and her torment soared, he could not be free? And how could he make her comprehend that while inner peace remained beyond Sera's grasp, it remained beyond his as well?

"She is beyond your reach, Serbaak." Teesha's dark eyes softened in her attempt at consolation. "All knew of Sera's affection for you. All knew that if it had been physically possible, if we of this clime were able to survive outside this hard land, Sera would have chosen *you* to return her home instead of the warrior Tolin. But Sera would not have you serve her only to see your strength consumed with every breath you breathed in Orem Proper until there was naught left of the man you had been—indeed, until you ceased to exist!"

Serbaak's fixed gaze grew piercing. "I am aware of the physical limitations of our race."

"Oh, Serbaak." Teesha's dark eyes filled as she moved warmly against him. He felt the brush of her rounded breasts against his chest, the warmth of her tears as she rasped, "Can you not forget . . . even as your flesh touches mine?"

Remorse surging strongly within him, Serbaak wrapped his arms around Teesha and drew her close. His lips against her hair, he whispered, "Specters of the past haunt me this night, Teesha, making consolation beyond me. Forgive me, for I must leave."

"Nay, nay . . ."

A few words more of comfort . . . a kiss, a promise . . .

* * *

Teesha's clinging embrace behind him, Serbaak walked the dark, winding corridors back to his chambers with a purposeful step. He dismissed the strained moments recently past from his mind; only one thought remained.

Sera needed him.

The cavernous walls of Zor's cave, slick with perpetual moisture, glistened with the reflected glow of the amber crystal under his hand. His concentration was intense; he felt neither the dampness of his abode nor the increasing heat of the mystical stone. Instead, he experienced the gradual surge of a power that had long evaded him.

With a wild pounding of his heart, Zor watched as the shadows within the crystal stirred. He called out, coaxing the elusive power in a voice grown hoarse with repeated incantations. His anticipation soared as the shadows became clearer.

Two figures drew steadily nearer. Their faces were unclear, their identities uncertain. He studied their forms, seeking, hoping, waiting.

Gone! Again they were gone!

Zor struck the stone with a shout of fury. Incensed, he pounded it again and again, catching his breath with pain when a sharp edge pierced his skin, causing his blood to flow. His attention momentarily diverted, he did not see the figures that flashed briefly clear—a woman with hair of a fiery hue and eyes of glowing gold and a man who was tall and broad, with hair so fair and eyes so cold as to be unmistakable.

Chapter Eight

The cobbled streets of the primary village of Orem Proper rang with the clatter of hoofed feet, the rattle of wagons, and the echoes of shouted greetings returned in kind as the caravan moved steadily forward. Riding in the back of the wagon she had inhabited during the extended journey, Sera peeked out through the drawn flaps, her heart pounding at the sights and sounds introduced to her view.

Home.

How many times had she reflected on this moment during her lifetime of exile? How many times had she dreamed of traveling these same streets and hearing these same sounds?

Sera reviewed in her mind the first signs of civilized habitation to which she had been introduced the previous day. Somehow, she had been unprepared for the simple dwellings of her people: the rough, thatched huts of the farmers living on the outskirts of the villages; the dirt floors visible through the open doorways; the mud and mire that seemed so much a part of their daily lives. She had viewed with concern small children working in the fields alongside their parents, their young backs bent in labor. Her concern had deepened when some had turned curiously toward the passing caravan, their faces drawn and their limbs appearing too frail for the heavy work to which they were set.

Orem Minor, for all the deprivations suffered and prejudices imposed, allowed no such treatment of its youth. A simple word to that effect had turned Tolin toward her with an expression that approached scorn. "You would have me believe that she who enters Orem Proper with thoughts of ascending to the throne concerns herself with the inconsequential affairs of peasant children, when she should instead concern herself with the threat that grows greater against her with each passing mile? If so, you would have me believe that woman a fool!"

Tolin's response had infuriated her, but she had known it would be futile to explain to one who could not see that in the welfare of the children of Orem lay the welfare of Orem itself, as well as its future.

Yet she had sought denial, telling herself that

the daily life of farmers beyond the villages did not truly reflect the lives of the majority of her people. It had become increasingly clear to her, however, that she had been wrong.

Consigned to the wagon with flaps drawn so she might not be easily seen, Sera continued to observe the half-bricked, half-timbered houses that lined the narrow thoroughfares they traveled, the congested streets, the throngs of people streaming through the crowded marketplace. All was familiar, as described in minute detail by Millith and in the written pages she had studied over the years. Yet all appeared somehow strange, as if she were viewing an aged painting in which faded hues, shadowed corners, and proud outlines were all that remained of a work that had once been a masterpiece.

For severe deterioration was the rule rather than the exception on the streets through which they passed. Houses lacked attention to the point of disrepair. Streets were deep in litter. The dress of most people appeared either worn or just beyond former glory. Upon closer view, the marketplace stalls held more empty shelves than filled, and those who lingered appeared reluctant to part with the contents of their purses, no matter how dire their need. She had heard running footsteps and angry shouts of, "Stop! Thief!" on several occasions since her arrival.

She had been taken aback, since crime was all but unknown in Orem Minor's frozen clime.

Her curiosity increased as the caravan turned down another street. Ignoring Tolin's stringent warning, Sera separated the flaps a little further. Tolin's intense scrutiny of her had deepened since their conversation in the wooded glade. He had grown more tense with each mile traveled, going so far as to refuse to allow her out of the wagon. She sensed disapproval or an emotion closely related to it, for a frown now seldom left his brow. She knew the drivers had mocked his apparent possessiveness. She had even heard one driver remark to another that he next expected the stone-faced Tolin to produce a veil to shield his wife's countenance from view.

Considering the remark to be of concern, she had repeated it to Tolin, only to receive a particularly cutting stare before he icily responded that the fools were free to think anything they wanted as long as they did not guess his true motives.

Sera purposely parted the wagon flaps wider. Tolin was overly cautious. Dressed so commonly as she was, her hair confined under a drab cloth as Tolin had instructed, she was almost indistinguishable from the women presently walking the streets around them. Danger was all but nil, she was certain.

Appearing abruptly beside the wagon, mounted upon his great warhorse, Tolin met Sera's gaze with a frigid stare. She sensed the anger behind his frozen facade as he snapped, "Unless you wish to cast your mission to the winds, you will keep those flaps closed!"

Sera's jaw locked. She who was born to rule, she who now knew the full scope of the sacrifice that had brought her there, would not be spoken to like an errant child!

Sera's response was delivered with a significant rise of her brow. "And if I choose *not* to close the flaps?"

Tolin urged his destrier so close to the wagon that the animal's breath was hot upon her as Tolin leaned forward, his low tone ominously clear. "You *will* close them."

Sera jerked the flaps closed with an angry snap. She stared at the rough curtain barring her view, her chest heaving as she struggled to control her ire.

Tolin was a tyrant as she would never be! A few more hours and she would be free of him!

Sera subdued a moment of disquiet at that thought. Her time of uncertainty would soon be over. She was *home*, where she was destined to be. She would seek out the Royal Advisors of Neer. They were still alive, of that she was innately certain. Millith had designated the exact street, the exact house, which had been the advisors' meeting place in the primary village, a location known only to an exclusive trusted few. The advisors would easily recognize her. She would obtain the vessel—the sheath Versa had left as her legacy—wherein all would be explained, and her quest would soon be fulfilled.

Sera's gaze took on a golden glow as the cadence of ancient words scrolled long before her time hummed softly through her mind:

Spirit of Neer confined in flame,
Crescent reborn to come again,
Vessel to seek, wherein the key
To bring the House of Rall to knee.

So much that had once been shrouded in uncertainty was now clear. Destiny was her ally. It had brought her to this point in time. She knew with unfaltering confidence that she carried within her all she would ever need to bring the prophecy to complete fulfillment.

That thought sustaining her, Sera sat back, silent and waiting, as the wagon rattled on.

Damned little fool!

Tolin scanned the surrounding street, silently cursing the remembered sight of Sera's beautiful face clearly displayed as she looked out the back of the wagon. It amazed him that for all the instinct and obvious intelligence Sera so often demonstrated, she could at times be so blind!

The busy marketplace past, their caravan had turned into an area of dilapidated inns, storage houses, and dwellings of ill-repute where women were kept for the enjoyment of men. The services offered in some of the houses of pleasure were varied, with no aberration denied if the proper coin was paid. The women who served there faded fast and were often gone overnight, never to be seen again. The demand for new faces was constant and questions were seldom asked when a new woman was delivered to the door.

The hard set of Tolin's jaw twitched. Those who lingered on these merciless streets did so with no honorable purpose in mind. He had been called upon to settle differences there many times while in the service of Rall. His sword had wielded justice without remorse. He knew instinctively that were he called upon to do the same in defense of Sera of Neer, he would not hesitate. He also knew, however, that to do so would to be to bring her to the attention of those he sought to avoid.

Tolin recalled the concern Sera had voiced for the children she had seen in the outlying villages. He knew only too well the plight of the child in Fador's Orem. Under Fador's callous disregard, too many children did not survive birth, and of those who did, an equal number did not live past the age of ten. The sight of small graves had become common, and the cries of innocent babes sacrificed to Fador's greed had tormented him endlessly. Helpless to effect change, he had had no recourse but to force the sound from his mind. In Sera's concern he saw no more than a repetition of his own former anguish and another in a long line of disillusionments to come for the heiress who sought to depose the House of Rall.

Tolin's strong frame tensed as he reminded himself that Sera's physical safety was his only concern. Intensely aware that the threat against her increased with each step they took deeper into Orem Proper, he had considered taking Sera from the wagon the moment the primary village had been reached. He longed to whisk her off to a place of safety. He had been tempted, but he knew that to abandon a wagon of considerable value and everything within it would have caused talk. Fador's spies ranged from the highest of the high to the lowest of the low. Nothing escaped his ears. Sera needed time and temporary anonymity if she were to effect her plan to reach the surviving Royal Advisors of Neer. When the time was right, he would then—

Suddenly conscious of the path his thoughts were taking, Tolin cursed once more. His days of dedication to causes had ceased! The terms of his pledge to Sera of Neer would soon be fulfilled and he would be free to go his own way.

Yea, free of his lust and free of growing concern for the safety of a woman who had not the sense to be afraid!

The caravan drew to a halt, bringing Tolin back to the present. He needed to find Rockwald and settle affairs with him. It could not be soon enough.

But in the meantime . . .

Tolin signaled to the wolfhound standing at his mount's heels. Leaping in quick response, the animal bounded through the flaps of Sera's wagon and disappeared from sight. The faint, feminine grunt of protest that immediately followed was unmistakable as Gar assumed his role of guard.

Determined to put a quick end to his liaison with the self-proclaimed heiress, Tolin turned his mount toward the head of the caravan where Rockwald waited.

"Again you fail me!"

Fador's shouted accusation struck Filnor like a whip. Summoned again to the tower room where Fador had begun spending longer stretches of time each day, Filnor had entered to find his father enraged.

Filnor's temper flared as well. He had bargained with the most vile of Orem Proper's inhabitants in accord with Fador's orders. An unsatisfactory exchange with Kiray had followed, one which had forced him to chastise her physically. He had not visited her in the time since and had been prowling well known dens of iniquity when Fador's summons had reached him. Now another shouted accusation!

Noting a wildness to Fador's gaze that he had not seen before and a flush to his cheek that approached apoplexy, Filnor felt his rage drain to caution. He had accepted the harsh reality that there was no room for forgiveness in his father's heart. In the hours following their previous interview, he had hardened himself and cast aside all thought that he might ever earn Fador's favor. Instead, he now knew that he would do well to gauge his father's lucidity of thought, for surely Fador was testing the bounds of reason.

Rumors of heightening bouts of cruelty within Fador's household were rife. Seeing a reflection of his own tendencies in his father's intimate eccentricities, Filnor had formerly dismissed them, but the gap between irrationality and reason was rapidly widening. As heir to his father's rule, he was vitally interested in the matter.

"I have never failed you, Father," Filnor said, disguising his own anger.

Fador's reply was a snarl. "I have charged you with a task to which you have yet to respond!"

"A task?"

"Do not play the fool, Filnor! The white raptor of my dreams! Have you found it?"

Filnor's eyes narrowed. "Surely you jest! I have barely had time to make the necessary inquiries."

"Inquiries! When it is action I seek!"

"You are being irrational, Father."

"And you are being *obvious*, Filnor!" Fador laughed wildly. "Do you think I cannot read your thoughts now, just as I have since you were a child? Do you think I do not realize that you see in my agitation a way to claim the throne before your time? Nay, I am not insane, my son, nor do I intend to surrender my power to you one moment before it is due. Instead, I will warn you once more. You threaten Rall with your ambivalence toward the threat that descends upon us."

Filnor's jaw twitched. "You dreamed the dream again."

"Do not patronize me, Filnor! Yea, I dreamed the dream again, but this time it went a step farther. I saw the raptor circling. Great and white it was, with eyes as cold as death. It stared at me, keeping me mesmerized with its gaze as it circled closer and closer. Still impervious to threat, it carried the fragile vessel containing the flame directly over my head, then released it to burst into fire at my feet. The flames . . .

the flames . . ." Fador closed his eyes in remembered agony. "I can still feel them consuming me!"

"You are hallucinating, Father!"

Fador's eyes slowly opened. As black and fathomless as death they were as he rasped, "Would that I could let you see how clear my thoughts are at this moment. Would that you could feel how strong is my contempt for your overwhelming arrogance. Ambition blinds your instinct! Were it not so, you would feel what I feel. You would see what I see. You would know what I know, and you would not doubt me!"

Fear without basis. Irrational claims. Filnor felt a slow elation rise. Fador's time was fast fading.

"You are not yet seated on the throne of Rall, Filnor!" Fador's anger broke into Filnor's thoughts as he continued, "And you never will be, unless you heed my words!"

"Is that a threat, Father?"

"A threat? Why would I threaten you, my son? You have shown yourself incapable of recognizing threat, even when it hangs over our heads like a blade ready to fall!"

"The peril is in your mind!"

"My mind? You fool . . ."

The volatile exchange continued.

Furious shouts rang loudly, reverberating against the stone walls of the staircase as Zor continued his steady, winding approach to the tower room.

His wizened face pale, Zor breathed heavily. He knew little jubilation at the words he was to convey.

Arriving at the great oak door at last, Zor thrust it ajar. He stood stiffly, hardly more than a pale shadow in the opening as Fador's heated gaze turned toward him.

Fador glared, his fury at Filnor extending to Zor as well, unconcealed as he demanded, "What do you want, old man?"

Zor delivered his pronouncement clearly, succinctly, and without emotion.

"The Heiress of Neer has returned."

Rockwald dismounted with a grunt as the caravan came to a final halt on the darkening street. His bearded face drew into downward lines that betrayed the direction of his thoughts as he shouted to his drivers over the growing din around him.

"Your work is not done, you lazy louts! You will not receive a single castar of the sum due you until the unloading has been completed!"

Rockwald turned a deaf ear to the grumbling that ensued as he surveyed the filthy streets around him with a low snort. It was difficult to believe that this sector of the village could have deteriorated so markedly in the short time he had been gone. The doorways were filled with ragged heaps of humanity, and outstretched hands reached out from all quarters.

As for the shadows . . . Rockwald gave a harsh laugh. He had no doubt that the shadows were filled with watchful eyes awaiting a single, careless moment before the contents of the wagons were turned over to the protection of Fador's guard. The quick and deadly swords of Rall had all but eliminated the courts in their land, and he knew only that reality kept the occupants of those shadows at bay.

Rockwald caught sight of a great, pale-haired figure striding toward him, and he stiffened. His hatred for the leather-clad warrior was intense. His stomach twisted as he recalled the scenes he had observed over and again between the man and the tempestuous beauty he called his wife.

Wife? Rockwald gave a scoffing laugh. No husband he had ever known suffered the depth of lust for his woman that he had read in Tolin's gaze. And no wife he had ever observed was as responsive to her man as that hot-blooded witch. The wench's squirming, sensual reaction to Tolin's touch had often stirred his blood to boiling, tempting him to risk Tolin's sword for a chance to show her what he could offer in Tolin's stead.

But Tolin—bastard that he was—had been

unrelenting. His scrutiny of the woman had been so consistent and the threat in his gaze so deadly that neither Rockwald nor the boldest of his men had dared offend him.

Unable to resist as Tolin halted a few feet away, Rockwald taunted, "So you have abandoned your bride's side in this unsafe quarter of the village. I would have thought you valued your woman too dearly to risk the dangers threatening her from every shadow."

The gray eyes looking down into his became daggers of ice as Tolin responded in a tone that was soft for all its undisguised menace, "What is mine, I keep. My sword speaks those words as clearly as I, and like me, it knows no fear."

Rockwald pressed his offense. "Your woman is alone. How can you be sure someone is not stealing up to your wagon right now?"

"Alone? Nay, never. A faithful friend stands at her side, one known to tear human flesh to ribbons."

Rockwald sneered. "I have heard of your beast's prowess. Vicious as he is, I am surprised that you trust him with your woman."

Tolin's smile was cold. "With her he is as gentle as a lamb."

"Of that I have my doubts."

The ice in Tolin's gaze became razor sharp. "To doubt my word in any way is to err dangerously."

Sensing a turn in the conversation that he had not anticipated, Rockwald drew himself up stiffly. "Enough of inconsequentials. Why do you approach me now?"

"A settlement of accounts."

Rockwald raised his hairy brow. "Meaning?"

"A fair price for my wagon and its contents."

"Which includes?"

Tolin's hard smile flickered. "The horses and all within—with the exclusion of my wife, personal articles, and my two animals."

Rockwald's gaze narrowed as he recalled the comforts of Tolin's wagon, which put his own traveling accommodations to shame. Voicing for the first time a suspicion long held silent, he pressed, "Does that include the store of zircum you have secretly transported?"

Tolin's hand moved slowly to his sword. "Fador has outlawed personal transportation of zircum. Do you accuse me of illegal dealings?"

Rockwald's expression hardened. "You would have me believe that you and your bride undertook a journey to Orem Minor and back—without profit of some kind?" Rockwald laughed harshly. "I am not a fool! I ask only a fair portion of the proceeds."

"All profit I had hoped to make was lost with the caravan on which I arrived. My wife and I count ourselves fortunate to have returned with our lives." Tolin paused for effect. "But tell me, is the zircum you have personally secreted in your wagon not enough for you?"

Tolin's reply caught Rockwald by surprise. Rockwald shook his head in vigorous denial. "Nay, nay, I carry no zircum for personal profit! Fador's punishment is heavy in that regard! All casks are weighed and the numbers carefully noted before being loaded on my wagons."

"And you think me less cautious of the law than you—I, whose blade has run red in the execution of Fador's harsh penalties?"

Stonewalled, Rockwald silently cursed. "How much do you want for the wagon?"

"One hundred castars."

"Fifty."

"Seventy-five."

"Done."

Withdrawing his money pouch, Rockwald counted out the required coin. Determined not to allow the great brute total complacence at having bested him, he smiled snidely. "When you tire of your *wife*, I bid you remember that I will offer this amount and more to have her delivered to me."

Blood rage suffused Tolin's countenance. "I issue you final warning. Another word so spoken will be your last."

Tolin then turned and walked away. Trembling in the big man's wake, conscious of the stain that darkened his leggings to end in a puddle around his feet, Rockwald watched Tolin's retreat.

The snickering of his men flushed Rockwald's face hot with humiliation. Turning his back on them, he sneered. Let them laugh! In that last fleeting instant, he had read his mortality in Tolin's eyes. Were they he, they would have been just as ineffective against that savage's fury! And no woman—*no woman*—was worth his life, not even the red-haired witch who had so tormented him.

Rockwald raised his head higher. They would get what they deserved, the two of them! As for himself, he was glad to be rid of them!

The wolfhound lay quietly beside the mattress where Sera sat; he had not moved since his ungainly leap through the wagon flaps a short time earlier. His huge head resting on his paws, he maintained his unwavering stare as Sera noted once more that unlike the smaller household pets she had known, this great beast had never shown even a hint of undisciplined emotion. Sera considered the thought. He was so like his master. She wondered exactly how the service of Rall had drained the two so completely of feeling.

Saddened, Sera stretched out a hand to touch Gar's wiry head with her fingertips. She then stroked him gently. She sensed that Gar was a stranger to a gentle touch, that his brave heart had known little satisfaction but that of service to his master. She wondered if the absence of human consideration and gentleness in Tolin's life had made him the man he was.

Or had it been the slaughter?

"Death's Shadow . . ." The name had not been easily earned, she was sure, but somehow, for all Tolin's severity of manner, for all his coldness, she could not envision him shedding innocent blood. Nay, that implied a lack of nobility, a blackness of the soul that she did not sense in Tolin, despite his harshness, just as she sensed no true viciousness in this beast which lay at her side.

A rustle of movement at the rear of the wagon raised Gar growling to his feet. The beast's lunge was unexpected, freezing Sera motionless as he leaped through the wagon flaps, briefly exposing a man crouched there before he disappeared from sight.

Quaking at the shrieking cries and sounds of violent struggle that ensued, Sera moved cautiously toward the rear of the wagon. She parted the flaps to see one of the drivers pinned to the ground with Gar's slavering jaws at his throat.

Retreating as a deep voice cracked in command, Gar maintained growling vigilance from a distance as Tolin stepped into view.

"Get up!" When the fellow remained on the

ground attempting to stem the flow of blood from a ragged gash on his cheek, Tolin repeated, "Get up, or Gar will finish the work he started!"

The driver scrambled unsteadily to his feet. His eyes were wide with fear. "I—I meant no harm! The woman—I but meant to speak to her!"

"You were warned."

"I meant no harm!"

His rage apparent, Tolin rasped, "This time you escape with your life. Next time, you will not! Leave now, before I give my beast full rein!"

"No, wait!" Sera's interjection turned Tolin sharply toward her. His gaze darted to her hand as it moved toward the pouch she wore fastened at her waist. "This man is bleeding. I can help him."

"He does not need your help!"

Swinging Sera out of the wagon and onto the saddle of the great destrier nearby, Tolin was mounted behind her before she had time to catch her breath. He was turning his mount out of the line of wagons when she questioned haltingly, "Wh—where are we going?"

"Our association with this caravan is done."

"But the wounded man—my personal belongings!"

Reaching through the wagon flaps, Tolin grasped the bundle Sera had wrapped hours earlier and hooked it onto the saddle behind him. Without another word, he spurred his powerful mount into a sudden leap forward that would have thrown her from the saddle had not the strong wall of his body supported her.

Stunned at the rapid progress of events as they galloped through the darkening streets, Sera felt a wild desire to laugh. Just minutes earlier she had reflected on the heart of the wolfhound now following at the horse's hooves, contemplating a gentleness that had not truly existed.

Like beast . . . like master.

Tolin's arm tightened around Sera almost to the point of pain as he spurred his mount to a faster pace. She knew the reason for his sudden impatience. He was anxious to settle her into a place of safety so he might be free of her at last. A tremor moved down Sera's spine, and a strange sadness ensued as the thought lingered.

Cold rage filled Tolin as Sera and he climbed the stairs of the Wayside Inn, one in a line of common inns in a sector of the village where the comings and goings of travelers were met with little scrutiny and less conversation. He had paid his coin for a room moments earlier and now turned back toward Sera where she stood concealed in the shadows nearby, so deeply wrapped in her mantle that nothing more than a gleam of golden eyes peered back at him. He had then grasped her arm and jerked her toward the staircase with a force that had almost raised her from her feet.

Entering the room and slamming the door closed behind them, Tolin turned toward Sera. His face frozen with fury, he stripped her mantle from her and demanded, "What do you carry in that pouch at your waist?"

Sera's hand sprang protectively to the soft leather pouch she had attached to her belt shortly before their arrival in the village, responding flatly. "That is none of your affair."

"Is it not?" Tolin took an intimidating step toward her. He could not truly explain the feelings that had exploded within him when he returned from his conversation with Rockwald in time to see Gar's attack. A fear unlike any he had ever known had leaped through his veins. In the few moments it had taken him to reach the wagon, he had suffered myriad fragmented pictures of Sera in distress—Sera in pain—Sera helpless in the hands of the vermin of the streets—Sera calling out for him!

Then he had seen Sera standing in the back of the wagon with a look of horror on her beautiful, faultless countenance. He had been hard put not to snatch her up into his arms then and there, so he might hold her close and assure himself that she was well and whole and had not been abused. He had wanted to tell her that he would protect her from any and all who sought to do her ill—only to be stunned into incredulity when Sera had stepped forward to voice concern for the same man who had sought to do her harm!

Then he had seen her reach for the pouch at her waist.

Tolin rasped, "Tell me you do not have zircum secreted in that pouch, heiress! Tell me you did not intend to openly reveal yourself on the street back there by offering to treat the wound of that brigand with zircum!"

"That *brigand* is one of my people, and he was bleeding!"

"That brigand believed you temporarily unprotected and was attempting to kidnap you so he might deliver you to one of the houses nearby where you would bring him a tidy sum!"

Sera went momentarily still, then responded, "Whatever his intent, he was bleeding."

Tolin was incredulous. His gaze flicked to Sera's waist once more. "Do you not realize that the personal transportation of zircum from Orem Minor, no matter how small the amount, is a crime? Do you not know that no common woman could use zircum as you intended using it, that for all its utilizations in Orem Proper, zircum holds no healing properties in any hands save yours? Can you not comprehend that your open use of it in that manner is tan-

251

tamount to an open declaration of the identity you seek to conceal?"

Sera shook her head, obviously surprised by his words. "Surely no one would report actions proffered in so humane a service!"

"You are not in Orem Minor any longer, heiress!"

The gold eyes that had so bewitched him scorched Tolin as Sera hissed, "Nay, it appears I am not! In Orem Minor my desire to cure would be respected, not held in contempt!"

"That brigand was not worthy of your concern!"

"All who suffer, whatever their illness or injury, are worthy of concern!"

"Nobly spoken!" Tolin felt an urge to shake the beautiful woman standing before him to within an inch of her life. He continued harshly, "But spoken with a disregard for reality that is astounding in view of the trials you are soon to face. Tell me, heiress, what is your *true* purpose in coming to Orem Proper?"

"You know my purpose!"

"I am not certain I do!" Tolin took another step toward Sera, directing the intensity of his gaze into hers as he strained for control. "I know only what you have told me, that you aspire to the throne of Orem, to depose Rall's cruel rule so you may install the House of Neer in its stead. I know only that you lay claim to a prophecy that many consider nothing more than a child's amusing song or the pathetic battle hymn of a small, fading core of Neer supporters."

"How dare you despise that for which so many have given their lives!"

"I dare, heiress, so I might discover the truth!"

"The truth is exactly as I have related it to you!"

"Then let me pose another question to you." Tolin's next step brought him intimately close to the beauteous pretender, so close that the familiar scent of her filled his nostrils, intoxicating him in a way he fought to ignore as he continued, "If your quest is as noble as you would have me believe ... if the future of Orem depends upon it as you would have me believe ... if your heart is filled with that purpose and that purpose alone, as you would have me believe ... why do you endanger it at this crucial moment?"

Sera did not respond.

"Well?"

"I did not consider the danger."

Tolin's incredulity soared. This could not be happening! This self-proclaimed Sera of Neer could not truly be so naive as to attempt to gain the throne of Orem simply to fulfill a prophecy that would ensure the future of her people! Nor could she truly believe that since she was finally "home," the hardest part of her journey was over and virtue would thwart the evil of Rall simply because it *should* be so!

"Sera . . ." Unconscious of his use of her given name, Tolin pressed, "Do you not realize that your peril was never greater than now, since you have arrived in Orem Proper? Are you not aware that the path you pursue could easily lead to your death?"

Sera's gaze did not waver. "My path is true. I will survive."

Clamping his hands onto her shoulders, Tolin shook Sera hard. He saw the flush that suffused her cheek as he rasped, "You are flesh and blood, heiress. You are not immortal!"

"Unhand me!" At Sera's tone, Tolin's hands fell to his sides as if they had been scorched. Enraged, she continued, "Leave me be! I will listen to you no longer! Your pledge has been fulfilled and you are free to go your way! I have been delivered to this place of relative safety, and I will make my way from here alone! I do not need you anymore!"

Sera's words cut deep. The first drops of blood drained from the wound as Tolin replied, "Do you not, heiress?"

"Nay, I do not!"

Tolin squared his shoulders against the strange trembling that began inside him. "Then it is done. My hands are washed of you."

The echo of his voice still ringing behind him, Tolin wrenched open the door and then slammed it closed behind him. He had reached the first floor of the inn when the full impact of his words struck him for the first time, along with a truth he could no longer deny. The flame of Neer had struck a blaze within him.

Emerging onto the street, Tolin breathed deeply in an attempt to clear his mind. He needed not that tempting flame! His wants were simply defined: food to assuage his hunger, drink to quench his thirst, sleep to temper his fatigue, and the warm press of female flesh to sate his lust.

Turning sharply, Tolin strode toward the stable where his destrier was confined. He mounted minutes later, knowing just the place where all his needs could and would be filled.

The silent tower room echoed with the sound of Fador's pacing step. He was uncertain how much time had elapsed since Zor's startling declaration and swift departure earlier. Filnor had left shortly afterwards, following another violent clash between them, and he had since wreaked a devastation on the tower room that was matched only by the devastation that had been wreaked within him that fateful night so long ago.

Dragging his hand roughly down his face, Fador felt bitter fury flare once more. He was afflicted with a son whose royal blood had been so diluted that only ambition survived! He was plagued with a royal guard so lacking in strength and direction after Tolin's desertion that he could no longer depend upon its worth. He was cursed with the continued deterioration of his life which had begun that night so long ago when he had lost the flame that was his only true love.

Striding to the window, Fador paused, grasping the stone sill as he looked out over the darkened village beneath him. The flicker of lamplight twinkled in glittering display, much like jewels on a velvet cloth, bright, glowing, breathtaking to behold. Yea, Orem was his, but there was no longer any joy in his possession!

The ecstasy of total rule had faded through the years. He had sought to recapture it in the accumulation of wealth wrung from the sweat of Orem—but it eluded him. He had attempted to restore it through an ever-tightening grip of power that was now so strong and absolute that his people had all but lost the will to oppose him—but the pleasure slipped from his grasp. He had fought his growing depression with a wash of blood, with a feast of debauchery, with the satisfaction of every physical desire—all the while knowing that it was not a physical need that taunted him.

The Heiress of Neer has returned.

Even now Zor's words filled him with a perverse joy mixed with pain. The spirit of Versa reborn? Versa's beauty, her courage, the unmatched glow that had radiated from within, the spark so strong that it would not die—could it ever be equaled?

Nay, never!

And yet he hoped . . .

Again the pain and the despair!

Versa, his lovely Versa, whom he must again seek, whom he must again find . . . whom he must again destroy.

Fador closed his eyes, his mind appealing to the fiery-haired image so clear in his mind.

Versa, will you not spare me this final torment?

Versa, must I shed your blood once more?

Versa, please . . .

Fador opened his eyes to the silent response flickering in the lights of Orem's lamps below him.

A flame that flickered still. A flame that would not die. A flame he must extinguish once more.

She was beautiful. Her skin was smooth and sweet. Her hair was dark and gleaming. Her body was naked and yielding.

Tolin's gaze raked Silva's flushed face, then followed the graceful movement of her voluptuous form as she approached. Full, darkly crested breasts swayed gently as she neared. Curved hips moved in a sinuous dance. Her arms slipped around his neck. They were warm against his skin as she drew him close, as her husky whisper sounded in his ear.

"I have missed you greatly, Tolin. No other arms have held me as tightly since we were last together. No other lips have thrilled me so. No other body has sated mine as completely as yours. I have yearned for you. I have dreamed of your return, and now you are here."

Silva's mouth touched his, coaxing his response, and Tolin's arms closed around her. Yea, he remembered Silva's comforts well—the relentless heat of her, her endless indulgence of his desires, the satisfaction that sparked in her eyes at his gasps of culmination. She was a master of her trade who sought to make each man believe he was her favored one.

Neither believing nor caring to believe the fantasy Silva aspired to create, Tolin drew her closer. He joined the intimate play of her kiss. He felt the taunting thrust of her full breasts against his chest, and he pressed her closer still, cupping her buttocks to hold her intimately confined against his bare flesh. He felt her momentary jolt of surprise, then the caressing hand that slipped down between them to tease his flagging member. Her experienced touch stiffened his reticent manhood slowly. But his mind wandered again from Silva's deepening kiss until he realized with dismay that his member was becoming reluctant once more.

Drawing back, Silva slanted her gaze up to meet his. Her full lips pouting, she whispered, "Do I not please you tonight, my sober warrior? As always, you must know your wish is my command."

His response an almost feral growl, Tolin swept Silva from her feet and carried her to the draped bed nearby that awaited them. Laying her upon it, he followed her down to lie beside her, fiercely pressing the pursuit of his passion.

Smooth skin . . . moist heat . . . a hot, familiar female delta awaiting him . . .

Jerking back from Silva, Tolin cursed aloud. His powerful shoulders were broad and stiff, unlike the part of his anatomy essential to his intimate quest. He glanced down at it with disgust, then drew himself abruptly to his feet. He glanced back at Silva's staying hand. Her gaze was a plea that matched her words as she sat up and whispered, "Do not be upset. You have traveled long and you are tired. Come, rest beside me until your passion freely soars. I will wait." Silva stroked him gently. "And I will pleasure you however you wish to be pleasured."

Somehow touched by the patient whore's words, Tolin paused, then responded, "It is useless to pursue that which so determinedly evades me. I waste your time this night."

"Nay . . . nay." Silva drew herself to her feet beside him, her arms clinging. "I would rather lie with you than any other. I would not have you seek someone else to sate you."

Stroking Silva's cheek briefly, Tolin withheld comment. He disengaged himself from her embrace and turned to his leathers. Facing her fully dressed minutes later, he slipped a gold coin into her hand, frowning as she pressed, "Will you return to me?"

Tolin strode from the room without reply. The front door snapped tightly closed behind him as the answer Silva had sought sounded in his mind.

He would be back. He would be back again and again until fiery strands no longer replaced Silva's dark hair in his mind . . . until he again saw Silva's brown eyes instead of eyes of glowing gold . . . until the press of Silva's sweet flesh again offered consolation instead of an aching yearning for another.

Damn her! Damn the witch of Neer!

He was done with her!

The night had been long and dark. Sera was grateful as it neared its end. She glanced toward the door to her room, a shudder running down her spine, and anger surged. Tolin had done this to her! He had sowed the seed of fear within her, a seed that had gradually taken root as the shadows of night deepened.

The constant traffic down the hallway of the inn, the boisterous male voices and shouts of laughter as staggering men filed past her room—or worse, as they had hesitated briefly there—had gradually coaxed that seed of fear into bloom. She had awakened countless times from a light doze to feel fear flourishing within her.

More daunting, however, were the memories that had followed; Tolin's cheek pressed against her hair as he curled himself around her in sleep; the familiar, male scent of him that had so warmed and consoled her; the unexpected comfort of his callused palm resting against her breast; and the instinctive knowledge that despite the often harsh words between them, she had never been more secure than when she had lain in his arms.

But it was not a need for security that had dug deep into the pit of her stomach through the night, causing the heated discomfort there. Rather, it had been the recollection of the way Tolin's lips had trailed her neck, her cheek, had captured her mouth—of the way his long fingers had slipped into her hair, splaying out at her temples as he held her motionless under his kiss—of the whisper of a sigh when their lips had separated at last and the reality that she was still uncertain whether that sigh had been her own.

She recalled the way Tolin's gaze had lingered, snapping away when caught unawares, only to return to warm her again with an emotion she could not quite define.

She had ached with that undefinable emotion and wished with all her heart that she—

Angered by her straying thoughts, Sera had reminded herself that Tolin's caressing touch, his kiss, his possessive posture, had all been affectation. She had told herself that she could not afford the weakness of indulging memories that meant so little as to be dismissed with a flash of cold gray eyes and his harsh, final words.

My hands are washed of you, then.

Through the remainder of her wakeful hours, she had attempted to focus on the moment for which she had planned and waited all her life.

That thought lifted her gaze toward the window once more, and Sera was relieved to see the first streaks of light creasing the night sky. Her heart leaping, she arose, walked to the washstand, and poured water into the bowl. Her simple toilette was complete by the time morning fully dawned. Her tightly wrapped mantle allowed little of herself to be clearly viewed and her shoulders were stooped in the posture of one far older than her years as Sera walked down the staircase to the first floor.

With her heart pounding so loudly that she was certain it could be heard on the deserted streets, Sera wound her way slowly toward the location she sought. Badger . . . Whipple . . . Fox . . . all were familiar street names, learned from a map of the primary village that she had committed to memory long ago. Yet she was astounded by unexpected sights and sounds. The moans coming from ragged heaps in dark doorways . . . the stench accompanying their presence . . . the canines that roamed the streets, so skeletal in appearance as to seem but a step from death . . . and the harsh shouts from windows above that preceded the emptying of buckets of waste, fouling the streets through which she walked.

Glancing from side to side, uncertain in an atmosphere that was both stirringly familiar and disturbingly foreign, Sera recalled the re-assurance of Tolin's stalwart presence at her side. She longed for the possessive strength of his arm around her and the respect it com-manded from all. But most of all, she missed the feeling, which she now knew had no basis in truth, that he had really cared.

Turning the corner, Sera emerged onto a broad, cobbled lane. She glanced up at a street sign to see the sign of a faded crescent. Unconsciously slipping her hand down to the mark on her thigh, Sera held it briefly there before continuing on.

Sera's breathing grew more rapid. She would recognize the house when she saw it. It was the fifth house on the street. It was large, with two floors and a sloped tile roof, and it stood behind a stone wall that was a head shorter than she.

Her pace increasing as she moved along the lane, her confidence growing, Sera counted. She walked past the first house, the second, the third, the fourth. She halted abruptly.

Unwilling to believe her eyes, Sera stared at the charred remains of the fifth house. Crumbled stone, blackened timbers, weeds of considerable height, and the refuse of years signified that the fire had not been recent. Sera glanced helplessly around her.

A flutter of movement in a doorway nearby caught Sera's eye, and she started toward it. At her knock, the door cracked open. A hoarse female voice inquired suspiciously, "What do you want?"

Sera attempted a smile. "Can you tell me where I may find the people who lived in the house next door?"

The suspicious gaze turned cold. "Nay."

The sharp crack of the door slamming closed was a sound that was repeated at each remaining house on the street.

Finally turning back in the direction from which she had come, Sera raised her chin against her disillusionment. Her people were a downtrodden lot who had become so concerned with survival in Fador's Orem that they no longer dared to offer simple human courtesy or good will. She could expect no help there.

Sera raised her chin higher. She had suffered a setback, but she had not been beaten. What had she learned? The house on Crescent had obviously been destroyed years earlier. The fact that the house had not been rebuilt indicated that whatever had happened there was meant as a lesson to be engraved into the memories of all.

Yet she knew that not all her people would submit to Fador's intimidation. She would search out one brave enough to share that memory with her, and she would proceed from there. It was but a matter of time.

Sera's determination briefly faltered. Time, when she had already waited so long; time that would hang heavily on her heart and mind without someone with whom to share it; time, all that was presently left to her as she turned the corner of the street and the Wayside Inn came again into view.

She was hungry. She was tired. She was lonely.

Ignoring the lump that rose in her throat, Sera breathed deeply. Just a little longer.

Chapter Nine

The baying of the hounds stirred Fador's blood as he rode through the dense green of Orem's forest, his private guard behind him. A brilliant morning sun filtered through the trees, touching shrubbery that was colorful and dense and sparkling on dew-drenched wildflowers scattered along the trail. But Fador saw none of it. Intent on the hounds' call as they fanned out in search of prey, he clutched the reins of his snorting stallion cruelly tight.

Fador's frustration knew no bounds. Zor's sober announcement in the tower room three weeks earlier still echoed in his mind. He had reacted instinctively, turning a furious wrath on Filnor. His words had been a vicious denunciation and a stinging ultimatum as he had

267

charged his son anew with the responsibility of finding the "flame reborn."

Yet three weeks had passed, and Filnor had uncovered nothing at all.

Suspicious of the effort Filnor expended in his behalf, Fador had contacted a personal spy. With a demand for secrecy and a promise of grandiose rewards, he had sent the man out into the villages on the same quest, only to have him prove as unsuccessful as Filnor.

Fador had then reviewed in his mind the decision he had made shortly after the fall of Neer so many years ago, when his search for the Royal Advisors of Neer had ended at the house on Crescent Square. In the time since, the charred remains of that once great house had served as a constant reminder of the danger inherent in even speaking the name of Neer.

He had pondered long over the fate of the Royal Advisors themselves. In the end, he had decided it would be unwise to establish them as martyrs to Neer's name. Instead, they would prove valuable hostages against any insurrection by Neer loyalists in the future. His sadistic bent had known great fulfillment when he had reduced them to humble conditions and total humiliation, forcing them to live in squalor, and his enjoyment had known no bounds when he had made it his personal cause to see that they suffered Neer's defeat every remaining day of their lives.

Confined to a narrow part of the primary village worse than any prison, where they lived as did the idiots and swine who shared their circumstances, the advisors had been kept under close surveillance since that time. No covert activity had been uncovered over the years. That fact had at first pleased Fador, then angered him, as he had finally come to comprehend that their lack of subversive activity resulted not from an absence of hope, but from a deep belief that the prophecy would prevail.

The Heiress of Neer has returned.

That simple sentence had effected the dispatch of the aging advisors to the deepest dungeon of the village prison, where the "heiress," despite the reputed powers of Neer, would be unable to reach them.

Unless Fador allowed it.

His distraction had still remained so intense, however, that he had been scarcely able to choke down a bite of food or a sip of drink during the days since. Awakening that morn with an agitation so acute as to be almost staggering, he had known there was only one way to assuage his distress.

Fador's lips tightened. There had been a time when filling his bed with female flesh—first one, then two, and then three who might simultaneously pleasure him—had given him relief from such fits of frustrated fury, but those days were long past. He still used women well and was not averse to the employment of boys for diversity at times, but he had discovered that the thrill of the chase and the shedding of blood was the only true release left to him.

For that reason, his hounds were extraordinarily well maintained. The kennels were swept clean each day and sprinkled with fresh straw. An ample supply of food was delivered for the animals' consumption each morn, and keepers charged with the dogs' well-being were required to sleep with the animals to ensure their comfort. He had heard it reported that the populace objected to the accommodations and care afforded his special canines, saying their care far exceeded that accorded the children of Orem Proper.

The tight lines of Fador's bearded face moved into a hard smile. Perhaps that was so, but it bothered him little. His canines served him well in the excitement of the hunt, that pleasure far exceeding any enjoyment he had ever received from the filthy waifs of Orem's streets.

Glancing behind him, Fador saw Filnor riding just ahead of his guard, and his smile became a grimace. He had sensed his son's gaze hot on his back, and he had reveled in his son's fury. He had commanded Filnor to accompany him on the hunt, seeing not an opportunity for companionship, but a chance to prove to his son anew, in the heat of the chase, that Fador of Rall's physical prowess had not waned, that his mental competence was still superior to all, and that he would *not* be vanquished!

A subtle change in the tenor of the baying alerted him, and Fador tensed. Muscles poised, he was ready to charge when the sharp, excited barking and the frenzied dash of his hounds announced the sighting of quarry.

Fador spurred his mount forward. Hot on the heels of his canines, he leaned low over his stallion's neck as the animal's legs stretched out into a full gallop. Neither knowing nor caring if Filnor and his guard followed as he dodged leafy branches and avoided strangling vines, he covered the uneven terrain at a breakneck pace that put the surefootedness of his frothing mount to the ultimate test.

Fador glimpsed it briefly then, a great stag larger than any he had ever seen before! His mouth growing dry with zest for the kill, he plunged on, gradually becoming conscious of a rider at his shoulder. Turning to see that Filnor was gaining upon him, that his son was pushing his mount to a life-threatening pace in an effort to take the lead, Fador laughed aloud.

Never, Filnor! Never!

Fador whipped his stallion harder, laughing louder as the animal's eyes bulged with strain.

Fador heard it then, another change in the

baying that he had been awaiting: the sound of the pack had become snarling growls and yelping barks as it trapped its prey.

In a moment he saw the great stag pinned against a stone wall, fighting for its life!

Fador reined his mount to a sliding halt, his rush of exhilaration unequaled as the valiant stag lowered his antlers to lunge again and again at the ferocious jaws attacking from all sides.

The blood . . . the breathlessness . . . the heat!

The moment of truth had come!

Snatching up his crossbow, aware that Filnor was close behind, Fador knew he had but one chance to send his arrow true—one opportunity before Filnor would attempt to purloin his triumph just as he sought to purloin the throne of Rall.

Never, Filnor. Never!

His crossbow raised, Fador sent the arrow winging, shouting out as the great animal leaped with the force of the missile that struck its breast.

The blast of the horn from behind drew the hounds back from their quarry as the stag twitched in the throes of death—not a moment too soon as Fador raised his bow against the slavering canines, determined not to be cheated of his final glory. Clutching his knife, Fador then leaped from the saddle, kicking the last, straggling hounds out of his way in his excitement to reach the mortally wounded animal's side.

Standing over the stag in brief, silent triumph, Fador then kneeled and slashed the animal's throat. Blood gushed from the wound. Hot and warm, it splashed his face and clothing, raising Fador's excitement to near delirium. Without a pause, Fador slashed once more, opening the underside of the noble animal, reaching within to rip free the heart that was still beating.

He consumed the heart greedily, blood dripping from the corners of his mouth as he turned victoriously toward Filnor, who had dismounted behind him. Wiping his arm across his lips, Fador then shouted at his son so all might hear.

"So, Filnor, once again you fail to best me! Once again I consume the trophy of the hunt, taking within my body the courage of this brave lord of the forest. And so I charge you while the blood of victory is still hot on my hands and lips: *Remember and beware!*"

Standing, his shoulders boldly squared, his expression triumphant, Fador signaled two of his men toward the downed stag. He returned to his panting steed and remounted, the open rancor in Filnor's gaze further excitation as he turned his mount back onto the trail.

Elation sang through Fador's veins as his guard fell in behind him.

Still in control! Still unbested!

His elation abruptly fading, Fador grew grim with resolution. He had sacrificed the woman he loved for the mantle of rule. Rather than surrender it a moment before his time, he would sacrifice his son as well.

And if ghosts haunted him, so be it.

If his suffering was without end, so it would be.

He had killed, and he would kill again to reign supreme.

Three long weeks.

Sera walked slowly, feigning the stoop of the aged as she clutched her mantle over her head and shoulders. She looked up as the Boar's Head Inn again came into view. The need for her disguise had grown more dire after each successive outing in the village. Suspicion, distrust, and fear were rampant on the streets, and as uncomfortable as her disguise had proved, she had quickly learned that an old woman was easily dismissed from the memory of most.

But the day had been long and her inquiries fruitless, as had been the many days and inquiries preceding it. Sera's spirits lagged.

Somehow, in coming "home," she had not believed she would find herself so alone.

Going over the day's futile search in her mind, she recalled the blank looks which had met her questions, the fear which had flashed at the mention of Neer, the haste with which most departed.

Somehow, in coming "home," she had not believed she would be so lonely.

Through the long days and nights past, Sera had thought of all those she had left behind—Millith, Impora, Alpor, and dear Serbaak. Strangely, almost painfully, she had finally admitted to herself that it was not those who had raised her, or those who had stood by her and advised her until she came of age, whom she longed most to have beside her.

Tall, unsmiling, pale hair bright, light eyes intent, Tolin had been the specter who had endlessly haunted her dreams. Uncertain of the moment when she had become so dependent on his silent strength, she only knew that apart from him, she felt somehow lost and incomplete.

She had quizzed herself relentlessly during the long nights past: Was it fear that had kept Tolin's image ever present before her mind? Mayhap. Was it hunger for the prophecy's fulfillment which drove her to long for his return? She was uncertain. Or was Tolin's image conjured up by another, more driving need?

I do not need you. She had spoken those words harshly, learning too late of a nameless need, formerly a stranger to her experience, which she would suffer because of them. She had grown more familiar with that need each day, a need which caused an inner voice to cry out with no thought of Neer, even as the future of her world crumbled around her.

Adjusting her mantle more tightly around her head, Sera entered the inn and climbed the staircase toward her room. At first, her silent comings and goings at the Wayside Inn, where Tolin had delivered her upon reaching the primary village, had raised little curiosity, so long as she paid her coin. Then had come a subtle change, a turning of heads and quizzical glances whenever she passed. She feared that whether she was believed aged or young, she had become an oddity that would not go unreported much longer. And so she had left the Wayside and moved to another inn a short distance away. She had followed that same procedure every few days, arriving at the Boar's Head that morn.

Yet, no matter how determined her efforts, her quest remained fruitless. At an impasse, she had also arrived at a point she had never reached before—where the path to her destiny eluded her.

Sera entered her room. Closing the door behind her, she straightened up and discarded her mantle without bothering to reach for the lamp nearby, choosing instead to lean back against the door and submit to the shadows surrounding her. It was nearing time for the delivery of her evening meal as she had arranged that morning, but she felt little hunger. There was comfort in the semidarkness, a gentleness that held at bay the hard press of the present, allowing her a momentary limbo.

"Sera . . ."

Sera started as a shadow in the corner stirred to life and moved slowly toward her. The shadow was massive in size, broad and towering against the setting sun shining through the window. A glowing shaft glinted on fair hair as the room vibrated again with the deep tone she recalled so vividly.

"Sera . . ."

Sera swallowed, and then managed to ask with difficulty, "What are you doing here?"

The sober gray of Tolin's eyes was suddenly clear. "You called me."

"I called you?" Sera shook her head, her heart pounding. "I did not."

"You did." His hand on her shoulder, his callused palm cupping her cheek, Tolin whispered, "When we parted in anger three long weeks past, I was determined never to look upon your face again. I despised you for the words you

277

spoke, and I despised myself for having allowed the emotions you raised within me. Determined to purge you from my mind, I sought refuge in the devices I had effectively used before to set me free of torment, but my efforts were to no avail. Failing, I struck out for the provinces, certain that in the wild lands there, where the challenge would often be simply to survive, I would lose the image of you which would give me no respite. But it was not to be. For it was then, in the silence of the night, when there was naught around me but the raw night shadows and naught above me but the endless darkness of the night sky, that I heard you call my name."

"I did not call you."

"Yea, you did." Tolin paused, his voice dropping a husky note lower. "I sought not to answer your summons, but your voice tore at my heart and deluged my mind with its sweet sound until the truth from which I fled could no longer be denied. I returned to the primary village then, only to find you gone from the Wayside Inn and to pass a day of frenzied searching that delivered me here to you this night."

Tolin paused again, continuing, "That truth which could no longer be denied, that truth which will allow me no respite save one, is this, heiress. You have worked your way deep inside me. You have left me helpless against your need, just as you have left me needing you."

"Needing *me*?"

The incredulity of Tolin's words became a slowly dawning joy as he drew Sera closer. A heat in the deep, inner core of her, and a trembling unlike any she had ever known, beset her as he whispered, "You have bewitched me."

Uncertain of the moment when her arms slid up to return his embrace, Sera pressed herself against Tolin's familiar warmth. A remembered beauty soared even as she protested, "I cast no spell over you."

"Yea, you did. Your eyes invade my dreams. Your lips speak silent words of love. You awakened a part of me I had thought long dead and wished never to revive. There is a price to pay for that possession, heiress."

Sera shuddered as Tolin swept her up into his arms. His power closed around her as he covered the distance to the nearby bed in a few swift strides.

Tolin leaned over her as he laid her down. Features once so cold and hard were soft with emotion. Eyes once brittle shards of ice were soft velvet as he whispered, "Look at me, heiress. Read in my eyes what you have awakened in me. The life, the yearning you see there, can be sated only by you. You have come to rescue your people, but in your coming, there is one whom you must first save."

Tolin's words were balm to the ache which

resided within Sera. She saw a flicker of pleasure that was almost pain move across Tolin's features as she touched his cheek, then followed the fine white scar down to his lips—the lips that had warmed her, taunted her, raising emotions that she had fought to ignore. She whispered, "Tell me who that person is, Tolin."

Tolin's cheek twitched. His gaze remained intent. "Heiress . . . surely you know. That person is I."

The song soared again within Sera. Its brilliant melody grew sweeter, louder. It rose to a brilliant crescendo that joined the pounding of her heart and the dulcet strains of overwhelming yearning as she reached up to draw Tolin gently down against her.

Tolin's muscled weight enclosed her with joy as Sera spoke words emanating from a point of light within that grew stronger with each syllable she uttered.

"Show me how I must save you, Tolin. Teach me the way, for at this moment I have no greater desire than to give to you as you would have me give, to make you feel as you would choose to feel, to bring to you in the deepest measure all you hope to discover once more."

Tolin's heart pounded against hers. Sera felt the quivering of his frame and the longing he restrained as he cupped her face with his hands, as he trailed his lips against her cheek, as the pain in his gaze grew.

"Sera . . ."

Perceiving the reason for Tolin's hesitation, Sera whispered, "Nay, do not read nobility into my words. You see, Tolin"—Sera's voice briefly broke—"I wish to give all this to you, because I know you will return the same to me."

Sera paused, eyes of glowing gold growing moist. "You heard a voice calling you while we were apart. I denied that voice was mine, but my denial was false. The cry you heard was that of my loneliness. You suffered the emptiness within me that your parting left behind. You felt my heart call out to yours, a spontaneous call born of a need I dared not define."

Her throat thick, Sera continued, "Tolin, you see before you the Heiress of Neer. The course of her destiny is clear to her, and she is determined to follow it at any price. Although the path temporarily eludes her, *she needs no one*, for the flame within her is self-sustaining, and it will prevail."

When Tolin stiffened at her words, attempting to draw back, Sera stayed him, continuing, "But inside this heiress lies another woman. This other woman is filled with need. During her separation from you, she was tormented by the same malady you suffered, but was ignorant of the cure. She chooses to be ignorant no longer. *Teach me, Tolin.* Teach me so I may know and understand, so the Heiress of Neer, who loves her people, will know the deeper love that will make her whole again."

The moment of silence that followed Sera's fervent plea became long and strained. It worked a change on the harshness that had briefly tensed Tolin's face. The transformation raised a well of jubilation within her as eyes of gray velvet consumed her, as lips so often tight curved gently, as Tolin swallowed, then whispered raggedly, "Yea, heiress. Come to me, for you are the stuff of my dreams, and only with you in my arms will I ever earn peace again."

Tolin's mouth covered hers then, and Sera's lips separated lovingly.

The sweet parting of Sera's lips, her faint sigh of acceptance, her taste, her scent, struck a fire within Tolin. Her simple gown was a hindrance soon overcome as he stripped it away to reveal the glorious silk of Sera's flesh. The heat of his yearning met hers and his heart sang. For too long that song had been dead within him. For too long he had followed the dictates of soulless need, feeling naught but the satisfaction of a bodily function easily sated.

Never again.

Kissing, caressing, leaving no part of her feminine beauty untouched, Tolin followed the passionate route of his loving hunger. Sera's lips were responsively warm . . . her virgin breasts his alone . . . her slender hips sweetly yielding . . . her delicate hands so gently seeking. Yea, the stuff of his dreams, the joy of his life, *the breath of his soul!*

The rose-colored crescent on Sera's thigh was clearly outlined in the meager light, and Tolin traced it with his kiss. The exquisite outline scorched his lips, fanning the fire within him, igniting a compulsion so strong that it could no longer be restrained.

Sera, who filled his mind.

Sera, who filled his heart.

Sera, who had become a part of him.

Sera's female delta was warm and moist against him as Tolin raised himself above her, hearing again the strains of her siren call. Fiery hair sparkled in the limited light, beckoning him. Golden eyes alight with inner heat drew him in. Words of love foreign to his tongue raced across his mind. They registered deeply, yet went unspoken as he eased into the well of joy awaiting him, then plunged fully within.

The widening of Sera's eyes, her sudden gasp . . .

Magnificent Sera.

His own.

Covering Sera's mouth again with his, Tolin breathed her in with a silent whisper, with a voiceless promise. Her lips separated, accepting his unspoken words, freeing him to begin the rhythm of loving that would make them one.

Loving fervor . . .
Rapid crescendo . . .
Bursting pleasure . . .
Matchless ecstasy . . .
Shuddering fulfillment!
Stillness.

With a moist veil of mutual passion still slick between them, Tolin clutched Sera close. He had lived no greater moment than that which had just passed. He had known no sweeter rest than within this woman's silken flesh.

A single regret nagged at Tolin as he looked down into Sera's beautiful face, as her eyes slowly opened and held his.

"Would that I could have gone more slowly, that I could have allowed you more time . . ." He lowered his mouth to hers. He drew deeply from it, savoring its taste before speaking again in a voice touched by both wonder and anxiety. "You have awakened a beast within me, heiress. It would not be denied."

Sera's gaze tenderly searched his. Her mellifluous voice soothed the ragged edges of his concern as she whispered, "But it is a loving beast, a beast that brings comfort and peace. It is a specter that I do not fear, for I recognize it within me as well."

Sera's golden eyes grew bright. "While we are together, until my time comes, we will indulge this beast of which you speak, Tolin." A tear slid down her cheek as Sera whispered, "And when my quest has been answered and I must follow whatever course has been preordained for me, your place will be forever secure in my heart."

Her voice dropping to a slender thread of sound, Sera raised her lips to his. "As for now, my very loving beast, I invite you—I implore you—to love me more."

His throat too tight for reply, Tolin crushed Sera in tender embrace.

His Sera.

Nay . . . Sera of Neer.

Sera who, for a time however short, would be his own.

Sinbald was not happy.

Shielded by the shadows at a corner table of the inn, he adjusted his ragged garments on his shoulders. He remembered a time when his dress had been stylish, carefully sewn to his individual proportions, and meticulously clean. The jingle of coin in his pockets had been constant, and he had looked toward a future bright with promise.

He had lived well as one of Fador's personal spies, and he had served well. Seeking out and reporting each and every infraction of Fador's law, as well as those who paused even briefly in contemplation of such an act, he had earned Fador's appreciation and trust.

Then Filnor had come of age.

Sinbald's yellowed teeth ground together. How he despised the arrogant Heir of Rall! The animosity between them had been deep, for Filnor had been threatened by the strict and unwavering allegiance Sinbald accorded Fador. Filnor had been determined to undermine Fador's confidence in him. Lies and false accusations had followed, and in the end, Sinbald had been dismissed from Fador's private service. His life had deteriorated rapidly afterwards, but he had determined during the years of suffering that he would one day pay Filnor back in kind.

Rubbing his unshaven cheek with a hand that had not seen recent washing, Sinbald then scratched at the oily strands of graying hair that hung on his furrowed brow. He had been settled into his life of misery and want when, a few weeks previously, he had been astounded at a secret summons to attend Fador once more.

Sinbald's frown deepened when he recalled Fador's disgust upon observing the physical change in his person. But his physical deterioration had not affected his wile, and Sinbald had managed to impress that fact deeply enough upon Fador to regain his ruler's confidence, however temporarily.

Grasping his cup of mead, Sinbald drank deeply, then slapped it down in frustration. *The Heiress of Neer reborn* . . . He had been stunned into speechlessness when Fador had stated that belief! He did not believe it for a moment! Yet, the task Fador had set for him had sounded so simple. He had only to report any suspicious personages found abroad in the streets.

Simple, yea . . . but when each report ended in disappointment, his stature in Fador's eyes had deteriorated further. It had finally come to him in the hours most recently past that he had arrived at the position where the misery of his former life was now preferable to the threat of Fador's heightening displeasure.

And the coin in his freshly filled pouch was dwindling.

Cautious not to call any undue attention to himself, Sinbald signaled the barmaid nearby. He sneered at the twitch of her nose as she neared and the obvious distance she kept between them as he ordered his cup refilled. His thoughts did not linger on her unspoken insult, however, as other, more pressing reflections filled his mind.

He had walked the streets of the primary village with dogged intensity. He had canvassed inns and roadways to no avail. He had even approached houses of pleasure with inquiry, only to be turned away with his questions unanswered. He knew Filnor's spies were searching as actively as he for this same wraith whom they did not name—with the same fruitless results.

The situation would be laughable were it not so dire! How did one find a figment of Fador's raging imagination? How did one find an apparition seen only in Zor's aging crystal?

And how did he escape the fate awaiting him if he failed?

Accepting his refilled cup, Sinbald raised it to his lips and again drank deeply. The night grew late, and the comforts of life remaining to him were few. He had all but completed his survey of the inns of the primary village. He would proceed from here when he had taken a few hours' rest, for this inn was as good as the next in which to drown his sorrows. Even its name was somehow prophetic of the pig sty that had become his life.

Yea . . . The Boar's Head . . .

The lamp was lit. Its glow flickered against the stained walls of the room, casting into elongated shadows the bed on which Sera and Tolin lay, but Sera saw naught but the warmth of Tolin's gaze as it held hers.

His long, muscular length was curved intimately against her, but Tolin was silent in his scrutiny as she raised her hand to stroke the silver-gold hair back from his forehead. She slid her fingers through the lustrous weight as she had so often dreamed of doing. There was a beauty in Tolin's gaze that filled her heart to bursting. It reflected the splendor that rose within her as their naked flesh touched more warmly and Tolin pressed his mouth to hers.

His kiss lingered. He trailed his lips against her fluttering lids, then whispered, "Did I hear a contented sigh? Tell me, was it the Heiress of Neer or the woman within who made that sound? You must advise me, for I wish to address my compliments to her."

"Compliments?" Sera grew breathless as the gentle wash of Tolin's kisses continued—the fleeting dusting of her brow, her temple, the bridge of her nose, the teasing circling of her mouth as her lips parted, growing eager for his. She swallowed, questioning again, "Of what compliment do you speak?"

A slow smile grew on Tolin's face. Suddenly realizing that she had never before seen Tolin truly smile, Sera watched as Tolin's countenance softened into a gentility of feature formerly concealed, as his cheeks creased into deep indentations of joy. So, it was true. The bliss within her was reflected within Tolin as well—a happiness and hope they had both lacked while apart.

Tolin's smile faded into thoughtfulness. Lifting a fiery lock from her breast, he wound his hand tightly in the silken strands. He drew her closer, holding her there as he looked directly into the golden citron of her eyes.

"I would compliment the woman I now hold on her loving, but I hesitate. Is it the Heiress of Neer to whom I now speak? My mind tells me it must be so, for no youthful virgin without the powers of bewitchment could have brought so much beauty to the moments between us. No common woman could have touched me so deeply with a word, with a sigh, with a touch. No simple maid could still hold me so firmly within her thrall."

Suddenly as sober as he, Sera queried in return, "If you would have my response, you must first tell me who this man is who now holds me so intimately close? Is he the same Tolin of the frozen eyes and heart—the same Tolin who was called Death's Shadow?"

Not as hesitant as she, Tolin responded swiftly, a hint of harshness returning. "Yea, it is the same man. These eyes that now cannot get their fill of you were once lifeless and cold from the devastation they had viewed and the blood they had seen spilled. This heart that now brims with longing was once hard and callused from wounds too deep to heal. This Tolin you see before you was once called Death's Shadow for the carnage he wreaked."

"Stop!" Tears suddenly brimming, Sera averted her gaze. "I do not believe these terrible things you say of your past! They are not true!"

"Look at me, Sera." Tolin turned Sera back toward him as he went on. "I would have you know the complete man who lies beside you. Ask the questions you wish answered. Ask freely, for this must be cleared between us once and for all."

Sera hesitated, suddenly aware that Tolin had realized before she did herself that the question she was about to voice had never been far from her mind. She whispered the words he awaited.

"Did you shed innocent blood in the name of Rall, Tolin? Did you slay my people needlessly?"

A brief tic of his cheek was Tolin's only betrayal of emotion as he replied, "I served Rall without question. There was no innocence when Fador's rule was threatened."

"You made no distinction between youth and age, the strong and the weak . . ."

"My arm served Fador blindly. My sword slashed at Filnor's side. There was no right or wrong that did not come from Rall."

"Nay, Tolin, nay!" Tears suddenly falling, Sera clutched Tolin close. "This cannot be, for a monster such as you describe could not have captured my heart so truly!"

Tolin separated himself from her. She heard the echo of his distress as he whispered, "I have answered your questions with truth. I ask you now to do the same."

Sera struggled to bring her emotions under

control. When she spoke at last, her words were filled with torment.

"You wish to know if it is the Heiress of Neer you now hold, or the simple maid within. Tolin . . . my very dear . . . you see before you the simple maid who loves you with her whole heart. She wishes never to be without the warmth of your arms around her or the promise of our bodies closely entwined."

Her voice momentarily failed her, but Sera forced herself to continue, "Also before you is the Heiress of Neer. This heiress needs you, too, but . . ." Sera's voice dropped to a tortured whisper. ". . . to her everlasting sorrow and pain, this heiress is uncertain if she can forget that the innocent blood of her people stains your hands. I fear that stain can never be washed away."

His gaze depleted of its former joy, Tolin did not immediately respond. Sera felt the slow shuddering that began within him as he digested her words. She waited with growing anguish until he broke the silence between them with a hoarse whisper.

"Then there is only one recourse for us, Sera, my love." Tolin's throat worked convulsively as he paused, then continued, "The Tolin who now holds you close, the man whose arm protects you and whose body worships yours, will love the simple maid within. He will press from his mind the heiress whose heart is closed to him and who will one day send him away. And he will cherish their time together, however brief, for it is more than he ever dreamed it could be."

"Tolin . . ."

"Nay, say no more."

"I must." Her words rising from an overflowing font of love, Sera drew Tolin's lips down to hers as she whispered in return, "This woman whom you now hold, this woman who must respond to her destiny, will always be yours in her heart, wherever she may be."

"Wherever she may be."

And the loving began anew.

A tense silence hung over Kiray's opulent, scented boudoir as the anxious whore stood before her mirror, shifting impatiently to better view her reflection in the shadowed glass. Turning sharply toward her servant, she ordered, "Bring the lamp closer! I must be certain of what I see!"

Irritation expanding as her servant stumbled, Kiray eyed the old woman harshly. Nay, she would never be like the crawling witch who now scrambled to do her bidding! Were she not certain it was true, she would never, in her wildest imaginings, believe that the shapeless heap of bones and graying hair that served her had once been the favorite of Orem's wealthiest merchants, a woman whose beauty and talents had been legendary in her time, and of whom it was reputed that once a man spent a night in her bed, he would never forget her.

Kiray's smooth face twitched as she recalled the day the woman had come to her, begging her favor. She had taken the hag in with a thought in mind that was far from the compassion with which most credited her. The drooling crone was a lesson to her, nothing more than a daily reminder tht one such as she could not take the present lightly, that she must work diligently toward her future, without relenting.

Filnor's handsome form sprang before Kiray's mind, restoring a smile to the image in the glass. Filnor was her love. Filnor was her future. Filnor was the man who would keep her with him always. To that end she had dedicated herself, allowing her other patrons only a portion of that which she saved for him.

Kiray raised a graceful hand to her cheek. She trembled as she touched the bruise disguised there, concerned that others on her arm and back were not as well concealed. Frowning, she recalled Filnor's obvious agitation when he came to her, hours earlier. She had been upset to see him so incited. In her desire to console him, she had unwisely pressed him for an explanation. Receiving the response that he had spent the morning at the hunt with Fador, and aware of Fador's reputation of cruel encounters with his noble son, she had made the error of voicing her thoughts.

Kiray closed her eyes briefly against the remembered specter of Filnor's rage. His blow had knocked her from her feet, but she did not fault Filnor for his abuse. Her audacity in speaking so plainly to his royal personage, the personal affront of her imprudence, had been a mistake.

Filnor had stormed from her chambers without a word, leaving her with tears and regrets. But she had determined in the hours since that she would erase any anger that still remained in the way she knew best. Filnor could not resist her in that regard. He was intrigued by her endless sexual dexterity.

Kiray's heart began a slow pounding. She had never held Filnor's physical mistreatment of her against him. Nay, the truth was that his innate savagery excited her. It drove her to excesses of her own that evoked the only true ecstasy she had ever known! Ecstasy for ecstasy—that was her bond with Filnor and the base on which she would build her future. As for the brief lapse which had driven Filnor from her earlier that afternoon—she would overcome it tonight.

Kiray scrutinized her reflection more intently. Her body was faultless, her skin without blemish, her diaphanous gown tauntingly revealing. Picking up the small jar of scented salve, Kiray unconsciously stroked the smooth glass. She had had it prepared especially for Filnor. With it she would bring him rapture without end. She would go to his quarters now and surprise him. When she had finished sating his every deviant need, he would forgive her.

Kiray slowly smiled. When the time was right, Filnor would overwhelm the aging Fador and assume the throne. She would be at his side then—or mayhap standing slightly behind him, wherever he chose to place her. For the truth was that Filnor was her love. He was master of her heart and soul. She would do anything he asked her to do.

Except leave him.

That thought lingering, Kiray donned her mantle and started for the door.

Harsh, grunting sounds . . . feminine whimpers . . . low laughter . . . a gasp . . .

His body damp with the exertion of the hour past, Filnor grasped the thick, dark locks of the naked woman who attempted to scramble from his bed. He yanked her backwards, laughing aloud at her screech of pain. Rather than eliciting anger, this experienced whore had raised him to new heights of titillation with her attempts to escape him.

True, he had been in a foul mood when he had sent his servant for a woman. True, the hour past had been spent more in physical torment than in physical pleasure. True, the whore's white skin was marked with bruises.

But it was also true that he was paying well to vent the feelings running rampant within him.

Fador had done this to him!

The humiliation of that morning renewed, Filnor heard again the ring of Fador's words as he harangued him with the blood of the hunt still dripping from his hands. It should have been *he*, Filnor, who had sent the arrow into that stag's heart! It should have been *he* who tasted that noble animal's heart! And it should be *he* who held the throne instead of the madman who was his father.

Obsessed by a woman, Fador had been a fool!

Obsessed by a flame, Fador had been ludicrous!

Obsessed by a flame now supposedly a woman reborn—*Fador was insane!*

But Fador was clever. He knew where his strengths lay. He knew fear was his greatest weapon, and he cultivated it. Dependent upon his guards' loyalty, Fador carefully preserved his facade of invincibility. He was not averse to sacrificing all toward that end, going so far as to demean his own son when he felt it was to his benefit.

But there had been a time when Fador's strength had begun to flag and Filnor's power had begun to bloom. Tolin had been at his side then, as he had been from childhood. They had fought in the same shadows. They had been drenched in the same blood. With Tolin at his shoulder, Filnor had been invincible, and even Fador's personal guard had begun to look toward him for guidance!

Fury flaring anew, Fador whipped the whore flat on her back, his grip on her hair unyielding. But Tolin had deserted him! He had proved himself a coward, turning on him and leaving the service of Rall behind.

Had Filnor had his choice then, he would have pierced Tolin's craven hide with his sword and watched with glee as the last spark of life faded from Tolin's eyes. But he had not had his choice. Fador had chosen to let Tolin live, to let him walk away so he might linger in Orem, and with his presence forever remind his people of the weakling Filnor had once embraced as a friend.

Hatred soaring, Filnor threw himself upon the sobbing whore, enjoying her grunt of pain. He bit her cheek and lip savagely. Unsatisfied until blood was running, he drew back to whisper tauntingly, "You are a whimpering bitch, Parta. I must tell your master how greatly you disappoint me with your pathetic efforts to entertain. Tell me, what will he do to you if you fail to please me?"

The whore's teeth were stained with blood as she spat in return, "My master knows I seek to please his customers!"

"You do not seek to please me."

"You do not wish to be pleased!"

"Oh, yea, I do."

"You wish to inflict pain!"

Filnor laughed again. "*Pain* pleases me."

The whore's trembling increased, and Filnor's excitement heightened at her shaken plea.

"Let me go, Master Filnor. I will return to my master and he will send another in my place—Aretta, who will happily indulge your wildest fantasy in that regard."

"Aretta . . ." Filnor's desire flared. "I will remember that name, but first—"

Raising himself suddenly above her, Filnor jammed his swollen member into the shaken whore. Satisfaction surged as she cried out aloud. He allowed her no respite as he plunged into her again and again, panting, "Let me hear you cry, Parta! Let me hear you beg to be released! Your anguish pleases me, and you want to please me, don't you?"

Fury surged within him when Parta emitted a whimper, and Filnor pinched her full breasts cruelly. She screeched with pain and Filnor's passions soared. Yea, he had needed that sound! He had needed to hear the shriek of one as impotent as he! He had needed to hear a cry of pain that matched his own!

He had needed—

Turning at the sound of his chamber door opening, Filnor went abruptly still.

* * *

Rigid, Kiray stood in the doorway as Filnor turned toward her on the broad bed she remembered so well. She had heard them as she approached. The shouts, the cries, Filnor's laughter—she had known what he was about, and jealousy had turned to white heat inside her.

Kiray perused Filnor's naked form as he remained joined with the blotchy-faced whore beneath him. Choking on her fury, she started toward him as Filnor shouted, "Do not take another step!"

The look in Filnor's dark eyes, the revealing flush of his cheeks—Kiray knew the warning signals. Filnor was at the edge of control. The bitch beneath him had obviously suffered his frustrated wrath and was anxious to escape him. Fool! Did she not realize that her fear stiffened Filnor's rapacious member more surely than any of the ancient tricks her master had taught her?

Determined to dispossess the bitch of her position beneath her raging lover, Kiray took a contrary step forward that elicited Filnor's vicious hiss.

"Leave this room now!"

"Help me, Kiray!"

Filnor's blow halted Parta's pleas. Blood spurted from the whore's nose, staining the bed linens, but Filnor paid it no mind, his gaze intent on Kiray as she remained unmoving.

"Are you so bereft of reason that you cannot understand me when I speak?" Filnor shuddered with fury. "I warn you, should you force me to withdraw myself from the warm rest I have found, you will pay a steep price."

Determined to prevail despite the chills crawling up her spine, Kiray responded, "You do not need that soiled piece lying beneath you, my magnificent Filnor! Look here!" Kiray stripped off her mantle, revealing her lush form. "See how that woman pales in comparison to the many delights I offer."

"Delights! You flatter yourself! I have lost my taste for the banquet you would set! I seek new, exciting fare that will stimulate my appetite out of the doldrums you create!"

Kiray's face flamed as she persisted, "You have but tasted the first of the many courses yet awaiting you at my hands. Think. Remember. Recall how I indulged you, how I brought you to culmination over and again, how truly you—"

"Out! I command you!"

"Nay, I will not go!"

On his feet and beside Kiray in a blur of movement, Filnor struck her a sudden blow that sent her staggering backwards. Kiray remained upright only to feel Filnor's fists pound

301

again and again until she could no longer stay on her feet.

Darkness loomed as the blows continued, leaving only a small tunnel of light as Kiray felt herself raised from the floor, then thrown through the air to strike the floor once more. She heard the slam of a door, the resumption of Parta's pleading cries, and Filnor's laughter.

Time passed. Uncertain of its duration as she clung to the spot of light remaining, Kiray listened. She heard it then, the door opening, a heavy thud nearby. The darkness enclosing her became her shield against the painful realization that Parta lay beside her in the hallway, discarded as was she—two whom Filnor had tossed aside never to use again.

The shadows shifted. The night deepened. Beyond the window of the Boar's Head Inn, the sky was a swirling ocean of somber tones lit by a brilliant crescent moon. The silver shafts of light flickered and blinked, streaming down to penetrate the darkness of the room, where, flesh against flesh, heart against heart, Sera and Tolin lay tightly entwined.

Their breaths mingled in sleep.

Two who had been bereft had found joy.

Two who had found joy had found peace—however temporary—as the night lingered.

Chapter Ten

Sera awakened to the light of morn with a brush of warm lips, with a stroking touch, with eyes of silver grey searching hers for a sign of regret. But she felt no regret. Instead, she indulged those lips, that touch, the searching gaze, and her heart soared.

The joy of Tolin lingered as Sera dressed in her drab shift and heavy shoes, then turned to see his broad shoulders again sheathed in leather, his long, strong legs similarly clothed. He had scraped the night's growth of beard from his face, his hair had seen cursory grooming, and he smelled of the scented soap she had purchased in her travels through the village as her one concession to all she had temporarily cast aside in coming "home."

Tolin reached for his sword and Sera frowned. Somehow it was not the sword at his side or the knife at his waist that gave Tolin the appearance of an impregnable force and turned heads automatically toward him. Nor was it solely his powerful size and the contrast of hair as pale as moonlight against skin colored by the sun to a golden hue, or even the strong, regular features composed in an expression that revealed a strength within. Rather, it was the manner in which he moved, with an inherent might and confidence that all immediately recognized . . . and some feared.

But the threat in that silvered gaze, the ice that had encased it, was gone. Their glances mingled, and Sera felt again the sweep of an almost debilitating emotion.

Taking a stabilizing breath, Sera forced emotion at a distance. With morning had come the return of responsibility. Sera faced it with mixed feelings as Tolin cupped her chin and drew her face up to his.

"It is a new day, heiress. Our quest continues."

"*Our* quest, Tolin?"

Tolin drew her closer. His strength encompassed her as he responded, "I turned my back on you and tried to tell myself I had fulfilled the bargain we struck, but I could not cast you out of my mind or heart, no matter how I strived."

Tolin's expression grew pained. "I knew you sought to find the Royal Advisors of Neer. I also knew that alone, you would not find them."

"You knew?"

"I knew they were discovered in the house where you thought to find them shortly after Rall assumed rule, and that Fador had ordered the ground charred black where that house had stood as a reminder to all of the supremacy of Rall's rule and the danger of even speaking the name of Neer. I knew the advisors have been held prisoner these many years by Fador, but as one of Fador's royal guard, I was sworn to secrecy. An oath such as that is not easily forsaken, heiress."

Stunned that Tolin had kept a matter of such crucial importance from her until that moment, numbed at the thought of the time unnecessarily lost, the effort uselessly expended, and the hours of despair that could have been avoided, Sera responded, "But you knew the import of my mission!"

"I knew only the mission and the nobility to which you laid claim. Years of training under Rall were no more easily discarded than my oath."

"And now?"

"And now, heiress?" Tolin's voice became a husky rasp. "I realize that there is no loyalty, no vow, no force in Orem that is stronger than my love for you."

The magnitude of Tolin's soft declaration momentarily stole Sera's breath, precluding the words that rose to her lips as she was inundated with bittersweet joy. Were this another time, another place . . . Were she another woman and Tolin another man . . .

But they were not.

Sera drew slowly back from Tolin's embrace. The heiress within her spoke.

"Then you can take me directly to the advisors?"

Surprising her, Tolin shook his head. "Nay, I cannot. It is too late."

Sera's heart went still. "Too late?"

"They have been moved."

"Why? Where?"

"I do not know. Those who know will no longer share that information with me." Tolin paused. Strangely, Sera thought she saw a flush of color briefly rise to his cheek as he continued, "But there is one who might. I will inquire."

"I will go with you."

Tolin paused again, then nodded. "If you wish."

Tolin reached for Sera's mantle. He adjusted it over her head and shoulders with obvious regret.

"Hair of fiery red and eyes of glowing gold are too easily recognizable in Orem." Tolin's gaze softened. "But I will mourn the loss of those flaming locks from my sight, however briefly."

Brushing her lips lightly once more, Tolin opened the door of the room. Sera heard the thread of amusement in his voice when she stooped to resume her disguised posture and he said, "Come, old one. I will take you to the street and guide your way."

Tolin's hand brushed her hip with a caressing touch. As Sera glanced back at him, he responded, "I beg your indulgence. It is difficult to resist you."

Yea, resisting was difficult, indeed, Sera thought as she started for the stairs. She was halfway down, the public room within view, when she sensed Tolin stiffening and turned to follow his gaze. She saw him watching the lad who walked toward the fireplace, struggling under the weight of a large, steaming pot.

Sinbald started, coming suddenly awake. Lifting his head up from the table, he groaned softly at the pain that ensued, struggling to clear his blurred vision. The public room of the inn was just stirring to life. He shook his head, cursing as the throbbing intensified. Where was he? Oh, he remembered. What he did not remember was how many glasses of mead he had consumed before consciousness had slipped away.

Sinbald drew back farther into the corner. He had been wise to sit at a table where he was all but invisible in the shadows. He supposed he had to thank the swarthy, overweight merchant who had caught the eye of the barmaid for not being tossed out onto the street at the end of the evening, as was his common fate. The wench had become so enamored of the merchant's fat purse that she had left her less savory customer behind in the corner, totally forgotten, when departing with the fellow. The shadows had done the rest, allowing Sinbald shelter when he might have had none, and an opportunity to gather his thoughts before the day began once more.

His thoughts . . . Fador . . . Sinbald groaned. What he had viewed as a possibility at redemption a few weeks earlier now hung over his head like a waiting blade.

Sinbald smelled the gruel before he saw it. The aroma caused a spastic jerking in his stomach that he struggled to control as he looked up to see a lad carrying a great, steaming pot toward the public room fireplace. The thought occurred to him that the innkeepers were fools to trust a child of that size with such a task. If the boy were to spill the contents, the work of hours would be lost and the income of the day greatly reduced.

As if in confirmation of his thoughts, the youth stumbled momentarily on a raised floorboard. Sinbald could not help but snicker as the boy regained his footing with a frightened expression, then continued toward the fireplace.

Sinbald snickered again. The lad was not only young, he was also clumsy, a dangerous combination in a place where profits were measured in small coin. He had half a mind to tell—

A slick spot on the public room floor—the lad saw it a moment too late! Before Sinbald could utter a shout, the boy's feet went out from under him, the steaming contents of the cauldron splashed across his legs, and he fell to the floor.

Oh, the screaming and the howling! Brought abruptly to his feet, Sinbald swayed unsteadily, his stomach churning. Unable to move lest the churning erupt, Sinbald watched the sudden burst of activity that ensued—the innkeeper's rush from the kitchen, his wife's frightened gasp, the arrival of the barmaid—as all the while the lad kept screaming.

Sinbald took another step forward, and then he saw them. The two stood on the staircase arguing. The man—he could be no other!—was Tolin, formerly of Fador's guard, the deserter who had brought such shame upon Filnor because of their former close association. No one could miss that great, hulking size and pale hair! The last he had heard, the fellow had left on a caravan to Orem Minor. Word had it that he was not expected to return.

Yet, there he was, struggling on the stairs with a hag bent in half with age!

Were the din not so great and his stomach so

poorly set, Sinbald would have been tempted to laugh at the fight the woman was putting up as Tolin sought to subdue her. Surely the great Tolin was not—

Gasping, Sinbald stepped back into the shadows.

"Don't be a fool, Sera!" Tolin's grip tightened as Sera struggled to escape his hold. "We must leave this place before attention is drawn to us! The boy will be all right! You can do nothing to help him."

"I can! I can treat him and reduce the pain of his burn." Sera's eyes turned up to Tolin's. "Look at him! He suffers, and he is but a child!"

Tolin retained his grip, his expression hardening. "We must go."

Sera's gold eyes took on a fierce intensity as she turned fully to face him. Her beauty abruptly halted his protest, thrusting aside concern for the boy still crying with pain, the frantic activity of the innkeeper at the child's side, and the screeching of the barmaid as they stripped away the young fellow's leggings, peeling away his flesh as well.

"Unhand me, Tolin. I will go to the boy!"

Yea, she was the Flame of Neer reborn. Tolin had never been more sure. He read it in the set lines of her flawless countenance as she opposed him, in the incredible glow of her eyes that reflected an innate love for her people—even for a suffering boy she did not know—and in the strength of will that demanded she risk all to help him.

Releasing her, Tolin felt a rush of love, pride, joy, fear—unfamiliar emotions all—as Sera forsook her disguise, allowing her mantle to slip as she dashed down the staircase to the screaming boy's side.

Following close behind, Tolin scrutinized the immediate area. He saw the surprised innkeeper look up. He saw the innkeeper's wife refusing to yield her place at the boy's side. He saw the barmaid whose hysterical howling had not yet ceased.

His order was concise. His tone brooked no argument.

"Let her through."

The lad was no more than eight or nine years old. Shrieking with pain, he looked up at Sera as she crouched beside him. He shrank back as she reached toward his legs, where raw flesh oozed from knee to ankle.

Sera took the trembling hand the boy stretched out to ward her off. She gripped it tightly as she spoke.

"Nay, do not be afraid. I have come to help you."

The boy's dark eyes bulged. Sera felt his

panic, knowing he was fast losing control. A familiar voice from within prompted her words as she continued in a soothing whisper, "You are Martek, son of Abrila and Caven, are you not?" She smiled. "I will ease your pain and start you on the road to healing. It is my gift, and I will share it with you. Take courage. You will not suffer much longer."

The boy grew silent, and Sera turned toward the women behind her. "Quickly, a bowl of water, and cloths—*clean* cloths."

The barmaid and the older woman rushed to do her bidding and Sera turned to address Tolin. "The boy must be lifted to the table where I may treat him."

The innkeeper shook his head, speaking for the first time. "Nay, nay. We must take the boy home! His mother will tend to him."

Sera turned sharply toward him. "*I* will tend his injury! You will take him home to his mother when I am done. But I warn you, if you ever again press this child beyond his strength, you will suffer my wrath!"

Dismissing the innkeeper from her mind, Sera stepped back to allow Tolin to lift the lad to a table nearby. Her heart filled with the boy's pain, Sera glanced toward the kitchen, toward the two women returning with the items she had ordered. She stroked back the boy's fair hair, noting his pallor and the trembling of his lips as he bravely sought to restrain tears.

"You have great courage, Martek. One day you will serve me, and serve me well. But on this day, I serve you."

Sweeping up a cloak lying nearby, Sera folded it under the boy's head as the trembling barmaid put the bowl on the table and piled the cloths beside it.

A silence fell over the small group as Sera withdrew the pouch from her waist and poured the glittering zircum dust into her palm, as she sprinkled it on the water in the bowl and stirred it lightly with her hand.

Zircum, the substance which served the Heiress of Neer as she served it.

Sera dipped the first cloth into the bowl, then lifted it out to cover the raw flesh of the boy's burns. She heard him catch his breath, but she did not hesitate, repeating the process until his legs were completely wrapped.

In the silence that followed, Sera looked up at Martek, noting that he was calm, but her task was not finished. Her face whitening, her heavy lids closing, Sera grasped the boy's wrapped legs tightly. Ignoring his whimper and the protests of those around her, she spoke silently to the power of the flame.

Heal, as you would be healed.
Save, as you would be saved.
Serve as you would be served . . . evermore.

313

Opening her eyes, Sera heard gasps around her as the wrappings on the boy's legs glowed with a brief green incandescence, as the cloth under her hand heated to scorching, then grew cool once more.

Removing her hands, Sera whispered to the sober child.

"Your pain is gone."

The boy nodded.

"Your wounds will be healed by week's end."

Sera turned to the innkeeper. "Take the boy home to his mother now. Tell her to leave the wrappings on for the allotted days. Tell her to treat her son well, and to cherish him, for he is marked by fate to leave an imprint in time."

Sera paused, then added solemnly, "I caution you not to speak of what has happened here this morn to anyone, for the future of Orem lies in the balance."

Tolin observed all in stoic silence as Sera took up her mantle and wrapped herself once more, then turned to him.

"It is time to go."

Sera saw the almost indiscernible flicker in the steel gray of Tolin's gaze the moment before he slid his arm around her and they turned toward the door.

In the shadowed corner of the public room, Sinbald stood trembling as the sober crew lifted the boy gently and carried him toward the rear of the inn. Forgotten was his pounding head, his queasy stomach, his discontent. Instead, excitement soared within him.

There was no mistaking her! It was the Heiress of Neer reborn! He had seen her! He had watched her perform her magic! He recalled Versa well, remembering that as a young man he had thought never to see a woman to match her in beauty. But this one—what had Tolin called her? Sera? She was Versa's match, and more!

Sinbald fought to control the wild laughter rising within him. While hours earlier he had thought his death was sealed by Fador's insane obsession, he now knew he had been redeemed!

His euphoria gradually subsiding, Sinbald drew back and glanced around him. He was fortunate that the hour was early and the public room was empty, but he knew the event he had just witnessed would not remain secret for long, despite the heiress's admonitions. Filnor's spies were as busily at work as he. He needed to reach Fador before word spread or there would be little celebration for him.

Slipping out of the corner, Sinbald moved quickly toward the door. Mayhap his reward would be twofold when he delivered not only the heiress Fador was seeking, but the traitor to Rall who was aiding her cause.

Good fortune was smiling on him! By this time tomorrow his future would be assured!

Contemplating the many joys that would follow, Sinbald stepped anxiously out onto the street.

She knew what kind of place this was.

Still clutching the mantle over her head and shoulders, Sera straightened up slowly. Tolin and she had entered the house through great double oak doors a short time earlier. They stood silently in the spacious marble foyer amongst milling groups of men who were drinking and laughing loudly. The men were dressed casually, to the point of abandon, with bare chests abounding and a lack of weaponry that suggested a place of total relaxation.

A great stone staircase wound down from a balconied second floor where she had observed women appearing individually, at scattered intervals, at which time one of the men below would break away to start up the staircase toward her. No one had to tell her where they went or what they did after meeting at the top of the stairs and disappearing from sight.

Sera stiffened, avoiding Tolin's gaze. She had heard that the bordellos of Orem Proper were often luxurious places where men went to be indulged in their fantasies as well as their perversities. She glanced covertly at Tolin. He seemed so comfortable here. She wondered—

The thought was forced from her mind by the appearance of a tall, exotically beautiful woman at the top of the staircase. Sera had never seen anyone quite like her. She realized belatedly that the woman was probably one of the race of people who wandered at the edges of the villages, nomads from the beginning of time, keeping to themselves, marrying within their bands and thereby perpetuating their distinctive appearance.

Sera stared. The woman was so tall that she was probably only a few marks below Tolin's height. Her hair was black, her eyes provocatively slanted and heavily lashed, and her features small. In womanly attributes she was more than adequately endowed, a fact made obvious by a sheer garment that left little to the imagination.

All eyes turned toward the woman as she paused at the head of the staircase. Startled when Tolin grasped her arm and urged her with him up the stairs, Sera felt a slow, pained tightening within, unlike any she had ever known. This woman and Tolin were not strangers.

Sera felt herself stiffen as they climbed, as she realized that the woman was even more beautiful upon closer scrutiny. The woman stepped forward when they reached the top, her pleasure obviously sincere as she touched Tolin's arm lightly.

Sera fought her surging emotions. This woman was one of her people. She could not submit to the suffocating anger that rose in her as the woman caressed Tolin's arm with her well-tended hand and addressed him in a husky feminine whisper.

"I am pleased you have returned." The woman glanced at Sera, her expression growing strained. "Why did you bring this woman with you?" Her dark eyes searched Tolin's face. "You have never been one of those who sought to—"

Tolin halted her mid-sentence. "It would be best if we speak in private."

The woman's gaze flew back to Sera before she turned and walked toward a nearby doorway. When inside the lavishly draped bedroom with the door closed behind them, the woman turned to Tolin again. Sera saw mirrored in the woman's eyes the same feelings now raging inside her, and her heart dropped to her toes. She needed no further confirmation of her suspicions as the woman spoke.

"Tolin, I did not expect you to return with a woman. I thought that we—"

Turning abruptly toward Sera, Tolin threw back her mantle, unveiling her to the woman's view. She heard the woman's sudden intake of breath as she stepped backwards with a spontaneous hiss.

"So, it is *she*!"

* * *

Silva's reaction was exactly the one Tolin had been awaiting. His heart began racing.

Sera . . . his magnificent Sera. He had dared not tell her how deep was her danger, that for the sake of a child on whom Fador would not have wasted a moment's thought, she was perilously close to losing the dream toward which she had worked all her life.

The mixture of pride and despair he had experienced at the wonder of Sera's healing hands, as well as the worshipful awe with which the boy had viewed her after her ministrations to him, were with Tolin still. There was no doubt that the lad was now Sera's willing slave forever—however short Sera's forever might now be.

When the healing was through, Tolin had longed to take Sera into the protective circle of his arms and spirit her away where no one might find them, but he had known that could never be. Sera, born to her destiny, could know true fulfillment in only one way.

Time was short and growing shorter by the moment. The innkeeper, his wife, the barmaid—he had no doubt one of them would pass along word of Sera's astonishing gifts. He had known he must find the Advisors of Neer quickly, before Sera's time was gone.

Tolin searched Silva's pale face. "You recognize her?"

"I do!" Silva's tone turned accusing. "It is true, then, what was said of you—that you carried with you a wish for death after resigning from Fador's service! Why, Tolin? Did you not believe that someone could make your life worthwhile? Did you not know that with a word *I* would have—"

Frowning, Tolin interrupted Silva. "You say you recognize this woman. Tell me who you think she is!"

"She is the woman for whom Fador has set his spies to searching, the woman of the coloring he so prefers who is rumored to have been fool enough to steal from Fador after their business was done and Fador was peacefully sleeping! That spy was here recently, hoping to uncover word of her. I can only hope no one saw her with you, or you will doubtless not live past the morrow!"

Tolin gave a disgusted snort. "Look at her more closely, Silva. Tell me what you see."

Silva's small features twitched with annoyance. "I see a woman—a young woman who is beautiful and whom you hover over protectively as if she were a precious jewel!"

"Look more closely!"

Silva frowned at Tolin's agitation. She scrutinized Sera more closely under Tolin's intense regard. He saw true recognition dawn as Silva's eyes opened suddenly wide and her face drained of color.

Tolin pressed again. "Tell me what you see."

"I see . . ." Silva faltered. "I see hair of fiery red and eyes of glowing gold." Silva swallowed. "Surely it cannot be *she!*"

"It is."

Silva raised a delicate hand to her temple. She took another step in retreat. "Fador will kill her."

"Nay." Tolin's words took on the solemnity of a vow. "Not on my life."

Silva's eyes grew moist. He saw her swallow and heard the pain in her voice as she asked, "What do you want of me?"

"Word that only you can give me." Tolin paused. "If you will."

Silva raised her chin. He had always admired her pride. It had set her above the others, and he would always remember her for it. Yet he waited, uncertain.

"Tell me what you want to know."

"The Royal Advisors of Neer have been moved from their domicile. I seek to find them."

Silva's smooth face twitched again. "What makes you think *I* know where they are?"

"Silva . . ." Tolin's gaze lingered. "You are a favorite of Fador's guards. There is not a man among them who does not confide in you."

"True . . . not a one but you."

Aware of Sera's subtle movement beside him, Tolin waited expectantly for Silva to continue.

He did not have to wait long.

"You will never be able to reach them."

"Why? Where are they?"

"Fador was agitated. The guards did not know why, but he ordered the advisors thrown into the deepest dungeon of the village prison, with no intention of release."

"The dungeon." Tolin was momentarily speechless. "You are sure?"

Tolin saw the parting of Silva's lips and the familiar light in her eyes before she responded in a voice of remembered intimacy, "Do you doubt me, Tolin?"

Nay, he did not doubt her.

Taking Silva's delicate hand, Tolin raised it to his lips. Her eyes filled. She did not speak until he took Sera's arm and turned toward the door.

"Not that way. It is unsafe."

Moving to a doorway disguised in the wall, Silva drew it open. Tolin halted as Silva addressed Sera directly for the first time.

"Goodbye, heiress. The heart of the man on whom your life depends is good and pure, no matter what is commonly said of him."

Sera's reply was gentle. "I know."

With a brief touching of hands, the women parted, and relief surged through Tolin. Two women, both so different, yet both so true.

His arm curling around Sera's shoulders, Tolin urged her down the dark staircase toward the street. Halting at the bottom, Sera turned back to him. He saw the uncertainty in her eyes.

"Tolin?"

Cupping her chin in his palm, Tolin whispered, "Silva is . . . a friend, but there is only one woman I have ever loved."

Filnor paced in agitation. Fador sought to humiliate him once more! He had summoned him to his quarters with instructions to wait until his return, and had then gone off with his guard!

Filnor's lip twitched into a snarl. He had no doubt where Fador now was. His servant's smile had been revealing. He was carousing, searching for a new titillation to stir his jaded appetite! His father would dally with true enjoyment, knowing his son waited for him in his rooms like a disciplined child.

Filnor slapped his palm down on the nearby table with an angry crack of sound. He would not wait! He would gather his guard and show his father that he had erred when he—

Filnor drew his raging thoughts to an abrupt halt. Nay, the risk was too great should he oppose his father now. His father doubtless thought to force him into such a hasty step, but he would not fall into the trap. He would be patient until the time was right.

The sound of a hesitant step at the door

turned Filnor slowly toward it. Neither guard nor servant would walk so stealthily, and no one without Fador's confidence would be allowed into this portion of the castle, unless . . .

Filnor's hand slipped to the sword at his side. He remained poised and ready. The cautious knock that followed narrowed his gaze further as he responded with a gruff bid to enter.

The door opened.

Sinbald!

Filnor's inner agitation swelled. He was aware that his father had secretly employed the aging degenerate's services. He was also aware that the despicable fellow would not have come to Fador now unless he had succeeded where the wretched Molta and his fellow spies had failed!

Sinbald's shocked dismay was the first pleasing note of the day. Filnor gripped his sword more tightly and offered coldly, "Come in, Sinbald. You come to report to Fador, do you not?"

"Nay, nay . . ." Sinbald's rheumy eyes widened with exaggerated innocence. "I but came to speak to him, to offer my aid should he be in need of it."

"In need of aid—from you? Surely you jest!"

Sinbald shook his head, the oily strands of gray flying out almost comically as he took a step backwards. "I but hoped to serve, but if Fador is not here—"

"Stand where you are!" The antipathy ever present between them soared as Filnor advanced. "I recall a time when you felt yourself above the young heir to the rule of Rall—when you dismissed him with ridicule whenever he addressed you and drove him away with the laughter you raised against him! How the mighty have fallen! You are naught but a filthy shell of the man you once were, while I am still the heir to the House of Rall!"

Sinbald cowered. "Nay, I never ridiculed you. You misunderstood me!"

"I misunderstood nothing! Nor do I misunderstand your reason for coming to my father's chambers now." Filnor paused, his knuckles whitening on the handle of his sword. "You have a report to deliver! Deliver it!"

"I do not!"

Filnor drew his sword.

"Wait!" Stretching out trembling hands in an attempt to shield himself, Sinbald pleaded, "Fador admonished me to tell no one! I fear to suffer his wrath!"

"It is *my* wrath you will suffer if you do not speak!"

Shaking so severely that he could barely form the words, Sinbald rasped, "I . . . I saw them."

A slow anxiety crawled up Filnor's spine. "Them?"

"Tolin is back."

Filnor went suddenly still.

Sinbald shuddered. "He has the *flame reborn* with him."

Filnor's stillness erupted into sudden rage. "Do not mock me!"

"I do not—I vow that I do not!" Sinbald stuttered, "I saw her! She is beautiful, the image of Versa of Neer, yet different in a way I cannot define. I saw her magic, and then I knew there was no doubt!"

"Magic!" Filnor scoffed. "You think me a fool!"

"Nay. I saw her lay her hands on a child who was burned and I saw her cure him! I came here to inform Fador as he commanded because I knew she was the one he sought!"

Filnor eyed the aging spy. There was no doubt Sinbald believed what he said. He was too frightened to lie. The dampness on his leggings was ample proof.

Filnor took a step back, his nose twitching at the odor emanating from Sinbald as he pressed, "Where did you see these two together?"

"At the Boar's Head Inn. They left shortly before I did, but they will doubtless return. They think they have bought the loyalty of the innkeeper and his wife with their treatment of the boy."

"That is all you have to report?" Filnor

paused, his gaze narrowing. "Take care of what you say, for should I discover you have held back . . ."

"I have not! I have told you all!"

Filnor hesitated, then nodded. "You may leave."

"Leave?" Sinbald appeared momentarily stunned. His lips moved into the semblance of a smile. "Master Fador promised a reward."

"Your *reward* is your life! Leave now, or I may yet revoke it!"

"But Master Fador said—"

"Leave!"

Withdrawing his sword with a sweep, Filnor took a threatening step forward that turned Sinbald abruptly toward the door. With a brief backward look, Sinbald disappeared from sight.

Sheathing his sword as the door snapped closed behind Sinbald, Filnor gritted his teeth. Sinbald had revealed himself in his parting glance. He would report the meeting between them to Fador at his first opportunity. Fador would be infuriated by Filnor's actions.

Filnor's eyes grew cold. There was only one thing for him to do.

Emerging into the castle yard minutes later, Filnor signaled his guard.

Panting, Sinbald continued down the street at a pace just short of a run. He glanced behind him as he searched for signs of pursuit. Seeing none, he paused, gulping air into his tortured lungs as his mind raged.

Damn the foul twists of fortune! Why had Fador's servants not warned him that Filnor waited in Fador's chamber? Had Filnor bribed them? Nay, he was too stingy with the coin in his purse! Well, it mattered not! Sinbald would be more cautious next time. He would wait and watch for Fador's return, and when he did, he would take the first opportunity to report that Filnor had forced the information from him. Fador would believe him. Fador would *want* to believe him, for he had never borne true affection for his heir.

Fador would then compensate him well because he would realize that, in truth, he could trust Sinbald farther than he could trust his own son!

Momentarily satisfied with that thought, Sinbald slipped into a nearby alley. He sat abruptly on a discarded box and closed his eyes. He was still trembling from the specter of death in Filnor's eyes. Yea, the cold-blooded pup had come close to slaying him, and Sinbald would not forget it! When the time came, he would see that Filnor—

A footstep.

A rustle of sound.

Sinbald snapped his eyes open.

328

Too late!

The sword of Rall fell, closing Sinbald's eyes forever.

Concealed nearby, Molta shuddered at the rasp of Sinbald's final breath. Crafty spy that he was, Molta had lingered near the castle when Sinbald appeared, suspecting that Fador had set his former spy to the same task that Filnor had set Molta and his fellows. He had noted Sinbald's barely restrained excitement as he approached the castle and had cursed at the thought that Sinbald had been successful where he and his fellows had not.

Wishing to be prepared for whatever would follow, Molta had concealed himself in the shadows until Sinbald emerged minutes later, scurrying fearfully. When Filnor appeared at the door of the castle shortly afterward, calling for his guard, Molta had seen the shadow of death hovering.

Perspiration dampened Molta's brow as his shuddering grew more intense. Filnor had punished Sinbald for being successful where his own spies were not. Molta knew instinctively that the same shadow of death now hovered over his fellows and him as well, because of their failure.

Molta's mind began a frantic reeling. What to do? Where to go? The time remaining before their fate was served grew shorter with each passing moment. He needed to find a way to avoid the merciless blade of Rall now hanging over their heads!

A thought occurred. There was one way he might save himself and his fellows.

Fador.

Their nefarious ruler might well be very grateful to hear from his lips that Filnor had gone so far as to kill Sinbald in order to conceal from Fador the information Sinbald sought to deliver. Fador might be so grateful that he would reward him and his fellows with a greater sum than the niggardly Filnor would ever have considered.

Molta appraised that thought further.

Yea . . . and then he might not.

Molta swallowed the bitter taste of bile that rose in his throat. The risk was too great. There was only one recourse for men such as he and his fellows when faced with a catastrophic threat like the one now looming.

Yea—quick and effective disappearance from the scene of impending disaster!

Molta scanned the surrounding area, then slipped back out onto the street. His decision was made. Within the hour the primary village would be behind him forever.

Molta hurried off without a backward glance.

Behind him Sinbald remained, pooled in his own blood, forgotten where he lay.

Chapter Eleven

The afternoon waned. Tolin was increasingly conscious of Sera's lagging step beside him as they walked through the winding streets of the primary village. Aware that her disguise made walking difficult, Tolin had attempted to spare her the stress of the long, fruitless search, but Sera had been adamant that she remain with him.

Turning a corner, Tolin breathed a silent sigh of relief as the Boar's Head Inn came again into view. He would deliver Sera there and have food brought up to the room so they might sup together. He would go out again on his own under cover of darkness to confirm what they had learned.

Tolin's stomach knotted painfully. It was

true. The Royal Advisors had been sent to the dungeon of the village prison as Silva had said. He had been able to learn little more about them, except that they had been delivered there apparently uninjured and had been thrown into a communal cell. His endeavor that evening would be to define if any friends of Neer were numbered among the prison guards.

Tolin looked down at Sera again, suffering her torment. He had sensed each time her spirits sagged, as well as each time her hopes were raised, only to be dashed once more. He was determined that he would find a way for her to contact the advisors that night at any cost. He did not fear for Sera's safety while he was gone. With Gar brought in from the stables and left to guard Sera in his absence, she would be safe while he was away.

And when he returned . . .

Anticipation of the night to come, when he would again hold Sera in his arms, set Tolin's heart to pounding.

At the steps of the inn, Tolin pushed open the door to allow Sera to enter. The weariness of her step as she climbed the staircase ahead of him was almost more than he could bear.

Waiting only until they were out of general view of the public room, Tolin swept Sera off her feet and up into his arms. He heard her gasp as her mantle dropped away from her head, as her fiery hair swung free and the glorious gold of her eyes met his.

His Sera . . . *his* heiress . . . *his alone* . . . for a little while longer.

Brushing her mouth with his, Tolin continued up the staircase toward their room. He thrust open the door and then pushed it closed, shutting out the world behind them.

Concealed at the foot of the inn staircase, Filnor stood paralyzed with incredulity. His mouth was dry. His heart was pounding. His breathing was erratic.

A childhood enchantment returned, surging to new life within him!

He remembered the flame. He would never forget its beauty. He had held it in his hands, mesmerized as it danced within its crystal prison. He had felt its weight. He had experienced its heat. Unlike his father, he had not railed at it or mocked it, but he had been no less bewitched as the iridescent colors that had induced such rapture within him splayed against the glass.

The thundering of Filnor's heart increased. He had thought Fador mad in summoning him with talk of prophetic dreams and the return of Neer, but everything was different now. He had recognized her immediately! She was the magnificent image who haunted his dreams . . . the flawless embodiment of female allure and promise without a name . . . the matchless ideal by which he had measured all women to find them wanting.

She was the flame reborn!

Filnor struggled to bring his raging emotions under control. He had disguised himself as a commoner hours earlier and made his way to the Boar's Head Inn, determined to test the validity of Sinbald's report. He had waited in the public room, his attention unstraying from the entrance as time slowly passed. Hatred had soared when the door of the inn opened and Tolin stepped into view. The stooped woman at Tolin's side had puzzled him at first, but Tolin's protective stance, his watchful eye, and the way in which the cold warrior's gaze had warmed as never before when he looked in the woman's direction had raised Filnor's anticipation.

Following their progress up the staircase with his gaze, Filnor had been momentarily paralyzed with the impact of the moment when Tolin had swept the woman up into his arms, causing her hair to blaze free as her mantle slipped from her head. He had glimpsed it then, when the woman's face had been briefly exposed to his view for the first time. He had glimpsed the flame that had enraptured him so long ago, flickering in the supreme gold of her eyes!

He had longed for that flame. He had lamented its loss. He had denied with every ounce of vigor within him the indefatigable hope that he might hold it once more!

Filnor's joy turned suddenly cold.

But it had not been *his* lips that had touched the flame reborn! It had not been *his* arms that had swept her up and carried her close to his heart! It had been Tolin who had held her—Tolin, the bastard friend, the cowardly deserter, the traitor to Rall!

Malice swelled within Filnor. Tolin was not worthy of the beauteous flame that had filled the Heir of Rall's boyish dreams, the flame that had burned in a corner of his mind, never to be forgotten!

And Tolin would not have her.

Cursing the time that would be lost before he could return to the inn with his personal guard, Filnor moved quickly toward the doorway. Were he to obey the inclination pounding through his veins, he would mount the staircase without hesitation and storm through that upstairs doorway to tear his flame from Tolin's arms.

But he must employ patience and caution.

He could not chance losing her again.

An hour—no more—and she would be his.

"I will come with you."

Sera was adamant, but Tolin could not be swayed.

335

Grasping her shoulders, Tolin held Sera immobile as she attempted to rise from the bed on which he had placed her after carrying her into the room a short time earlier. It had been one of the most difficult things he had ever done to sit beside her when he had wanted to do so much more. But he had known there was much he must accomplish before they could find loving rest in each other's arms. His mistake had been in relating his further plans for the evening.

"Release me, Tolin! I will not be treated as if I am truly the aging female I have pretended to be through this long day! This quest, however demanding, is mine, and I will meet its test!"

"Listen to me, Sera!" Marveling at her beauty and dauntless spirit even as he spoke, Tolin continued forcefully, "You will be a detriment to the course I would pursue tonight. You would bring suspicion upon me by your presence. Without you I might pretend to visit former comrades at arms, mayhap affect a regret for surrendering my former life, and thereby be allowed to enter areas where I would otherwise be forbidden."

"I will wait in the shadows."

"Nay."

"I will follow you!"

"Nay, I say!" Pausing to regain control, Tolin whispered, "Can you not see that my concentration would be impaired by fear for your safety?"

"What difference would it make if I were here alone, or there alone?"

"You will not be alone here. Gar will remain with you."

"The innkeeper will object to an animal's presence in these rooms!"

"No one refuses Gar."

Tolin was unprepared as Sera leaned toward him unexpectedly, her eyes softening to melted honey as she whispered, "Tolin, do you not see? I fear to be separated from you."

"Fear?" Tolin studied her with suspicion. "Sera of Neer, afraid?"

Sera's voice was a soft plea. "Tolin, do you not yet understand? Sera, the woman without, is fearless; but Sera, the woman within, fears the threat you face in her name."

Tolin responded with corresponding intensity, "Sera, do *you* not understand? The only threat *I* fear is the threat to you. To spare you such jeopardy, I would—"

The sound of heavy footsteps in the hallway outside the door halted Tolin's words abruptly. Springing to his feet, sword drawn, he turned in its direction the moment before the door burst open with a crash of splintering wood.

Tolin met the leather-clad warriors rushing toward him with a warring stance. His arm was raised to strike when a familiar voice sounded unexpectedly.

"Halt! Put down your sword!"

Sliding Sera behind him as she scrambled to her feet, Tolin shielded her with his massive frame. His gaze narrowed as Filnor stepped into view to speak again.

"Surrender your sword and your life will be spared!"

Tolin grated in return, "By what right do you enter here and disturb me when I am with my woman?"

"Your woman! Do you think me a fool that I do not recognize her?"

Observing the lust that flashed in Filnor's eyes as Sera stepped out from behind him, Tolin spoke words of warning filled with menace.

"She is mine."

Filnor's startling response rang with jealous rage. "She was *mine* before she was yours! She will be mine again!"

Tolin shook his head, incredulous. "You are insane! You know not of what you speak!"

His eyes black coals of furious heat, Filnor rasped, "I know well of what I speak! This woman is the flame reborn. It is *I* who set her spirit free that night so long ago when her crystal prison shattered. *I* am responsible for her rebirth, and she is mine!"

"Nay." Tolin attempted a note of reason. "You err. Sera belongs to no man. She belongs to Neer and to Orem. She has returned to fulfill the prophecy."

"Traitor! You seal your death with your words! There is no future for Orem without Rall! This woman you protect with your solitary sword has bewitched you, but she will not bewitch me! And she *will* be mine!"

"Never!"

"Cease!" Her voice echoing in the sudden silence of the room, Sera faced Filnor with eyes blazing. "I have not returned to my people so that blood might be shed in my name! Nor have I returned to serve as a plaything for one so arrogant as to believe that *he* accomplished the work of destiny, when in truth, he was merely destiny's pawn! Were you a different man, Filnor of Rall, you would recognize the greater power which controls this universe, where fates are decreed and must be obeyed for the betterment of all, and where it is the duty of all to serve as they would be served!"

"Fool's words! I accept no fate except that which I work with my own hands!"

Sera's gaze grew cold. "Hands that are covered with blood."

Filnor laughed aloud, holding up his hands. "Yea, mistress, these hands have shed blood, the same blood your protector has shed for Rall as well!"

Sera stiffened. "Tolin is not the man he was. He has been cleansed."

Filnor's smile grew carnal. "Cleansed by the

flesh of the flame." He took another step toward her. "I, too, would be so cleansed, mistress."

"Knave!" Tolin's sword glinted as he advanced a step further. "Touch her and you breathe your last!"

"It will not be I who breathes his last!" Filnor met Tolin's threat with a venomous hiss. "We will settle this now, Tolin, *formerly* of Rall! Your sword against mine—as it should have been the day you turned your back on your vow of allegiance."

Sera protested, "I will not allow this madness!"

"You have no choice, mistress!" Filnor's handsome face drew into evil lines reminiscent of his sire's as he turned back to Tolin. "What say you? Your sword against mine as it was meant to be."

"Tolin . . ."

The desperate note in Sera's plea crawled up Tolin's spine as he responded, "And the woman?"

"To the winner go the spoils."

Seeing no other recourse, Tolin nodded abruptly. "Done."

"Tolin!"

Ignoring Sera's plea, Tolin turned toward the guard nearby. "Hold the woman back. See that she does not interfere."

Retiring to the hallway where they could move more freely, the two men crossed swords.

* * *

Struggling against the rough hands that held her captive, Sera moved out of the room and into the hallway overlooking the first floor of the inn. Unaware of the crowd forming below, she felt only a sense of dazed incredulity.

She had not wanted this! She had not believed for a moment that her return to rule would be accomplished by the spilling of blood! Nay, her dreams, the voice that had guided her path, the visions that had grown gradually clearer in her mind, Tolin's arrival in Orem Minor—all had contributed to an expectation that included a bloodless coup d'etat.

Sera's heart was pounding. Her voice was frozen in her throat. The lamplight glistened on Tolin's heavy pale hair and reflected off the midnight sheen of Filnor's dark locks as the two men prepared to do battle.

Like reverse sides of the same coin they were, both tall and muscularly proportioned, both handsome and intent, both bent on the destruction of the other.

The restraining hands on her arms tightened as the clash of swords sounded, and the mortal contest began.

Oh, the horror of it! The harsh grunts of ferocious lunges . . . the crash of clashing blades . . . the gasps . . . the echoes of stumbling steps!

Tolin advancing, then feinting under the onslaught of Filnor's renewed attack . . . Filnor's gaze of barbaric intensity . . . Tolin's cold, emotionless stare . . . mighty strengths pressed to the limits . . .

A strike!

Blood streamed from a gash on Tolin's arm and Sera went momentarily weak. Tolin! She could not lose him!

But Tolin did not retreat. He lunged strongly forward, once, twice, a third time. Unprepared for Tolin's rebounding assault, Filnor stumbled, falling backward, struggling to escape Tolin's slashing blade and the savagery of his powerful arm as it descended again and again with increasing fury. Filnor sank to his knees, then struggled to regain his feet.

Another crashing blow dislodged the sword from Filnor's hand, leaving him defenseless.

Silence.

Tolin's blade at Filnor's throat drew a single drop of blood. It trickled down the strong column of Filnor's neck to lie like a glowing red jewel against his warrior leathers. Unable to speak, Sera saw Filnor's eyes bulge, his lips locking tight in preparation for the final thrust. She glanced at Tolin to see his expression cold, his eyes grey ice. She saw the subtle movement of his arm and she caught her breath.

A sudden step beside her. . . .

With a shriek, Sera saw Tolin stiffen as he was struck a powerful blow from behind!

As if in a dream, Sera watched as the guard drew back from his ignoble act, as blood gushed from a wound on Tolin's head!

She saw Tolin waver.

She saw him fall!

Suddenly free of restraint, Sera was on her knees at Tolin's side. She stroked his face. She read his pain. She saw the anguish in his gaze as his pale lips whispered words she could not discern.

Panicking, Sera reached for the pouch at her waist, but it was too late! She saw it the moment it happened . . .

. . . *the moment Tolin slipped beyond her healing powers.*

A loud, screeching wail began within Sera's mind. It shut off all sound, all light, all feeling, leaving only darkness.

Chapter Twelve

Lamps filled with scented oils glowed softly in the silence. The sweet fragrance permeated the room as Filnor paced around his bed, his gaze returning over and again to the slender figure that lay so still on bedclothes trimmed in royal purple.

Frowning, Filnor sat again beside Sera and took her hand. It lay limply in his, almost as if the blow that had closed Tolin's eyes forever had ended her life as well. But she was alive. The pulsing of her heart was strong and even under his lips as he kissed her wrist gently. Her body was warm and inviting although it lay so still.

Were she another, Filnor knew he would have taken her where she lay, so powerful was his lust for her. But she was not another. She was the spirit of the flame that had lived in his mind, refusing to be subdued. She was the spark that would bring him the joy he had lacked since that night so long ago in the tower room. She was *his* spirit, *his* flame. He would take her with love. He would make her see that the destiny to which she referred had not ordained that she rule in the name of Neer, but that she was meant to return to *him*.

Filnor leaned closer to his beautiful flame.

"Sera . . ."

Her name was warm on his lips. To speak it gave him pleasure so intense that he could barely restrain his desire.

"Awaken, Sera . . ."

She must awaken soon, and when she did, he would prove to her what fate had truly decreed. He would prove it with his voice, with his lips, and with his body—all of which would be hers alone.

Sera awakened slowly. She felt a fleeting touch on her wrist and shuddered. She heard the whisper of her name, but the sound grated harshly. She heard a voice urge her back to consciousness, and she struggled against it.

The voice rang with the sound of death.

Sera awakened abruptly and saw *him*.

Anguish and sorrow flooding back in great,

overwhelming swells, Sera stared with horror as Filnor leaned over her, his gaze adoring.

Rage and a deadening grief emerged in a scathing rasp.

"Murderer!"

"Nay!" Filnor denied her accusation, sincerity shining in his dark eyes as he leaned closer. His lips were only inches from hers as he whispered, "I sought fair combat, nothing more. My guard acted hastily."

"For which you no doubt rewarded him handsomely!"

Incredibly, Filnor smiled. "Yea, I rewarded him. What man does not reward loyalty that saves his life?"

"A just man, a man who lays claim to nobility, does not reward a cowardly strike from behind!"

"Mayhap not, but a *wise* man values his life. As would a wise woman value the ardor of one who is powerful enough to make her life all she hoped it to be—a man who would take you into his life, Sera of Neer, despite the blemish that marks you."

Filnor dropped his hand to trace the outline of the rose-colored crescent on her thigh, exposed by a fresh slit in her shift. His touch physically nauseated her, and Sera commanded with tight control, "Remove your hand."

Filnor's eyes glowed salaciously. "Your skin

is soft. It was made for my touch, a touch that will give you pleasure beyond your wildest dreams."

Taking Filnor by surprise, Sera sprang to her feet.

"Butcher! Are you so vain that you think I cannot resist you? Are you so arrogant that you think I will believe your lies? Are you so overwhelmed by misguided self-esteem that you actually believe that I would give myself to you? *I* who am the hope of Orem? *I* who perceive you for what you truly are? *I* who know that you are of the same blood as the man who slew my mother without a qualm, the same man who took righteous rule from her and assumed the mantle of reign so cruelly?" Sera paused with a shudder. "*I* who saw your guard slay the man I love!"

Filnor's face flushed a deep red. He drew himself to his feet and advanced slowly toward her.

"So you loved Tolin?" Filnor's laughter was harsh. "You must pardon me if I disbelieve you, for you see, I knew Tolin well. A fine figure of a man he was, but there was nothing within. He was cold, devoid of emotion. He was no more than a weapon developed by Rall. You used him in the way he was intended to be used—as a means of defense. I applaud you for that! As for the other crimes of which you accuse me, my name is Filnor, not Fador! I do not walk in Fador's steps, and I am not responsible for anything that happened in the past—except for the freeing of the flame which gave you life."

Slowing his advance as he drew closer, Filnor lowered his voice to a whisper. "Tell me, Sera, do you really believe the hand of fate was not involved in that night so long ago—that we were not fated to come together as I would have it now between us? Would you not believe me if I told you that I regretted Tolin's death as deeply as do you, and that if I had the chance, I would restore him to life?"

"Cease your fatuous lies!" Sera's breast heaved with the fury of her words. "Had you your chance, you would not have hesitated to pierce Tolin's chest with your own blade, although he was reluctant to pierce yours!"

"And for that weakness, Tolin paid with his life, fool that he was!" Filnor laughed again, abruptly dismissing all attempt at pretense. "I am tired of this repartee! You have been sheltered too long, heiress! It is time you face the true facts of life! Living is for the strong, and death is for the weak! Fool that Tolin was, he allowed himself to weaken. I will not make such an error, for I learned long ago the necessities of survival—as will you!"

Sera's reply reflected her contempt. "It is clear to see that integrity is a word to which you are a stranger!"

"Integrity! You would have me believe that your precious Tolin was possessed of integrity? Was it integrity that earned him the name Death's Shadow? Was it integrity that struck fear in the hearts of all those who would oppose him, save me? I truly doubt that, heiress. But since Tolin still lingers in your mind, I will allow your delusion a little while longer."

Filnor paused, continuing with a twist of the lips, "Now, just this *first* time that we come together, I will allow you to pretend that my hair is of a faded shade instead of shining black, and that my eyes are pale instead of darkly hued. But I promise you that when I take you into my arms, when our flesh meets, when you are hot and moist beneath me and I sink myself deep inside you, you will not mistake me for another. Nay, you will call out the name Filnor, and you will find a satiation you have never known before! You will beg me never to leave you!"

Pausing again, his breathing heavy, Filnor continued in a throbbing tone, "And I will promise you then, as I promise you now, my beautiful Sera—my incomparable flame—that I will cherish you, in my heart and in my arms, to the end of time."

Sera stared at Filnor with disbelief. "You speak of death and you speak of love in the same breath! You boast of the blood on your hands while seeking to convince me of the place

I hold in your heart! Yea, you have succeeded in convincing me of the error of my ways. Where before I despised you for the acts you committed in Rall's name, where before I could envision no greater justice than to have you struck from life as Tolin was struck so cruelly . . ." Her control threatening to collapse, Sera breathed deeply, then continued, "Where before I felt an antipathy so intense that it threatened to overcome all my former teachings in favor of burning vengeance, those emotions are now stricken from my mind. What remains is *pity*, pity for one who has been stripped of all humanity!"

"Pity, is it!" Livid, Filnor lashed out at her. "You may feel pity, or whatever else you please when you lie beneath me—when I spill my seed into you and begin a new generation of Rall's rule!"

"Never!" Shuddering, Sera felt the heat of a new fire stirring to life within her. "Your seed will never grow within me!"

"Yea, it will, heiress!" Filnor stepped closer. "And as it grows, you will learn to cherish me and my seed." Filnor reached out for her. "And through it all, I will—"

Gasping aloud as he touched the flesh of Sera's arm, Filnor snapped back as if burned. Startled, he remained staring at her for long seconds before grasping her arm again. Jerking back anew with a pained hiss, he then threw both arms around her, only to wrench away with a growled warning.

"Witch, you singe me with your fury! Turn off this spell you have cast, or you have my oath that you will pay for this offense!"

When Sera did not reply, Filnor attempted to embrace her again, only to recoil at the burn he suffered. His handsome face distorted with rage, Filnor spoke in a venomous whisper.

"Sorceress! Bitch! To the prison with you then, where you may join the rabble of Neer rotting in the dungeon there!"

Sera stood firm as Filnor shouted for his guard, as the burly fellows grasped her arms and took her prisoner without suffering any singeing. Filnor's fury had reached near apoplexy as she was dragged from his chambers.

Strangely, however, Filnor did not linger in Sera's mind as the door of his quarters slammed shut behind her. Instead, she saw only the image of Tolin's pain as he lay prostrate before her, of his pale lips as he struggled to speak, of the light dimming in his eyes. She suffered again the excruciating pain of seeing that light fade.

Tolin . . . Tolin . . .

Sera fought to dislodge the guards' oppressive grip on her arms, to escape so she might vent her despair, so she might eliminate from her sight the soulless warriors who had ended Tolin's life!

Sera did not see the blow coming. She felt only the burst of pain that stunned her and the grip of callused hands supporting her roughly as she weakened. She heard only the echo of a derisive voice as it spoke words that trailed after her into the waiting darkness.

"So much for the Heiress of Neer."

The shadowed figure walked slowly along the darkened street of the primary village, staggering weakly. Pausing to draw himself erect, the robed man adjusted his hood to shield his face before entering a well-lighted inn a few steps away. He paid the price of a night's shelter, then climbed the stairs to the room assigned above.

Pushing the door closed behind him and throwing back his hood to reveal noble Minor Oremian features marked with distress, Serbaak gasped for breath. He staggered to the nearby table, his hand trembling as he reached for the flask at his waist and unscrewed the cap. He shook the glittering zircum dust within into the cup there, filled the cup with water from the pitcher nearby, and drank thirstily, the pale liquid streaming from the corners of his mouth in his haste to consume it.

Draining the cup, Serbaak placed it back on the table, realizing as he did that an increasingly stronger dose of the elixir was needed each time to restore his strength. The time was fast approaching when it would have no effect on him at all, and he would succumb to his body's inability to adapt to conditions outside his native Orem Minor.

His strength returning, Serbaak cast those considerations aside. He did not recall the exact moment he made the decision to come after Sera, discarding Alpor's fears for his life and Teesha's pleas that he remain. He knew only that the scenes from the past enacted so vividly and unexpectedly before his mind as he had lain in Teesha's bed—scenes of Versa of Neer's life and death—had unleashed a driving force within that had dispatched him to Sera's aid.

He started his journey immediately afterwards, cursing himself for allowing Sera to depart Orem Minor without him. He had been consoled only by the realization that as creatures indigenous to the harsh clime of Orem Minor who were not further hindered by the plodding pace of heavy ore wagons, he and his mount would traverse the distance between the two worlds of Orem in half the time it had taken the caravan to cover the same distance, and that he would soon be at Sera's side.

His strength returning, Serbaak's thoughts reverted to Sera, to the waves of shock, despair, and grief most recently transmitted to him since reaching Orem Proper. He felt a stirring of the same force within him which had dispatched him to Sera's aid, which guided his hand in the mixing of the elixir which strengthened him, and which had led him to the particular inn where he now stood. Placing his trust in that intuitive surge, he squared his shoulders under his concealing robes, his jaw firm with purpose. He was well and strong again. He would use his temporary strength. He would use the last spark of life within him, if need be, to rescue Sera from her despair. For him, it could be no other way.

Serbaak drew his hood back up over his head and turned toward the door. Downstairs in the public room minutes later, he sat and ate—and listened.

Hoofbeats echoed against the dark, cobbled streets as Filnor raced down the narrow thoroughfare at breakneck speed, a contingent of guards behind him. Unmindful of pedestrians scattering for their lives, he turned the corner to enter a dissolute quarter of the primary village with which he was familiar. His expression grew fierce as he passed the brightly lit houses.

Not the first house, nor the second . . .

Filnor drew back sharply on his mount's reins as they reached the third house, ignoring the animal's whinny of protest as he turned to the men behind him.

"We will amuse ourselves briefly here!"

A resounding clatter ensued as the guards dismounted, exchanging knowing glances. Stepping down onto the street beside them, Filnor straightened his attire and ran his hand through his hair. His lips tightened as he approached the door of the house of ill repute. He had been riding for hours in an attempt to alleviate his frustration, and he was much the worse for wear. Despite his most valiant attempts to the contrary, however, Sera's image remained before him, just as she had appeared when she had so scathingly refused him.

Witch!

Filnor glanced down at his palms where blisters from contact with her skin remained. The heiress had paid severely for refusing him. Rather than on his royal bed, she now lay in the filth and squalor of the prison dungeon. Rather than feeling the warmth of his loving caress, she now felt only the damp cold and the brush of the long-tailed denizens of that dank abode.

Fool! Did she not see that there was no future for her quest in this Orem now dominated by Rall? Did she not realize that her only hope for fulfillment lay in his arms?

Bursting into the house, Fador stood briefly framed in the doorway, coldly observing couples in all stages of undress and physical intimacy who barely acknowledged his arrival.

With a low snort, he turned toward the staircase and mounted the steps two at a time, his gaze intent on a particular doorway atop the landing.

He was in a vicious frame of mind and there was only one who would suit his present inclination. He had used Matier occasionally before when the mood had come upon him. Her perversions had adequately filled his needs.

Striding across the hall, Filnor kicked open the door. His lips moved into a twisted smile as he strode across the room and ripped apart the two naked forms tightly entwined. Grasping the man by the hair, he dragged him to the doorway and thrust him out into the hall, then slammed the door closed behind him. He then turned toward the woman, who had drawn herself to her feet beside the bed.

Matier's light hair hung limply against her naked back as she advanced toward him. Her eyes were bright with anticipation. Her flesh glistened in the limited light, her full breasts heaving with excitement as she reached his side. She pressed herself against him, raising her lips to his as she curved her hand around his head to draw his mouth down to hers.

Filnor smelled the warm, musky scent of her. He felt her hand move searchingly. He felt the brush of her wet lips.

Assailed by a sudden wave of revulsion so severe that he almost retched, Filnor thrust Matier abruptly away. Momentarily motionless, he stared at her confused expression. He was as surprised as she by his actions when he turned away from her, pulled the door open, and strode back down the staircase in the direction from which he had come.

Mounted on his weary beast minutes later, his men mumbling behind him, Filnor rode off at a savage pace.

The perpetual darkness of the dungeon enclosed Sera as she came slowly awake. A dampness smelling of rot and human waste assaulted her senses as she strained to acclimate her gaze to the shadows surrounding the cot on which she lay. Seeking to dispel the strange disorientation that afflicted her, she became abruptly aware of silent figures with indiscernible faces crouched beside her.

Total recall returned with a sudden stab of pain.

Tolin was dead.

He had sacrificed his life for her.

She would never see him again.

Sera closed her eyes, her heart wrenching. There were no longer two Seras of Neer. The inner woman who had loved Tolin so deeply was gone. Her life had ended with Tolin's, and in her place was a void where only grief remained. The grief was deadening. It sapped her strength. It devoured her joy. It consumed the last spark of hope within her. It left her little but the desire to close her eyes, never to open them again.

But there was no solitude in Sera's despair. The other Sera of Neer remained, reminding her that she had no choice but to continue her quest, to arise from her desperation and face the future now surrounding her in the darkness of the cell.

Sera slowly raised her heavy lids. She scrutinized the men around her. There were five. The faces beneath their matted, greying beards were lined with age and their robes bore the stains of confinement, but their gazes were clear and intent.

She recognized them immediately, as different as were their appearances from the vision she had seen of a time long past: Nako, Principal Royal Advisor of Neer; Gorum, second in authority; then Ektra, Dorball, and Whit—five who had offered the knowledge and wisdom that had been the young Versa's guide. They were five true and faithful men whose hearts beat solely for the welfare of Orem.

Sera drew herself to a seated position. Her jaw ached, reminding her of Filnor's blow, as she extended her hand in greeting to each man. Her voice was choked despite the affection in her tone as she addressed them.

"I had not thought our meeting would be in this foul place."

"Heiress . . ." Sera discerned both joy and despair as Nako managed a shaky smile. "There was not a moment when we doubted your return, but it was difficult for us when you were delivered here." The old man's mein revealed the strain of the momentous moment as he continued softly, "You were immediately recognizable to us, for Versa's beauty lives on in you, as does the aura of her spirit."

"And the royal crescent." Sera glanced down at the mark clearly visible through the slit in her shift.

"An unnecessary confirmation . . . which we yet sought to deny."

"To deny?"

Beside Nako, Gorum responded in his stead. "We had no desire to see you come at last only to meet a desperate end."

Sera threw her legs over the side of the cot and drew herself to her feet, and the others stood as well. She ignored the brief dizziness that ensued as she responded firmly, "I foresee no end to my quest because we meet here. Instead, I feel only elation at having found you at last."

At the uncertain looks exchanged among the advisors, Sera continued, "I was directed to you so I might fulfill the prophecy by finding the

Royal Vessel of Neer that was left under your protection—the sheath that Versa delivered to your care in that last hour before her death. It is the key to my people's liberation from Rall's rule. I yearn to see it, to feel its weight in my hands."

Nako shook his head. Sera read in his faded eyes the torment that stole his ability to reply, forcing Gorum again to speak in his stead.

"It is true, heiress, the Royal Vessel of Neer was handed over to our care. A sheath it was, encrusted with gold and precious jewels, but its worth did not lie in the outer casing. Its true value lay in what was contained within, the secret confided by Versa to the only true life Orem would ever know."

Sera waited, sensing a darker revelation to come. Her heart began a new pounding as Nako stepped forward to take her hand in his. "My apologies, heiress . . . but the vessel is gone."

"Gone!"

"Taken by Fador on the night he discovered us in the house on Crescent Square those many years ago! We do not know who betrayed the secret of the vessel's location to him, but there is not a one of us who will ever forget Fador's great glee when he flaunted it before us."

Nako's voice dropped to new desperation. "Fador displayed them both to us that night— the vessel he had stolen, and the crystal containing the captive flame of Versa's spirit. Versa's raging despair, her frustration, her need, were transmitted to us through the faceted glass. It echoed in our minds and in our hearts, and in that moment we vowed as one that we would do all in our power to bring the prophecy that had been written so long before our time to full fruition."

Nako's gnarled hand squeezed Sera's almost to the point of pain. "But we have failed you. In failing you, we have failed Versa as well. In the end, it is our inadequacy, rather than Fador's imprisonment of us here, that brings us true devastation." A tear slipped from Nako's eye. "Forgive us, heiress."

Forgive . . .

Nako's distress was clearly reflected on the faces of the other four, and Sera closed her eyes. Strangely, it was not Versa's image that appeared suddenly before her, but Tolin's—great and strong as he had been the last time he had stood beside her, the last time he had held her in his arms.

Forgive . . .

Forget . . .

Cast aside pain . . .

Sera was beyond it.

Silent, unable to do anything else, Sera withdrew her hand from Nako's and slipped into the obscurity of the shadows.

* * *

Fador smashed the flat of his hand against his desk. The sound echoed in the silence of his chambers as Zor held his gaze unflinchingly and Fador spat, "I do not believe it!"

Zor's pale, drawn countenance grew tight. "Do you again question my words?"

"Filnor would not dare the impropriety of which you accuse him! My orders to him were clear and succinct. If he found the flame reborn, he would deliver her to me!"

"I saw him clearly . . ."

"More of your delusions!"

"Nay, the images were distinct! I tell you that even now the Flame of Neer is confined deep in your own prison dungeon where Filnor cast her—in the same cell with the advisors!"

"Filnor would not be so great a fool!"

"Yea, he is. . . ." Zor paused, then continued, "He is obsessed by the flame as his father was before him."

Fador went still.

"He seeks to capture the flame for his own and keep her with him."

Fador gave a soft, choking sound.

"He cast her into the dungeon when she refused him."

Fador's voice returned with a hint of dark pride. "Refused him? Filnor would never be refused by a woman!"

Zor's patience snapped. "Believe me, or believe me not! The choice is yours, but I warn you now. The Flame of Neer is close by and her fire threatens Rall's rule. The flame must be snuffed, before it is too late! Do what you wish. My duty is done."

Turning stiffly, Zor disregarded Fador's command to halt. He allowed the epithets Fador shouted to fall on deaf ears as he followed a steady course out of Fador's chambers, his sober robes brushing the floor with his evenly paced step.

Behind him, Fador cursed the frail sorcerer who despised him despite his allegiance to Rall. He cursed his steadily growing belief that his son had indeed betrayed his trust. And he cursed the flame which yet consumed him with desire.

Striding toward the doorway moments later, Fador shouted for his guards, bringing them on the run as he prepared for the confrontation to come.

Serbaak moved into the dimly lit room and approached the unadorned bier in the center. He stopped short beside it and looked down at the body lying in state, at Tolin's ruthless features, imposing even as he lay lifelessly still.

An unexpected sadness overwhelmed Serbaak. The deadly contest between Filnor and Tolin was being spoken of in whispers all over the village. Tolin had given all to protect Sera. Serbaak had misjudged the cold-eyed warrior. Jealousy had blinded him to the man behind that grim stare, and Serbaak's regrets were overwhelming.

Serbaak closed his eyes as Sera's pain crossed the distance separating them to stab painfully at his heart. The pain grew stronger, more piercing. He suffered its torment, stiffening, his body growing rigid.

Serbaak stood so impaled for long moments as the force within him which guided his way in the new, uncertain path his life had taken stirred to life once more.

Growing ever stronger, the force gained a faint, almost indiscernible voice.

The voice was beautiful.

It infused him with strength.

It touched his soul.

The wonder of it growing ever stronger, Serbaak allowed the voice to guide his hand as he reached for the flask at his waist, as he removed the cap and filled it with zircum dust. Watching his own actions as if from afar, Serbaak set the cap on the bier and withdrew his flint. He struck it and touched it to the dust, his eyes widening as a strange mist arose.

Somehow insensitive to the heat, Serbaak took the cap into his hand as the voice within directed him. The strange green flame danced as he held it close to Tolin and blew the mist into Tolin's face.

Serbaak stepped back as the mist thickened suddenly, enveloping the bier and leaving it invisible to Serbaak's eye. He took another backwards step, then another as a strange, choking sound came from the smoke-enshrouded bier.

A growl of rage followed from within the mist, and Serbaak caught his breath as Tolin, *well and whole again*, emerged into the light!

Booted feet pounded down the stone staircase of the prison dungeon at a run. Leading his contingent of personal guards, Fador stepped onto the lowest level, panting as he sought to adapt his vision to the poor light. Turning toward the shaken jailer, he ordered, "The Advisors of Neer, take me to them!"

Signaling his men to follow, Fador fell in behind the jailer, his chest heaving. He had ridden directly from his confrontation with Zor to the prison, his thoughts churning.

If it was true . . . if it was true . . .

Fador's wrath soared.

If Filnor had indeed found the flame reborn and cast her into the dungeon, he would have done it for only one reason! Everything Zor had said would then be confirmed.

Filnor obsessed by the flame . . .

Filnor betraying him because of his desire to possess it . . .

366

Fador took a shuddering breath. He knew the strength of that desire. He knew the dangers inherent in it. *He* had been strong enough to do what was demanded of him those many years ago.

But Filnor was not as strong as he.

Filnor, his son, was a weakened seed.

The trembling jailer halted beside a cell door. Fador turned with a sharp command to the guard standing firm at his rear.

"Open the door and drive all within out into the light!"

The door creaked open, and Fador's heart began a thunderous pounding. His guard entered and the shadows within shifted, forming the outlines of the five men who emerged.

Fador was filled with contempt. The Royal Advisors of Neer—hah! They were no more than filthy old men who had outlived their usefulness. Were they not still valuable to him in other ways, he would have—

Fador's racing thoughts crashed to a halt at the emergence of another figure. He gasped with shock. The woman was as slender as a reed, and her hair was a brilliant red. Her skin paled as she stared at him, too overwhelmed to speak.

The words Fador sought became lodged in his throat as he looked down at the woman's thigh, then snatched back her ripped shift to expose a rose-colored crescent emblazoned there.

Eerie laughter burst from Fador's throat. It was she, the daughter of Versa's flame, yet he felt no warmth for her at all! He was free of Versa's spell! Total victory was within his grasp at last. Yea—at last!

Fador turned to his guards.

"Slay her!"

The shouted protests, the pleas of the advisors, were all for naught as the sword of Rall fell!

Standing over the lifeless body of the Heiress of Neer moments later, Fador watched dispassionately as the last drop of Neer blood drained onto the dungeon floor at his feet.

A slow satisfaction gradually growing within him, Fador addressed the advisors in a triumphant tone.

"Neer has been brought to its final end! As generous as I am, I will give you a few, final moments to bid adieu to your heiress." His smile evil as the men remained motionless, Fador then snapped, "Your time is up! Go back to your cell!"

The cell door slammed shut as Fador addressed his guard.

"Carry the body upstairs and into the courtyard! All will know this night that the prophecy has come to its final end, and the House of Neer has been erased from the face of Orem forever!"

* * *

The great blaze struck in the prison courtyard raged higher. Great tongues of fire licked up at the night sky overhead, roaring and crackling with ever-heightening din, expelling bursting showers of sparks over the heads of the crowd assembled there as Fador's guard continued to feed the flames.

The mumbling of the crowd grew in volume, the enforced number swelling as houses on nearby streets were emptied by Fador's relentless guard and the occupants ushered into the prison courtyard to observe the unknown spectacle to come. Young and old side by side; men and women steeped in timorous uncertainty; children clinging to their parents with fear; babes in arms whimpering . . . all quaking with expectation.

Watching from a position of unobstructed observation nearby, Fador smiled demonically. Yea, this was the moment he had waited for—the moment for which he had been born! This was the moment for which he had *sacrificed* all to *gain* all—a moment of supreme victory unmatched in all of Orem's history!

His jaw hardening, Fador observed the captain of the guard approaching. The officer's expression was grim as he halted his brisk pace a few feet away and raised his voice to be heard above the crackling of the flames.

"Master Filnor cannot presently be found. I request your permission to dispatch a larger contingent of men to scour the illicit houses in the lower quarter where it is rumored Master Filnor was seen earlier in the day."

"Damn him to hell!" His response erupting in a shout of fury, Fador continued hotly, "Cancel the search! It matters not that my son is not present this night to bear witness as the House of Rall celebrates its greatest triumph! It matters not that I will be cheated of the enjoyment of seeing him suffer as the body of the woman who enraptured him, only to refuse him, is served up in offering! For in truth, the relevance of this night outshines any minor disappointments that would stand to eclipse it!"

Surveying the assembled crowd once more, Fador turned back to his captain. The leaping tongues of fire reflected in the onyx depths of his eyes imparted a maniacal glow there as he snapped, "I am ready!"

Turning toward his men, who stood at the perimeters of the crowd, the captain signaled them forward. Fador watched with growing rapture as the townspeople were driven relentlessly closer to the flames, as their voices rose in shouted protest against the scorching heat that raised perspiration on their brows and fear in their eyes.

Satisfied when he was certain they could be

driven not a step closer, Fador signaled his men to halt. The crowd stilled at first sight of him as he stepped up onto a platform raised nearby. The ecstasy of true power rippled over Fador, deepening the mighty resonance of his voice as he shouted into a silence broken only by the crackle of the blaze.

"I, Fador of the Ruling House of Rall, have gathered all of you here this night so that I might share with you an event of great significance to Orem—one that will live forever in the annals of Orem's history! On this night—this *momentous* night—a myth has been destroyed, a pretender sent to final rest! The prophecy has been exposed! No longer will Orem be held in its thrall! No longer will its spare lines be recited in secret! For this night, the truth is upon us!"

Pausing in his demonic eloquence, Fador surveyed the assembled crowd more closely. He continued in a tone that was somehow intimate for all the force with which it carried as he rasped, *"Crescent reborn . . . to come again . . . "*

Turning toward a contingent of guards standing in a dark corner of the courtyard, Fador signaled them forward. He heard the gasps . . . the shocked cries . . . the sounds of growing dismay . . . the whispers that changed to shouts of enraged protest as the body of the slender, flame-haired woman was carried out into full

371

view and thrown on the ground before them.

Allowing the crowd long moments to observe the lifeless figure, Fador signaled once more, a depraved smile twisting his lips as his guard swept back the woman's shift to reveal the crescent emblazoned on her thigh.

Fador laughed aloud as acute horror swept across the crowd, rebounding over and over again in outraged shouts, sobbing cries, and pitiful laments. Indulging the sounds of mourning, reveling in the might they accorded him, Fador allowed long minutes for the significance of the moment to be seared into the minds of all before signaling his guard a last time. His heart pounding as the ultimate destruction of Neer loomed near, Fador watched as his guard raised the limp female form thrown so callously on the ground minutes earlier, and with a mighty thrust, cast it onto the fire!

Shrieking, weeping, and wailing rose in an uncontrollable swell from the assemblage—grown men sobbing aloud, outrage mixed with sorrow; women sinking to their knees with grief, tears streaming; mothers clutching their babes close with sorrowful desperation that came from the soul; as betwixt and between others tore at their hair and beat their breasts in unrelenting despair.

As Fador watched . . . and listened . . . and indulged the rapture of true triumph over all!

* * *

The echoes of tumultuous despair from the prison courtyard rang through the stone corridors of the prison, reverberating down into the hallways of the dark dungeon below. They rebounded still as a shadow within the dungeon corridor stirred and came to life in the form of Filnor of Rall, who had observed Fador's deadly work, remaining silent while the lifeless female form was carried up to the funeral pyre awaiting it, and the last of his foul deeds was done.

Stepping out into the light, his personal guard behind him, Filnor stared down at the pool of blood on the dungeon floor. He then turned abruptly, signaling his guard to follow as he strode to the last cell on the block and ordered the door opened. He smiled as his guard entered, emerging moments later with a bound, gagged, and furiously struggling Sera of Neer!

"And so, heiress . . ." His dark eyes glowing, Filnor carefully avoided physical contact with Sera as he continued softly, "Once more you owe me your life. Were it not for my foresight in having that useless, red-haired whore thrown into the cell in your place, and for my quick thinking in scraping a crescent mark onto her thigh so Fador might feel secure in his identification, it would be you, not she, who would be enjoying a brilliant funeral pyre."

To the heat of Sera's mumbled reply, Filnor responded, "Instead, we live to love another day, my beloved."

Laughing, Filnor directed his guards to carry his seething captive toward a concealed staircase in the rear of the corridor. Pausing as Sera was thrown over a brawny shoulder, Filnor met her gold eyes, which blazed with wrath.

Struck momentarily breathless at their matchless glory, he took a step closer. His handsome face aglow with the success of the deception he had practiced on his father, Filnor raised his hand to his lips and, with true ardor, blew Sera a kiss.

Tolin walked cautiously through the evening shadows of the street. His broad frame strong and erect, he frowned as Serbaak staggered weakly at his side. He remembered little of the hours most recently past, the time spent in the pale oblivion where he had lain as the slim thread of life remaining within him grew gradually weaker. He recalled only fleeting, unidentifiable specters—and a soft voice whispering indiscernible words of consolation that gave him strength. He remembered that, somehow, he had been *waiting*. His shock had been great when he had awakened from that strange netherworld to find himself lying on his own bier within a zircum mist, Serbaak standing close by as the recollection of Sera's danger returned.

Serbaak stumbled again, but Tolin restrained the urge to support him. Serbaak grew steadily weaker, but he could not afford to call attention to his condition on a street where Fador's spies could be anywhere. He knew Serbaak had risked all for Sera in leaving Orem Minor, and that in doing so, Serbaak had saved his own life as well. Tolin was also aware that the zircum elixir Serbaak needed must be taken soon or he might not survive.

Relieved when the inn finally came into view, Tolin crossed the threshold with Serbaak. He was surprised to hear the sound of a great uproar in the public room. Apprehension crawled up his spine when he saw that opposing factions were arguing with a vehemence that approached the point of rioting.

Turning to an observer nearby, Tolin inquired, "What has occurred to cause such tumult?"

The balding fellow looked up at Tolin with surprise. "Did you not hear? All of Orem is talking about the execution of the Heiress of Neer!"

Stunned, Tolin shook his head as the fellow continued, "Yea, it is a shock indeed! The supporters of Neer have concealed themselves these many years, clinging to the hope of the prophecy's fulfillment. They number many more than Fador realized, and they are incensed that Fador ordered the heiress slain!"

Serbaak swayed beside him, but Tolin was unconscious of the Minor Oremian's distress as the balding fellow continued, "Although there are many who mocked the prophecy, there can be no doubt that the woman was truly the heiress reborn. Her body was dragged from the dungeon and all were forced from the surrounding houses so they might view the crescent emblazoned on her thigh before she was thrown onto a funeral pyre."

Tolin's breathing grew short. His chest heaved. "Nay, it cannot be true!"

"It is true!" The fellow grew adamant as he pointed to a man arguing fiercely nearby. "Tritok witnessed all! He stood within a few feet of the heiress's body before it was consumed!"

Tolin swallowed, an unbearable pain expanding within him. Sera . . . Sera . . .

Unwilling to abandon his tale before it was through, the fellow continued, "Fador himself stood by until naught but ashes remained. He then ordered the ashes gathered and given to him before he rode away in triumph. But word of his despicable act is spreading quickly, and the people are inflamed!"

Tolin was frozen with grief as the turmoil in the public room grew louder, as altercations grew physical and rioting began.

"Tolin . . ."

Turning at the sound of his name, Tolin saw Serbaak stagger. He grasped Serbaak's arm and drew him up the stairs. Entering Serbaak's room moments later, Tolin pushed the door closed behind them. He watched numbly as Serbaak mixed the zircum elixir and drank it down, seeing instead of Serbaak's distinctive Minor Oremian features, the image of an exquisite face framed with fiery hair, eyes as gold and warm as melted honey, and lips that were sweet to the taste, although they spoke with the ring of destiny.

Sera . . . his love, his life, the course of his salvation . . .

Tears streamed down Tolin's cheeks as he sank to the bed. His massive frame rocked with sorrow as he covered his face with his hands, cursing himself and his failure to protect the one he loved more than life itself.

Serbaak's steady hand on his shoulder raised Tolin's gaze slowly to meet his fixed Minor Oremian stare as Serbaak whispered, "Sera is not dead."

Tolin's breath caught in his throat as hope surged to life. "But the reports—they came from witnesses. There can be no error!"

"Sera is alive." Though another spasm of weakness briefly paled his skin, Serbaak continued with unfailing certainty, "I feel Sera's anguish and rage even now. She is alive and well, and she is incited to fury."

Leaping to his feet as life surged anew within him, Tolin rasped a single word in reply.

"Where?"

Serbaak shook his head. "I do not know."

Tolin's expression grew grim as he acknowledged at last the true course destiny had charted for him. His deep voice resounding with hope, with love, and with the full vigor of the life recently restored for that purpose, he whispered, "I will find her."

Chapter Thirteen

How much longer would it take?

Filnor stared at his partially naked reflection in the silvered glass of his room, assessing it critically. Nay, Sera of Neer's continued refusal of him was not caused by his physical appearance, for he was unusually pleasurable to behold. There were few men with hair as black and gleaming as his, and fewer still with features so classically drawn. His brows were well shaped and dark, his eyes and lashes similarly so.

Filnor assessed himself in the broader view. He was taller than most men by a head, and broader of shoulder and chest than most by half again. There were few who met him eye to eye, with the exception of Tolin, who no longer provided competition. As for his more intimate physical qualities . . . Filnor smiled. He was more than ample, and possessed of an expertise that set even the most jaded of women into throes of groaning ecstasy when that was his aim.

His body reacted to the stimulus of his thoughts, and Filnor felt a familiar quiver move down his spine. Yea, that was his aim with the woman who remained confined only a few doorways down the corridor, although she still resisted him.

Filnor resumed his restless pacing. He remembered watching his father covertly as he held the glittering captive flame in his hand. He understood now, for the first time, his father's inability to extinguish the flame that had been Versa of Neer, for it was much the same with him. His fascination with Sera controlled him. He was unable to eject the heiress from his thoughts.

The threads of promised ecstasy entangled him, drawing him in, making his life a misery of frustration each time she was near. He longed to hold her as he had never held her. He longed to taste her mouth, her skin, to explore with full freedom the intimate female delta where he would bring his desire to full fruition. He longed to sink himself deep within her, to linger in the moist, velvet flesh that would enclose him. He longed to fill her with his seed so that he might claim her as his forevermore, so the progeny that would gradually grow within her would tie them together with a bond that could not be severed.

Somehow, he needed that assurance. Somehow, he needed Sera of Neer with a desperation beyond his wildest dreams.

Filnor turned toward his clothes, disdaining his warrior leathers in favor of a robe of royal color, unwilling to admit that he feared the warrior leathers reminded Sera of Tolin and the fate he had brought upon his former comrade-at-arms.

Filnor was fully dressed when he turned to view himself again. He was ready. He would approach Sera in the luxurious prison he had provided for her three days earlier. He would persevere, and he would eventually overcome her resistance to him. The fire that seared his skin each time he attempted to touch her would then cool, and the only fire that would remain would be the flames of passion rising between them. He had time—limitless time to work his amorous designs.

As for Fador . . . Filnor snickered. His omnipotent father was not as wise as he believed himself to be. With his public "eradication" of Neer in a funeral pyre, he had incited the people of Orem Proper against him in a way he never had before.

Fador knew he must proceed carefully in his dealings with the remaining elements of Neer. So appeasing had he become in order to quell the uproar still raging, that he had released the advisors from the dungeons that morning and returned them to a place of public residence where they had full freedom and all might observe that they still lived.

Filnor's snicker grew to laughter. Fador had said that he had done so to demonstrate his munificence. In truth, he had done no more than demonstrate his fear. Filnor would use his father's fear to his advantage. When the time was right, when his seed grew within Sera, he would present her to Fador with the announcement that her threat to the reign of Rall had ceased.

Sera would be truly his then, in the eyes of all.

Filnor breathed deeply against the rapid pounding of his heart. During the time since he had delivered Sera from the prison dungeon to her lavish prison down the hall, while he had been held at bay by the strange spell that seared his flesh each time he touched her, he had tried to relieve his frustration with other women. But his efforts were to no avail. Those who had before stirred him to heated lechery now merely filled him with disgust. He had only one woman in mind.

Filnor forced a smile. He would visit Sera

now. No woman had ever been able to resist him for long. He would win her over, and she would become his loving slave.

Time was in his favor. He would use it well.

Clothes of luxurious silk, lavish furs, magnificent jewelry, extravagance carried to the point of vice—Sera looked around her sumptuous prison, her heart aching. How gladly she would trade the opulence surrounding her for the dampness and filth of her dungeon cell if she could turn back time and return to life the innocent woman who had died in her stead. Even now the sound of the woman's screams lingered in her mind. Yet here she remained, her vision of the great future she would restore to Orem and to the House of Neer dimming more each day.

Tolin . . . Thoughts of him sliced viciously, bleeding her heart dry. Tolin had sacrificed his life to protect her, and a part of her had died with him. How many more would lose their lives in her name before this trial was through?

As for Filnor, would he slay again in his attempt to slake his infinite lust?

A sound in the hallway turned Sera toward the entrance the moment before the doors opened to reveal Filnor standing there. His smiling countenance brought her to her feet, eyes blazing. She waved her arm in a sweeping gesture as she rasped, "This is all for naught! You cannot buy me!"

"Buy you?" Filnor advanced into the room. Sera noted that he kept a few steps from her as he had been wont to do since he had been singed. Were she of a different frame of mind, she might have been amused at the grim irony of captor helpless against captive.

But Sera was not of a different frame of mind. Tolin's face flashed before her anew, as it had looked when the light of life had faded. She closed her eyes at the memory of blood gushing from Tolin's wound, opening them to Filnor's expression of feigned innocence. When she spoke again, her tone was filled with revulsion.

"Surely you cannot think me so much a fool as to believe you do not have ulterior motives for these indulgences you have lavished on me." Looking down at the pale silk garment that lay smoothly against her flesh, Sera sneered. "Had my own simple robe not been taken from me during the night, you would not see me so attired."

Filnor's smile faded. "You are beautiful, Sera. I wish only to see your surroundings reflect your beauty."

"As the policies of Rall slowly choke the life-blood from my people!"

"I told you, I am not responsible for the policies of Rall."

Sera gave a sharp laugh. "So saying, you again hope to deceive me."

Filnor's handsome face grew sober. "I have no wish to deceive . . . only to love."

"Spare me your lies!" Repulsed, Sera added, "Were everything you say true . . . if I truly believed your claims of love . . . even then I would turn my face from you. You are my enemy, Filnor of Rall! You are responsible for Tolin's de—"

"Cease! I will not hear that name on your lips again!" His loving expression abruptly abandoned, Filnor advanced to within a handsbreadth from Sera as he rasped, "Look into my face, Sera. See here the man who will possess you. See here the man who will claim you for his own. See here the man who is content to wait a lifetime to make that claim a reality!" His voice dropping to an intimate, softer note, Filnor continued, "Are *you* willing to wait a lifetime, Sera?"

Stepping back, Sera raised her chin in a manner that was instinctively regal. She replied in a soft voice that nonetheless rang with power.

"I have a voice within me, Filnor of Rall. That voice is the spirit of Versa of Neer, whose time was curtailed by Rall's greed. That voice has guided me and protected me as it does still. With its insistent whisper, it tells me that I have yet great things to accomplish for my people in

Orem, far greater than to become the concubine of the lascivious, corrupt Heir of Rall."

Her voice grew still softer, causing Filnor to strain so he might hear her words. "And even were that not so, even did not that voice remind me of the duties I must yet fulfill, I tell you now that I would gladly sacrifice the last light of life within me rather than spend a single moment of intimacy in your arms."

Filnor stepped back abruptly, as if struck. His chest heaved with the passion of his words.

"So say you after you have bewitched me! So say you after you have raised within me a yearning for you so strong that it dominates my every thought! So say you after you have driven all thought of other glory from my mind, save the glory which would be ours, together, if you were mine!"

Visibly quaking, Filnor closed the short distance between them. He breathed deeply of Sera's breath as it brushed his lips, taking it inside him as he deliberately reached out to grasp her hand.

Sera saw Filnor's pain as their hands met. She smelled his searing flesh. She sought to withdraw her hand from his as much to spare him the scorching she could not control as to escape the distress of his touch, but he would not allow it. Instead, he held her hand tight, his teeth clenched against the pain for moments longer.

Releasing her at last, Filnor held his hand up to her view. A tight smile dawned as she winced at the sight of the raw burns there. Filnor spoke as softly as had she, looking into the golden glow of her eyes. "I bear this wound gladly for the joy of touching you, even briefly. Do not underestimate my fortitude, Sera of Neer. Whatever your inner voice advises, you will be *mine*."

Gone in a moment, Filnor left Sera silent in his wake. She knew in her heart that the prediction he voiced would never come to pass, and yet . . .

Quietly observing in her place of concealment in the corridor outside Sera's chamber, Kiray drew back. She saw the door open as Filnor emerged from the red-haired witch's rooms. Jealousy swelled within her as Filnor turned to the guard at the door, instructing him in low tones before proceeding down the hallway.

Kiray followed Filnor with a longing gaze, her pain increasing. She loved him. She had always loved him. She wanted nothing more than to please him so he would keep her with him, but he was through with her. He had told her so with his words, with his fists, and with the cruel strike of his boot as she had lain prostrate before him.

Kiray stiffened. She knew who the woman was! She was the witch who was supposed to have been cremated in the funeral pyre, the pretended Heiress of Neer who caused Orem Proper to be torn with strife! Filnor had tricked Fador, faking her death. He now felt safe concealing the woman.

Kiray's lips tightened as her jealousy slashed deeper. She knew what had progressed behind those locked doors from which Filnor had just emerged. She could picture Filnor in her mind, his broad, naked frame shuddering, his skin moist with passion as he plunged his eager member into the witch again and again.

Nay! If Filnor did not want her, neither would he have this new mistress for whom he risked his father's rancor! Yea, he would have neither of them!

She would see to it!

With quick, silent steps, Kiray was gone as secretly as she had come.

"Trust you?"

Nako drew his frail frame erect. He and the other advisors had been delivered from their dungeon cell to a residence in one of the better sectors of Orem Proper that morning. They had been installed within public view by Fador's guards and had been accorded full freedom of movement, as well as all the comforts they could desire. But they took little joy in their new liberties.

The Heiress of Neer had disappeared.

In a painful quandary, the advisors had conferred, uncertain what to do. They dared not take any steps that might betray the trick that Filnor had played on Fador. They dared not allow a hint of the truth to be divulged.

But what was the truth? Always volatile in personality, Filnor had become devious and unpredictable as well. In spiriting Sera away only a scant hour before Fador arrived in the dungeons looking for her and installing an innocent woman there to be killed in her stead, he had left them ignorant of the heiress's true fate.

Where had Filnor taken Sera of Neer? What were his intentions?

Was the precious jewel of Neer still alive?

Oh, the anguish of uncertainty!

His weary heart aching at his ineffectiveness, Nako had silently prayed to the greater presence that guided all to send them a deliverer.

Nako shuddered.

Yea, but not *this* deliverer!

Nako gazed at the great, pale-haired warrior who stood before him, the man who had slipped into their residence unobserved and now stood before Nako with an unidentified, hooded man at his rear, demanding their confidence.

Tolin of Rall.

Nako shuddered again. The same eyes now staring into his had emotionlessly viewed the unpardonable carnage wrought by his blade in Rall's name.

Trust him, he had said.

"Trust you?" His thoughts forming into words without his conscious intent, Nako repeated the question, then shook his head. "Nay . . . nay, we cannot!"

"Fool!" Tolin took an angry step forward that deepened Nako's frown. "You know as well as I that Sera of Neer lives!"

Nako responded with spontaneous denial. "She has been slain! Her funeral pyre burned long into the night!"

"I will not tell you how I know Sera of Neer lives and that she now suffers great distress. I will only say that I know it is true beyond doubt—as well as I know that there is only one place she can be."

Nako glanced at the other advisors clustered nearby. They were as disturbed as he as he responded, "I know nothing of what you speak."

"I will not play this asinine game while Sera remains Filnor's prisoner and is subject to the caprice of his perverted whims!" Tolin halted, swallowing tightly. Nako was almost tempted to believe the cold-eyed warrior suffered at the thought of the heiress's danger as Tolin continued with a new harshness in his voice, "Were circumstances different, I would not deign to solicit your aid! I would storm Filnor's residence with only my blade as my companion, but Filnor's treachery demands caution. It demands that I raise a force equal to any Filnor might throw against me if I am to liberate Sera without any chance of harm coming to her."

"What makes you think I can help you raise the force you seek?"

Tolin's expression grew fierce. "Enough of these evasions! A word from you and the loyalists of Neer will rise! You waste time while at this very moment Sera may be at the point of Filnor's sword!"

"Nay . . . Sera is yet alive and well."

All eyes turned toward the hooded man who stepped out from behind Tolin, addressing Nako for the first time. Struck by a familiar chord in his tone that somehow ignited hope anew within him, Nako watched in silence as the man threw back his hood to reveal unmistakable Minor Oremian features. He met the man's fixed gaze as the fellow questioned, "Do you know me, Nako?"

Nako caught his breath with disbelief. "Could it be . . . is it truly you, Alpor?"

"Nay, not Alpor, but Serbaak."

"Serbaak . . ." Nako blinked, recalling the night the destination of a fugitive babe had been determined. The babe had been sent to the only place, to the only *one* who could be entrusted with the endangered Heiress of Neer—

391

Alpor of Orem Minor, who had one son, Serbaak.

Nako's throat grew tight. "Yea, I know you."

Serbaak swayed. He stayed Nako's responsive step toward him. "Nay, I need not your aid. Rather it is to Tolin you must lend your support."

"Tolin . . ." Nako glanced again at the leather-clad warrior. "This man who serves Rall?"

Serbaak shook his head. "Nay, this man who is renewed in the service of *Neer*."

"How can we be sure?"

"Trust him." Serbaak swayed again, but his determination did not falter as he rasped, "With the last of my fading strength, I entreat you to believe this man, for the future of Neer lies in the balance."

Nako glanced back at the massive warrior of Rall. Tolin's hard features were controlled, his gaze unyielding, as unyielding as death.

Nako shook his head. "I cannot!"

"You must!"

"Nay!"

The heated exchange continued.

Fador's enmity swelled as Zor stood in his chambers once more. A taste as bitter as bile rose in his throat. Orem Proper was in a state of turmoil as never before. His judgment had been faulty in forcing public witness to the final annihilation of Neer. Fador knew that now. But he needed no one, most especially this ancient fool, to question the wisdom of his actions!

The frail seer stood silent and resolute, and Fador's hatred soared. He knew, as he had always known, where the true threat to his rule lay. It had never been Neer, or even the flame reborn. Neither had it been his son, whose arrogance and conceit far outweighed his cunning or discretion. Instead, it lay in this robed figure who sought to control Rall with the power of his visions as his mentor had before him. But this time the man had gone too far in calling false a truth Fador had witnessed with his own eyes!

Fador swept Zor with a contemptuous gaze. "You have grown old! Your powers are as confused as your aging mind! She is dead, I tell you! I watched her blood drain onto the floor of that filthy dungeon and I saw her body consumed by flames! The Heiress of Neer threatens Rall no more!"

"You err, Fador. The red-haired one lives."

"Err? You say that *I* err—*I*, who with the final destruction of Neer have made myself invincible? It is *you* who errs, old man!"

Unable to abide Zor's piercing perusal a moment longer, Fador shouted, "Get out of my sight! Go back to your cobweb-filled cave and misty crystal and leave Orem's reign to me! You have outlived your usefulness. I need you no longer!"

Zor's continued scrutiny raised Fador's rage to new heights.

A solemn decision abruptly made, Fador declared in a voice trembling with hatred, "Hear me now, Zor of the Decrepit Seeing Eye! This is my final word. With this last assault on my judgment, you have overstepped your authority for the last time. I will suffer your insolence no longer! From this moment on, you are barred from the royal chambers. You are dismissed from the service of Rall—now and forever!"

Fador's irreverence for the power that had served him so well raised a flush to Zor's wrinkled face. The ancient seer replied in a voice that was soft despite the grave warning it conveyed.

"Think what you say, Fador. A step of this magnitude, once taken, cannot—*will not*—be retraced."

"You do not frighten me with your threats!" Fador did not attempt to conceal his fury. "Go! And remember—if you breathe a word of your foolish visions to anyone, if you stir anew hope that the Heiress of Neer lives, the words you speak in that regard will be your last!"

Zor turned away without response.

Incited to new heights of ire at Zor's unaffected facade, Fador shouted after him, "Feebleminded necromancer! I need you no longer!"

Laughing wildly, Fador watched with great satisfaction as Zor left his chamber, drawing the door softly closed behind him.

Zor paused, listening to the click of Fador's door as it resounded in the empty corridor. The finality of the sound touched the aged sorcerer with both sadness and a growing sense of outrage as he drew his thin frame slowly erect.

So Fador would mock his service to Rall and dismiss him forevermore, would he? Fool that Fador was, in so doing he had put Rall in greater jeopardy than it had ever known!

A rustle of movement in the corridor behind Zor interrupted his thoughts. A tight, knowing smile touched his lips, for he knew the identity of the person concealed in the shadows. He turned, head high, and started back down the corridor. It had not been the revealingly sweet scent which betrayed the one hiding there. Rather, the scent had been a silent confirmation.

Yea, the destiny which had become inevitable with Fador's dismissal of him drew steadily closer.

His step unwavering, Zor continued down the hall. The shadows behind him shifted as a slender form moved toward Fador's door and slipped over the threshold through which Zor would never pass again.

* * *

"You dare come to me with the same preposterous tale I have just dismissed—that the Heiress of Neer lives?"

Kiray watched in terrified silence as Fador grew livid. It occurred to her as she stood craven before her sovereign in the silence of his chambers that she had not realized how true was the resembling between the royal father and son. Nor had she anticipated that the mention ofthe Heiress of Neer would raise the same, fierce emotions in the father as in the son—or that in coming, she would place her life in danger.

That realization suddenly acute, Kiray proceeded cautiously, "It is true, Master Fador! She is alive! I saw her! Filnor spirited the true heiress from the dungeon and substituted another in her place because he lusts for her and wishes to save her from your threat. He now entertains the heiress regally in his quarters, to the exclusion of all others!"

"You lie!"

"By my life, I do not!"

"By your life, indeed!" Fador's eyes darkened with wrath as Kiray cowered before him, as his gaze traveled her trembling form with contempt. "You are the one known as Kiray, are you not?" At Kiray's nod, he continued, "So, my son's faithful whore betrays him to his father out of a need for vengeance."

Fador's jaw twitched. "Strangely, it is for that

reason that I am inclined to give your tale more credence than I do the ramblings of the addled fool who just departed."

Her gaze riveted on the lines of evil gradually deepening in Fador's countenance, Kiray felt a new quaking beset her as he continued, "Yea, I will visit my son with a full contingent of guards, and I will test your truth. In the meantime, you will wait for me in quarters befitting your service to the House of Rall."

Relief flashed briefly through Kiray the moment before Fador's lips tightened into a sneer. A quick pull of the wall cord nearby produced two sober guards whom Fador commanded sharply, "Take this woman to the dungeon cell vacated by the heiress. Confine her there. If the heiress lives as she says, she may remain in the quarters she has earned for the rest of her days. If the heiress is indeed dead, execute her!"

"Nay!"

Kiray's gasping protest turned Fador viciously back toward her.

"Did you expect more? The payment you receive befits your duplicity. It is my hope that you will enjoy that which you have earned."

The guard's hand fell heavily upon Kiray's shoulder as she stood shaken to the soul. Dragged from Fador's chambers pleading for mercy, the stunned whore realized with dismay that Fador had already forgotten her.

* * *

Filnor strapped on his sword, then adjusted his fur-trimmed robe across his shoulders. He glanced toward the window of his chamber at the sound of horses' hooves in the courtyard below. The coach had arrived at last.

Filnor looked out through his window at a sky where the last streaks of sun had set the horizon aglow with color. Night would soon fall, and with it the milder temperature of the day. It occurred to him that by the time they reached the secluded dwelling he had prepared for Sera in a deeply forested quarter of Orem Proper, it would be well into night, but that bothered him little. He would enjoy traveling with Sera beside him. He would revel in the time allotted him to continue his gentle courting.

The unwelcome memory of Sera's grief for Tolin briefly intruded, and Filnor frowned. During the time they passed in their new environs, he would gradually indoctrinate his beautiful heiress to the reality of his love for her. He would win her over and she would submit to him freely, thereby nullifying the force that singed him. He was as certain of that inevitability as he was that he had been born to rule, and that Sera had been born to be his.

That thought invigorating him, Filnor emerged into the corridor moments later. Clutching the elaborate fur cloak he had ordered fashioned for Sera, he signaled the contingent of guards waiting there to fall in behind him as he continued toward her chamber.

The door opened as Filnor arrived. He smiled as the serving woman he had dispatched earlier escorted Sera into the corridor beside him. He wrapped the lavish cloak around Sera's proud shoulders, careful not to touch her. Though she remained stiffly unresponsive, he took pleasure in the way the lush, amber-tinted fur enhanced her beauty. His desire for her, never dormant, surged to an aching hunger as he spoke.

"A coach awaits in the courtyard. Our life together will soon begin."

The glaring heat in Sera's gaze was a stinging response to his loving words. Smarting, Filnor responded directly, with a confidence meant to stab her in return.

"You will change, and you will love me, despite your present scorn. I tell you that with full conviction because I, as Rall's heir, will allow it no other way."

Signaling his guards to usher Sera along at his side, Filnor turned toward the staircase below. He knew the tack Sera now pursued. She hoped to antagonize him so he would cast her aside, but she would not succeed. He was a new Filnor, a man who saw his future clearly for the first time. Sera's face shone in that future like a jewel in the sun.

His jewel.

His treasure.

His alone.

Filnor stepped down onto the staircase, aware that Sera had not spoken a word, but secure in the knowledge that with or without Sera's accord, he now took the first step in the true vanquishing of Neer.

Despairing, Sera walked rigidly at Filnor's side, the rough hands of the guards determining her course. Three long, endless days were winding down into another night, yet there was no relief from the nightmare to which she had awakened in Filnor's chambers. The voice within had remained constant, but it somehow grew more dim with each step she now took toward her unknown destination.

Sera's mind silently railed. Surely it had not been meant to be thus! Surely she could not have met Tolin, could not have lain in his arms to become so much a part of him that their souls had joined, only to be sacrificed to the lust of Rall! Surely there had been a greater purpose in the melting of the ice that had encased Tolin's heart than to have his heart cease its beating within her view! Surely, the supreme wisdom that guided all had not intended that the love Tolin and she shared should end at the premature moment when Tolin's eyes had closed forever!

Sera's step faltered. The grip on her arms tightened, and anger replaced Sera's former despair.

And surely she was not meant to be led to the fate Filnor had decreed without the protest expected of the Heiress of Neer! In so surrendering, she profaned the memory of all who had suffered and died for Neer!

Nay! She would not profane them, at any cost!

Jerking suddenly backwards against the strong hands that restrained her, Sera shouted, "Let me go!"

"Do not be a fool, Sera!" Annoyed, Filnor signaled his men to a temporary halt. "You may walk to the carriage waiting below, or you may be delivered there. You may spend the next hours of traveling comfortably seated, or you may spend them bound. In any case, your ultimate arrival at the destination intended is assured. The choice is yours."

Furious at Filnor's autocratic tone, Sera pulled her arms unexpectedly forward, slipping the grip of the guards and darting down the staircase toward the courtyard below.

Breathless, her heart pounding, Sera was halfway down the winding stone staircase when she was caught from behind and jerked back to face an angry guard. Thrown roughly over his shoulder at Filnor's command, she fought fiercely, pounding at the guard's back with her fists and shrieking as he continued down the stairs.

The guard placed her on her feet when they reached the bottom of the stairs, and Sera turned to face Filnor. She read the intention in his gaze the moment before he raised his hand to strike her—the moment before a heart-stoppingly familiar voice resounded in the stillness of the yard.

"Strike her and you die where you stand!"

Sera gasped, incredulous as Tolin stepped out of the shadows a short distance away. Tall and straight he was, whole and exuding the menace of old as the setting sun glinted on his pale hair, and his light eyes glowed eerily!

Trembling, hoping with all her heart that the image she saw was not merely a specter fashioned by need, Sera was stunned into speechlessness as a soft chanting began in the shadows. The echo surrounded them, growing gradually in volume until it became a throbbing chorus of the name "Neer" repeated over and again until the courtyard rang with the sound!

A spark of joy grew to full flame within Sera. She remained motionless as armed loyalists stepped into sight and moved to form ranks at Tolin's rear.

Filnor paled. His shock was apparent as Tolin sneered, "Nay, Filnor, I am not an apparition from the dead. Did you not realize that the hand of Rall, of the house I served so long and well, would be powerless to end my life in so cowardly a manner?" Tolin's laughter was harsh. "Instead, the blow struck from behind that would have taken the life of another man, merely cast me into a breathless sleep, where I lay awaiting the proper vessel to heal me and to help me rise once more."

Transported from shock to fury in the space of a moment, Filnor rasped in return, "Specter or flesh and blood, this time you *will* die!"

"Halt your advance, Filnor!" Tolin commanded. "Look around you! Our force is superior to yours in number. You cannot win. Surrender the heiress and order your men to put down their arms so they will not be needlessly slain!"

Sera saw the hatred behind Filnor's slowly dawning smile as he responded, "You will take this woman from me in no other way."

Revolted at the slaughter about to ensue, Sera called out, "Enough blood has already been shed. I will see no more!"

"Nay, you have not seen nearly enough!" Filnor turned toward Sera, his gaze impassioned. "There is no price too high to pay to attain ultimate glory. *You* are that glory, heiress! Tolin knows that as well as I, and I will not surrender that final victory to him until the last life has been spent—until the last drop of blood has flowed—until I can no longer raise my arm in defense of my possession of you—*you* who are meant to be *mine!*"

Directing his next words to the guards restraining her, Filnor ordered, "Take the woman and hold her back!"

Struggling as the guards dragged her relentlessly backward, kicking and scratching, Sera saw only the hand Filnor raised to signal his men's advance. She shouted out again in protest, but the sound was overwhelmed by an unexpected voice thundering from the rear of the courtyard.

"So, it is true!"

All turned as Fador strode boldly into their midst, his personal guard marching at his flank as a wall of Rall warriors surrounded the courtyard and those within.

Halting a few feet from the two adversaries, Fador addressed Filnor in a tone filled with loathing.

"Betrayed by my own son!"

"Yea, Father, betrayed as you would betray me!"

Ignoring his son's response, Fador turned toward Sera. Remembered passion flickered briefly in his eyes as he rasped, "In seeing you now, it confounds my mind how I could have believed for a moment that the red-haired whore who met her end in the dungeon was of

Versa's spirit. You are exquisite, like your mother before you."

His gaze gradually hardening, Fador continued, "And like your mother before you, you have bewitched the heir of Rall with desire for you. But this time you will get more than you bargained for, heiress! In bewitching my son, you will achieve nothing more than carnage worthy of Rall itself!"

At Tolin's sudden, aggressive step toward him, Fador warned, "Stop there if you do not wish to see your heiress slain before your eyes! My archers have her in their sights."

Tolin glanced toward the perimeter of the courtyard, where Fador's archers stood with bows drawn. He turned back to Fador with a warning growl.

"This I vow, Fador of Rall—if the heiress is harmed in any way, there will be no force in Orem or beyond that will save you from my wrath."

Fador's sudden burst of laughter rang in the silence. "So, you too desire the Flame of Neer!" He laughed again, appearing to enjoy the dark humor of his thoughts as he continued, "But only one can have her. What is the answer? A fight to the death?"

"Only a fool celebrates annihilation!" Tolin's words were harsh with challenge. "I offer you another solution, one more worthy of two royal houses."

Fador's smile grew tight. "A solution?"

"A personal contest between Filnor and me—with the provision that should I win, I will meet you, or your champion, to determine whether Orem will go forward under the rule of Rall or Neer!"

Fador turned slowly, stretching out the tense silence before facing his son. "What say you, Filnor? You have always claimed yourself superior to Tolin in combat. An opportunity is at hand to prove your boasting. Do you accept the challenge?"

"On one condition." Filnor glanced at Sera with hot intensity. "When I win, the woman is *mine*."

Fador's expression grew sinister. "For what purpose?"

"For whatever purpose I wish!"

Fador went completely still, pausing long moments as a myriad of emotions flashed across his face. He spoke a single word in response.

"Done."

The battle lines shifted as Tolin stepped forward, sword drawn. Filnor turned to face him.

Sera struggled against the guards' restraining grip as the combatants moved into position, shouting, "Nay! I will not allow this contest in my name!"

"You do not command here, heiress!" Fador's snarl betrayed his unyielding malice. "Enjoy—

for indeed, the entertainment provided this day may yet be your last!"

Facing the combatants once more, Fador eyed the battle lines so clearly drawn: the loyalists of Neer standing grim-faced and determined in support of Tolin, Filnor's personal guard stationed unyieldingly at his back, and Fador's own troops—the superior force in number—surrounding all.

Fador raised his hand in the awaited signal.

Tolin stood with Filnor, swords crossed. He felt the intensity of Sera's gaze upon him. He knew she did not fear for herself in the contest about to begin, that her concern was for him and all who might suffer in any combat to come. A bloodless coup had been her aim, yet he had known that her wish could never be fulfilled.

Sera, whom he loved above all . . .

Fador's hand fell in command.

"Begin!"

Filnor's sword crashed heavily against Tolin's blade. Blocking the blow, Tolin leaped back under the ferocity of Filnor's attack, seeing a blood lust in his former friend's eyes that he recognized well.

And in that moment Tolin knew that the contest was to the death.

* * *

Thrust, parry!
Lunge, retreat!

The scrape of heavy footsteps against the cobbled courtyard!

The clash of blades became a resounding din that reverberated harshly in Sera's mind, as a scene she had witnessed once before was replayed before her horrified eyes.

Tolin, his face soberly tight.

Filnor, his expression filled with demonic fury.

Strength against strength.

Skill against skill.

Two sides of the same coin, evenly matched.

First blood!

Sera gasped aloud as Filnor clutched his forearm briefly, then swung powerfully in retaliation.

Jab . . . repulse . . .

Sera gasped again as Filnor's sword swiped at Tolin's thigh, letting blood there and sending Tolin staggering backward under a renewed assault.

Her heart pounding, her breathing short, Sera struggled against the hands that held her captive. She needed to stop this savage encounter! She needed to halt this potential slaughter! She needed—

A scream of terror rose to Sera's throat as Tolin's foot slipped on a slick stone. Unbalanced, he staggered under Filnor's attack. Another slip, and Tolin fell to the ground, the sword flying from his hand!

Sera saw Filnor's face in that moment of supreme power.

She saw his smile.

She saw his glee.

She saw him swing his sword mightily, his blade arcing out toward the defenseless Tolin.

Rolling so suddenly to the side that he appeared no more than a flash of light in the darkening twilight, Tolin emerged on his feet again, sword in hand!

Slashing, clashing, forcing Filnor steadily backward under his driving attack, Tolin was a relentless weapon of destruction that would not be denied!

Death's Shadow . . .

Sera closed her eyes, only to snap them open a moment later as a loud gasp rang out in unison from the spectators, as the clash of swords ceased, as Tolin stood over the fallen Filnor, his sword pressed to Filnor's heart!

Silence reigned in the shadowed courtyard.

With his blade pressed against Filnor's breast, Tolin felt his own heart begin a thunderous pounding. His blood surged hotly. A single thrust and it would be done!

Hatred flashed in Filnor's eyes, but Tolin remembered days long past.

Friendship . . .

Companionship . . .

Warmth . . .

All had dissipated in the donning of warrior's leathers and the wash of blood that had followed.

"Thrust the blade home!"

Snapped from his daze by Fador's harsh command, Tolin glanced up. Fador's countenance was rabid as he approached, his expression so coldly vicious as to appear almost bestial.

"Thrust the blade home, I say!" he shouted again. "It is a contest well won!"

Tolin's gaze narrowed as he saw in a flash of sudden insight the man he might have become.

Nay, nevermore.

Turning his back on Fador with slow deliberation, Tolin lowered his blade and extended his hand to Filnor.

Filnor stared. Incredulity, resentment, then relief registered in his expression as he reached for Tolin's hand.

The rush of footsteps behind him turned Tolin to see a heavy sword descending! Reacting spontaneously, he twisted to the side and thrust his blade upward, feeling the moment of contact and swift penetration as Fador was impaled upon his sword!

Standing over the fallen Fador, Tolin was not conscious of the long moment of silence before the stunned warriors of Rall lowered their weapons to the ground. Nor was he aware of

Dance of the Flame

the moment when Filnor's guard followed suit. Instead, Tolin heard only Sera's voice as she called out his name and rushed to his side. He felt only the joy of holding her safe in his arms once more, while beside him, Filnor fell to his knee beside his dying father.

Fador's chamber was dimly lit by tapers as his life slowly slipped away. Standing beside his pallet, Sera, Tolin, and Filnor, with Serbaak nearby, heard the rasp of Fador's labored breathing as he awaited death.

The shadows of hatred still burning in his fading gaze, Fador addressed Tolin with a weak smile that was strangely demonic.

"It is time for the final reckoning. You, Tolin, who have dealt me the fatal blow, believe you have vanquished Rall, but you have not. It is I, Fador, to whom the final victory belongs. With great pleasure I tell you now that while you live, Tolin, Champion of Neer, Neer ever stands under the threat of Rall. That same threat will keep your beloved heiress forever from your arms!"

The uncertainty and apprehension his words had stirred drew a virulent rattle of laughter from Fador's throat as he rasped, "Did you never guess, Tolin? Did you never wonder that you were pressed into the service of Rall immediately upon the death of your mother when

411

you were still a child? Did you never puzzle that you were accorded the same education as Filnor, the same privileges and advantages—everything but the name of Rall?"

Tolin's face drained of color as Fador's feeble laughter sounded again.

"The blood of Rall flows in your veins, Tolin! *My* blood—the same blood you have shed this night! I saw in you, my illegitimate son, a greatness the son of my wedded wife would never display! I could not send you away."

"Nay! That cannot be!"

Sera's spontaneous denial turned Fador toward her with obvious satisfaction. "Yea, heiress. Proof may be found in the birth records locked in the vaults of Orem. You have but to read to confirm my claim."

Watching as incredulity became belief on the faces of those surrounding him, Fador was suddenly exultant. "My death is my triumph! The threat of Rall remains! It is a dark cloud that will forever overshadow the 'glorious destiny' of Neer rule!"

The heat of Fador's gaze shifted to Tolin once more. "As for you, *my son*, the blood that flows through your veins will forever keep you from ruling beside the woman you love! It is fitting, is it not? As the father was denied, so shall be the son!"

Blood welled at the corner of Fador's mouth

with his choking laughter. It trickled down to stain his pillow as Fador enjoyed his sweet revenge.

The stunned silence that followed was broken as Sera addressed Fador stiffly. "The combat this night between the champions of Rall and Neer was legal and binding. It named Neer as the ruling house of Orem. Are you agreed, Fador?"

Fador gasped for breath, his dimming eyes suspicious to the last as he gasped, "You know that to be true."

Sera's eyes flashed. "By the power granted me this night through that mortal combat, and as heiress to the throne, I, Sera of Neer, demand the return of the Royal Vessel of Neer that was taken by you at the time of conquest."

Fador did not immediately respond. "The Royal Vessel . . . containing the Sacred Scroll of Neer?" He took a painful breath, his weak smile returning. "So, you would give me the ultimate victory. . . ."

Fador turned toward his legitimate heir, his strength visibly fading. "Filnor . . . in the desk . . . a key in the secret drawer . . ."

His expression sober, Filnor moved to the desk nearby, a twin of the one in the tower room where the key to the barred niche had been hidden so long ago. He pressed the hinge and the drawer sprang open to reveal a small brass key. He turned back as Fador rasped, "A loose stone in the far wall . . . the box hidden there . . . quickly . . ."

His expression sober, Filnor obeyed, returning with the locked box he found there.

Sera inserted the key into the lock and raised the lid to reveal a jewel-encrusted sheath within.

Reaching into the box, Sera took the sheath into her hands. Her heart began a rapid pounding as she repeated the words of the ancient prophecy.

Spirit of Neer confined in flame
Crescent reborn to come again,
Vessel to seek, wherein the key
To bring the House of Rall to knee

Fador's voice cut into her recitation, severing the thread of joy which had begun unwinding as he hissed, "The sheath is empty!"

Sera gasped. "Empty?"

"The scroll within crumbled into dust when I took it into my hand those many years ago!" Fador's evil glee was triumphant. "The secret of the final subjugation of Rall is lost forever!"

Sera's color drained. She closed her eyes as a litany of lament began in her mind.

To have come so far . . .

To have risked so much . . .

To have loved so deeply . . .

. . . for naught.

414

Nay.

The jeweled sheath warmed unexpectedly beneath Sera's palms as the faint echo of a familiar voice reverberated in her mind. Its heat swelled within her as the whispered words grew louder. The sound expanded until a sweet, familiar voice rang purposefully clear with a message heard by her alone.

Opening eyes that glittered with new brilliance, Sera walked to the corner of the room where Serbaak stood silently observing. She reached for the flask at her loyal friend's waist. Uncapping it, she sprinkled the last of Serbaak's zircum dust on the jeweled sheath.

With trembling fingers, Sera then unbuckled the sheath . . . to find a fragile scroll inside.

Fador's incredulous, dying gasp went unheard as Tolin and Filnor left his bedside to join Sera. They stood beside her when she withdrew the scroll and read her mother's words:

"To Sera, the daughter of my spirit,

My love to you, daughter. I have seen you only in visions, but I know you well. Your name, and the images which accompanied its revelation, have grown ever clearer. Your destiny has been revealed to me. This gift, normally bestowed upon the ruler of Neer only upon the birth of her heiress, is mine now because I will never walk the path fate decreed for me. My destiny was altered by the lust of Fador of Rall when he destroyed he who would make my power absolute.

I will not write the name of the man who was born to bring my life to full fruition, for he passed into the light to await me before you could be conceived. He was the man destined to rule beside me, the father you will never know. His name was written upon a scroll such as this and was revealed to me upon my coming of age.

As you must realize by now, my daughter, in each generation the revelation of the man destined to procreate the ruling progeny, to cause the royal crescent to be reborn, is the key to Neer's perpetual rule.

My dear Sera, as your destiny was decreed before you were conceived, the man who would make your power absolute, he who would procreate the next Heiress of Neer, was in like manner decreed.

I ask you not to question the predestination which comes to you as your inheritance. I ask you not to decry the fate which has mandated that through you, the blood of Neer shall be blended with that of Rall. You must accept, whether the decision fills you with sorrow or joy, for you must fulfill your destiny.

Rejoice in your glorious future, Sera, and in the peace which you are fated to bring to Orem! It is my gift to you. Do not look back in sorrow, but look forward to that which will be. And know that your glorious destiny forever lies with

TOLIN

My spirit will be with you always, daughter, as will be my love.

Your mother,
Versa of Neer."

The letters of Tolin's name glittered on the delicate parchment with a familiar emerald glow. In the stunned silence that followed, Sera looked up at Tolin to see her incredulous joy reflected in his gaze as well.

Standing hands and hearts joined as unspoken words of love flowed between them in a pledge as solemn as a vow, they celebrated in silent wonder the knowledge that so it had been meant to be, and so Sera and Tolin would reign, for all their glorious destiny.

* * *

Zor moved softly through the concealed entrance to Fador's suite that he had used countless times before. Unnoticed, he stood in the shadows, scrutinizing the three men who stood near the new ruler of Orem—she who had been awaited by so many.

Tolin, his arm around Sera of Neer, stood proudly and lovingly beside her, as they would rule.

Serbaak, loyal confidant of Neer, regarded them with peace in his fixed, Minor Oremian stare.

Filnor . . .

Zor's brow furrowed. Filnor's gaze lingered on Sera of Neer with excessive warmth. The heat in Filnor's look did not escape Tolin, and Zor unconsciously nodded. Opposite sides of the same coin were Tolin and Filnor. Opposite sides of the same coin they would always be.

Dismissing those disturbing thoughts, Zor turned to Fador's lifeless form. He had but one final duty to perform.

His faded eyes aglow with irony, Zor withdrew an iridescent crystal vessel from the bag at his waist and placed it over the heart of Fador which beat no more. He raised a gnarled hand to the darker power which had served him many times before, closing his eyes as he began reciting an ancient incantation. Fador's lifeless body twitched in the throes of progressing bewitchment as Zor's soft chant continued. The spasms grew more erratic, more violent, halting abruptly as a black flame burst to life within the sealed crystal!

Opening his eyes to find Sera and Tolin beside him, Serbaak and Filnor close by, Zor took the crystal and placed it in Sera's hands. Years of service to Rall tinged his tone with regret as he spoke.

"This is my wedding gift to you, heiress. It is similar to the gift I gave Fador many years ago when he assumed rule of Orem. Fador cherished the Flame of Neer and the spirit it held captive, but that spirit was too strong for him to deny. His ineffectiveness against it led to all that has now come to pass."

Pausing, Zor studied the heiress's sober face. Beautiful it was, as had been her mother's before her. He read her heart and found it pure. As for the man who stood beside her . . .

Zor hesitated. Eyes as cold as ice scrutinized him in return. But within that frozen stare was . . .

Yea, he read love.

Meeting the glowing gold of the heiress's gaze, Zor warned, "Guard this captive flame well, heiress. The fulfillment of your destiny now lies in it, where the spirit of Fador lives."

Turning away, Zor did not see Tolin take the

crystal from Sera's hands. Nor did he see Tolin hold it securely, protectively apart from Sera . . . in fulfillment of that which was meant to be.

Epilogue

The royal assembly room was filled to bursting. Petitioners, complainants, well-wishers, advisors, all speaking at once, raised a din that temporarily drowned out the words of the page who sought to identify the next in line.

Clad in a simple amber robe, Sera sat on the throne with Tolin standing beside her, where he had chosen to remain all the years of their life. She was the magnificent personification of the flame, all the more glorious in having become flesh and blood, and she was her people's savior.

Sera contemplated the many changes that had come about in Orem since the decisive day of the courtyard battle between Rall and Neer.

Serbaak had returned to Orem Minor with haste, due to his rapidly deteriorating condition. She missed him dreadfully.

Filnor had been dispatched with a sentence that suited the unexpected revelations unveiled that day. She missed him not at all.

The army had been liberated from the ruthless policies of Rall and from officers who had pursued them with malice of intent. A strong, fair command prevailed.

Steps had been taken to alleviate the want suffered at every level of Orem by elimination of the practices Fador had initiated to develop a consistent level of dependency among the populace.

The contents of the great zircum warehouses had again been made generally available to the people. All unnecessary restrictions had been removed so they might again use the precious substance to enhance the heat of their fires, the fruit of their fields, and the progress of their daily lives, as it was meant to be.

The prisons had been emptied of political prisoners.

Rescinded freedoms had been reinstated.

The reaction of the people had been an immediate upsurging of energy and hope that had added a new vibrancy in every quarter of the land. Orem was revitalizing, yet more time was needed to further develop plans that the advisors, Tolin, and Sera had hastily drawn.

Sera turned toward the pale-haired warrior

standing beside her. Amazement struck her anew that it had taken her so long to recognize the innate nobility of character so obvious in the carriage of Tolin's broad shoulders, and in the tilt of a strong jaw that signified an inner strength and integrity that Fador had temporarily suppressed but had not been successful in extinguishing despite his greatest efforts. In retrospect, she supposed the lifelessness in Tolin's eyes had distracted her from immediate recognition, a lifelessness that was now gone forever—although his present demeanor revealed a definite waning of forbearance.

An amused smile tempered Sera's expression as she addressed Tolin softly.

"The people of Orem have come alive again."

Tolin leaned close. His pale hair brushed her fiery locks as he whispered, "Yea, heiress, so much so that I fear the throne will never know a minute's peace again."

Sera's smile faded at Tolin's sober response. " 'Tis only the first month of my reign. Do you grow weary of the travails of rule so soon, Tolin?"

Tolin's gaze dropped revealingly to Sera's lips. "I grow weary only of the time wasted that we might even now be spending together."

"Together?"

"Yea, heiress." Tolin moved closer. The familiar masculine scent of him teased Sera's nostrils with remembered intimacy as his whisper deepened. "The distance enforced between us until the customary betrothal period elapses chafes sorely. It has been my thought the morning long that in this confusion, there are few here who would notice if you and I were to slip away, to return in a week's time when the advisors have had an opportunity to better organize the manner in which petitions are to be presented."

Tolin's voice grew husky. "There is a house in a secluded portion of Orem Proper that belonged to my mother's people. We may remain unmolested there while Gar patrols the land. We will be free to entertain ourselves in any way we find fit."

Sera's gaze lingered on Tolin's face. She recalled a time when she had been incited to fury at the protective and possessive stance he maintained at her side. Such conflicts were now past. Tolin deferred to her in all matters of rule—but in matters of the heart, there was only mutual thought between them. Yea, the loneliness of her imperial bed had also left her aching with longing.

A week with Tolin in his forest hideaway?

Nay.

But . . . three days?

Tolin's eyes warmed to grey velvet as he appeared to read her mind. "Shall we leave now, heiress?"

"Three days, Tolin."

Tolin's lips moved into a rare smile.

"Three days, my love."

Her heart thundering, Sera slipped her hand into his.

Filnor paced his chamber, his strong frame tense as frustration raged. Orem was in a state of near euphoria at the return of Neer rule! He had never thought to see the people so beside themselves with joy.

Filnor reviewed in his mind, as he had countless times before, the momentous events recently come to pass.

Fador was dead and no one mourned him.

No one but *him*.

Filnor's stomach knotted with surprising pain. Yea, he mourned his father—not the father Fador had been, but the father Filnor wished he had been. Curiously, he treasured still the picture he held in the back of his mind of the strong, handsome man who was his sire, and who would one day love him.

That day had never come.

Now it never would.

A familiar hatred soared as Tolin's image appeared in Filnor's mind.

Tolin, *his brother* . . .

Nay! Never!

Sera's image was not far behind.

425

They deserved each other!

Filnor halted at that thought. If that were true, whom did *he* deserve?

Filnor cast that thought aside.

It galled Filnor that he was a prisoner of Neer in his own chambers, that the guards standing outside his door holding him captive within were the same guards who had obeyed *his* orders only a short time previously. It vexed him even more to realize that his future lay in the hands of a woman whose heart was closed to him, although the mere thought of her still set his blood aflame.

Filnor's jaw locked with fury. The witch's enchantment prevailed! She possessed his thoughts, awake and sleeping.

As *he* would never possess *her*.

Tolin possessed her.

Tolin . . . his brother . . .

That thought was a blade which returned to slash him deeply. Filnor recalled Tolin's impassive stance beside Sera as she had pronounced sentence. The sound of Sera's voice lingered in Filnor's mind, as did the sobriety about her that had seemed somehow pained as she had spoken.

In pronouncing sentence on Filnor of Rall, Neer recalls the blood that flows in his veins, and the blood he caused to spill in Rall's name, as well as his enmity against Neer's ruling house.

Rall's name is profane in the ears of many, but destiny has decreed that the blood of Rall will join with that of Neer. For that reason, Neer will demonstrate its benevolence.

Thus, the first official act of the Throne of Neer is to place Filnor of Rall's fate in his own hands by imprisoning him under guard in his own chambers, where he will be held powerless over his present and apart from the general populace of Orem until such time that he is able to bring the warring within him to an end—until such time that he may stand before the Throne of Neer and vow his allegiance to it.

Filnor of Rall is now justly warned that should his quarters prove inadequate for this sequester, or should he demonstrate that his heart is so closed to change that he is incapable of such rehabilitation, he will be confined in the dungeons of Orem, there to live out the remainder of his days.

Sera had addressed him directly then, her eyes filled with a curious regret.

Neer is ever merciful, Filnor of Rall. We pray that you will allow it to show its compassion—for your sake and for the sake of those who will follow to rule with the blood of Neer and Rall forever mingled.

The blade of pain twisted cruelly once more as Filnor recalled Sera's final words. The Rall blood to be blended with Neer's in Sera's progeny was meant to be *his* blood, not Tolin's!

Filnor's pacing grew more agitated as the direction of his thoughts raised a carnal need within him. He ran a rough hand through his dark hair. He but needed an ally who was able to move freely on the streets of Orem, and Sera would yet be his.

Filnor brought his step to an abrupt halt. There was only one person who could assuage his intimate needs and serve as an ally as well.

Filnor turned to the door with a shout.

"Guard!"

His chamber door snapped open to reveal familiar faces now hardened against him as Filnor questioned tightly, "The whore, Kiray, where is she located now?"

The guard's response was cold. "She was released from prison along with all other political prisoners. She returned to her quarters where she continues as before."

"Send a message that I require her presence here."

"You are a prisoner, Master Filnor. You no longer command."

Filnor paused, agitation abounding as he grated, "My brother, Tolin, will approve my request. He is a very generous man."

The door closed behind the guard and Filnor all but laughed aloud. Yea, Tolin would grant his request, if only with the hope that it signified his lust for Sera had ceased!

Would that time ever come to pass?

Never!

But in the meantime, Kiray would do.

Filnor resumed his pacing.

The cruel wind of Orem Minor flayed man and beast with sharp pellets of snow as the caravan wound its way along the icy trail. Straightening his broad shoulders, Serbaak breathed deeply of the frigid air, suffering little at the unrelenting assault of the elements. Instead, he had grown stronger with each mile traveled deeper into the frozen land until, nearly at journey's end, he was again healthy, his strength restored.

Serbaak looked up at a familiar sky that was dark with heavily laden clouds. He then attempted to penetrate the curtain of falling snow ahead of him with his gaze. No more than a mile farther and he would be home again. He was jubilant at the thought, even as he silently acknowledged the part of him left behind in Orem Proper.

A pang disturbingly similar to pain quaked through Serbaak as he recalled Sera's joy when she first discovered his presence in Orem Proper. The contest between Tolin and Filnor had ended, Fador had been mortally wounded and removed to his chambers to die, and the opposing forces had surrendered their arms. It was then that he had stepped out of the shadows into sight and Sera had seen him.

Sera had rushed to his side and thrown her arms around him, joyful tears flowing. He had relived over and again in his mind the supreme exhilaration of that moment when Sera had openly confirmed her love for him. He cherished that love. He knew that although it was incorporeal and fell short of the depth of his feelings for her, it was heartfelt and true. He had dismissed Sera's concern at his condition, knowing that to hold her in his arms, to see her safe from the threat of Rall and at the pinnacle of her destiny, was worth any price he might pay.

Strangely, he did not realize until that moment how tightly fate had intertwined the course of Sera's and his lives. Nor had he realized how closely Versa's spirit had guided them both on that path.

Serbaak was uncertain when he first consciously recognized the whisper that had directed his solitary journey from Orem Minor to Sera's aid in Orem Proper. He knew only that the same voice had instilled in him the confidence to mix the elixir that had granted him temporary respite from his weakness so that he might go on.

That same whisper had led him to Tolin's

bier. It had grown louder as he stood over Tolin, believing him dead. It had guided his hand when he struck the flint to the zircum dust and raised the mist that allowed Tolin to rise whole and well once more. He was incredulous, even now, that *he* had been chosen the vehicle by which Tolin was to be restored to fulfill his destiny—thereby defining in a way which could not be denied the additional role he had been fated to assume in Sera's stead.

"Oh, Serbaak, why did I never see the truth of it all until this moment?"

Serbaak closed his eyes as Sera's words in parting returned to him. She had looked up at him, her glorious gaze glowing.

"Why did I never realize until now that you were the one for whom I so meticulously prepared my medical journal in Orem Minor, the one who would carry on my work there? I should have known! You were always closer to me than any other person—save one."

Yea, save one.

He had clutched Sera in tight embrace for long minutes then, whispering words he could not now remember. He had savored the sweet intimacy of the moment with the realization that a whole world of distance would soon be between them.

"You are so dear to me, Serbaak. A part of me is forever yours."

431

Those words had become engraved on his heart.

"When you leave, that part of me goes with you."

As a part of him remained forever with Sera . . . his dearest love. . . .

It had been all he could do to release Sera and allow her to step back into the protective curve of Tolin's arm. Granting him both pleasure and pain was the realization that for all her insight, Sera remained ignorant of the full extent of his love for her.

Closely observing their farewell, however, Tolin was not deceived. But the mutual respect that had developed during the trials Tolin and he had shared in Sera's behalf remained intact. It was reflected in the strength of their handclasp as Tolin spoke his parting words.

"You may set your mind at rest. I will keep her safe . . . and loved."

Safe . . . and loved.

The unique bond, the ability to sense Sera's distress which Serbaak had known from childhood, had been severed at the moment of Tolin's solemn words of commitment. Serbaak was strangely bereft without it. Yet he was innately sure that should the occasion ever arise when Sera needed him again, he would know.

Drawn abruptly back to the present as the familiar outline of Orem Minor's main village wavered briefly into view through the gusting snow, Serbaak felt his spirits rise. He pressed his mount forward with new enthusiasm as the caravan continued its plodding pace behind him. He was anxious to see Alpor again so that he might personally confirm the victorious dispatch that Sera had issued to her former home in Orem Minor immediately after the defeat of Rall. He wanted to report to his father the incredible resurgence of hope he had witnessed among the common people of Orem Proper after Sera assumed rule. He desired to set his father's mind at rest with the reassurance that Sera, *their beloved Sera*, was truly "home" at last.

Most importantly of all, however, he wanted to—

But . . . what was that?

A solitary figure had emerged from the gates of the village and was pressing its way toward the caravan through the battering of the storm.

Could it be . . . ?

Spurring his mount to an accelerated pace, Serbaak drew up beside the struggling figure minutes later. Leaning down, he swept a breathless but ecstatic Teesha up into his arms.

Elation . . . laughter . . . tears!

Serbaak clutched Teesha close, knowing true joy in a moment of revelation when their lips touched.

Drawing back from his kiss at last, Teesha spoke in a shaken whisper.

"I love you, Serbaak."

Teesha had said the words simply because she could hold them back no longer.

Serbaak whispered his response. "I love you, too, Teesha."

Yea, he did—with a love that did not impinge upon a greater love that could never be.

Accepting that reality, knowing he would serve it well and with honor, Serbaak urged his mount home.

The fragrance of flowers wafted through the window of Kiray's chamber as she walked toward her wardrobe and drew the door open. Choosing to ignore the reflection she saw in the glass as she passed, she stood before the colorful array of garments within. She needed no reminder that her appearance reflected only too clearly the horrors of the dungeon to which she had been subjected.

Filth . . . humiliation . . . pain . . . unrelenting fear . . . all had left their mark on her, both inwardly and without.

A step at the door turned Kiray toward her haglike servant. It occurred to Kiray, not for the first time since her release, that had not the unexpected reversal of Orem's circumstances effected her liberation from the damp squalor of the dungeon, she might have shared that hag-like appearance. That thought instilled a note of gentleness formerly absent in her tone when she addressed the woman she had formerly scorned.

"What is it, Odana?"

"The royal guard is at the door."

"The royal guard?"

"Yea." The old woman grew breathless. "Filnor requests your presence in his chambers. He desires you, mistress."

Kiray went abruptly still as Filnor's image came alive in her mind. Dark eyes that shook her to the soul, a powerful body that consumed her, and ecstasy . . . matchless ecstasy. . . .

Kiray's slender frame trembled. "He would have me come to him?"

"Yea, it is said that Filnor will soon be free, that because of the common blood Tolin and he share, Neer is forgiving of his transgressions."

Forgiving . . .

Kiray's trembling gradually stilled.

Nay, she was not as forgiving as Neer.

Kiray instructed coldly, "You may tell the guard that I know no Filnor of Rall, and neither do I care to know him."

Turning her back on the old woman's shocked countenance, Kiray continued her perusal of the contents of her wardrobe, Filnor, for all intents and purposes, forgotten.

* * *

The afternoon waned.

Kiray had not come.

Filnor's pacing continued with new agitation.

He cared not that the whore had deserted him! He did not need her! There was only one woman he needed.

The Flame of Neer's visage shone newly bright before Filnor's gaze, and he halted.

Yea, it was she, the flame who was his torment.

And his love.

The bedchamber of the forest hideaway was dimly lit. Featherdown mattress beneath them, luxurious drapes at the window closing out the world beyond, Sera and Tolin lay flesh against flesh, heart against heart, lips clinging. Drawing back, the pounding in his chest and the eagerness within him unable to be restrained, Tolin slid his powerful body atop Sera's delicate length. He heard Sera's impassioned gasp. He saw a new light of love kindle in her gaze, and he silently marveled that the matchless woman lying in his arms was truly his alone, at last.

Tolin's words throbbed with the passion he held at bay as he cupped Sera's face with his palms and whispered, "I have a secret I must confess to you, heiress."

"A secret?" Sera whispered in return. "What

secret do you wish to convey that suits this special moment? Tell me, for I lust for your response."

A gaze once frozen and without life bathed Sera's face with heated ardor. A strong face once devoid of emotion was alight with yearning. A powerful body once satisfied to know only physical satiation prepared to worship hers with love as Tolin responded, "I confess to you a misconception that I have allowed to prevail. I declare to you now that had not the words of the sacred scroll borne out the truth as written to be proclaimed to all, I would still have been convinced that you were meant to be mine."

Sera's gaze reflected tender skepticism of Tolin's words. "Hindsight and love are powerful allies, my dear Tolin. They clear a path which is often hazy and uncertain when faced from the other direction."

"Nay, I do not view the past from hindsight, but from the reality of my love for you." Pausing, Tolin brushed Sera's lips with a lingering kiss before continuing more softly than before, "Now, lying in my arms, do you doubt me when I say that there is no force in Orem or beyond that could have made me abandon my possession of you once you were truly mine?"

"In the inn you said you would yield to whatever fate destiny had decreed."

"Yea, those noble words . . ." Tolin continued earnestly, ". . . but the tongue that spoke those words did not belong to the man who had seen you wrenched from his arms by Filnor's lust. Neither did it belong to the man who lay for a brief eternity in a netherworld between darkness and light, awaiting the moment of renewal with only the thought of you to keep him from slipping beyond . . . nor to that same man who was ready to fight the entire force of Rall rather than have you slip away from him forever. Nay, heiress, that man would not have surrendered you to another—for *any* reason."

"And if the scroll had decreed otherwise?"

"I would have challenged destiny."

"Like Filnor."

"Nay! Never like him!" Tolin's demeanor grew intense. "Filnor challenged destiny with lust and greed. I would have challenged it with love, and with the purity of heart and purpose that *you* had brought to my life. For you see, heiress . . ." Tolin's pale eyes grew suspiciously bright. ". . . You gave me back my life when it was almost lost, and in doing so, gave me a reason to live as well. You *are* my life."

"As you are mine."

"You are my purpose. . . ."

". . . as you are mine."

"You are my flame. . . ."

"Yea, Tolin . . ." Elation unbounded, Sera whispered, "Brought to life so I might learn its full meaning in your arms, so together we might live and love and follow the course of a destiny that brought us to this matchless moment."

"This matchless moment . . ."

Words no longer sufficing, Tolin's lips met Sera's again with ecstatic fervor. Their bodies joined with love unequaled, as that which was meant to be was eclipsed by the wondrous splendor of that which was . . . and that which would always be.

The matchless moment unwound, becoming destiny fulfilled as . . . *in a deserted tower room high above the royal residence of Neer, in a barred niche within a stone wall, a flame enclosed in crystal flickered. It was a captive flame, the spirit of Fador of Rall. It was a flame as black as his heart . . .*

. . . and it would not rest until it was again free.

Dear Friends,

My husband and I were driving home through a deserted, densely wooded area of North Jersey late one summer night when the story of the captive flame came to me in a very unusual way. The road had no streetlights. The headlights of our car and a moon that darted in and out in a cloudy sky were the only means of illumination for miles. My husband was at the wheel and I was staring out the window into the woods beyond when I saw a spark flicker deep within the shadows. It floated high above the ground on an air current for a few minutes, glowing so brightly before it disappeared that it startled me.

I was intrigued. There were no houses in the area, no bonfires nearby, and the spark that had danced briefly on the breeze, then vanished,

441

had not been a firefly. I wondered what it had been and where it had come from.

I thought, what if . . . ?

We arrived home a short time later and I went immediately to my computer. I worked long into the night as the story of the captive flame flowed as easily as truth, and the characters of *Dance of the Flame* and the two worlds of Orem came alive.

I was exhilarated when I completed the outline in the early morning hours of the following day, and I enjoyed every minute spent in fleshing out *Dance of the Flame* into a completed novel. I hated to say good-bye to that mysterious flame. I regretted leaving Sera and Tolin, Serbaak and Teesha, and the despicable duo, Fador and Filnor. Then I wondered, what if they . . . ?

Are you wondering, "what if they . . . ?" too?

Thanks so much for all your letters. I enjoy hearing from you.

Sincerely,

Elaine Barbieri

P.O. Box 536
West Milford, NJ 07480

Enchanted Crossings

Three captivating stories of love in another time, another place.

MADELINE BAKER
"Heart of the Hunter"

A Lakota warrior must defy the boundaries of life itself to claim the spirited beauty he has sought through time.

ANNE AVERY
"Dream Seeker"

On faraway planets, a pilot and a dreamer learn that passion can bridge the heavens, no matter how vast the distance from one heart to another.

KATHLEEN MORGAN
"The Last Gatekeeper"

To save her world, a dazzling temptress must use her powers of enchantment to open a stellar portal—and the heart of a virile but reluctant warrior.

__51974-7 *Enchanted Crossings* (three unforgettable love stories in one volume) $4.99 US/ $5.99 CAN

Dorchester Publishing Co., Inc.
65 Commerce Road
Stamford, CT 06902

Please add $1.75 for shipping and handling for the first book and $.50 for each book thereafter. NY, NYC, PA and CT residents, please add appropriate sales tax. No cash, stamps, or C.O.D.s. All orders shipped within 6 weeks via postal service book rate. Canadian orders require $2.00 extra postage and must be paid in U.S. dollars through a U.S. banking facility.

Name_____
Address_____
City _____ State_____Zip_____
I have enclosed $_____in payment for the checked book(s).
Payment must accompany all orders.☐ Please send a free catalog.

MADELINE BAKER

Beneath A Midnight Moon

Winner Of The *Romantic Times* Reviewers Choice Award!

He comes to her in visions—the hard-muscled stranger who promises to save her from certain death. She never dares hope that her fantasy love will hold her in his arms until the virile and magnificent dream appears in the flesh.

A warrior valiant and true, he can overcome any obstacle, yet his yearning for the virginal beauty he's rescued overwhelms him. But no matter how his fevered body aches for her, he is betrothed to another.

Bound together by destiny, yet kept apart by circumstances, they brave untold perils and ruthless enemies—and find a passion that can never be rent asunder.
_3649-5 $4.99 US/$5.99 CAN

Dorchester Publishing Co., Inc.
65 Commerce Road
Stamford, CT 06902

Please add $1.75 for shipping and handling for the first book and $.50 for each book thereafter. NY, NYC, PA and CT residents, please add appropriate sales tax. No cash, stamps, or C.O.D.s. All orders shipped within 6 weeks via postal service book rate. Canadian orders require $2.00 extra postage and must be paid in U.S. dollars through a U.S. banking facility.

Name_____
Address _____
City _____ State_____Zip_____
I have enclosed $_____in payment for the checked book(s).
Payment <u>must</u> accompany all orders.□ Please send a free catalog.

An Angel's Touch

Where angels go, love is sure to follow.

Don't miss these unforgettable romances that combine the magic of angels and the joy of love.

Daemon's Angel by Sherrilyn Kenyon. Cast to the mortal realm by an evil sorceress, Arina has more than her share of problems. She is trapped in a temptress's body and doomed to lose any man she desires. Yet even as Arina yearns for the safety of the pearly gates, she finds paradise in the arms of a Norman mercenary. But to savor the joys of life with Daemon, she will have to battle demons and risk her very soul for love.

_52026-5 $4.99 US/$5.99 CAN

Forever Angels by Trana Mae Simmons. Thoroughly modern Tess Foster has everything, but when her boyfriend demands she sign a prenuptial agreement Tess thinks she's lost her happiness forever. Then her guardian angel sneezes and sends the woman of the nineties back to the 1890s—and into the arms of an unbelievably handsome cowboy. But before she will surrender to a marriage made in heaven, Tess has to make sure that her guardian angel won't sneeze again—and ruin her second chance at love.

_52021-4 $4.99 US/$5.99 CAN

Dorchester Publishing Co., Inc.
65 Commerce Road
Stamford, CT 06902

Please add $1.75 for shipping and handling for the first book and $.50 for each book thereafter. NY, NYC, PA and CT residents, please add appropriate sales tax. No cash, stamps, or C.O.D.s. All orders shipped within 6 weeks via postal service book rate. Canadian orders require $2.00 extra postage and must be paid in U.S. dollars through a U.S. banking facility.

Name _____

Address _____

City _____ State _____ Zip _____

I have enclosed $_____ in payment for the checked book(s). Payment <u>must</u> accompany all orders. ☐ Please send a free catalog.

An Angel's Touch

Time Heals
SUSAN COLLIER

Tired of her nagging relatives, Maeve Fredrickson asks for the impossible: to be a thousand miles and a hundred years away from them. Then a heavenly being grants her wish, and she awakes in frontier Montana.

Saved from the wilderness by a handsome widower, Maeve loses her heart to her rescuer—and her temper over the antics of his three less-than-angelic children. As her angel prods her to fight for Seth, Maeve can only pray for the strength to claim a love made in paradise.

_52030-3 $4.99 US/$5.99 CAN

Dorchester Publishing Co., Inc.
45 Commerce Road
Stamford, CT 06902

Please add $1.75 for shipping and handling for the first book and $.50 for each book thereafter. NY, NYC, PA and CT residents, please add appropriate sales tax. No cash, stamps, or C.O.D.s. All orders shipped within 6 weeks via postal service book rate. Canadian orders require $2.00 extra postage and must be paid in U.S. dollars through a U.S. banking facility.

Name _____
Address _____
City _____ State _____ Zip _____
I have enclosed $_____ in payment for the checked book(s).
Payment <u>must</u> accompany all orders.☐ Please send a free catalog.